J.A. St Thomas

A WALK IN THE PARK

THE CANNABIS CHRONICLES

Library of Congress 2018911256
ISBN 978-0-692-17249-0

Acknowledgements

I pay humble tribute to all of my Muses, with eternal gratefulness to my husband Thomas and our daughter Elektra – my greatest loves and constant inspirations.
I must also give thanks to my Fates; Eugenia Parry, Jean Weiss, Ruth Lopez, Kathryn Gaitens, and Michelle Rutt – for wielding the knife with temperance and grace.
Trish White - I am beholden to the unending encouragement you bestow.
To my Brother Steve Alikas, you're right, it's A Walk in The Park.

Preface

In 1996 The Lynn and Erin Compassionate Use Act was passed in the state of California, allowing citizens of the U.S. to utilize the benefits of marijuana to treat debilitating physical conditions, setting a precedent for the nation.

In 2010 the state of Colorado amended their constitution to protect their citizens' rights to access marijuana by legislating and regulating medical dispensaries (stores), producers (cultivators), and (MIPS) manufacturers of edible products.

In 2012 Colorado became the first state to legalize recreational use for 21 and older, thus originating the Green Rush.

In 2017 there were between 20,000 and 28,000 cannabis businesses in the U.S. grossing over seven billion dollars with no ceiling to be had.

By 2018 the pioneers and innovators are holding on by a thread or partnering together to stave off big pharma takeover. Corpocracy is running rampant. The potentate is out of control, emboldening the worst characteristics of mankind. Voices and actions of classes are harshly divided, spurring a new wave of heroes. They don't have capes or super human strength. They have ideals and the passionate hope that this brave new world can be a better place...

But these are merely the facts this fiction is based on.

Chapter Song list

The music that inspired the chapter titles were as much as an inspiration as the actual experiences depicted. SCAN TO LISTEN to playlist. Ebook chapter titles are live.

1

Part I

SLIP INTO SOMETHING

Waking to the clatter of bird and monkey sounds that have become the norm, a cacophony of life stirs the imminence of dawn. But there is something wrong. She hesitates, instincts on full alert, waiting in exact silence not moving or blinking to be sure before she warns, "They're coming!"

Survival instincts kicking in, everyone is running torn from sleep, this group of eight women, stick together with great purpose. This is an ideal time for an ambush, they will need the strength of their numbers if they hope to survive. Pushing through the underbrush, they all know what to do. They have gone through this scenario many times. Delta, their leader is taking them further into the jungle. Only the sound of their feet weighing down on the fallen leaves is heard, followed by the eerie push of wind coming from above. It is not a storm, it is worse than a storm. Storms pass in the night with the angst of teenagers, tempests on the shores. Storms are welcome, they are the only time of rest, a truce of worlds.

Struggling to keep up with her, each woman of this family, pushes herself, not allowing panic to take hold, when a roar like thunder grips their hearts. They must reach the river mouth but suddenly, Delta is overcome by a foul unusual smell, "That's new."

Shaking it off, she wonders how she could explain this to anyone outside of the hell they know. The comfort and strength they give each other and most importantly the hope they share. This is her family now and she feels the deepest responsibility for these women, this bond is all they have.

Running full out, away from the gagging odor and sound of rushing wind, just a quarter mile more, they must make it. Panic increasing their reflexes with each step, they can almost feel the brutal wind. It smells of doom and death, filling them with despair.

Reaching the openness of the river mouth, Delta leads them, skirting along the shrunken river banks, always staying undercover. The rains haven't started yet, making the river quite manageable. Not far to go, guiding her family they finally stop, panting and bent from exertion, beads of sweat layering their skin.

It's unnerving, how little she knows about each one of them and yet it doesn't matter as she looks from one woman to the next.

Pulling dry reeds from the ground and snapping the roots off anxiously, they begin to wade in. Moving toward a small densely treed island in the middle of the river, a little over fifteen feet from shore.

Carefully Delta scans for signs of predators, any wake or dark shadows in the water could be a problem, as their only weapons are the sharpened sticks they carry. Once waist high, the women begin to swim, reeds in mouths, like dogs retrieving sticks, carefully aware not to disturb the surface. Each stroke feels like an eternity as another loud roar careens towards them from behind. Taking the reeds into their mouths like straws and supplicating themselves into the waist high water protected only by the canopy of thick mango branches, they are careful not to spread out. Eyes wide with terror they slip into the water before their heads go under, gun shots ring out, all birds take flight.

2

STONEYRIDGE TERRACE

Our room awash with morning light, my eyes open slowly, while from a distance the big blue Pacific greets me as the familiar friend she has become. The surface of the sea ripples as a thin layer of fog continues its morning retreat to the eternal horizon.

Silently stretching, I twist over on my side admiring the sleeping man beside me. I have loved Remy for more than half my life. We are the people we have grown into, because of each other. Smiling at this, tracing his face, I am captured by the long thick lashes that frame his intense hazel eyes. They can be blue, or green depending on his mood and the clothing he is wearing, reflecting his moods and thoughts. But now that his blond locked temples are turning gray, his eyes dare to match, nudging him from drop dead rock star looks to Richard Gere sexy reserve. I know every line on this face, every mark on his body. His chiseled features are those of a roman statue, although he claims to be Irish and Finnish.

I have kissed his lips a thousand times, yet they are as mysterious to me today as they were twenty years ago.

"Morning Sweetie." His sleepy carefree mouth turns into a smile that melts my heart.

"Good Morning," I add finding his warm lips with mine. "How did you get so sexy? Men are supposed to look old and withered at your age?"

"Steph, you are a flirt."

I move over so he is on the edge of the bed, his hands finding my waist pulling me closer, "Now who's flirting?"

"Hmmm", there is no more talking, we greet the day with each other.

Our new town house in Laguna Beach is small with a view to kill. We had to choose a place in the U.S easily accessible by air for work as we spend most of our time travelling, pushing our cannabis infused coffee company, Mad Hatter Coffee & Tea.

Of course, my husband Remy's only requirement is that it be a surf-able break or at least close to one. I married a California boy, with a golden mane of hair and all. Found him in New York, he would say he was window shopping and found me but fate had ultimate control over our destinies, we were meant to find one another. I consider this as I watch his body move across the room, every muscle accentuated in the pink hued light. Looks aside it's Remy's calm that draws me to him along with an inner strength that verges on mythological.

We would have preferred an older house, but we are both considering this move temporary, so it really didn't matter. Originally, we had wanted to live in Encinitas, where Remy grew up. We spent a couple of weeks there before he realized going back may not be the best thing.

"This is no longer the little surf town I grew up in." I remember the sadness that overcame him while he spoke, "Look there, the old little sea cottages that used to line the coast, torn down to make way for Mc-mansions. They've pulled out by the roots the aged fruit trees and sentinel bougainvillea's, to build their three car garages on the entire lot line. It's too horrible to bare, no dogs on the beach, no horses on the beach, no bon fires. God forbid you have a car that's not new and shiny, you're a moving target. I try not to judge sweetie, but it's difficult to understand how people en mass can move to a place for all the simple virtues it offers, only to condemn those virtues as base or illegal", Remy propounded sincerely out of breath and heart, "We have to get out of here before we become one of them!"

"I know," I remember saying, shaking my head, for he was right, we just don't fit in here in the United States, and what may be worse is that it doesn't bother us. We'll find our tribe, somewhere.

"Let's put our time in, make the best of it, rent the house out and go south." Remy's mantra so clear.

"I'm in."

"We're so close sweetie. If we can just close one of these deals, we could breath." He deliberated with the obvious need to provide.

"We will," I confirmed.

One day we will make the jump and perhaps the pool will appear. Until then, we chose Laguna Beach California, because neither of us had lived here, it's fresh and unknown, we won't miss the secrets that have already been exploited. While courting we had stopped at Harry's Bar and Grille a couple of times throughout the years, Remy's nickname for the Krishna Temple here in Laguna. You could dine with devotees, and be entertained by dancing and marigold lei's, it was awesome. But that was the extent of our history in Laguna till now.

"Come on my little muse, let's go for a paddle."

This invitation ends my reminiscence as both of us walk through the house naked, into the garage, thank goodness all the windows are in the back of the house and look out to the sea from a hillside that gives us a good view of the whole bay. Our bare feet pad on the concrete floor as we slip into wet suits. It's May and the water is cold. The morning air will feel disturbingly tight, as we walk out of the gate to load up the boards. I brace myself for the morning chill. I like surfing, but for Remy, it's part of his physical make up, it keeps him balanced. We have both been so busy with Mad Hatter and the daily drama the cannabis industry creates that is constantly infiltrating our daily lives, neither of us have any time for creative outlets. Unless you consider spread sheets creative, which I do not. Of course, Remy being the alchemist of our cannabis infused beverage company has a tremendous amount of time experimenting in his lab with infusion processes, which he is highly regarded for. I suppose my creative time is spent working on the marketing and branding aspects of our baby. The point being, throwing ourselves into the sea every day or so, cleanses our souls and recharges our batteries, sort to speak.

No one is stirring on our street; the hive has not begun to buzz as we putter off in post dawn's light. There are perhaps fifteen to twenty people on the whole beach in fact when we arrive, it's a short drive from our house without traffic. The morning fog is still hanging over the sea like a shroud. But it doesn't deter Remy, he delights in the fact it will burn off unmasking another true California day, as usual.

I, on the other hand, find myself drained by the endless perfect days, my east coast upbringing is genetically coded for gray skies and rain. Once every two weeks or so, I draw the curtains in our bedroom, bake bread and make soup from scratch and watch old movies on grainy VCR tapes, just to align my system. Not Remy, he is solar powered, I think to myself smiling as he tosses his 8'x 6" board into the sea strapping the tether to his right foot. I giggle that surfing with your left foot forward is considered "Goofy Foot", he is anything but goofy, he is old school, carving the waves with elegance and liquidity.

"Steph, no wet hair this morning!"

"Yeah, maybe for you."

The sound of the sea is now wholly impressed upon me. It swallows me and pulls me into a moment of time where primal instincts rule, for if you are paddling or sitting in the lineup and goose bumps appear out of nowhere, pick your feet out of the water, I remind myself, you are now in the food chain! Of course, the same holds true for the cannabis industry.

As I cough out the first wave that smacks me squarely in the face, thoroughly drenching my hair, Remy is already in the lineup. No one is out this early, and hardly anyone knows of this secret spot. Remy found it as a kid before we met. It seems surfing entailed lots of driving in those days, scouting the waves at each break, a part of the morning ritual as much as waxing your board. I keep telling myself just a couple more waves to dive through, when he comes charging at me on Big Red, "Wooo hooo", I hoot.

"Ramming speed matey!" accompanies the biggest smile I have seen since this morning's wake up call, laughing I keep paddling.

Finally, I make it through the sets of waves to the lineup, laying down on my board, a 6'4" tri fin, I trace the sea foam green turtle tracks striping the center to the tip. Gaining my strength back from paddling out, Remy is already upon me, "This one's for you, Sweetie," he nods towards a whomper coming in.

"Right." *Oh shit!* Panic-paddling towards the wave in the hope of not getting hammered while Remy just turns his bad ass boat around and careens towards shore. The wave thankfully passes me as I turn and look. I can't see Remy only the roll of the back of the wave, they look a lot smaller from the back.

Sometimes I think the only reason I surf with him is to watch him, certainly, it's to share something he loves.

Looking out to the horizon, I can see dolphins in the kelp beds. I don't know why, but I feel safer when they're around. Smiling, I pull my board around and take the next feasible wave I can manage. Someone had once said to me, "When women get dressed, they ask themselves, how can I feel my best today? When men get dressed, they ask, how can I not look ridiculous?" The latter is how I feel about surfing. I enjoy it, I love being in the water, but I am very self-conscious.

I manage to stand up and as I pass Remy paddling back out, he cries," Wooo, how much for the legs?"

Slapping my bottom in response, I drop down to my knees and with my arms out, make my way to the beach. Plopping my board belly up on the sand, removing my tether, I lay my wetsuit on top of my board and enjoy the sense of newness the water creates.

I may be self-conscious about surfing and the primitive poses I strike, but I am not self-conscious about my figure. I am damn proud of it. I have never been thin. I have a Greek figure, rounded hips, wide shoulders, proportioned breasts that are more than a handful, and a little pot belly found to be replicated in Greek classical sculpture, I remind myself often. I am particularly proud of my legs, however lean, muscular and well- shaped, I inherited them from my mother. At 37, I fill my two- piece bikini and wear it with pride. We spend quite a bit of time on planes, at our home office and in hotels, where it's easy to get off our routines. It takes discipline, but it's really our play time; bicycling, surfing, swimming and a little yoga that keeps us fit and balanced.

I head back in, swimming is my favorite exercise. Charging out through the breakers I own a renewed self-determination. Flipper-less, I stay out of the big surf. Today is a typical California day, if it were one foot higher, it would be two feet high. I'm following Remy out on what must be his hundredth wave. We make it out to the line-up, and I start swimming around him. He keeps his toes up on his board in a sitting position, all that bravado, *but I know his secrets.*

"Beautiful day." I comment on the blue sky beginning to peak through the haze of morning.

"It looks like it. It doesn't get better than this." Remy manages before he turns around and takes off, his preoccupation wholly sincere.

The sea is quiet outside the breakers. Unless you have the courage to come out here, it's not something anyone can describe to you. An unknown depth, the shore in perspective and nothing but a vast ebb and flow. It could take you in a second, I guess that's part of the allure, the willingness to lose control. Floating on my back I watch the last wisps of fog surrender to the sky above. It is this peace that gives us both strength to push what seems like a never- ending rock up hill.

When Remy and I started Mad Hatter in 2007, we knew it would be tough, but nothing could have prepared us for the rollercoaster ride we bought a ticket on. We were one of the first, certainly the first coffee company. In eleven years, we have grown from two blends to thirty- three, available in eight legal states. We've certainly seen a lot and been through a lot but surprises are always around the corner.

Back then in Colorado, there were little to no regulations, and no licenses to apply for, save a business license. You needed a food handler's certification and could make your products in your home. It was the wild west back then, I recall fondly, *the good ole days*. Anyone that had a good business sense and branding skills could kill it. We were among those.

Remy had been making hash infused coffee for friends and family for some time at home. He comes from a long line of coffee drinkers, 1 of 10 kids, I am surprised his Mother didn't walk around with an IV full of it.

When we had first moved back to California from the east coast where we met, his brothers would come over for coffee klatch whether Remy was home or not. We would sit and chat, gossip really, but it was good clean fun and there was always coffee.

"Whew, did you see that tube?" Remy pulls me from my daydream.

"Did you get tubed?"

Scowling at me but distracted by newcomers he replies, "Looks like company, fifteen more minutes, I want to see who it is, ok?"

"Sounds good." I wave him off.

Spinning his board around like it doesn't weigh 45 pounds he paddles like he's pushing air before the next wave scoops him up and delivers him to the crest with the pride of a competitor who has met her match.

Floating on my back I contemplate how different the cannabis industry is today. For the good, and for the bad. Is it really that hard to make good legislative rule decisions when you are faced with exponential growth of an industry? Probably. I am sure alcohol was similar. I've read about prohibition, with the hopes of finding some kind of connection and ultimately a window to a thriving industry. Neither are apparent. Most industries regulate themselves. This fact is little known to the public, the fracking industry drew up their own regulations and created a list of chemicals they would be allowed to inject into our earth, they devise their own transport and refuse standards. I shake my head, when citizens cry out, "How can they do this?" They do it because they regulate themselves, there is no THEY other than THEM. It makes me laugh out loud at the fact that we have to manifest each wholesale delivery of our product. We literally have to inform the state what streets and at what time our delivery of cannabis infused drinks will be transported, within a 24- hour window. Nuclear waste isn't even monitored for transportation as carefully as marijuana! It doesn't stop there, scanning each ounce of pot for seed to sale tracking and my all- time favorite mandatory in most states for medical and recreational purposes to lab test and fully disclose on a label affixed to the product what type of materials the marijuana was grown in, bacteria and pesticide residual as well as a cannabinoid breakdown. The cannabis industry is the ONLY industry in the United States that calls for mandatory labelling. Not even vitamins, food we eat, or medication we take is subjected to this. Not that that is a good thing, there should be labelling laws, but this witch hunt is obvious. Leave it to the stoner business people to make life harder for themselves. If only we could organize.

"Come back to the moment", I say to myself through gritted teeth, paddling around. *No, this industry is a bastard child, one that is still nursing from a kind woman but neglected, oppressed and denied any true affection.* I turn my head and swim for the beach, hopefully shedding the negativity I feel.

Already drying off, wetsuit zipped down and fallen to just above his pelvis, Remy catches my lascivious thoughts.

"Oh, really?" he simmers.

I laugh. "Who was that?" changing the subject nodding to two men with boards walking down to the tideline.

"You remember that old guy out here about a month ago?"

"Yes, the retired car dealer?"

"Hmm, yeah he and his son. Visiting from all places, Jersey." He manages while quickly pulling off his suit and drying his naked ass before he pulls on sweat pants and a Mad Hatter t shirt, that says; This is the earth, beautiful and terrible things will happen, don't be afraid, there is Mad Hatter. *Only Remy.* His sarcasm towards New Jersey is playfully aimed at me. I grew up there, what seems like eons ago. I may have escaped New Jersey and without an accent, I may add, but you can't take the Jersey out of the girl.

"Really? What exit?" I retort. An insider joke, to anyone that lives off the Jersey Turnpike or the Parkway, which is three quarters of the population. My soggy husband replies with a cheesy grin.

Wrapping up in my towel I slip into my flip flops, refraining from exhibiting my personals to the entire beach. *I am not a prude, just private.* "How old is he?" I ask.

"Seventy- seven."

"Wow, that's great." I admire the senior as he paddles out on his knees.

"I am starving. Let's get some burritos."

"We have to be online for a conference call by 9." I remind him.

"Then we better move." He says while picking up both our boards and making tracks in the sand.

Remy places the boards on the racks of our 71' Volkswagen Camper van, affectionately known as Trixie. She's in mint condition, red and white with a covered tire on the front, bedazzled with her name. I also made covers for all the seats with red, white and micro striped beige sunbrella fabric, to hide the hideous original beige vinyl, that stuck to my ass every time I got in. She's loud, we find ourselves yelling at one another to be heard. Hard to turn, almost impossible to park without power steering, and no AC but she is adorable. It was Remy's idea to buy a VW van and use it as a mobile hotel before we could afford to fly to our conferences. We would pull her into our booth at conference centers and set her up like an ice cream vendor. With her awning out, she draws a lot of attention to Mad Hatter. Of course, we are promoting cannabis infused coffee and tea so we really don't need much to draw attention to ourselves.

Five years ago, we were often the only edible company attending cannabis conventions. Penned in by extractors, security systems, insurance agents, indoor light companies, and of course the hordes of marketing companies that were largely the main attendees. We were an anomaly, I recall. We would draw the largest crowds and sweep up the press without any effort. Our constant attendance and exposure made us darlings and expanded our brand in ways we never could have imagined. By the time most edibles companies were still organizing their first kitchen operation in one state, we had expanded into 3 additional states. Our business model, in retrospect, truly brilliant, but mostly instituted out of necessity.

We had started in Colorado, the birth place of cannabis as business eleven years ago. I remember what it was like, people were wrapping brownies in saran wrap and taping a label that said brownie on it that had been hand written with a sharpie. It was pretty bare.

Watching the California landscape roll by the van window, which mostly consists of over- crowded housing, I remember the days we launched with sweet nostalgia. Remy went door to door, like a travelling sales man, goods in the trunk. He visited every dispensary in Colorado. Out for a week then home for a week. I handled the cold calls, getting the managers on the phone and bluntly asking them if they would be interested in infused coffee. We termed it, 'The original wake and bake'. No one said no to either of us, except one or two hippies holding on to the golden age, poo pooing edibles like a dying fad. Today, what was once a dying fad is now 80 percent of the billion- dollar market share.

"Do you remember when we decided to lab test out drinks before they made us?" They being the state, I ask Remy as we pull into the Burrito stand parking lot.

"Yeah, we had some balls then."

"You still have balls, my dear, that's why I married you, for your big balls." That statement, which I use often, always gets me a mixed response. I laugh.

We were the first edible company to figure out how to consistently dose our products, so people could rely on them with confidence. *Who hasn't had a miserable experience with a loaded brownie?* It all made sense, they were natural steps, no one would buy our products if we couldn't promise them, they wouldn't be fetal for days from drinking it. With that in mind, I say to Remy, "You know looking back we seemed pretty proactive and forward thinking, but actually most of it was pure common sense and survival."

"Yeah, what's on your mind Steph?"

"Well, nothing really. I was just thinking that sometimes when you look back at the past, it can sometimes make you look smarter than you are."

"Red or green?" He answers contritely.

"Red", *I always get red chile in my burrito,* "Cheese inside, no rice."

"Yes dear. Are you saying we look smarter than we are?"

"Did I say we?" I ask with a smart alik lift of my brows. "No, I think we are pretty damn smart."

"That's why I married YOU." Remy teases me while sipping his coconut.

"I thought you married me for my money?"

This intercourse reminds me of the scene in the movie Casablanca, where Rick (Humphrey Bogart) the American café owner, is asked by the Nazi Major, "Why did you come to Casablanca?"

Rick answers, "I came for the water."

"Water, there is no water here, it's a desert." The Nazi Major, replies as he shovels caviar into his mouth.

With bogart cool, Rick replies, "I was mistaken."

We scarf down our burritos, sitting in the van with the little table up and the sliding side door wide open looking out onto Ocean Blvd. We have only just moved to the neighborhood, we don't know anyone except the burrito truck owner Miguel from Jalisco and a couple of other surfers up at this hour.

"I've got to work on my backside," I manage between bites, recalling how difficult it is for me to choose a wave that is going to break to the right, I just like going left.

"Why don't you let me worry about your backside." Remy quips as he wipes red chili from my chin. "Have you sent the numbers over to Colorado for their blend yet?"

Referring to our Licensee's in Colorado that manufacture Mad Hatter. They order all coffee and tea blends from us, un infused of course, including packaging.

"No, I should be finished today."

"The sooner they get the numbers, the sooner we get paid." He reminds me.

"I know," I mumble nodding my head and rolling up my burrito wrapper. "Let's go."

I love my husband, he's sexy, smart, funny, kind, strong and innovative. But I think to myself, I hate when he reminds me of a task I have to finish when I am working as fast as I can already. It makes me feel like a failure. I know that's not his intention, he is just being a helpful male. With that in mind, I brush off the question and change the subject. "I got a text from laure last night."

"How's she doing?"

"Good." Laure is my oldest friend, we met in college. I dragged her into this industry, I remind myself, "She's adapting well to San Francisco. She looks great."

"She find a man yet?"

"No, not yet."

We pull into the driveway, Remy grabs the boards off the roof and washes them down while I pull some weeds in the garden outside of our front door. I haven't really tackled the front yard yet, I think to myself, but at least everything is alive and well. The previous owner's fondness of rhododendrons and begonias is a bit old lady for me, I am thinking Belladonna. It's good to surround yourself with poisonous and hallucinogenic plants, it keeps you on your toes, after all, we live in their world.

Our call is with the CEO of Hammer Industries. An old family run fortune 500 company, that has been breaking into the cannabis industry for 3 years and doing a fine job, until a week ago. Most of the time newbie companies just want to pick Remy's brain, under the pretense of partnering. His network of people and his talent for connecting them is almost legendary. Not to mention he isn't afraid to Innovate at the cost of a crazy idea. He isn't afraid period. It's Remy's creative approach, and humor that separates our company from the stoner companies and the white label companies found today in the cannabis industry. With blend names like "Third Eye Chai", "Army Intelligence", "Family Reunion", "ImmortaliTea", "Freudian Couch", "DeiTea" – he really nailed the fact that we are not just offering a medication, we are enabling our patients to manifest their own well- being. The reality is, our products take people on a trip, with the proper guidance it can go beyond the physical body.

Remy is out of the shower and pulling on his pants as his nostalgic pinball ringer hails us from across the room. But this is the real deal, this company seems sincere, as sincere as corporate America can be.

"Mr. and Mrs. Beroe, it's Miles Venery. I hope you are both well today?" Miles can sound a bit turn of the century, something that bothers Remy. I find

Miles a bit of a romantic, an old fashion gentleman. He is the third generation to hold his position and I am sure his daughter will follow. Miles is a viral seventy something, with a sharp long nose and large intelligent eyes, never ostentatious, although his breeding is always an underlying tone in his movements and actions. I have never, not seen him in a suit, he's old guard and although that can be comforting, it also makes me very wary.

"Fine thanks and you?" Remy replies, raising his eyebrows at me.

"Very well, indeed. I thought it might be a good idea for all three of us to chat about the present nasty business." Miles continues.

"Stephanie is also on the line." Remy adds.

"Good morning Miles." I offer.

"Good Morning Stephanie. As you know, we have been the leading innovators in cannabis research in the U.S. for the past 3 years. We also lead the nation in food and drug innovations that span the globe. I'll get straight to the point. We are as taken aback as I believe anyone that has had any relations with our company is, with the editorials that appeared in print last week."

I see Remy's brows furrow. My hands start to sweat, I had read the stories in The New York Times, and Newsweek. Who had not? With sources like that it's hard to refute the accusations, which were, that Miles was courting smaller cannabis innovators to merge with, only to repress their new ideas and control patenting, to secure the innovations now in play. This is how capitalism in the U.S. reincarnates itself through the ages, *I get it, we just don't want to be victims of it.*

"It would be good to hear what you have to say, I found the stories, troubling." An understatement from Remy, who in fact found the stories more than troubling. When he read the article from the New York Times, he threw his cell phone across the room. We had just finished eight months of negotiations. We were set to go.

"God Dammit!" I heard from the bedroom and then a loud bang. Poking my head in to see what was going on, Remy was sitting on the edge of the bed, staring at his feet.

"Are we totally idealists? What the hell is wrong with us? Why couldn't we see this? Man, I tell you I feel like a fool. Again!"

"What happened?" I gently prodded

Remy likes to glean the news, I determinedly avoid it. My system of order cannot survive the glut of fear and hatred that is pointedly focused to draw our attention as good little viewers and followers. It damages me, tears at me, diminishing my faith in mankind, which lately is always teetering on empty. Remy's skin is tougher than mine, he keeps us connected, I like to think I keep us grounded.

Walking over to his phone he blurts, "Read this", while burning a hole in my skull. I took the phone, not taking my eyes off his. When I looked down, I noticed the screen shattered.

"Let me get my pad." I offered retrieving my device and handing it to Remy. After a moment, he tossed it back to me. The front -page highlight of the business section read;

Hammer Industries - Takes Aim at Cannabis Industry Innovation.

Although the article only notated an anonymous source from Hammer Industries itself, it clearly stated their monopolizing intentions, as a positive play in the business world. It practically encouraged while commending mergers with small innovators, only to gut them as good business practices. My stomach churned. I shook my head, eyes closed. I couldn't look at it anymore, only barely managing refrain from throwing it at the closet door as well.

"We just wasted eight months, almost a whole year negotiating with these clowns! We don't even have a back up to turn to!" Remy's words scared my brain.

"I can't believe H.S. and his group DBS are any better." I blurted out.

Remy rounded on me from the manic pacing he had fallen into, as I referred to the first large company to court us, a year ago, that had also come, to an abrupt end. I knew better than to say anymore, I 've learned when he's pissed, you just let him go.

"Sometimes, I think we just aren't good business people. We should have stayed in the arts! If we had put this much energy in your music or my paintings, where would we be now?"

I took this as rhetoric and firmly held my lips together. We both had budding careers in our twenties and early thirties, Remy as a fine artist and me as a singer song writer. We lived in New York City then. Remy had interest in his work by some of the big boy gallery owners, and he was smart, art smart. It was only a matter of time.

I had already charted in the top ten with my band, we were local darlings of the city and blooming but something happened to both of us after my mother died. The game became disenchanting, our priorities changed binding us together in the aftermath. Besides, we had been through this many- times;

second guessing our life choices now, at what would have seemed the bottom of a bumpy road, would have been, to say the least, counterproductive.

"We do have protections written into our contracts," I replied without thinking.

"Are you kidding me! Our contract won't be worth the paper it's printed on once they own us! That's why it's so important we find people we like, that are like minded. Don't be naïve, Steph."

It hurt, but it was true. I knew it, I had been hoping for the best. No other company had come close to our point of view like Miles and Hammer Industries; H.S. and his cronies at DBS were despicable, in I am sure more ways than one. But that one, was enough for me.

"So now what?" I asked letting the wall behind me bare the weight.

"I don't know Steph, I just have to think for a while," Remy stated, walking over to the window.

Think he did, for three days I could not break the barrier of depression that enveloped my usually positive spouse, his favorite expression, "It's all good." A friend embroidered on a pillow for him as a Christmas gift, his ever-contagious mantra, forsaken.

I attempted a positivity that was not unfeeling to his low depths. It was important that one of us maintained hope, or the ship would have sunk. On the third day, I recall, like a nail in the coffin, a small article in Newsweek appeared, Hammer Prowls Nascent Innovations.

"It's over, we have to find another partner." Remy glowered from the couch.

"Ok, any suggestions?"

"Well, there is H.S."

I noticeably recoiled at the suggestion.

"What? I don't understand what turned you against them so quickly. What was it?" he sat down next to me, his green blue eyes intent with concern, placing his hand on mine.

I looked at our hands, his strong yet gentle, and mine rather large for a woman, both showing the signs of maturity, intertwined.

"Steph," his tone was gentle and coaxing, "What happened? Please tell me."

I raised my eyes to meet his imploring gaze. I had looked into his handsome face over these years and found the strength to survive my biggest life's challenges, I reminded myself. What made this so hard? My lips parted with an attempt to betray the guilt in my heart. *The guilt*. Closing my eyes, I lost my nerve. The words were there, but I couldn't or didn't want to say them out loud. The repercussions would have been …unforgivable. "It was too good to be true, you said it yourself." I managed.

Narrowing his eyes, he let go of my hand and walked away.

"Rem", I reserve this endearment for moments of intimacy usually, "You know so many people, there MUST be someone else." I implored as he walked through the doorway.

"God damn it!" He growled. "What do we have lined up for this month, conference wise?" His attempt at control apparent, his back still turned.

"Well my dear," I replied with as much sincerity as humanly possible," I am in New York at the Javits show, and B.C, the end of next week. You are in San Francisco the end of the month, then we both go to Germany the following week."

"Put some feelers out." His tone more of a command than a statement. I could feel the shift, we were moving into new territory.

I slid up next to him in the doorway. "This is not the end," I remember saying placing my hand on his back, "We have faced so much worse together. We will rise from the ashes, we have the technology, we can rebuild it." I continued while singing the song for the Six Million Dollar Man. Finally cracking his smile, relief waved through me, like a mountain spring. "What tide is it?" I asked tilting my head.

"I was thinking the same thing, but first a station break." Pulling me towards him, Remy and I melted into our private world, where no one and nothing else existed, if only for precious few moments.

Pulling myself back into the present, I take a large breath, we had not heard from Miles or any of his staff until yesterday, a week after the editorial. This silence did not play well with Remy. When we finally received a text from Miles yesterday, asking if we were available for this conference call today, Remy almost didn't reply. It took considerable coaxing on my part, "We have nothing to lose." I offered.

"Our time is worth a lot, Steph."

"Yes, let's just hear what he has to say."

He shrugged with a look like, "Don't tell me what to do." *Scorpios*.

"Well, we are certainly open to hearing your side of this *scandal*." Remy uses a hard inflection on the word scandal. I can see his temper beginning to flare already. Without holding his hand over the speaker, and purposely not whispering he turns toward me and says, "He is wasting our time."

I reach over and push the speaker phone.

Miles ignores the statement and continues, "The truth is, we don't know who was quoted, but I can assure you we are placing a great deal of effort into finding the culprit, and the motivation." He notes with Zen like calm, I read to be forced, continuing, "It is pure libel, we do not have any intentions of controlling your patents. We have meticulously placed verbiage in our agreement to prevent it. You are the innovators in this scenario, our relationship with you is the most important aspect of this deal."

Remy throws his head back at this, then jumps up vehemently pointing his finger at the speakerphone. "You mean to tell me that both The New York Times and Newsweek Magazine release practically the same story, the same week, glorifying; "*the adeptness of your company prowess as hunters in a caged zoo*", Remy quotes the article as I cringe, "on the eve of our signing a partnership agreement with you? And it's utter bullshit? Seems like the only thing that went wrong, was the timing, perhaps the story got released a day or so early!" Remy, torrently continues, "Come on Miles, everyone in our industry is following this partnership, it is the first of its kind! What do you take us for?"

Directness in situations like this separate the men from the boys. Although his voice is raised, Remy still holds a reserve that emanates hidden calculation. Had I not felt as if our world were rapidly escaping our hands like a balloon rising towards the boundlessness of the sky, I would have been taken by the inner strength expressed on my spouse's handsome determined face. Drawing me to him like a moth to light, he is inescapable, his personal power is awesome.

"Remy, you have a right to be angry, the position we are in does not look good. Especially since we have only known one another for a short period of time. I can only tell you" Miles pauses correcting himself, "ask you, for the opportunity in person, to show you that it is NOT true."

I interrupt, "I think THAT is a good idea."

Remy turns on me with an expression of horror, as if I just drilled a hole in his longboard. I place my finger to my lips quietly. An awkward silence fills the air.

"Thank you, Stephanie." Miles intercepts seeing the opening," I can be in Long Beach this afternoon. Where would you like to meet?"

Miles knows we work out of our home, the entire first floor is designated to our stations. He also acknowledges it would not be appropriate at this time to meet here. I note the civility.

"Today is not good, I have meetings all day." Remy bursts, placing his finger to his lips with the relish of a teenager. "Tomorrow is better, in the lobby of La Casa del Camino Hotel at 11."

We could have insisted he meet us at the top of the Eiffel Tower with a pink carnation in his breast pocket, and he would have acquiesced, however, power is not what we are looking for. We have learned with our early years of running our own business, that not desiring to hold power in a relationship, encourages the other party to prove themselves all the more. I nod my head while staring into his now piercing blue eyes, I can guess what he is up to.

"Tomorrow then? Thank you for this opportunity, both of you." Miles replies with dignity and humility, I find sincere.

Remy disconnects the call without looking up, "We need a day to figure out our strategy. We can't go in there like sheep."

"Well, what is our strategy? Do you believe a word he is saying?" I get up to get a glass of water, "Do you want anything?"

"No… I mean no, I don't want a drink. The problem is I WANT to believe him. God damn it!"

Thinking that H.S. and D.B.S are our only alternative, I murmur to the sink, "So do I."

3

BOX CUTTER EMPORIUM

Finger depressing the speaker phone, Miles Venery rises out of his chair. The hand he sees in front of him looks disturbingly like his father's, weathered and aged. Crossing the room, the view of the Empire State building looking south, banded by the East River, captivates his thoughts of sabotage, *am I too old to play this game anymore?*

Competition, the cornerstone of capitalism, an ever- driving force has rarely been his foe. Looking downtown from the Hammer Industries executive offices on the 65th floor of the Chrysler building, Miles is reminded of the competition between three previous millionaires in 1928 to build the tallest skyscraper in the world; The Chrysler building, the Empire State building and the Bank of Manhattan Trust on Wall Street. The principals were architects and financiers, innovators at a turning point in U.S. history, but Walter P. Chrysler took competition to a new level. A friend of his grandfathers at the time, Walter Chrysler was obsessed with building, and had confided in Mile's grandfather, the plans Chrysler and his architect William Van Alen fashioned to secretly out build Van Alen's former partner and architect for the Manhattan Trust building,

H. Craig Severance. They secretly delivered and assembled the crown of the Chrysler building inside the top floor then hoisted it up and riveted it on in absolute secrecy. Their merits overshooting the Manhattan Bank building, which had been two feet taller, by over a startling, one-hundred feet, heralding the Chrysler building into history as the world's tallest skyscraper.

Miles can hear his father's voice retelling the story, a man who rarely showed emotion consumed with excitement, as he claimed, "That same year the Yankee's led by Babe Ruth, won the world pennant for a historical two years in a row. The world was watching New York City, Miles."

He loved this story as a child, sitting in this very same office he now occupies, begging him to retell it almost daily. His father's exhilaration matching his own while they recounted every detail of the secret plan. Miles was hooked, allured by the deviant prestige bestowed upon the prevailer.

Today as Miles Venery looks down over the sixty fifth floor of Chrysler's architectural giant, he is reminded the building was designed and modelled after the Chrysler automobiles that bare the same hood ornament as the Eagle gargoyles stationed at each corner of the building, and by continuing to compete with rivalling innovators Chrysler was also pushed to create and install Airtemp, making the Chrysler building the first fully air- conditioned skyscraper in the world, a landmark for eternity, and a curious little known fact, but a huge economic strive for Chrysler, ensuring his legacy.

Three sets of eyes watch Miles intently from across the room, waiting for a sign of mood or decision, following him back to the Art Deco desk his fore fathers commanded before him. Known for practically Anglophilic reserve, Miles like his father has never tended towards impulsiveness. At seventy- two his trim physique and strong jaw counteract a well- maintained head of gray hair. Unfolding his hands from under his chin staring in his own reverie to a silent room he thinks to himself, *it could be someone in this office.*

His silence frightens them. Anne Mallory his assistant, a tall lithe dark haired Irish hearted woman with fiendishly squared off finger nails, has been with him for more than twenty years, *we couldn't be closer if we were married,* he reminds himself, *in fact, I spend more time in her presence than my wife's.*

David Dixon, Hammer's Chief Operations Manager, a towering man in his late fifties, has had a rough year, losing his eldest son to cancer, but he has held fast in fifteen years and has not waivered.

Elizabeth, the Vice President of Hammer, is after all his daughter. His instincts assure him it is not anyone in this room.

"Do we have anything on this editorial?" Miles breaks the silence with controlled agitation, turning his deep- set eyes on the group.

"Father, I have been digging." Elizabeth begins in her eager and rapid fashion, "I have talked with each reporter from both rags, they won't divulge a thing."

"If only the New York Times and Newsweek were rags, we wouldn't be having this conversation." Miles reminds them.

"Shall I book you out for your meeting with the Beroes?"

"Yes Anne, I would prefer something roomy on the seaside, at the Casa del Camino."

The stylish, late sixty something, well- bred woman nods, picking up her device.

"Alright David, what do you really think about all of this?" Miles asks staring into David's creased face. Seated on the arm of the sofa lounge across from him, Miles notes the qualities of his good friend and colleague. A natural with people, David's relaxed almost laisser faire personality disarms with a sense of familiarity. David's eyes, always issuing calm in the stormiest of seas, he is a natural leader. Miles can't help notice David's shoulders are hunched. Helplessly watching his child die, has left its mark. David is not the same man he was last year, more withdrawn, pained.

"Honestly Miles, I don't think it came from inside. When you really dissect the article, it doesn't even read from any employee I know. We just don't think that way."

"That is precisely what I was thinking. I would like a list of the top five companies you would suspect. Who can we put on this full time?"

"You mean who have we pissed off lately?" Elizabeth interjects.

Miles nods at her, today corporate competition is a wearisome, but necessary evil.

"I have the right man for the job," David adds.

Knowing he would, in ten years there has never been a job too small or big or too tasteless, Miles remembers with uneasiness.

"Father, what will you say to the Beroes?"

"I don't think I need to say anything, I believe I just need to hold their hands. Isn't that a Beetles song?"

All eyebrows raise.

"Elizabeth, have you ever known me to be at a loss for words?"

4

DICTAPHONE'S LAMENT

By noon grace our assistant walks in with a cobb salad for me, and a
burger and fries from the tavern down the street for Remy. I had thought
to text her we were hungry and weary, but she is always thinking ahead. Grace is
a new addition to our world. At first, I fought Remy about the idea of having an
assistant. Perhaps I was seeing it as a sign of inadequacy on my part. After all, I
had taken care of all our little details as well as some of the larger ones from the
beginning.

"Sweetie, you ARE Super Woman," Remy chortled," but even she needs
help once in a while. Besides, I need a lot of help, and I don't want to lean on
you, your plate is full."

Always observant and forward thinking, I could not argue with his
reasoning. We did need an assistant. I placed an ad online about six months ago,
through a cannabis specific employment network. With the industry growing
exponentially there is a glut of people trying to get a foot in the door. I had a
folder on my desk filled with resume's that have been sent via our website. The
task was daunting, so I placed the ad just to cover my bases. I recall I had

reviewed half the applicants in my folder when I received an email that the agency had successfully screened an applicant. Having placed strict pre-requisites on the site, which is easy to do when you are filling in a box on a form, I was excited. In person, I get wishy washy.

Grace graduated from Purdue, which always seems funny to me, so old school, from an upper middle- class family, so she says, although at times I feel she may have escaped a white tower. Grace met all our requirements, on top of that, she is well spoken. Most importantly she successfully shields us from time wasters. That was my idea, installing a live filter for email, and calls so we could alleviate the "Drainers" as Remy puts it. Grace, fields all voicemail and email, that we are not acting on at the moment. The last two months have been an incredibly smooth transition and a chain breaker for both Remy and me.

Just a hair shorter than I am, she is a fit very pretty purposeful blonde, with blue eyes and well- tanned skin tone in her mid- thirties. She could be mistaken for a California girl, but for her droll East coast demeanor, a dead giveaway. Playing her beauty down, with metrosexual clothes and very little makeup, she is obviously bright and well read

"Thanks Grace, you saved us again." I smile as I head for the table. Remy is on a phone call, facing the window that looks out to the sea. I pour a little white wine for both of us. A civil notion in a complex world, I think, with just a trace of guilt.

"How are you today Grace?"

"Wonderful," Stephanie, "Thank you, and you? What have you been up to today? There seems to be a little tension in the air."

"Yes, well Miles called. We will be meeting him tomorrow at 11." I state plaintively.

"Really, that is interesting. How exactly did he manage that?" Grace is, of course, privy to our business life, and we keep her abreast of the agreement situations with all potential licensees, it's necessary although a little nerve racking to share at times. I am not used to having an outsider in the equation. She is not privy to our personal life, no one is. Remy and I confide in each other, at least we did.

Before I can reply, Remy walks over to the table while closing his conversation on the phone, the smell of burger having lured him over sub consciously.

"Hey Grace, when did you get here?" Grace and I eyeball each other and smile. As we eat, Grace goes down to the office floor of our townhouse and organizes our lives. Thank God.

Clinking our glasses together we toast. "Cheers sweetheart."

"Cheers my love."

Managing luncheon without one word of business, Remy is focused on property in Costa Rica. He is gleaning information every spare moment he has. "Putting a cost on the dream", he says.

Of course, we don't have any money to buy anything in Costa Rica or anywhere else. All our cash is either invested in this town house or Mad Hatter. Both money pits. Dare to dream, I think to myself and certainly know better than to play Debbie downer.

"We can still buy property on the beach, right on the water for under a hundred thousand." The excitement in his eyes is undeniable.

"That's encouraging," *It might as well be a million,* "have you narrowed any areas down?".

"A couple, I estimate it would take us a month to drive down, and then another three months looking around once we get there."

"Sounds like a great trip. I am just having a hard time wrapping my head around it right now." I say using my hands to make a wrapping gesture in the air to accentuate my point.

"That's why it's important to have dreams, sweetie." Remy reminds me with a profound gentleness, "We are nothing without them."

Oh, those eyes. "I know," I say taking a moment to appreciate his unerring ability to continue forward momentum regardless of obstacles. "What else do you have today?" I ask while moving my mixed salad greens around with my fork, they are a bit wilted.

"Hmm, I have a two o'clock then I have some tests to run later today in the lab. How about you?"

The lab is in our garage, Remy experiments with preliminary ideas for infusion and processing here at home. Once an idea has been proofed down, he runs the real testing at our licensee's lab facility. We are never more than a couple of rooms apart from each other unless there is a conference attendance that divides us or one of us is training licensee staff. Unlike most couples, we live and work together and always have. We spend all our waking hours well within the vicinity of each other, it works for us. Lately, I have noticed we don't need to speak in order to talk anymore, we just know what the other is thinking, with that thought I smile. "I am revamping our display boxes today, I would like them to be printed and ready to ship within the month. Remy looks at me with a parental glance. "I am also wrapping up the blend estimate for Colorado." His face relaxes upon my announcement. "Oh, also I forgot to tell you I received a text message from Francois, he mentioned again he would like to work with us, on a CBD line of products. I am going to see him next week, he will be at the L.A. show."

We met Francois at a small gathering of interested parties and curious seekers, that was intended to introduce Nevada to the Cannabis world, prior to it rolling out it's legalization of Medical Cannabis usage. After that, we teamed up with his company at several conference booths. We work well together. They have IP for a crystalized water dispersible CBD or Cannabidiol infusion that would be beautiful for bottled drinks. Hemp CBD although it is controlled like most nutrient products, can be shipped globally as it does not make you high, but it alleviates pain and stress. It is receiving world recognition for treatment of seizures and Parkinson's. We have tossed around the idea of partnering with them. Our brand their IP, combined marketing and distribution channels, it seems like a good fit. It should certainly be an easier line of products to promote as it is not a federally regulated schedule one, meaning a lot less state and government interference.

"I wish there were two of us, we need to focus on this partnership predicament first. Then we can sit down with Francois."

"Two of you?" I muse, "That sounds interesting." He leans over and kisses me, warm and confident.

"It's all good." He whispers in my ear.

"Ok you two, break it up," Grace emerges from the stairs, "Are you ready for your call lists?"

"Lay it on us." Remy grabs his phone, pushing back his chair.

She gives us the low down on who has called and why. Divvying up the list of call backs we have Grace handle the left overs, literally.

We retreat to our work stations for the day on the first floor, one of three floors in the house. The garage/lab and offices are on the first. The office is an open loft space that we have divided in half. I work on one side and Remy on the other. The offices share a wall with the lab, but the door to the lab is outside. A large table in the middle is our communal space, usually strewn with paperwork, prior to Grace. She tends to command the center table. The entire west facing wall is glass and looks out to the sea, we can almost see the entire bay from our vantage point. There is no need for artificial lighting during the day, both of our desks face the big blue.

As I reach the bottom of the spiral stair, I notice how very different our work areas are from each other. My antique maple and rose wood sewing table I use as a desk only supports my lap top. There are no drawers, just a top with two hand carved legs on each end, stabilized by a wooden bar that I like to rest my feet on while sitting. The Yoga ball I use as a chair, I note, needs inflating.

Every other surface in this space is covered with brochures, card board displays, flow charts and folders of bills, evidence of a growing business. Boxes of post cards and packaging with large black hand printed letters that clearly mark the territory they will be sent to, line the walls. Ideally, we need a storage area, I think to myself, making my way through the maze.

I have three calendars hanging on the wall, one is a regular calendar with images of Ancient Greek temples and the dazzling Mediterranean behind them, this is reserved for family birthdays, and holidays. Remy is one of ten, between siblings, nieces and nephews this calendar is pretty full. The second is a white board blend calendar, listing dates for continued blends of our products for each of our 8 territories that outlines marketing time frames, packaging issues, sales quotas, and holiday preparation. The third written out on black board paper attached to the wall, is for conferences, listing where Remy and I will be two months out at any given time. I admonish myself for this old- fashioned system, but we are both visual people and seeing it on a handheld device just doesn't do it for us. When I had explained it to Grace, so she would understand how to keep them up to date, she looked at me with her head slightly tilted, "You do have a calendar on your phone?"

"Yes, of course, we both do." I replied, "And they will need to be kept up to date as well," I replied in defense, "they are all synced together," I added attempting technological savvy. "These individual calendars allow us to see things compartmentalized. Free time, ghost time and face to face time. We wear different hats for each. Pun intended."

"Got it," she said with noted trepidation. Two months later, Grace is familiar with our eccentricities.

Settling in to my space, after inflating my yoga ball, I have three different types of display mock ups in front of me. One is tin, the other cardboard and the last is wooden. My intention is to choose which of these based on price, quality, and innovation of design will be our new sampler box for wholesale clients to receive their initial order in that can also be used as a counter display. It doesn't sound all that interesting, but in store marketing is key. It is grass roots and you cannot put a price on receiving counter attention.

"Sweetie," Remy calls to me from the stairs, "can you send me Francois' phone number?"

"How much is it worth to you?"

"I'll let you live." He whispers while grazing my ear from behind, sending goose bumps down my spine.

"You are so dangerously close, my love."

He laughs, "No, really."

Grace having followed him, a loyal puppy, quickly texts him the information, putting an abrupt end to our negotiations. I am not oblivious to the fact that Grace has a crush on Remy. I cannot blame her, I do too. Most women that come in contact with him are affected the same way. I am used to it, and since I don't have to share, it's not a problem. If anything, it's a little ego boost for him, half the time he doesn't even pick up on it. All the same, I keep my eyes open.

A large flat screen, that we use to get our presentations together via blue tooth and to view packaging, marketing, and promotional materials in large format hangs on the wall behind Grace, not the ideal position with the glare of the ocean, but the block out curtains I managed to sew has reconciled the oceans attempts at distracting us. My spouse's work space, which is in my direct line of sight over several large boxes of T shirts ready to ship to Nevada, is spotless. No boxes, no brochures, his desk, a vintage doctor's stainless- steel behemoth is immaculate albeit a little dusty. All surfaces are devoid except for a pair of binoculars, and a half a dozen art books and science journals neatly lining the shelf that sits on the north side wall with a photograph of Lee Friedlander's hanging behind him that I had given him as a birthday present. A black and white image taken in a hotel room in the 60's while Friedlander was a traveling sales man. In frame is a radiator, and an old- style television on an aluminum stand with wheels, just a corner of the unmade bed in the fore ground. Everything in the room of this photograph is the same tone, the carpet, the bedspread, the wall even the radiator. On the television is a scene with Marlon Brando on his motorcycle, the head light of the bike coming toward you in the night, from "The Wild Ones". Perfect, I think to myself. It reminds us both of the days we first started Mad Hatter, I would set up cold call sales meetings and Remy would go in and pitch the products. For the first two years, we did this, with him travelling all over the state of Colorado. Like any artform, sales is the tricky part. Creating the products came easy, Remy's unusual way with words has become the hallmark of our brand, satirical poetry if you will. Creating the blends was and is the fun part, researching ingredients, homeopathic remedies, eastern medicine, and Amazonian herbs to pair with the perfect flavor and aroma as a cross section to create complex recipes is Remy's forte. Like a sommelier, he has a gift for it.

Yes, this stackable townhouse suits our needs for the moment, the kitchen and living room on the second floor have a deck that expanses the back of the townhouse, I have managed to keep a lemon tree alive in a large pot just outside the living room slider, what it lacks in leaves it makes up for with lemons, and reminds me of a painting Remy did just after we met. I recall it was brightly colored and rather large. A very small terracotta pot with an overgrown lemon tree growing out of it sitting on pink patio paving bricks. The branches are laden with large lemons, although the tree bares only a handful of leaves. Behind the tree in the painting is a decorative floral brick wall. I don't know why I like this painting so much. At first glance, the plant is terribly confined by cement, while thriving, despite its confines. I make a mental note to ask Remy to find that painting in storage and re stretch it, I would like to live with it again. *Art predicting life?*

Behind the real lemon tree, there are several flower boxes of herbs and one bright pink tea rose in a clay pot up against the wall of the town house, the pot has four three dimensional faces each balancing the other looking out as sentinels. I made it a year ago, sculpting the lovely faces onto the coiled pot. Our last house was surrounded by overgrown pepper trees, the pot fit in there, nymphs in the woods waiting out time.

The second floor is pretty open, a well- designed modern kitchen looks out to a wall of glass with a view of the southern side of town, edged by the sea. Our furniture is a mish mash of my life, Rem's life, and my Mother's life before she died. A curated blend of elegance, eclectic and recycled treasures, creating a bohemian chic, seldom rivaled, so I'm told. A petite cocktail baby grand in the corner with family photos on top in un-matching but interesting frames, homemade drapes, and pillows add an air of Eastern Indian influence while art from all over the world, including Remy's paintings, pick up the overall cache'. My sculpture and organic goodies we rescued from the elements, blend everything together nicely. It's comfortable and unique.

Our bedroom and small catch all room on the third floor is our private domain, not even Grace has been invited into our sanctuary. No one goes up there and we can sometimes stay there for days at a time, only retreating to the kitchen for food, when we have returned from intense travel schedules. I recall that our last retreat required a day's rest from our intimate activities. That was before H.S and Miles, I think to myself, holding fast to my resolve.

My phone rings, Grace picks it up. "Mad Hatter Coffee & Tea, this is Grace, how can I help you today? Hi Beth, how are you? Hmm, that's odd. Let me give the bank a call and I will get back to you. Sure, no problem." She hangs up.

"What's up?" I ask.

"That was Beth from Vermont, she said the wire transfer they sent you for this next blend was returned."

Before I can suggest a strategy, Grace has already dialed Bank of North Americans and asked for a supervisor.

Remy is on a conference call to Hawaii. A group that has applied for a license to produce MMJ, that knows a good friend of ours, has been testing the waters while expressing interest in licensing Mad Hatter. All three men are multi- millionaires if not billionaires. Remy puts his phone down and sits in his chair, staring at me, without seeing me.

"What's wrong?" My intuition screams, my voice barely audible.

"I've got to tell Burgess not to send anymore newbies my way. They just want to pick my brain, glean as much information as possible, waste my time. These guys are so cheap, once you bring up a consultation fee, you never hear from them again." He picks his phone back up texting furiously with one finger.

Poor Burgess, I think to myself. We met him in Nevada, his out the box approach to life, bonded him to us. Networking is his strength, we have worked together on many projects, some positive others not so much, but that's business. You never know when something is going to click until you give it a try. I feel for Remy, the newbies or new comers to the industry can be a real drain.

I have printed out mock design layouts for the exterior of the display I am working on. While I am hacking them on the paper cutter, I recognize the look of eternal hold on Grace's face. I look up at her and she just shakes her head with a shrug. The Marijuana Industry is plagued by many ridiculous regulations. The fact that marijuana is a schedule one substance means, the federal government looks at it as illegal to prescribe to patients, illegal to sell, grow, purchase and possess. All states where Marijuana is legal for patients and recreational adult use are protected by their own state laws only. Some states, I remind myself have gone as far as to incorporate the access of marijuana into their constitution, giving them further protection from the feds. Due to this Federal and state snafu, a good majority of MMJ industry companies have been thrown out of banks, simply because the banks are federally insured, causing a conflict with the federal government should they desire to impose the federal laws. We have been thrown out of five, none of them would even disclose why, but we knew. The Obama administration stated they would not direct funds towards any legally licensed marijuana operators in legal states. Which is helpful but they certainly could have gone further. The next election could be a game changer, again.

Three quarters of our industry have no banking solutions. So, here we are attempting to be good little children, transparent, tax paying legal business owners, with no bank accounts. The irony is almost too much for Remy. I look over at him, he is gleaning something on his phone.

"The feds will take our tax dollars for our business, but they won't regulate access to banking. What a bunch of losers. I hate banks." I am probably not remembering his correct terminology, I laugh to myself, but Remy is right. All of us in the industry have changed our corporate names to acronyms in the hopes the banks would not catch on to what we do. Signing up for a new account you have to be vague you don't need to lie, but you don't need to tell the whole truth.

Grace walks over to my desk and writes on a post it, *being transferred to the risk department*. I wave at her to give me the phone. After fifteen minutes of excruciating infomercial details on how B of NA can make my business run more efficiently, a woman comes on the line.

"This is Kanisha Jones, how may I help you today." Her voice is steady and devoid of emotional contact.

"Hi Kanisha, I was checking on a wire transfer that was returned to my client from our business checking account. It should have cleared three weeks ago, I was under the impression that wire transfers take 2 business days. Now I have been transferred to you."

"Yes, Mrs. Beroe. Can you confirm some account details for me please?" After going through the rigorous I.D confirmation for the third time, since Grace placed the call she asks, "Can you tell me what type of business you have?"

"We are wholesalers, consultants and develop real estate," I reply with equitable emotionless calm.

"What did you describe your business as when you opened your account?"

"I just told you."

"Well, It seems we cannot verify the payee of the wire transfer."

What does that have to do with our business intentions? "That's odd we have been doing business with them for over a year now, regular payments. What's the problem?"

"Can you please hold?"

"Sure," I reply, knowing this is not good. Remy is looking at me from across the room he is doing his Caesar thang, thumb up or down. I raise my hand with a thumb down.

"Shit." He mutters.

Grace is sitting on her big round desk, watching all the gory details unfold, until I hear her phone go off, she walks up- stairs talking rapidly, probably to Beth. Beth's company in Vermont uses their full name on their account, High Valley Dispensary. Probably due to the fact that Vermont is so cool, their small savings and loan doesn't care about federal pressure.

Five minutes later, Kenisha returns, her voice is stern, motherly. "Mrs. Beroe, we have attempted to contact the payee, but there is no answer for verification."

I fall into the trap, "Ok, well the owner is on my other line. Would you like me to dial you in?"

With a little more friendliness, Kenisha replies, "That won't be necessary, we have deemed your account as high risk. We are closing your accounts, effective immediately, we do not have to disclose a reason, based on the paperwork you signed when you opened your account. You will not have online access, we will not transfer any funds in or out of your account. Any checks you have out on your accounts will be returned. You will be required to physically go into a branch and withdraw your money, in cash or a bank check."

Closing my eyes, I repeat, "Accounts?"

"Yes, all of your accounts, personal and business."

When I open my eyes, Remy is standing over me.

"Wonderful, what a great help you have been." I reply perhaps with a little too much sarcasm and continue, "You do realize that you and your company are acting in prejudice to our business because we service the Medical Marijuana Industry? We are no different than a light company, or lawyer, or security company that brings a service to the industry. We don't touch Marijuana, *not completely true,* we don't hold a license to grow or sell marijuana. We wholesale tea and coffee recipes and branding to state license holders, period." I can see Remy ready to blow, I shake my head.

"I am not at liberty to discuss this with you. Is there anything else I can do for you today?"

"No. You've done enough already," I say hanging up. *Touché*!

"God damn it!" Remy hits the desk with his hand.

"I've got to go withdraw all of our money from the bank, even our personal accounts." That means no more debit cards too." I say looking at him for a solution.

"You gonna hire an armored car for all that cash?" He retorts, planting himself on my desk, having sensed my attempt at control.

I roll my eyes. Of course, he is kidding. From the outside, Mad Hatter looks like we are doing very well. Cutting edge technology, incredible niche products, booming industry. We would be feasting too, if we hadn't decided to expand. The expansion is taking the bulk profit out of our hands and into a licensee's hands. Unfortunately, most of the licensees have not rolled out yet. Things take longer in this industry, we see a two- year period from signing contracts to product on the shelves. We have been hand to mouth for the last year, somehow always moving forward, but it is beginning to wear on both of us. This is the sixth bank to close our accounts and the first time it has affected our personal accounts.

"Here we go again," I say, tossing my pen into the pile on my desk.

"I'm sorry Sweetie, this is not what I envisioned." Remy takes my hand and looks at it.

"I know, neither of us did. We knew it would be tough."

"Damn it, it always seems like we are being tested."

Those blue eyes searching. "It does." I manage before he looks into my face and kisses me, soft and warm.

Dashing out to the bank, I give Grace instructions to notify all of our clients, that we have had a banking issue and direct them to pay monthly payments to our online Friendpal account in the interim. My mind is full to the brim. I am in the middle of a $120,000 blend between 2 states. Each state licensee is required to purchase their uninfused, or what we call raw tea and coffee blends, and packaging through us, to maintain quality control. We pre-blend the raw products in our small kitchen facility and ship them out by weight, thus protecting our IP and standardizing consistency at the same time. They infuse the product with cannabis in their state licensed facility.

I now have about $210,000 in cash to pull out of our account. *Cash! What the hell am I going to do with all that cash? I can't deposit it into Friendpal!* Attempting rationale, I take a breath as I am grabbing my purse and sun glasses, I pause laying them on the sink counter of our bathroom. Remy follows me in, as I pull down my panties to take a pee.

"You want me to come with you?" He asks a bit sheepishly, but I know what he is thinking.

"Are you kidding? No, I don't think that's a good idea."

"What?" Replying lifting his eyebrows in mock surprise.

"The last thing we need is for you to be arrested because you had an inkling to voice your opinion on Bank of North Americans business practices, I can see the headlines now," I say wiping my ass.

"All press is good press." *Classic Remy style.*

"You realize, I will be bringing about $210,000 in cash home? Oh, and I am in the middle of our biggest blend yet and have no idea how I am going to purchase $80,000 worth of goods from our suppliers, without a checking account or a credit card?" Panic now seeping through my retort, my throat becomes dry and coarse.

"Can't you just put it in the Friendpal account?"

I turn to look at him pausing to control my impatience, "Sweetie, there is no way for me to deposit into our Friendpal account that is not electronic. I am going to lose my mind if I have to pay everyone in money orders. Not to mention I am going to feel like a drug dealer at the post office buying all of them."

"You ARE a drug dealer."

I open my mouth and close it.

"You'll figure it out," he pats my behind, as I walk out the bedroom door, "you always do."

Most males would be uncomfortable with their wife handling ALL the money, taxes, bills. Not Remy, it really doesn't matter to him, money is not what motivates his being. I love that part of him. Most of the time Remy doesn't even know if we have money in our account. Which is good, I think to myself as he is extravagant with his gifts to his wife. If we have $4000 in the account that he knows of, he doesn't think twice about buying me a piece of art, or a car and spending every cent. I smile thinking of the beautiful Jean Lowe papier mache' books and book shelf, he bought me for my 27th birthday, not three months after my mother had died. I love that piece. A wonderful San Diego artist, very insightful, sarcastic environmental social commentary of corporate greed and the shallowness of mankind, *right up my alley*. My favorite book in the series is titled in her hand writing, "Not on My Dime." The bookshelf and all 10 books are an anchor in our living room.

With a quick look in the mirror, I retrieve my bag and dash down the stairs. Grace is at the office landing, awaiting instructions, as I am sure Remy has just updated her.

"Try to look up secure credit cards. See if I can buy a card at the grocery store and how much cash I can put on it. I need to be able to load $50,000 on to a card somehow in the next three days." I say to Grace.

"Got it."

Remy walks me out to Trixie, "Now you come back to me, all that cash… I bet Costa is looking pretty good?" He is purring in my ear.

I let out a blurt of amusement.

"No, seriously, come back to me."

"Always." My reply in earnest.

Jumping in the van I head off down the hill, B of NA is on Ocean Ave. and Beach street about a seven- minutes- drive from the house. Turning off the radio and rolling down the window, helps me clear my mind. *Just another hurdle.* I remind myself, if we can hang in there, we will be set. A California zephyr greets me as I wait at a stop sign, I read it as a good omen breathing in the warm air and letting it push the tension out of my body. "Breathe."

Parking the van in the lot across the street from the bank, I walk into the lobby of the faceless building. The interior has always been dark and dingy, but today it feels ominous. The line is out the door, one teller is working. I take off my sunglasses, I don't recognize anyone. I feel uncomfortable, out of place… GUILTY. Yet, I have done nothing wrong. Anger welling inside me, suddenly my emotions draw me back. *Guilt.*

Striding up to the teller, 20 minutes later, I place my glasses on the counter and hand her a sheet of paper with our account numbers on it. Swiping my card at the atm terminal to initiate the transaction, I turn to the teller and in the most controlled, unemotional voice I can muster state very clearly, "You have closed our accounts. I need you to withdraw all of our money from these accounts AND make sure they are all closed."

The twenty something looks at me with a mixture of empathy and alarm, "Certainly, Mrs. Beroe."

After an exchange with her computer, she looks at me and states, "I don't have that much cash in my drawer."

"That is not my problem," I affirm steely eyed and ready to pounce.

The manager comes over, obviously picking up on my vibration, Remy says I can vibrate at such a high level, he can hear the hum, at this moment so can I.

"Can I help?" The manager demurs.

The teller repeats my saga, I can feel the attention of everyone in this bank on the back of my head. I am determined NOT to make a scene, only because *I know it won't help!*

The manager, writes the figure down on a piece of paper, she looks over the counter that is barely lower than her chin and asks, "How would you like this?"

"Do I look like I care?"

She winces and heads for the vault. I look at the teller and state firmly, "I am going to need a couple of bank bags, and I would like the guard to follow me to my car."

"Certainly." Locking her drawer, she picks her 110- pound figure out of the seat and meanders over to the security guard, that has been watching me with increased interest. The teller's braces gleaming in the fluorescent light, she is wearing a flimsy white blouse, that is badly made with high waisted synthetic black pants pleated on both sides of the button. I note the only style this girl has is bad. I am no snob, I shop at thrift stores mostly, there is always a bargain to be found. I pride myself on unique, one of a kind clothing, that I procure from the discards of shop a holics. There is no reason to dress badly today, there are just too many options.

Listening to the money machine counting our hard- earned cash, I remember when bank tellers were women, dressed impeccably. But those were the days American Corporations hired lifetime employees on salary, instead of minimum wage part timers without pensions and benefits. *How much money do you need?*

Watching the manager return with a shoe box sized mound of cash wrapped in marked paper bands. "Ok Mrs. Beroe," attempting friendly, she proceeds to un-band and place bundles of five thousand, one hundred- dollar bills into the electronic counter. Once the first bundle has been processed, I request, "I would like to count it by hand as well," before she re-bands the pile.

"Certainly," She replies in surprise as if a machine has never made a mistake. I take a bundle and start counting, with the precision of a Vegas dealer. Once I'm finished the teller re-bands the bundle. Both women are amused by my proficiency.

"Lots of cash in my business," I state batting my eyelashes.

"What business is that?" The teller responds, her manager gives out a little cough to snap her underling back into place.

"I'm not at liberty to discuss that with you, my dear," I retort with a moment of satisfaction.

Shoving the cash into the bank bag another twenty minutes later, I turn to the guard who follows me out the door. My guilt has now turned to pride, after all how many people in this line looking at me or sitting behind this counter, like the thief they believe me to be, has $233,874.99 in the bank?

As the guard and I approach Trixie, he remarks, "Sweet bus."

"Thanks," I respond over my sunglasses.

"Well, have a nice day," He offers.

I just shake my head. We ARE all in this together, it's really US against

THEM. WE are the peasants of the ruling class, we just have modern amenities and shiny new cars, to make us feel good about it. Instead of clamping us in chains in fields and factories, they complete our false package of freedom with the idea of choice and hope. Forcing us to buy all their crap by making us feel like failures if we don't have as much virgin jungle toilet paper as our neighbor has stock piled from floor to ceiling in his garage. "This really is The Matrix!" I mutter as I fire up Trixie. "We've GOT to get out of here!"

5

KOTA

For what seems like an eternity, they wait under the brush and protection of a mango grove in the waist high water. Even in the terrible light of midday sun, the river is murky with the sand it carries from the mountains miles away. After months of seasonal drought, the storms have finally begun up mountain. If only they could approach those mountains, they would be safe, Delta thinks to herself in vain.

Knowing it will pass again, it's random but always comes more than once, she considers they are safe for the moment at least. The group of seven women huddled around her are dutifully scanning the dirty water. Surrounded by foliage so incredibly dense, she can only make out the shoreline from her perspective across the river mouth. The air heavy with moisture but the aroma is unmistakable. Unable to see the smoke, she smells burning flesh.

"We are just going to sit tight." Talking more to herself than the others. "This is safe. Watch for any movement on the shoreline." Normally preferring higher ground, Delta had seen the reed thing in an old James Bond movie. What she would give for a martini right now. Life had changed so fast, she barely knew who she was anymore, or why she keeps going. Looking around at her small group is her affirmation. She is THEIR only chance.

The warm water soothes her aching muscles, it will also keep the dogs off them. All of their senses heightened from the rush of adrenaline.

Ora sees it first, her beautiful face overcome with anguish and discernment.

"Ora what is it?" Delta asks.

A nod her reply in the direction of a shadow of movement, but it's enough.

Silently signaling the group to submerge again, everyone obeys with- out question, except for one, defiant and dictatorial as usual. A momentary look into Pitt's eyes is proof. This was going to come to a head soon, but not now. For now, the best defense is a good offense, hide when you can, fight when you must.

The water offers a false calming silence. Breathing through the reeds is not as easy as the movie made it seem. She has to pinch her nose in order to keep a good seal between her lips and the bamboo reed. Delta cannot see the women next to her, but she can feel them. Their touch in the murky milieu is comforting. She has come to love each one of them, *well perhaps not all of them*. Watching their struggle for survival, helping them adapt to their new life has created a strong bond. They are family now.

6

THE SHIP SONG

Remy is in the bedroom, attempting to fold the clothes he is taking for his presentation in San Diego later today, by rolling them. I shake my head and start refolding everything when he's not looking after throwing the bank bags on the bed, now strewn with his wardrobe hopefuls. I look about and quietly pick out sensible but inimitable attire. I can't talk him out his high tops, nor would I. They are turquoise blue with bright orange accents and orange laces, they don't go with anything and at the same time, match everything. Just like Remy.

This is an insider industry event, not a blown- out cannabis cup with dabbers falling to their knees, and public looking for free samples of dope, *as if?* Just another notable difference from our industry and pharmaceuticals, I remind myself. No advertising on T.V. or print in some states including T shirts or online and no samples. At some point, all of us had been kicked off Facebook, which is peculiar as the CEO gives millions to the MMJ legalization fund in California, *yada yada yada*…

Remy will undoubtedly dazzle them with his new process for sprayed infusion, that is fully activated and standardized for dosage as well as water soluble. The latter being the most impressive, as THC oil and water don't naturally mix well even with most emulsifiers.

We spend most of our time traveling to these types of conferences. I hold my end up in marketing and branding events, with the intention to ever expand, while Remy works the innovation side.

"Two hundred G's baby. Whatta ya gonna do with all that money, while I'm gone?" Remy jests, shirtless from the bathroom door.

I raise my eyebrows in reply ignoring him, "So, I will see you later tonight?"

"Yes dear."

"Got everything you need?"

"Think so."

"Knock em dead. Remember, it's a walk in the park," we both say at the same time smiling at each other. My brother coined the phrase years ago when he would come into NYC and roadie for my band. Just before I went on stage he would say, "A walk in the park, kid."

Walking my husband out to our practical commuter car, a Subaru Cross Trek. I remind myself of when we used to make fun of people that drove Subaru's, they just had to have all wheel drive to get back and forth to the grocery store. A glorified shopping cart that identifies them with an active outdoorsy crowd. With all the driving we do to Denver, Oregon, and Washington we had to give in, at least this is a hybrid. We bought it gently used, a Doctor's wife didn't like the color on her special order, I remember with a smirk. Turning to face Remy, glad that is not my life I say, "Come back to me." While fixing his shirt collar, but really just attempting to hold on to him for a few more seconds. His smell, his warmth, his strength.

"Always." He kisses me gently on the forehead, and as the car pulls out, I hear Nick Cave groaning about bridges and ships.

I have roughly nine hours to myself, I contemplate my plan of attack walking back to the front door. Because Remy and I live and work together, and would have it no other way, I must admit I do enjoy the occasional moment when the whole house is mine. Of course, today I will spend most of my time finding an alternative banking situation. "Damn it!"

"Are you ok?" Grace overhears me thinking out loud and expresses her concern.

"Yes, I'm fine, all things considered. Grace, could you go down to the grocery store and buy a couple of the secure credit cards you looked into, I don't care about fees right now. I just need something we can deposit high sums of money onto. Hang on a minute." I run upstairs and grab a money bag from the bed and return with it under my arm. Handing her a crisp one hundred-dollar bill from my new stash. Grace takes one look and responds, "Wow!"

"Exactly, the sooner I get this out of the house the better." Collecting her things, she graciously asks, "Do you need anything else?"

"No, I'm good sweetie, thanks." *We should have installed a safe.*

Walking down the stairs to the office, I realize Remy and I were so distracted by the bank, we forgot to pow wow about Miles and our meeting. Making my way over to my desk through a mire of boxes, I decide to write out a list of my pros and cons for Mile's company, Hammer Industries. The most obvious cons first; deception, greed and lack of morality are followed by lack of definition of operating control in the contract, and feasibility of our severability, should things go wrong from our perspective. My pros; lack of history known to me of Hammer having done this in the past. Get grace on this, I make a mental note.

My phone dings, Remy texts; Sweetie, think about an approach for tomorrow, we can talk tonight.

I'm on it, please keep both hands on the wheel XOXO. How spooky it is that we are continuing each- others thoughts from a distance. Shaking my head, I get back to my list, adding; sterling reputation prior to articles, genuine intentions, no flares. I stare at no flares, immediately our conference call with H.S from DBS comes to mind…

The pin ball machine ring tone from Remy's phone accelerated our anxiousness about the call, a huge opportunity for our company.

"Remember, let's see what their intentions are before you offer any services." I blurted out as Remy slid the ringer over on his cell and tapped the speaker phone.

"This is Remy."

"Remy, good morning this is HS." His voice resonant with familiarity. H.S., the CEO of DBS, was in his early seventies, we found his over confidence a clear statement of his success in the business world, although we both found it a bit unnerving, we also considered it an unavoidable fact.

Physically H.S. brandishes a roundish face and carries his most unusual physical attribute, a flat nose that must have been broken several times, proudly giving him the air of rough and tumble. His blue eyes and fine gray hair were usually combed to the side to complete a very put together, if not handsome man.

"Good morning, Stephanie is on the line as well," Remy announced.

"Good morning Stephanie, how are you?"

"Fine, thank you."

"H.S.", Remy began," You know what we have to offer, we have sent you our prospectus, and outline of what we are looking for in a company to partner with. What do *you* have to offer Mad Hatter?" Never at a loss for words Remy goes right for the meat.

H.S. coughed, "Remy you understand that our conglomerate can assist your company's development in dozens of ways. Just being able to access our marketing and promotional staff would alter the way the world would see your company over night, and not just in the U.S."

"Hmm, well I think our marketing and promotion kicks ass for a small underfunded company. Steph manages quite well."

"I didn't mean to say she did not, I wouldn't be talking to you now if I didn't think both you and Stephanie were talented and markable in your industry."

Markable, I thought to myself, what a strange word to use, as I hear other people in the room with him on speaker phone, I could only assume they were not being introduced as they were temporary bystanders. At least that is what I hoped.

"H.S., I am not offended." I intervened, looking at Remy, "I think our biggest concern is that being annexed into a large conglomerate, even with a moderate budget, could get us lost in the family, and we do not wish to become a step child." *I had had similar experiences in the record industry, having been signed to Retro records in my twenties, a subsidiary of the multi- national Russell Brothers Records, it was difficult to negotiate for tour support, video funds… without being a favorite of an executive, you wallowed.*

"I assure you if I did not intend for our partnership to be a priority for both myself and DBS, I wouldn't have initiated negotiations. Why don't you let me impress you? Do you have some time next week? I can fly you out to NY, you can tour the home office and then we can take you to the lab facilities in Connecticut. Be my guests of honor."

"I would like to see the facilities." Remy confirmed, rubbing his chin. "That sounds good, let me check our calendar."

"Oh, by the way on the fifth of the month we are hosting our V.P. annual celebration in the Caymans. I think you would both enjoy this. I will have my people send over the details, you will be our guests, we will handle all the travel arrangements."

I gulped, "Sounds wonderful."

"Great I will be in touch." H.S. hung up.

Remy and I looked at each other as he disconnected, "What do you think?" I asked.

"I don't know, he is definitely determined to impress us. Oh shit, I gotta go." A penchant for being on time, Remy prepared to leave for a meeting with a grower slash extractor in San Diego. As I walked him to the door, his arm around me, I remember saying, "Give us a kiss. Come back to me."

His eyes meet mine, "Always."

I am staring off at the wall across from me as Grace returns from the grocery store, having completed her errand, as I am sending her an email asking her to look into Hammer Industries, our new best choice for our future's past for examples of takeovers, while she lays the bag of assorted credit cards on my desk.

"I bought four, they are all different, but these two have the highest limits, America serve by Mastercard. I had to put money on them when I bought them, so I just divided up the hundred you gave me, I am going to register two for you and two for Remy."

"Great thanks. I sent you an email about Miles as well." I say looking at the plastic cards in front of me, with printed numbers instead of raised credit card numbers.

"Ok."

The front door rings, I look at the clock on my screen and know who it is without thinking.

"Do you want me to get that?" Grace offers.

"No, I got it." I manage, walking to the front door, I see the face of my adorable mail man. He is sixty, very fit and wrinkly from walking door to door for years in the California sunshine, he reminds me of Jack Lalane. Jimmie's walking route gives him ample time to cabitz with all the stay at home workers. He just loves our company and prefers to hand deliver the mail when he sees a car in the drive. Handing me the mail, smiling from ear to ear he begins, "Hello, I have a new one for you today."

His penchant for questionable jokes is endearing. "Ok, let's have it," I say taking the mail from him as inconsequential.

"Why are New Yorkers so grumpy?"

Fully aware I am from New Jersey, I can see he is really enjoying himself. I think for a moment, but the only obvious reasons are property taxes, smog, and traffic, none of which are funny. "Why?" I surrender.

Pleased he stumped me again, Jimmie responds with relish, "Because the light at the end of the tunnel- is New Jersey."

I laugh, "That may be your best yet."

"Oh, I love a challenge. See you tomorrow."

"Have a good one." He's lucky Remy didn't answer the door, I think to myself walking back to the desk, he knows every punchline, he's a regular Sphinx, it's uncanny. He's the same way with presents, you cannot surprise him, although I have tried, he always guesses it.

I bring the mail up with me to the kitchen to grab an orange and a glass of water, *maybe a smoothie?* As I am removing all fresh fruit from the fridge, my eyes float to a small box on the lower corner of the front page of Cannabusiness Global, a quarterly insider magazine that also promotes conventions. *Who's not promoting conventions these days?*

The box is a highlight for an article dubbed, *Pot-Luck Problems.* I read the sentence that draws my eye again. *Mad Hatter Coffee & Tea, Cannabis Pioneers fall on hard luck.* Blinking I close the fridge and grab the magazine, scattering blueberries on the floor, groping for page 10. It's a byline article with a picture of a 1950's wife in a handmade apron over a crinoline dress, holding a casserole dish smiling vacantly.

Many Cannabis industry mom and pops have partnered with larger corporations for access to capital that the standard banking business market will not or cannot fulfill. Mad Hatter Coffee & Tea Co. is one such company. An insider from the pioneering company informs Cannabusiness "They (Mad

Hatter Coffee & Tea Co.), are courting several large corporations presently in food and pharmaceutical fields.

My stomach lurches as I read the word pharmaceuticals, NO ONE in this industry is a proponent of big pharma. This is persona non grata, a four- letter word. I sit down. The article continues;

Unique IP and strong branding have enabled most of these partnership agreements as well as market share in multiple states driving potential growth. A competing coffee company Dr. Joe's, who has recently launched with success in California told Cannabusiness, "The beverage industry is still wide open, there are no leaders in the markets yet." Their intentions to broker several licensing deals in other states by the end of the year is a clear main objective. "It's all about the price points, no one cares that it isn't genetically modified or organic or solvent free, they want the biggest bang for the buck, we give the people what they want." Dr. Joe's CEO, Dean Blackman told us from his office in San Francisco, a family run business. It would seem success in this industry is based on what you bring to the table, not what corporate America shoves down your throat. Most retailers and customers are not interested in a pot luck. By Gregory Howes

"Ouch, What the hell, who is this guy, and when did an insider from Mad Hatter talk with him?" My first impulse is to contact the editor and chew him a new asshole. I walk over to my phone on the counter and pick it up. I should wait for Remy to comment before I kick up dust, he has a way of handling things of this nature concisely, I reassure myself.

Grace walks in the kitchen, "What's wrong?"

I know I've gone pale. "This day just keeps getting better and better," I say handing her the article. I've lost my appetite now but fill a glass with water and chug the whole thing without taking a breath, placing the glass down rather roughly.

Grace looks up at me, "Oh my."

"Yeah, I think I need to sage the office or have an exorcist in, this is getting crazy."

"It's a small article, perhaps it won't get a lot of attention."

"Do *you* want to tell Remy that?" There's no need for her to reply. I turn and head down the stairs, wondering what the hell is next? Ignoring the squished blueberry trail, I am leaving behind, I contemplate, Dean Blackman from Dr. Joe's. He is a pig, having met him at several conferences I decided to never be in his company again. He's not in cannabis for cannabis. "Family run business my ass!" Like so many others, he retired with a golden parachute from wall street and was able to raise over five million to start up, his family run coffee company without even possessing one product to sell. Seriously if you can't successfully launch an edible company with five million, you never intended to do so in the first place. He doesn't imbibe, it's the perfect scary scenario for what the future of this industry could become. *We need to get out!*

I look up Gregory Howes on the internet, his face is unfamiliar to me. To his credit, he has a popular blog, but this is the first cannabis article I see with his name on it. *A newbie.*

7

CURSED MALE

NYC at Lenox Hill, on 69th and Park avenue, two Maserati Quattroportes pull up to the valet of The Union Club like high school boys racing along the summer strip at night in their daddies' cars, oblivious to the pedestrians canvassing the sidewalks. The valet, a middle-aged Italian immigrant discretely steps back and up to the curb nearly avoiding being clipped by the matching dark blue sports cars, squealing to a stop before him. Dashing around to the driver's side to open the door, Emilio is not taken aback by the aged man who attempts to dislodge himself from the car with noted effort.

Warren Bazel has been a member of The Union Club since he graduated Duke University in 1967, a graduation gift from German industrialist immigrant parents. He holds tightly to his heritage and his accent, as points of power. Short in stature as well as patience, he steps away from the door, a look of contempt clearly expressed for the man now holding his keys. Bazel's small leering eyes are complimented by an utter lack of hair and squat physique, creating the façade of mistrust and shiftiness. A financial guru, luckily most of his business is transacted over the phone. He is known for his acute conveyance of algorithms that have enabled him to predict trends in the global financial markets. He can be charming until his third drink.

The second car is emptied just as gracefully, by Richard Bannock. Consistently dressed in mismatched, outdated suits. The seventy something is the fourth generation to command his family company Bannock Industries, said to own an actual percentage of the property on earth. Dyed dark hair, sits atop his bloated somewhat European face. The constant need to prove he does not suffer from erectile dysfunction drives his un ending desire to conquer young beautiful women. To overcompensate for an average IQ and complete lack of business savvy Bannock's convoluted desire to be recognized as important, verges on other worldly. He is known to order Maître' D's to spoon feed him desert, especially when they are women.

Both men greet each other silently and walk toward the stone facade building. No gym bags are required for their weekly drink and game of backgammon.

The womanless club, considered the second oldest in New York and perhaps the third oldest in the country is known for its conservative membership and distinctly old blood. Deciding not to turn out confederate members during the Civil War, an indicator of its lack of moral discernity. Portraits of John Jacob Astor IV (who died on the Titanic), J.P. Morgan, Cornelius Vanderbilt, Dwight Eisenhower, and Ulysses S. Grant adorn the card room, all former members. The great entrance hall adorned with a Greek cross domed ceiling and columns is crowded with non- members waiting for their Paige, the holding pen for civilians awaiting their sponsors.

Both men charge through the crowd with the alacrity of fettered horses, stopping at the bar momentarily to ascertain attendance for the evening and order scotch.

"Dick, see anyone you know?" Warren Bazel taunts his only friend, his German accent cutting off each word like a scythe.

"Not anyone I wish to talk to," Bannock responds, a smirk positively audible on his weathered but well- tended face.

Moving through the evening crowd passing the library with its Saturn inspired light fixtures, they enter the backgammon room like hero's returning from war, of course, neither of them have ever served. Their regular table has been reserved for them as usual.

"What will it be tonight?" Dick asks surveying the room.

"Let's make it interesting," Warren responds with a glean in his eye. "Let's say dues for the year?"

"Yummy," Bannock replies while setting the black ebony checkers on their appropriate points. Warren Bazel mimics his ivory checkers on opposite points. After rolling a large die to decide who will go first, they settle into their game. Gambling on games in the club is of course, strictly forbidden.

"Tell me, Dick how's your new girl?" Bazel inquires, referring to Bannocks parade of office assistant's comings and goings.

"She's delicious. Wide- eyed and bushy, literally." Bannock responds to his opponent while snapping his fingers at the barman for another drink. His new assistant has been with him for two months, she's lean, dark, full lipped and heavily stacked. Thinking about the last "conference" she was required to attend with him, he can feel a rise in his mind. *She hadn't struggled too much, just enough actually.* Occasionally, it's difficult for him to get excited, it's become increasingly more difficult. *These vignettes are exactly what the doctor ordered. Real passion as stimuli,* he muses, *that could be the motto for our new club!*

"Where **do** you find them? This is what, your fourth in nine months?" Bazel's strained accent chides as he rolls doubles.

"A year Bazel. I have my sources." Bannock looks up at his friend with a sly smile, continuing, "So do you, from what I understand." Playing a hunch with an attempt of distraction.

Rolling doubles again, Bazel avoids eye contact, a glimmer of concern crossing his face as he has never revealed his secret to anyone. Neither his estranged wife of 40 years nor any of his fleeting friends would understand. When he hunts, as he likes to call it, he hunts alone. The raunchy bars he frequents in Alphabet City and Hoboken are not in danger of being patronized by his colleagues or club members. "Shall we double the stakes, Dickie?" Bazel asks, spontaneously responding with the ploy of changing the topic.

Bannock sets his crystal glass down with a clatter. Pursing his lips momentarily while taking stock of the board in front of him. *How many doubles can he roll?* "What do you have in mind?"

"I'll take your wide- eyed bushy gal... for this."

Bazel slides his 48-carat gold cellphone across the table. On the screen is a picture of a decorative shot gun in a case.

Bannock's eyes widen with recognition and delight. "Is that what I think it is?"

"It is indeed."

"You're on."

Continuing their game with the fervor of the men they wish they were, has drawn some attention in the room. Johnathan Handel an old- school chum of Bannock's, stumbles over, rye in one hand and cigar in the other. He has the stature and temperament of Napoleon, the custom suits he deigns give the illusion his legs are shorter than they are, a critical unwitting mistake, creating a midget affect. Always in gray to match his waning head of hair that is worn slightly long and combed over to the left side of his head, at 74 he is the definition of excess. His disproportionately large mouth is a launch pad for persistently pouting lips. When he speaks his jaw almost seems to disconnect and over extend, giving him the appearance of a ventriloquist's dummy.

"Bazel, Dickie." Handel's Connecticut drawl breaks both names into two hard syllables.

"John, you are just in time to watch a complete shut out." Bazel gloats as he rolls his third and unknowingly final doubles for the evening. Noting the displeasure on Bannock's face.

Draining half his glass and rattling his ice at the barman before responding John comments, "You're very pithy tonight, must be unusual stakes."

"You know there is no betting allowed in the club," Bannock replies flashing a renegade smile to match his sarcasm. "I hear YOU have a new FEEDER?" Bannock never at a loss for information asks Handel, while stripping four pieces off the board and rolling a consecutive double six.

"Ah yes, you are well informed." Ash from Handel's cigar falls unceremoniously unto the plush carpeted floor. Recovering quickly, he adds, "Yes, I am prepared for our next excursion."

"I hope this one is from better stock. Your previous feeder lasted what? A week?" Bazel throws in, denying the fact he may not win this game tonight, with unpleasant surprise.

Taking a defensive pose, Handel puffs up his child sized swollen chest replying, "The last one was injured during transport," he stammers, "making it difficult to adapt to the new environment. You know how difficult assimilation can be for the species."

"Yes, of course," Bannock nods with a sidelong glance to Bazel. "Up for a side bet?"

Eyebrows raised, Jonathan Handel blinks, "What do you have in mind, Dickie?"

"Two hundred and fifty thousand, your feeder doesn't last the week." Bannock entreats thinking he needs to make up for his losses tonight.

Handel takes the bet out of pride. He chose his feeder due to weaknesses, not strengths. Listening to the last of the backgammon pieces clipping into place, he has a momentary lapse of conscience, clearing his throat with the sting of alcohol, he thinks to himself, *just one more week.*

8

YELLOW

By four o'clock, my office walls feel like they're closing in, I have only managed to place $4000 between four secure bank cards, after countless conversations with countless customer service agents.

It seems you first purchase a dummy card, that has a maximum of $1000, these are a one- time fill after registering each card. You cannot load any additional funds until you receive your new mock credit card in the mail, two weeks later. Not a success and my premonition of completing an $80,000 blend with money orders is becoming clearer. *God, I hate banks!* I stop myself, rubbing my face, "Think positive Steph" I can hear Remy's voice in my head, "Watch what you manifest." He is right of course, but a little self-pity will go a long way today.

Thinking of Remy, I look at the clock, he should be wrapping up the conference soon, I have yet to discuss the "Pot Luck" article with him, why send him on a rampage while he's in front of people? Besides, if Cannabusiness, the morons that printed the stupid pharma article are attending the conference, he would probably throttle them.

My stomach churns loudly, I have had a piece of cheese, a wilted salad, and an orange since breakfast. I place the new credit cards in my drawer for tomorrow. "Paying our mortgage is going to be fun," I say out loud. Grace looks up from her notepad, "What?"

"It's nothing, let's call it a day."

"Sure thing, I'll see you tomorrow."

"Have a good night Grace."

Following her to the door, I am overcome by a familiar wave of exhaustion as it closes, with a click. A bath sounds like a perfect remedy, hiking up the stairs to our bathroom, I am flooded with questions about who could have spoken to Cannabusiness. Sure, we have competitors out there, but we don't have enemies. The industry is too small for that. We have certainly dealt with scoundrels who do have enemies, but it's just not our style. The customer is always right. It always seems the better choice to take the higher ground. Not be stuck in the mire, just walk away. This motivation allows for a lot less baggage and a lot less negative energy.

I'm Greek, we barely forgive, and NEVER forget, but Remy takes the Buddhist approach. It is one of his characteristics I admire most, his even calm when forced into confrontation. He must get it from his mother, how could you survive ten children otherwise? I remind myself to ask her.

Turning on the water to the tub I add a little olive oil and a couple of dashes of lavender oil. As soon as I remove the cap and inhale, I feel the day's tension dissipating. It is amazing how that works. A glass of wine would be good right now, I look over at my phone on the dresser, it's 4:20. Laughing I text Remy, *Pouring a glass of wine and a hot bath... how about pasta with sausage and kale for dinner, table for 2?* Xoxo.

Instantly his reply, *I Love you, CU @8,* appears. I smile, wrapping a towel around me, to fetch the wine. The one thing I can see that could really bother me about this house are the split floors, I am constantly going up and down. Today I am just worn out. I trek back down to the kitchen, there is a lovely pinot Gris in the fridge calling my name.

My phone rings as I return to the bathroom, the sound of the tub filling the room.

"Mad Hatter Coffee & Tea, this is Stephanie, how can I help you?" An automatic reply to a number I don't recognize.

"Oh, hi. We were wondering where your store is?" A middle- aged woman asks.

I sit on the edge of the tub, with a smile. "We are wholesalers, we don't have a store. If you let me know what zip code you are in or visiting, I can lead you to a dispensary that carries our products." I reply with candor.

"Great, thank you. We are in downtown Denver."

"Ok, are you looking for recreational 21 an older marijuana or do you have a medical prescription card?"

"Recreational."

"Are you looking for anything in particular from our line?"

"Yes, I wanted to try your Third Eye Chai, and your Mushroom Elixir Teas."

"Wonderful, let me check inventory and I will text you a dispensary name and address."

"Wow, really? Thanks."

"No problem. Enjoy."

I disconnect the call, and text Jennifer the kitchen manager of operations for our Colorado licensee, she had worked for us while she was an employee at BB Edibles, our first licensee in Colorado. I could log in to their inventory sheet, but I just don't have the energy to go back downstairs to my laptop.

Client looking for rec mushies and Third eye in downtown area, any suggestions? I rest the phone back on the counter, reach for my wine and sit on the little wicker stool next to the tub. Usually, I have soaps and body scrubbers sitting in an abalone shell on the stool, but Remy likes to come in and talk to me while I'm in the tub, so most of the accessories wind up on the floor instead.

Thoughts of Barbara the owner from BB Edibles, our last licensee in Colorado now floats through my somewhat overfilled brain. So much hubris, she would not take any suggestions small or large about our product line and sales when they licensed our products in Colorado. What a lesson we learned there, *NEVER let anyone else tell you about your own business. If it's not broken don't fix it.* My phone dings, *Native Roots tell them parking is one block east of the building.* She follows this with their address. I thank her, then forward the text to the newbies, a term I coined for anyone new to our industry, it's not derogatory, I tell myself taking a nice cold sip, it's strictly descriptive.

Dimming the lights and lowering the shade to block the glare of the sea, I ease myself into the tub, feeling the worries of the day loosening their grip. Placing a wash cloth over my face I breathe, "That's it, let go."

By the time, I see the lights of our car pull into the drive, I have cooked the sausage with onions, kale and sundried tomatoes in olive oil and just filled the spaghetti pot with water, setting it on the stove. The table is set on the deck, linen and cloth napkins and my Mother's Japanese china. I have a nice salty parmesan cheese and rustic loaf of bread laid out on a 1930's molded glass plate surrounded by fruit for an appetizer. Hearing the door shut from below, followed by Remy's familiar footsteps on the stairs, I am relieved to hear his voice.

"Hey, sweetie," he calls out.

"Hey," I answer walking over to steal a kiss. "How did it go?"

"It went well, I met a couple of new people from Canada and Australia. They seem genuinely interested, even though they're slow tracked for roll out."

"Great," I answer taking notice of Remy eyeing the table outside. I am wondering how to bring up the article. I side step pandering and just blurt it out. "Did you read Cannabusiness today?"

"Yeah, I read it. Those assholes. They were at the conference. I had a little chat with them." A notable grin on his face amuses me as he removes his wallet and phone and places them on the counter. I pour him a glass of wine and bring the cheese plate over to our 1950's green glass kidney shaped cocktail table we bought in Oceanside when we were first married.

"Oh really, tell me about it. What did you say?" Coaxing, curling my legs up under my prized yellow wrap around vintage halter dress, on the couch.

Enjoying my amusement, Remy takes a moment to drink his wine, not taking his eyes off me. "You are so beautiful, you know that?" He whispers while sitting down next to me.

"Really?"

"Yeah." Warm lips soft on mine.

I melt, puddle on the floor, just like in the movie Amelie. Taming the heat inside me, before continuing, "Did you give them hell? Because it was a derailment I could have done without today."

"I found them in the press room, cowering."

"I bet they were." Thinking you do not want Remy on a direct course with you. It's downright frightening.

"I had just finished an interview with CFN, the pod cast will be released next week."

Cannabis Financial Network is a cannabis news and marketing firm. They have been working with us for years. I like Franz their director, he isn't as pay to play as most of the marketing scoundrels out there.

"Great. Go on."

"Oh, I talked to a writer from Forbes today as well. She is putting together an article on global branding in cannabis. She wants to speak with both of us next week."

This is our industry in a nut shell, I think to myself listening. One step forward two steps back. "Sounds good, what about Cannabusiness." I remind my tangential spouse.

"You know Mark, from the Cannabusiness conferences? He had the nerve to greet me as if he had no idea that the article even mentioned us."

"So, what did you do?"

"I slapped him on the chest with a copy of it and said, "What the fuck bro?"

My eyebrows fly up involuntarily. "What did he do?"

"He just blinked at me, the asshole. I reminded him our company is three people, and that none of those people had spoken to anyone from his pimp paper. I redefined the words libel and defamation, in my usual poised and self-controlled manner," he adds while cutting the parmesan cheese.

Those last words would conclude everyone in the building heard him. Once he swallows, Remy surmises, "I told him he needed to fix this, quickly."

"Well done, darling. I knew you would handle it effectively."

"How did your banking problem work out today." He asks changing the subject while grabbing a piece of bread and dipping it in olive oil.

"It didn't." I brought him up to date.

"It could be worse."

"Please don't say that."

Remy reaches over, squeezes me and murmurs. "I like you in yellow."

9

ADD IT UP

Taking aim from the safety of their luxury custom train, the men look at each other with uncontrollable excitement. The floor to ceiling windows have been retracted, leaving only the warm humid air as a curtain between safety and the jungle before them 20 feet below the tracks. The hunters, as if on cue begin boasting about the reaction they are causing on the ground.

"The packs are moving for cover." Someone warns aloud in a sing song voice to his club members in the train car with less regard for the creatures below then would be had for a swarm of ants. The small bit of spittle collecting at the corner of his mouth drips with anticipation. They set their sights, like a gruesome amusement ride, as the train follows the frightened pack scattering from the men's gunfire.

He has one mission this afternoon, to make sure his feeder is dead. This is a contrary move, normally club members bet heavily on their own feeder. Their concentration is usually honed to shoot as many feeders of the other club members as possible. Bets are in place, as usual, several hundred thousand here, a million there.

All twenty-four of the club's exclusive members, gather in their elegantly tailored hunting attire, having cleaned their collection of guns with liturgy prior to departure while catching up on gossip. Single shot only, no automatic weapons or assault rifles, "though far more substantial than any handgun, and certainly the symbols of endemic warfare, killing hundreds with one twitch,

(as Stalin infamously jested), is a statistic – not a tragedy." They are after all gentlemen.

Each member is quite familiar with the somewhat eccentric club rules and regulations that are imposed upon them for membership. This club has only three rules, he recounts to himself while regarding his club members, the most relevant are; Absolute silence by pledge of death and no connections with the feeders. Everyone adheres to the first rule for obvious reasons. The second rule has become more of a guide-line, he muses to himself while reloading. Scouting from every side of the train, which runs silently, scanning every crevice for his feeder.

During the construction of this train, built for the club's unsavory tastes, the members requested it be as silent as technology permitted, cost was obviously not an issue, the rare and even extinct hides, as well as human hides used in the décor, is the ultimate show of immunity from any law.

Desperate now to find his mark. He had been proud of his choice of feeder, a waiter from his favorite restaurant. Strong and virile the curly mop headed know it all, had corrected him one too many times, he recalls. Young and dumb, the perfect combination, he was on the top ten list. The final straw was the evening he had invited several business associates, guests from China to dinner. It was the final meal of a week- long wooing.

One of his chemical companies was clinching a deal with TB Chemicals in Beijing to create wholesale distribution for Alpha-PVP. Although the DEA has since then banned several versions of the schedule one drug, used to create Flakka, (also known as the zombie drug, as users have been found eating live animals and attacking people in psychotic states), his new partners in China would modify the particulate just enough on a regular basis to allow importation into the U.S. circumventing any law changes. Their subsidiary would then distribute the particulate, completely within the confines of the gray area of the law. What people do with it once it's here in the U.S. isn't our problem, he thinks to himself. Being highly addictive, this sector of his chemicals production has quadrupled in the last quarter. *Give the people what they want.*

Having had many dealings in Asia over the past thirty years, he has partnered with the Chinese dozens of times. There is usually a fine line of legal standing to tread, but if you are willing to find the gray areas, the returns are staggering. *You don't keep teams of attorneys on staff for their conversation or company.*

Li Ma, the CEO of Taipen the parent corporation over TB Chemicals was on his original list as a club member. A billionaire like the rest of them, Li Ma's love for the exotic hunt is notorious plus his added penchant for the peculiar only a Chinese king pin could cultivate was notable. However, dis-trust for the Chinese compelled him to pass Li over.

The company had secured the public library in NYC for the closing dinner of seven months of negotiations, a small party of 30 guests with 30 concubines, (common party favors when closing a deal with the Chinese) catered by one of his favorite restaurants at the time, Norma's. Known for its signature thousand-dollar frittata and proclivity for pretentiousness he finds entertaining.

He recalls after what seemed like an hour of introductions for the umpteenth time, they were finally all seated at the circumspect oak table he had flown in from Bedfordshire England or some such nonsense. The fool of a waiter then proceeded to remove his napkin from the table with a flamboyant crack and place it over his lap, as if he had forgotten to place it there himself. The sound of the snapping napkin echoed for centuries in the marbled temple where they convened. The look of fatality in his eyes, not enough incentive for the young phalanx to desist. Breaking the uncomfortable silence with an attempt to redirect the table, he inquired from the sop, "Which wine are we serving first for our guests?"

"You're not," The waiter's dramatic reply then followed with, "We are pouring Iordonav Vodka, with your lobster frittata topped with Sevruga caviar." The young man followed this with a dramatic pause as if awaiting a round of applause.

He had all he could do, to not jump out of his linen wrapped chair and wring the lawn fairy's neck. This disrespect continued when his scallop dish arrived, he was the only guest at the table who received three scallops instead of four, when the main course arrived, he was plated three medallions of boar rather than four. It was deliberately malicious and he was not the only person at the table to notice the slight. Li made the closing comment around the young man's noose after surveying his host's wanting dish.

"Tā xūn hēi nǐ de liǎn".

Which loosely translates to, "He blackened your face." All of Li's entourage broke into indulgent inexorable laughter. Chinese are notorious for saving face, "Mianzi" it is called unless it is at someone else's expense. A difficult cultural tradition to understand for most American's, as confirmed by the blank expressions of his inadequate American staff at the table. The final nail had been driven into the pine box.

Having survived for five months so far, the curly haired feeder has proven to be a good choice. Having won over a hundred million on him so far, only one other warrior has survived longer and she is a shadow player, rarely seen during the hunts, definitively smarter than her abductor.

Yes, he had made a solid choice of feeder, but nothing like his new one. Cursing below his breath, still not having sighted him, he was running out of time. Shots ringing out in all directions, breaking the silence, as he makes mental notes of the injured below. The train would stop at the station allowing the hunters to reload, change weaponry and brag over drinks and meticulously prepared hors d'oeuvres before they take their next pass around the park. If he couldn't get a clear shot before the break, he would have to resort to plan b.

The team of "handlers" they hire to keep the feeder packs, as they like to call them, moving below is an effort to reduce their prey's ability to hide and survive. By means of dogs and fire crews on the ground, the handlers redirect the feeder packs without actual interference.

The park is, of course, monitored at all times by this elite group of mercenaries, hired by the club at an outrageous cost through one of the members, John Jameson's military defense corporation, Habistram. *Murder is expensive, and tax deductible,* he licks his lips while refilling his crystal glass with bourbon and ice, catching the eye of his biggest competitor, of course he would never admit to that out loud.

"John, how is the shooting today?" He asks John Jameson, saddling up to the ivory tusk stool his opponent occupies covered in albino lion skin.

"Very exciting." John replies with genuine enthusiasm and eyed suspicion, pausing before following with, "What have you done? Brought someone down?" John's thin lips draw up to a leer, in an attempt at a friendly smile.

"I have a proposition for you." He states as calm and blandly as if asking for a fork.

"I'm listening." Absently mindedly John refills his glass with Balvenie, forty-year- old scotch.

Only the best and most expensive will do for the prodigy. John Jameson is the youngest CEO in their elite hunting club. He is fit, with a full head of black curly hair that is envied by all the members; an excellent marksman, flies his own jet and gives charitably to his own Cancer Foundation since he lost his devoted mother to breast cancer a year ago. Always mentioning how important family is to him, is a poor smokescreen. Although no one in the club discusses it, they all know for a fact Jameson's feeder at the park is his younger brother Thaddius.

Running over Jameson's profile in his mind, the younger man's lack of scruples can only be matched by his penchant for winning, with companies notorious for constricting free markets, they both have many similar traits. Jameson's parent corporation Habistram, having been awarded the majority of military arms contracts for both the United States and Russia in Syria, confirms John's dynasty is thriving at a gluttonous rate. A fact he finds hard to swallow, in fact, he would like to see the look on John Jameson's face once they release the details of his company's latest deal.

Unbeknownst to the people of South America, one of his own subsidiary companies has successfully cinched control over all mining rights in eight of the twelve countries on the continent including the majority of the rain forests.

What makes this deal unique, is that the mining rights clearly include all property above ground as well as below. Meaning they now have control over mineral, air, sun and rain rights. A brilliant coup, and perhaps his legacy.

Heightened by his own acumen he turns to Jameson with a proposition, "I will put up my vessel for anything you like, that I take your feeder down before you can take mine, today." He wagers to Jameson, clearly enjoying the look of shock on the younger man's sterile face.

At this offering, the entire train car responds with silence. Cash bets are the norm, with stakes as high as tens of millions of dollars, sometimes mistresses and wives are proffered as well, but his custom built, three hundred and seventy- million-dollar luxury yacht, that has graced the cover of every yachting magazine and hosted every living president and royal statesman alike… she is a show stopper.

Jameson can feel the room staring at him, awaiting his reply. This is too good to refuse, he could hear himself bragging to adoring sycophants, *I won it from that poor old schlep on a hunting bet.* Scouring his mind for a trinket he could stake, *after all, they are all trinkets when money is just paper with and you have a never-ending supply, the only valuable commodities are power and status.* Feeling perspiration on his back, Jameson contemplates whether he is being set up. *Was his feeder, One wounded?* They had decided to name them by number it would be easier to keep track of them that way, once your feeder was killed you would replace him with a new feeder but keep the same number. John thought he had caught a glimpse of One running full speed into a rock crag.

All of the members are now hovering around both men with baited breath.

Watching Jameson hesitate is almost worth losing his ship. This is what brings them all here. Their flagrant disregard for the laws and morals that mortal men adhere to, need not apply to them. *This place is proof of that. Belief makes something intangible real, doesn't it? Isn't that the basis for religion, democracy, and Santa Claus?* He recalls using that ploy with each and every member, including Jameson before they were inducted into the club. Creating their own reality was the only thing money could buy them of value anymore. Not one of the men hesitated, once he fed their eschewed egos. "We will create our own world, we will have ultimate control over all of the creatures within it. We will be Gods!" He reminisces before continuing to bait Jameson, "Of course if it is too rich for your blood, perhaps someone else would care…" he adds turning away from the youngster, looking around the train car at the startled eyes surrounding him.

"What do you say I stake my new Boeing." John blurts out.

The world knows John Jameson's pet project. A commuter jet, similar to a commuter car. With the ability to land and take off on any road, the wings fold up and the plane becomes a car, unlike most of the commuter prototypes, however, Jameson's car/plane can fly to Europe on Hydrogen. The ultimate James Bond toy. The first prototype has successfully cleared rigorous testing. It's worth well over a half- billion dollars, he is sure Jameson considered this, before counting on his own unparalleled marksmanship.

"Done." He professes, turning away from the crowd, a smile concealed on his lips. He had already won, now all he needed to do was wait for their next train pass. *The yacht is insignificant,* he reminds himself, having designed and built it with his latest conquest, a young Swiss debutante with a large family fortune. Gabrelle's father would boast in confidence about his family ties to Nazi treasure, and how the International Law was written to protect the plunderers of war, as he gifted the unbalanced couple several masterpieces to display on their ship. He would have liked the old man, only 7 years his senior, if he hadn't had such fowl breath. Anyway, Gabrelle was too fond of chintz at the time and he has no desire to redecorate, besides no cost would be spared for his new plan.

He can't help but over hear the conversation in the bar car, inspirationally taken over by side bets as to which of the two men will down the other club members feeder first. Walking to the barman, there is no need to ask for a drink, the barman assumes he will have a glass of Yamazaki, 35 year- old malt whiskey, a private reserve he only shares with his closest friends. *Luckily,* he thinks to himself, *I don't have any.*

The interior of the bar car is reminiscent of the orient express in the good old days between World Wars, he reflects, enjoying his drink and admiring the bedlam he has created. Lush dark skins covering the walls, meticulously dyed and cut to create the most unique custom wall paper. The floors are covered in giraffe hide cut and patterned into a basket weave parquet. Winged club chairs are covered in sheered orangutan with walnut cocktail tables that are mosaiced with pangolin scales as well as the facia of the bar, lending an air of a gentlemen's club, it could be the Olympic in San Francisco or the Union Club in New York, both of which he is a member. All of the hides, gifts to the club from members, trophies of previous hunting expeditions. The wall sconces are genuine Edison lamps and bulbs, the bulbs are obscured by a perfect circle of feeder skin stretched between a hand hammered copper ring. The skins had to be tanned just right to allow for the correct opacity of light reveal. Getting them to match was tedious but worth the time, he comments to himself.

There are several Masters paintings, well- lit and hung in the bar car, his favorite is a small Rubens of "Hercules and the Nemean Lion". *The first task to his path of immortality,* he thinks smacking his lips with the taste of whiskey, remembering his last skinning. Most of the club members are a bit squeamish when it comes to skinning their kill. Sending off their prizes to be cleaned and prepped, by ground crew. For him, the most integral part of the process is rendering the hide from the body. In rare circumstances, he has been able to master the process while his prey is still alive, wounded enough to render them incapacitated of course. *The look in their eyes as their flesh is ripped from their body is par non,* he considers. *They become practically lidless, gaping increduled and helpless. That is godlike, to give and take life as you deem.* The pair of white rhino tusks, he removed from the filthy animals he shot last spring, that he had fabricated into sconces behind the bar, he notes, looked better than he had imagined.

A small library of rare books on exotic hunting activities through the ages and an even rarer collection of snuff books decorate a pink ivory wood custom bookshelf with round molded leaded glass. The talk of this expedition, however, are the new framed glass boxes on the main wall behind the bar in this windowless train car. A prized collection of historic guns bought by members at auction or family heirlooms and contributed to the club. The .44-caliber Smith & Wesson that drilled a hole into the back of Jesse James's head glows under a spotlight behind the bar. He was of course killed by a double-crossing gang member, Bob Ford who secretly negotiated James' murder for reward to the Missouri governor; They all know the story, after breakfast on the morning of April 3rd, 1882 as James paused to straighten a picture on his wall, Ford shot him in the back of the head. The gun, is a gift to the club by a club member, an emaciated gangster of the banking world himself, rumored to have abducted his daughter's boyfriend because he just didn't like him. Like all of the members, he believes he is a man in charge of his own destiny.

Next to the Smith & Wesson is another club member's gift to the club, Teddy Roosevelt's double-barreled shotgun made for his 1909 expedition to Africa by The Fox Gun Company. A beautiful piece of American workmanship with the original case and oil cloths. A brass hunting dog is inlaid just over the trigger, a fleur de li embellishing the chamber, it is truly considered a work of art. The letter Roosevelt wrote to Fox thanking them for the gun is under glass next to it, in the spirit of the hunt, he finds it amusing Roosevelt cared more for the gun than the tens of thousands of animals slaughtered with it. *Roosevelt blathers on,* "The double-barreled shotgun has come, and I really think it is the most beautiful gun I have ever seen. I am exceedingly proud of it. I am almost ashamed to take it to Africa and expose it to the rough usage it will receive. But now that I have it, I could not possibly make up my mind to leave it behind." Several original photographs of "The Lion" and his conquered game adorn the 24 suites on the property, (not his choice but the club is a blend of all of their tastes or lack of), contained in the resort area created to house their Park's club members and guests. He doesn't care to bring guests to the park, mixing passion with politics is not his cup of tea.

The piece de la resistance, however, and underlying conversation of this hunt is his latest contribution to the wall. A gold plated 7.65 Walther semi-automatic pistol with the initials A.H. inlaid in gold on the ivory grips. Having paid a pittance for it, a little over a hundred thousand dollars. *It is priceless to me,* he covets his prize as Garrison Levitt joins him.

"I was researching the provenance of your little gun." Levitt churns out. "You realize, it is believed he never even fired it?"

Directing his head slowly towards the incipient fool now sitting next to him, he turns an amused glare at Garrison Levitts's puffy round face. Levitt immediately reaches for the ridiculous ascot he wears as an overture to his British roots and adjusts it nervously, an annoying tick. The CEO of The World Bank is a terrible disappointment. Giving the witless man's chilled cheek two playful little slaps, he walks away, reminding himself to drill a hole in the back of Levitts's feeder's head before the end of the day.

It's a good rule, that weapons aren't allowed in the bar car, restricted to the shooting gallery, the last of the only 3 rules of the club. The second rule he will break for a second time. No one will ever know, he reassures himself, surveying his club members. Even if they did, the first rule cancels out his rule breaking. Absolute secrecy upon death.

10

THE MATING GAME

Waking the next morning refreshed and lured by the California dawn, I rise, quietly putting on a pair of shorts and a tank top with a light jacket, leaving a note near the Italian coffee pot for Remy that I went for a bike ride.

I drink a glass of water, fill my bottle and hop on my bike. I am not fond of bikes with curled over racing handle bars, it hurts my back to bend over like that. I prefer a mountain bike, staying off the roads and staying on paths or the beach. It' early, but the morning commuters are already in full swing. The hum of the hive starting to throng, I take the back streets toward the old part of town then finally get on the sand. It's still chilly, no sign of the sun behind the morning fog. Zipping my jacket up to my neck, I head North on the beach, a slight wind in my face. The beach is already busy with morning dog walkers and joggers. Forcing myself into a higher gear, the burn of the sweat exactly what I need to clear my mind from yesterday. Of course, Remy was successful in clearing my mind last night, the memory of his gentle warm hands on my skin, brings a flush to my face, giving chase to the morning chill.

The tide is coming in, so I stay close to the water line. La Casa Del Camino the hotel we will meet Miles today, is coming up on my right. What a sweet romantic old place. Remy and I had stayed there before we bought our town house. The roof deck restaurant is vacant. *Take a deep breath Steph, this will all work out,* I tell myself. *Maybe I should get a shaman in to cleanse our house? It couldn't hurt.* I can feel my hands starting to grip the handle bars as I flip through the details of today, Miles being the most imminent. It is going to be difficult to convince Remy that he means no harm. I really don't see how or what Miles could say that would put Remy at ease, at ease enough to give him a one third share of our company. *Why does it always seem as if things have to get worse to get better?* Shaking my head with an attempt to shake off my concerns. I turn around at the next headland as I do not wish to go into Irvine and turn back with a tail wind.

Remy should be paddling out by now. I put the bike in gear and really amp it up. The little cove we like to surf has difficult access from the road, which keeps it quiet. The few locals that live nearby and don't mind the steep ascent with a board under their arm surf there, that narrows the lineup for California. On my approach, I can see two surfers, neither of them is Remy. I stop and look around, it doesn't look like anyone is coming down the path either, so I head home, finally enjoying my sweat.

Remy is on the couch, eating a bowl of granola with nuts doused in green goo when I return. He is unusually quiet. "Hey, no surfing for you today?"

"What? No. You may want to sit down."

"I am definitely finding a Shaman."

"What?"

"Never mind, now what?"

"Have you been online today?" My spouse looks at me with calm reserve, that scares me to death.

"No. I just got back."

"Before you read this, you should check your emails and messages."

"Rem, what the hell?"

"Steph, just check for me first, please. It's on the kitchen counter."

"Ok," I say trying not to panic, I turn on my phone and wait. Phone in hand pouring a glass of grapefruit juice and mixing it with water, I feel the numerous vibrations from my phone signaling the cache of emails and phone messages received. I swipe to email first; every licensee has checked in today, not the norm. I open an email from Jennifer in Denver first. *No recall here, everything is fine. Please let us know what is going on? Jenn.* At the word recall, my stomach drops.

I open the next email from Vermont, there is no problem here, just wanted to let you know.

Oregon, Nevada, Washington and Illinois Licensee's all stating the same thing. No problems. I look over at Remy, he is looking into his almost finished bowl, scraping the bottom with his spoon.

"Check your voicemail."

I have fourteen voicemails, seven are from licensees, concerned about the article but reporting no RECALLS. "What the?"

Remy interrupts, "Steph, the Marijuana Daily Business Journal reported, we had a massive recall. All products. Didn't specify a state or a reason."

"Can they do that? Let me see it!"

Through gritted teeth, Remy hands me his phone, Mad Hatter Coffee & Tea Co. RECALL all products by request of state. We were unable to attain a statement from Mad Hatter at the time of printing.

I look at my partner, "What the hell is going on here?" Anger wells inside me, "Yesterday with big pharma now this? This is a real problem! Even if there isn't a recall, people will think there is! Dispensaries will want to return product, and retail clients will stop buying just because we are associated with the word recall! We have been tainted!" I feel a rant setting in. Remy is sitting quietly, he hasn't moved since I walked into the house. I let his energy calm me. "What are you thinking?" I ask bringing my voice down and throwing myself on the couch.

"This is no coincidence. We are being set up, Steph. We have to find out who and what is behind this."

"So, what's the plan?" My hands are shaking.

"First, we talk to the journal, demand a notice of false statement in print. Then I am going to make a couple of calls." Remy places his cereal bowl in the sink, turns around and walks upstairs without another word. I know better than to follow, his line of fire is not directed at me so I will stay out of range. Tears running down my face, I look out the window as the sun is starting to break through. *Seriously?*

Once Remy works his way downstairs, I go up and shower. Peeling off my odorous clothes, I turn the shower on as hot as I can take it. The water stings my skin. We have had our battles with rivalry companies. New coffee companies sprout like hydras, one goes out of business and nine more launch. We have had our share of business relationships go bad, I recall but we have always kept a positive profile with those companies or people. We have never gone rogue. If this is a plan to ruin us, we might be in serious trouble.

Last year, I remember through the spray of water, our layout person withheld our original files. We had worked with him for years but had not signed any operating agreement, we were friends as well as associates. He was withholding the files in lieu of a bill he had invoiced, without any breakdown of what time was spent on, just a tally of hours. I had no idea which of 8 states the work was for and therefore had no possible means of invoicing my territories or verifying hours. When I asked him to breakdown the bill, he was offended that my request was questioning the validity of the time spent. I did question some of the hourly time, as I had worked side by side with him. I redesigned our variety packs, they needed sprucing. I added thumbnails on the back of the packages and cleaned up all the branding. Hans was good, he could move things around easy enough in Illustrator and he took my directions well but he had questionable taste and he wasn't incredibly creative. He could have never created our logo or our packaging designs on his own or even revamped them without my direct guidance. I had a very good idea of how long it took. $2000 worth of a $3000 bill was in question. This was the beginning of the end of the friendship and worse, he sent a bullshit cease and desist letter to our printer, claiming he owned our artwork, virtually shutting us down until our lawyer got involved. He then attempted to sue us for $13,000 and claimed the artwork was his, and Mad Hatter would have to pay to use it. It was all bullshit, and he knew it. The year it took to defend ourselves and win the case, was a waste of time and energy, not to mention the $14,000 dollars in legal fees and the almost six months of no income due to the lack of original files for packaging. Our world came to an abrupt halt while I rebuilt every label from scratch with a new design company, I don't even wish to recall the emotional drain and feelings of betrayal the entire episode erupted. *Could this be Hans?* It wouldn't be hard to call anonymously and provide a juicy tip to a writer. He had been ordered by the court to pay us for the hiring of an additional layout person to set up our files from scratch, he had not been happy. Hans seriously believed he was going to walk with $3000 over the limit civil court allows and our files, shaking my head still in disbelief that someone could be so contemptuous, someone that had been in our inner circle. I jump out of the shower. Remy is on the bed waiting for me.

"Do you think it could be Hans?" I ask, drying myself off standing on one foot.

"No. It's not Hans."

11

STRANGE FRUIT

Out of breath, Manaya is still standing, she waits to see how many of her family will return. Had she lost one or two to the flames? There was no possible way of knowing or anticipating what had happened. Running over the scenario again in her mind. The sound of the train sent them running for cover, scattered, divided and vulnerable.

Manaya's group had been tracking Delta's family pack for three days, it was the closest they had ever been to ambushing them. While waiting for the pack of women she hunts with to appear from the emmeshed jungle, the words of the nameless faces that brought her to this awful place resound in her head, "You kill the other group and you can go home. Don't you want to go home?" The deep resonating man's voice echoed in her head.

"Yes, please. Please just let me go. I don't belong to a group, I don't even know where I am!" Her reply coursed with sobs only yielded laughter from her captor in the dark.

He repeated, "You will. Kill the others, then you can go."

"I can't kill anyone." She replied her voice strangled by her attempts to breath.

"Then you are already dead." The voice said ominously, before brutally pushing her out of the back doors of an enclosed truck with his feet onto the unforgiving ground.

She had landed on her back, instantly relieved she was away from her captor, only to be swallowed by the complete darkness of night. Afraid to move, she just laid there and waited for her breathing to calm. The night closed in, the air was heavy, much heavier than home in the summer. Unable to see the sky, she assumed she was in a forest. Crawling on hands and knees, she felt naked although she still had her work clothes on, but completely defenseless. Scraping her knee on a sharp rock, she stopped to wait for her eyes to adjust. Nothing, it was completely black, she could not see her hand in front of her face. Gripped with primordial fear, beginning at her spine and creeping up her back, she slowly moved to find a tree or a large rock to sit up against, anything to keep her company. The sounds of the night now over coming all her other senses, sounds she had never heard before, desperately straining to see anything in the pitch. Imploring all the Gods, she could name, before finally finding a tree trunk, pulling her knees to her chest and curling herself into the smallest form possible, Manaya cried herself to sleep.

It seemed like an eternity since that first night, she thinks to herself as she counts the women coming out of the under- brush today. "Five." Manaya states aloud looking to each of the women, she now considers her family. All five shake their heads, no one speaks, still trying to catch their breath while listening for sounds of impending encroachment.

Suddenly, a twig snaps, followed by more rustling, it's moving slowly whatever it is, but definitely in their direction. Everyone forms a line, sticks and or clubs in their hands. Half of them turn North the other South, facing the intruder, bodies tense with fear and anticipation. They all smell it first, looking to one another, eyebrows pinched.

Pushing through the brush, the sound moves forward towards them, the smell overpowering. A small black figure finally emerges, one of the women in Manaya's line- up falls to the ground gagging, a reflexive response to the barfola odor of burning flesh. The figure finally stops moving, her eyes the only decipherable fragment of her body, as she reaches out a hand, and irrevocably falls to the ground.

12

I WILL POSSESS YOUR HEART

Grace arrives at 9 o'clock on the dot, I have already been at the computer for 2 hours, working on the Colorado blend. It always seems as if our clients can't wait to see the estimates, they can't be created fast enough. Yet when it comes time to pay for the blend and consequently all the time spent configuring units, pounds, ounces and gram weights of all the ingredients, no one is in a hurry. It's a thankless job. I remind myself how much I love spread sheets!

Grace looks over, "Let me guess a blend day?" She smiles at me. Of course, she knows it's a blend day because it's written all over the white board behind me!

"I am going to finish inserting the new menu for them, with the new ingredients for the CBD tea, then it's all yours, you lucky gal," I say, happier now that I know I won't be spending my entire day doing this. We are preparing to launch a new line of CBD (cannabidiol – one of many cannabinoids or chemical compounds found in cannabis that alleviates pain, seizures, and stress among other things without getting you high) mixed with THC

(Tetrahydrocannabinol – the most prevalent phyto-cannabinoid found in cannabis that makes you high) infused tea for our marijuana markets. They would still be restricted to dispensary store purchasing as they will contain THC. For pain relief as well as tumor reduction blending the two together has almost unlimited possibilities, with little to no side effects accept getting high and having the munchies. Eventually, we will launch a CBD only line, probably with Francoise, it will be a refreshing change to handle products that are not federally regulated. *Dare to dream.*

Remy had left early for a desperately needed paddle session, I declined as I wanted to get this blend off my list of to do before our meeting with Miles. I now hear his footsteps upstairs and the sound of his voice on the phone, reminding me I have to cancel all of our auto debit transactions online and make this month's payments with either our Friendpal card or the new temporary cards. With our travel schedule, paying bills online is the only option for us; *This bank conspiracy is cramping our style.*

Remy floats down the stairs as if he hadn't a care in the world. Smiling at me, then nods over at Grace, "Hey Grace, how's it going?"

"I'm good. And you?"

"Great." He replies, with a devilish grin.

I wait.

"What's your schedule?" He asks sitting on my desk, his back to Grace.

"I'm wrapping up a few things, should be good in an hour."

"Make it before ten." His request is a murmur, my curiosity piqued. Remy turns around and heads back upstairs. I don't see him again.

After completing all of my menial tasks, I walk up to the kitchen where Remy is sitting, in the middle of a text.

"Let's go outside, I want to talk to you about our strategy for Miles." He leads me outside. We have forty- five minutes before we need to leave.

"Ok, what's going on? Why all the secrecy?" I ask sitting down at the small patio table, noting the view of the bay.

"What? Oh, we'll talk about that later. First Miles, I made a list of concerns, I want you to look them over and see if I missed anything? If we are really going to look at this as a second chance, I want to make sure all of our bases are covered." Handing me his phone, I note that his list is longer than mine, but IP is Remy's specialty;

Control over patents stays with Mad Hatter

Control over Mad Hatter stays within Mad Hatter, except for overall budgets

Only IP and patents that pertain to Mad Hatter product manufacturing applications are contained within the partnership

Trial period that both sides can get out, up to 3 years

The lab has limited access, including security videos

Any actions deemed as controlling or inhibiting by the partnering corp. can be seen as a breach of contract, with steep penalties

I look up at my husband after scanning the list. "This is thorough, you've been busy."

A smile is his reply.

"This looks good, of course, it's all in the approach," I state raising my eyebrows just a tad. "I had Grace research Hammer Industries, see if she could pull up any previous partnerships or situations in the past that would give substance to the accusations in the articles in Newsweek and The New York Times. Nothing." I say shaking my head in confirmation.

"What did YOU find?" Knowing me better than anyone else, his conclusion that I would not leave this to someone else entirely is correct. Or is there more to it than that, the look in his eye is, unusual.

"I couldn't find any history of corporate rape on Hammer, they have had two business dealings with smaller companies go awry, but when you consider they've been in business for over eighty years, that's pretty damn good."

"Hmm."

"Personally," I continue, "His daughter works for him, and his key staff has been with him on average of fifteen years or more. He doesn't fit a profile for eating small companies, although he does enjoy big game hunting and lives the life of excess on his million-dollar yacht and numerous residences."

"You like him."

I was going to argue, for the sake of arguing but decided against it, "Yes, I do." I say hesitantly, "I hate to say it, I know it sounds completely naïve, but I trust him, he seems honest and sincere to me."

"You don't think that gentlemen air is a tactic?"

I sigh heavily, "If it is, it's a good one," After a moment's pause." no, I don't think so."

Shaking his head with a look of despair, I rarely see, Remy replies, "Neither do I. The thing is, I want to believe."

My Phone rings, I look at the area code, 212. "It's New York, do we have anyone from NY that you are talking to?"

"No. Let it ring"

I pick up the call, "Mad Hatter Coffee and Tea, this is Stephanie, how can I help you today?" My voice pleasant and as carefree as I can manage. Remy is watching for my reaction.

"Hi, my name is Sveta Russher. I am the Chief writer for CNN Money. I am collecting information about a select group of edible companies, for a story for tomorrow. I was hoping to speak with someone at Mad Hatter."

"Hi Sveta, I am sure I can assist you, what would you like to know?" Remy's inquiring eyes, demand I write down who is on the line on a sheet of paper. Giving me the caesarean thumbs up he taps an invisible watch on his arm, we have twenty minutes before we need to leave to meet Miles. I nod.

Sveta begins, "I have spoken with several companies in Colorado, who have all recommended Mad Hatter as an innovative industry leader." She continues, obviously unaware of the recall blasphemy.

"Yes, well it's nice to be well thought of." *Thank goodness someone out there is still thinking kind thoughts about us.*" My husband and partner is the man behind the innovation, Remy is the alchemist."

"Wonderful, would it be possible to speak with him today?"

"Yes, after one, he'll be available."

"Great, in the meantime can you tell me a little about the company?"

The interview takes eighteen of my twenty minutes. It's the same story each time. She had no back-round information, hadn't looked at the website yet. Most of the high- profile magazines and papers, still really have no grasp of our industry. They write about it because they have to. The economy of it alone demands attention. Unfortunately, I have yet to meet a name brand writer that has either the time or the capacity to really excavate the true nature of the real aspects of the marijuana industry that are not superficial. I supposed to myself while looking for my purse and glasses, THAT is the difference between a writer and a reporter. I would hope a reporter gets down in the dirt. If you are writing about marijuana, you better try an edible, tour some dispensaries, and shadow an administrator. Then I recall the onslaught of interviews for the music industry, my old music partner and I would succumb to. Hiking up to the record company offices at Rockefeller Plaza for weeks on end, lining up for one interview after another, normal protocol after releasing an album. More than half of the writer- reviewers, hadn't even listened to the album! How do you interview someone about their music, if you haven't listened to it? It was at that point, I realized getting up and walking out was better than dragging someone by their nose.

Making my way down to our office floor, I text Grace all of Sveta's info. Asking her to follow up with printable logos, and blend pictures for the article, as well as checking the writer out. You never know? It might be someone you don't want to share with. Remy is waiting in Trixie. I jump in, and he looks me in the eye, "Are you ready?"

"Yes, I'm ready." I lean over and give him a kiss on the cheek, regardless of how this meeting goes with Miles, life is still good. "I set you up for 1 o'clock with the writer, she's oblivious by the way."

"Yeah, I figured."

We head down the hill, it's a beautiful day a slight breeze, perfect temperature, especially for a car without ac. I have resigned myself to just have messy hair. You can't drive around with all the windows down without it.

We turn right on Ocean Blvd. both of us quiet, running over approaches for our meeting with Miles, no doubt. Remy finds a parking spot around the corner from the hotel and pulls in. This is not the busiest time of the year. The water is too cold for tourists and most locals, you definitely need a wetsuit in May. The Pageant of the Masters is the big draw in Laguna. Held in the original town amphitheater, it's known for its tableaux vivant, where scores of people pose to recreate master paintings. Costumed and painted they hold perfectly still, true to the painting, it's over the top and lasts all summer long as an art festival. We are looking forward to it, as we moved here in January, after the tragic presidential election.

I come around the van and take Remy's arm.

"A walk in the park, kiddo." Only I would notice his breezy words not matching the concern on his face.

I could be walking into a hotel anywhere in Mexico. Large archways on either side of the main doors, the hotel sits on the beach but is unassuming if not decorative. The large wrought iron light fixtures and heavy dark wood furniture give the lobby an elegance of the past, perfectly blended with modern convenience. Remy looks around as do I, without spotting Miles. He leads me to the sitting area with a couch facing two chairs and a large coffee table in between. Pulling out his phone, he texts Miles; *We are in the lobby.* After a moment Remy gets up.

"I'm going to get a cup of coffee. Would you like anything?"

"No, I 'm good sweetheart thanks." His gray eyes smiling at me as he walks over to the café at the far end of the hotel lobby.

I watch as two women travelling together check out my husband as he walks by them. I smile with pride, while his easy gate disappears into the café.

I feel my phone buzz, so I pull it out and take a peek. It's our Licensee in Colorado, wondering where the blend breakdown is. In reply I answer; *Jennifer, working on it now, will have it to you by Friday morning for approval.* Then I text Grace, *Please, prioritize Denver blend and send to me for final review,* I am feeling anxious about the blend breakdown, as it is out of my control for the time being, as Grace works through it.

Got it, will do. Grace replies instantly, lowering my stress level to Defcon 3.

Remy returns with two croissants and a cup of coffee with a saucer. I devour the croissant he hands me in wax paper. Taking a moment to look around the lobby. Except for the management, most of the staff look like Irvine college students. Clean cut and well spoken, but young.

"Wouldn't it be great if the staff were old men, like Peter Luger's in New York?" I ask Remy.

"Peter Luger's," he repeats nodding his head in reminiscence, "it's been a while since we ate there. Yeah, that would be good, I feel like an old man compared to the kids they have working here."

"You are no old man. What time is it?"

Risking a quick glance at my phone on the table, Remy then pulls his phone out of his pocket. "It's ten after." Before I can reply he adds, "We'll give him until 11:30."

I get up and walk over to the front desk, thinking perhaps Miles has his phone off. How hard is it to reply to a text to someone you have just flown two thousand miles to see? The gal behind the desk is cute with sparkling brown eyes and clear white teeth.

"Miles Venery please."

"Certainly. Who may I say is calling?"

"Stephanie Beroe."

She picks up the phone and dials, a sweet smile lightens her face. I can hear the phone ringing three, four, five rings.

"I'm sorry there is no answer."

I feel a pang in my stomach, "Did he leave a message by any chance?"

"No Ma'am, I'm sorry. Would you like to leave a message?"

"No thank you. Could you try again? He flew in last night to meet with us today."

"Sure," she redials. "I see he is checking out late today." Again, five rings, again no answer.

"Thank you." I turn and walk back to Remy, just finishing his cup of coffee.

"That was the worst cup of coffee, I may have ever had."

"Worse than Nicaragua?" I comment absent mindedly flicking a piece of croissant off his lip but wondering why he drank all of it.

"Yeah," Remy mutters, now noticing my expression. "What?"

"He isn't here."

"He never checked in, or he isn't here?" Remy asks with a tone of one who is controlling his emotions.

"Miles checked in last night, stated he would check out late today. I rang his phone twice in his room, no answer and no message."

"God damn it!" Looking at his watch, he relieves himself from the couch and takes my hand, "let's go."

Except for the purring engine of Trixie, the ride home is silent, but we know what the other is thinking; Miles had read the articles and decided to pass. It makes sense, although the way he did it, does not. It's so easy to blow someone off these days, the age of technology is the age of turning tail and running, people divorce by text but it just doesn't seem like Miles' style to me.

Remy heads directly upstairs upon our return, I don't force anything. I go back to what seems these days, like my hole in the basement. It's amazing how two terrible days can make you see your surroundings. I nod to Grace, without conversing and put my headphones on. I don't want to listen to any music, I just need a moment of non- engagement, while I scour my email for any sign of Miles' excuse or apology for standing us up. Our licensees are still freaking out about the "Recall" that never happened. So, I decide to draw up a note to calm them, with our promise to demand correction in the false statements pertaining to Mad Hatter. I also have a great idea and ask them to send any tips of peculiar phone conversations or meetings with anyone in the last two weeks, that may be the cause of all this nonsense.

Emailing Grace, I ask her how the blend estimate is coming along, even though she is within my sight, *very age of technology*. I look at our calendars; today is Tuesday, May twelfth, Remy and I are due in San Diego on Thursday, then he is off to San Francisco Friday morning for a three-day event. The timing couldn't be worse for bad press, way too much exposure. I take a deep breath and let it out, probably louder than I realize as I have head phones on.

"Everything ok?" Grace attempts interaction by yelling across the room.

"Yeah, it's all good," Remy answers from the stairs, looking at me in acknowledgement.

Resting my chin on my folded knuckles, baring up as the British say, I comment, "We have a busy week ahead." Remy walks over to his desk and assumes his casual self. I look on in amazement but take his cue. Pulling off my headphones and smashing them, "How 'bout some music?" I ask Remy gently Within seconds I hear Gibbard from Death Cab for Cutie yearning, "*How I wish you could see the potential, the potential of you and me, it's like a book elegantly bound, but in a language that you can't read just yet.*" I look over at my husband, my eyes revealing the title of that song, he already possesses my heart.

13

Part II

IT'S A BEAUTIFUL DAY

What did you say?" I ask Grace a second time. Hoping with every pour, that the feeling of dread creeping through my body is misconceived. The walls coming down around me, are a melting hallucination of reality, my knees buckle as she very slowly reiterates.

"Stephanie, Remy did not show up at the conference this morning in San Francisco, he was scheduled to speak an hour ago, although he called en route, he physically never appeared. I have been emailing and texting him, with no response."

I hang up and call him myself, thinking perhaps he just changed his mind and didn't want to explain himself to Grace or anyone else. All the bad press we had acquired recently could create unpleasant conversations at these events.

Each ring echoes in slow motion with eternal silence in between; one, two, three, four, no answer. I start texting. *Where are you? Are you ok? What happened at the conference?* I wait.... no reply. *There is something wrong, I know it.* Looking around the dingy Coaster Metro train car for my bearings I think to myself, *I am sure he just... what? Changed his mind!*

For the remaining fifteen- minute ride, my phone, I realize is not the magic ball I thought it was. I feel helpless, but worst of all, I feel a very important piece of me is missing and there is nothing I can do about it. *This cannot be happening!*

As the train begins to pull into the station, I find my car and decide to email everyone close to us, that may have been at the event. Since I wasn't appearing at the event, I hadn't bothered to connect with anyone that might be. The list is short, Joan our friend and the organizer is at the top but, nagging at the back of my mind is the fact that Remy decided, for whatever reason, not to appear, so I decide not to contact Joan. It's completely out of character, but Remy not checking in with me is a God damn omen! I shudder, perspiration starting to trickle down my back. My breathing is shallow and loud in my car. As I sit in this plastic, iron bubble watching a silent world outside go by, I have no connection with, I can't help but notice, the sun hasn't changed, the blue sky is not faltering, the sea is still ceaselessly ebbing. *How can there be anything wrong?*

Forty- five minutes have passed since Grace first called me. She's on the phone and hangs up as I enter our offices. I throw all my junk in a chair, and march over to Remy's desk, looking for a hint that might suggest what the hell is going on. There's nothing, a couple of sticky notes with reminders of people to call, none of them worthy of missing a conference lecture.

"Get me a flight out. I'm going to San Francisco," I say to Grace as I head upstairs to collect a couple of things to take with me. The living room is flooded with light, but an obvious emptiness intensifies my feelings of helplessness as a wall of tears grips me at the doorway to our room. All I can do is stand there and let them flow for a moment, hit by a new uncertain reality. Finally taking a deep breath and wiping my face, I push myself and my worries through the threshold.

Underwear, comfortable shoes, toothbrush, I'm on automatic pilot, a clean shirt and pants, a light jacket and a stack of $100 bills from our money bag about an inch thick. Not knowing how long I will be gone, I look around for a good hiding spot for our money. I decide the bottom of the overflowing laundry basket, is not only the safest place but also in keeping with most state and federal regulatory agencies assumptions. I also fill a couple of boots and place a flat layer of cash under the shower rug, *it's always good to break things up,* then I lock our closet, bathroom and bedroom door. I will stash about ten thousand in my office for Grace to get the Colorado blend going. She is going to need purchase cash for our purveyors.

On my way back downstairs, I instinctively go to the freezer and grab a tincture of Indica oil. I medicate only when my stress levels are unhealthy. *Now seems like a good time.* I throw it in my bag, 30 grams of raw oil should be a five-years supply for me, as I use about enough oil to coat the head of a toothpick in my tea per serving, but I don't have time to move it into a separate container. I'm not worried about flying with the meds, as I have my medical card and California, as well as Oregon and Washington, have allowed transportation on airlines within the state as long as you have a prescription. *How kind.*

Grace is waiting for me in the living room as I come back up the stairs from our offices with my overstuffed purse over my shoulder, a bottle of CBD oil that I lifted from her table, it won't get me high but you never know what you might need.

"Maybe we should call the police?" Grace begins as she rises up from the couch and places her arm around me protectively, a look of alarm on her face.

"I can't call them for 24 hours, Grace. Besides, what if it's just a mix up and I bring the police into this? My husband is not a fan of the police. What if he's been in an accident? No, I should be there."

I hop a plane to the last point of communication, the conference hall in San Francisco. The flight is only an hour from Huntington Beach, my brain feverishly recounting the last 24 hours for any details that might give me a clue as to why or what. We had both spoken at a conference for the Native Americans Medical Cannabis industry in San Diego the day before and decided to stay the night as a treat in La Jolla, it was Remy's idea. The week had been so stressful with Miles blowing us off and the bad press, we both needed a change of atmosphere. We had dinner at an old haunt, The Beach House in Cardiff, from our courting days, a beach front seafood restaurant, where we had enjoyed many a happy hour when we first met.

I ate the steamed mussels and Remy had the salmon, we finished the meal with a hot lava cake, then drove down to check out the sea lions and the surf in

La Jolla ending up with drinks overlooking the sea as a night cap. We returned to our room around midnight, a cute nightly rental walking distance to downtown La Jolla. My eyes close recalling our playful intimacy of the previous night;

"You were amazing today." I offered, truly attempting to not allow anything between us.

"You were pretty good yourself." Remy smiled taking off his shirt as he continued, "My favorite line, was when you answered that guy from Canada that asked you what kind of advice you could give to a small company jumping through the hoops, you said, *"set them on fire and take a running start, because it's not going to get any easier.""* We both laughed with considerable delight as he threw himself onto the bed.

"Did you see his face?" I recalled, "Like a doe in headlights. Jesus, having money and a business degree doesn't make you qualified for this industry." Dropping on the bed next to him, he propped his head up with his hand, his blue eyes so soft and encouraging, "Anyone out there I should be talking to?"

"No." I replied, "The fact that they are all different Nations, only adds to the regulatory nightmare. I think we should wait until the dust clears, we don't want another California on our hands." Reminding him of our failed launch dampens his romantic inclination momentarily. In California due to its size, sheer numbers of clients and lack of state regulations, it creates a county and city regulatory nightmare. You could have clients in a fifty- mile radius that have completely different local codes for packaging, dosage, and verbiage requirements. It was a manufacturers black hole.

We had launched without a ground crew, several years earlier in California and is was a disaster, not something we will ever do again. Avoiding his eyes, I asked, "Are we going to be ok?"

Remy took my face gently in his hands staring, silently for what seemed a long moment. "This will pass, it's just growing pains." His voice slow and steady very assured, a tonic. "Are you happy?" he asked while moving a stray hair from across my face.

"Yes, my love, I'm happy."

Taking one last countenance of my face, he replied, "Good." Then he turned out the light and slipped under the covers. While climbing into bed next to me, I asked him, "Do you remember, how simple life was before we started Mad Hatter, before the cannabis industry?" The only light in the room, was the moonlight and a street light through the window, perfectly highlighting his profile.

Yawning he replied, "Yeah, I remember." Placing his arm around me, my head on his shoulder, his breathing, steady and strong.

"Do you remember the day of that big swell? When you drove me all over the coastline from Encinitas to La Jolla, watching the big rollers coming in, with that extraordinary stormy gray sky above?"

"Yeah, remember that old guy we watched paddle out from above the cliffs of La Jolla?" He added while absent mindedly stroking my head before he continued, "The swell was huge. Ten- foot waves at the La Jolla cove at least, a day to remember."

"No one was out in the line- up," I recalled, but many people like us were crowded against the lookout above the cliffs to watch the big rollers come in.

"Yeah!" Remy continued excited now by the precious memory, "Out of nowhere that guy with long gray hair, no wetsuit, just old-style shorts and the longest beat up board I had ever seen, jumped out on to the receding tide from the stairs on top of his board. He got up on his knees, and started paddling big kahuna style, remember that? Both hands just digging in while he sat straight backed on his knees!"

The crowd had doubled in size with anticipation, I remembered. "Yeah, he paddled out," I continued, "straight through, like a channel opened up just for him, his hair dryer than mine, then he pulled his board around and without any hesitation, effortlessly took off on the next huge roller. He rode it all the way in, no tricks, no hoping, he just carved his way in like Poseidon himself. At first, the crowd was struck mute, remember? We were speechless! Then we all started hooting in unison, as he took the wave all the way to the beach and I will never forget this, he picked up his board plopped it over his head and disappeared into the bushes. It was magical, wasn't it?"

"A perfect California moment," Remy added.

"It was amazing," I confirmed. "Like you Rem."

"Hey now. I thought this was a work trip?"

"Ah, all work and no play…" I managed to say before I can't remember what I was saying, and neither of us cared.

This morning, I headed home by train, while Remy continued by plane to S.F. *Can he really be missing? Missing? No.* The only thing that would keep Remy from an appointment without contacting me, would be an accident. Or intervention, could he have been side tracked? By someone or something? I start perspiring. *Could he have been taken? Get a grip Steph, who in their right mind would take Remy?* He is not particularly tall, but he is a well- oiled machine. Surfing, snowboarding, and biking have left their admirable marks, he is strong. Probably from paddling that tree of a longboard I had given him for his 30th birthday. I remember having it made in Encinitas by a board shaper that was a friend of friend. Remy dubbed it big red. 8'6" cherry red with a black balsa streamer and black rails, it's old school with a glassed-in single fin. The shaper fought me on the black rails, said they would get so hot in the sun in the line-up, they could burn him. I remember thinking, that's the point, love is like that.

How many times have I looked for him in the line- up? With his blue surf cap strapped to his head and beat up t shirt as a rash guard? Watching him take off, he makes it look so effortless, so natural. All that paddling, my least favorite part of surfing, is no doubt what sculpted his chest, arms, and back. He always says, "It's all about the paddling." *Isn't it though?*

Maybe he was in an accident? Maybe he got sick? I give word for Grace to check with all the hospitals, emergency care, and police stations, while I am on the plane.

Hitting me like a wall, nausea swelling in my throat, *what if he found out? What if someone told him out of spite?*

Tears slowly begin trailing down my cheek, the taste of their salt on my lips. *Who would tell him such a thing? No one else knows.* **He** *certainly didn't want Remy to know, it would be suicide.* Hiding my face from the stranger seated next to me, I focus all of my energy on control, the weight of my guilt making me the focus of all the passengers in my mind.

As the plane begins its descent for our approach, I wipe my eyes and settle back in my seat, taking a huge breath with effort. *Maybe something or someone else is at work here? We had been suffering for a good month from bad press and events, more bad luck than usual for sure. The banking fiasco… it goes on and on. One thing is for sure, I'm going to find out who or what is behind this.*

Continuing with alternative solutions I press my faculties. What are the facts so far? It's not like Remy to be late, never mind not show up at all without word. It is not like him to **not** answer his damn phone! Recalling, how he regards phone and computer technology with great distaste, although it has allowed us to travel without need for a work schedule, he claims regularly he would love to throw his phone away. Which may happen at some point, but this would not be the time. *It better not be!*

When we hired Grace to assist both of us, it was our desire to place a buffer between ourselves and the new throngs of phone calls and emails we were inundated with. We spent more time sifting through voicemail and email than should be legally prescribed. It was draining and hindered our creative process. Grace weeds through the bulk, makes initial contact and based on criteria we set down, places call backs in priority where necessary. Of course, our criteria vary immensely; Mine is geared towards marketing, branding, potential partners, overall business operations. Remy has more of a " No time wasters" approach. Therefore, Grace spends a good deal of time vetting possible drones out of his path, which is not easy, a good deal of it is based on instincts. Our motto being, it only takes one conversation, one person to change our life.

By the time I hear the wheels deploy for landing, my breath fogging the oval window, I am struck by a profound thought; *How could anything truly sinister happen on such a beautiful day, could life be that ironic?*

14

INERTIA CREEPS

Looking up from his New York Times, morning edition and placing his coffee cup down on its saucer, he takes a moment to reflect on his incredible life. Having created a global dynasty, there isn't a head of state that doesn't know who he is. Favors are bought and sold with financial gains larger than most state budgets. Playing both sides of the fence has been a key aspect in his foreign strategy, selling armament and telecommunications to both sides of any war, guaranteeing success.

Let's hope Dante was just a crackpot, he thinks with amusement to himself, smirking. Justification comes much easier now than in the earlier days. His web is so thick, he has become an integral pillar of the economic system, in fact, he is the economic system. Immune to society's laws because he creates the people that make them. He is not subject to anyone, he considers himself a God among men.

Wiping his mouth on a linen napkin before throwing it on the floor, the thought of having to sustain himself with food and drink like the rest of his race, becomes momentarily appalling.

Daryl, his butler from childhood enters the dining room noiselessly and retrieves the napkin, placing another clean napkin on his lap. The Dining room has just been painted white, three tones of ultra-white at his wife's request. The custom-made Lucite table and hand carved chairs she went on about for months that were flown in from Germany are not to his taste. In fact, the entire room is not to his taste, it looks like a white stark cell a laboratory rat would live. He makes a mental note; *my wife is no longer to my taste. I will need to do something about that.*

"This came for you by messenger, Sir." Holding out a small envelope on a silver tray his initials type written on the front.

"Thank you, Daryl." Daryl, has been with his family since he was a boy of 17, Daryl's parents had worked for his family before he was born. They are barely ten years apart in age. He muses to himself, *born into slavery,* as a smile pierces his thin lips, still bitter with coffee.

"More coffee Sir?"

"Yes." He replies while using a marmalade knife to open the envelope, waiting for Daryl to fulfill his needs and take his post by the door. The blank note card simply reads. *Phase 1 complete.*

'Perfect. Daryl, have my hunting attire packed and sent to the plane, I depart in an hour." He announces, knowing there is just one more little thing to do.

"Yes, Sir. How long will you be gone, Sir?"

"Five days."

"Very good Sir."

"Yes, very."

15

LOVE WILL TEAR US APART AGAIN

The mandatory time allotted prior to calling the police when you suspect someone is missing is 24 hours. Grace informed me via email after she checked the local police stations in San Diego. I confirmed that on go ask Jeeves, multiple times then requested that she find a private detective to meet me at the airport once I land, to run down details with me. *Two sets of instincts are better than one when your husband is MISSING!* She texted me the detective's info with a picture so I would recognize him.

Deplaning, I gather my large purse, the only item I had time to bring with me stuffed with overnight items, and brace myself as I walk out to the baggage claim area designated for my flight.

Kurt laddington, is no Columbo, much to my chagrin. My guesstimate to his age, around thirty- five years old. He informs me, he had been a police officer for 10 years, when he was wounded in action. Now he specializes in missing persons on his own time. He seemed a bit resentful of the lack of pension and medical attention he was subjected to, who could blame him.

My initial assessment finds laddington, a touch narcissistic, too much of a dandy, over dressed and over coiffed. His perfect metro- sexual hair do, is kept by more products than I own. Manicured fingers and toes I can assume are not just polished but sealed with a clear gloss coat, gives the perception of an investment banker. Large very brown bright eyes can only be matched by Laddington's intensely bleached white teeth, rigid grinding jaw and perky demeanor that are either a byproduct of energy drinks or cocaine, *perhaps both.*

Unfortunately, being judge-mental has become a part of my business instinct. However, whereas most business people judge a lack of hygiene and expensive wardrobe and coiffure as a detriment or sign of lack of status. Remy and I shoot from a different perspective, both of us being artists, for the good part of our developing years, surrounded ourselves with creative people, writers, musicians, artists, poets, thinkers. We've grown accustom to our peers proving themselves with substance versus costume. Having migrated into the business world with our cannabis infusion company, we understand that costume is interchangeable with posture armor. Remy is an absolute rock star in a suit, head turning, jaw dropping, stop a conversation. I can't make up enough excuses to get him in one. On occasion, he indulges me. We are simple people, however, a stuffy office and certainly, an airport are not the place for armor. Making a mental note that armor is a form of protection, I chalk up my new best friends' appearance to life in a big city and move on.

"Mrs. Beroe?"

"Yes, Mr. Laddington?"

"Please call me Kurt."

After the customary niceties, we walk to his car, a brand new, Saab. Private detective work pays well it seems. Laddington opens the passenger door for me.

"Your assistant filled me in on your situation. I must say, you sure aren't wasting any time. In my experience in a case such as this, the person in question usually turns up of their own accord, albeit under the influence of nerves or indecision, or drugs." He did not look at me while he spoke.

"Nerves and indecision are characteristics of all creatures on earth Kurt, but neither would portend my husband into failing to perform and or communicate with me," my solemn response, ignoring his quip about the drugs. Then the detective starts asking the questions I don't want to hear with a neutrality I find repulsive;

"Are you both happy? Could he have left of his own accord?"

I can't even answer. Yes, Remy and I are happy, at least we had been until I started withdrawing from the only person in the world that mattered to me. In my heart, I know Remy would never leave like this, if ever. Our bond is un severable, only death could tear our love apart. "I appreciate your gesture." I finally respond to Laddington's inquest, my head reeling with a mixture of confusion, grief and a touch of guilt, that I immediately tell myself not to acknowledge. "But something has happened to my husband, and I need to know that you are on board, or we are just wasting each other's time."

"I am on board, Mrs. Beroe." Without taking his eyes from the road he continues, "I have made an appointment with Ms. Holland, the event coordinator at the West Bay Conference Facility. The conference is still in session but she has agreed to meet with us."

I nod, *that is precisely where I want to go.* Before he adds, "You realize the police will ask you the same questions?"

At the sound of the word police, I feel ill, a wave of heat runs through me. I don't reply. It's been five hours since Grace had received the call from Ms. Holland the event organizer, that Remy had called to check in with her before he disappeared. Laddington will run down all the lyft, airlines and credit card charges. The only credit card Remy could have used is his debit card from Friend pal, thanks to our closed bank accounts. I have already checked that card statement online. Grace is running down my findings.

Trapped in the worst traffic, I have perhaps ever encountered, we drive to Fillmore St. driving past the Jazz district, releasing memories of Remy and I in San Francisco twenty years prior. It seems like we have been on a never- ending tour of conferences for the past five years, but this memory is very different. Intimate and soft, no pervading haze of the Marijuana business, just us and nothing else mattered. We were young then, early twenties, unstoppable. Everything so intense, our love was charged with youth's unknown bounds. I remember just brushing up against Rem's body, his hand or arm, would send a flush down my spine. The power of innocent love drawing us together with its invisible tendrils. We were never more than inches away from one another. Family and friends poked fun at us for eating with one hand, we heard a lot of "Get a room", from my Brother and his wife. We had become part of each other, that early.

My face flush as I shake my memory, quickly dabbing my eyes and fumbling for my phone to check yet again with hope that Remy has answered my texts and I can be rid of the man sitting next to me. A barrage of emails line my inbox, none from my husband, several I cannot ignore.

Our new licensee in Illinois is incredibly confused. As standard practice, several weeks ago I inquired as to whether their state regulatory board that oversees Cannabis compliancy, needed to approve our packaging. Not unlike the alcohol industry, there are standardizations for labelling and packaging. Unlike the alcohol industry, our standardizations vary from state to state drastically, in some cases certain cities and or counties within each state have stricter definitions. It is a never- ending ball of minutiae. Their initial response was no. So, I sent them a proof and asked for confirmation on compliancy prior to templating all of our products packages for their market. With timelines for launching in place, I oversee all layout and printing deadlines. The kicker is that although we have licensed our products to a state authorized producer, the great state of Illinois does not allow any logo on the packaging other than the state licensed producer. Meaning our logo cannot be on the packaging. With that in mind for the last almost two months, I have had to recreate packaging from scratch for them, that maintains national branding for Mad Hatter while being compliant minus our logo. Since it is also unlawful to include any imagery that designates what is in the package, *why should people know what they are ingesting, right?* So, you got it, no coffee, no tea, no chocolate images, actually no imagery at all except the logo of the state authorized license holder. Might I add, their logo was snatched off of Microsoft clip art, completely un altered. You don't need to be a design snob, to hate their logo. So, I reworked their logo to at least make it uniquely Mad Hatterish, then painstakingly spent hundreds of hours of my time finding textures and colors that simulate our national brand as well as the product identity, for thirty-three products. Our contract agreement states that they, our licensee pay for any layout change charges to alter our packaging for state specific compliancy issues. My time, however, is not covered, it just becomes part of the process. Knowing this, I read our licensee's email with the subject: *State labelling approval.*

Dear Stephanie,

It has come to our attention that our packaging for every product must be approved by the state regulatory board. Please send a malleable document that is high resolution, so we can print it out and walk it over personally for approval.

Thanks for your attention to this matter.

"Are they kidding me?" I ask out loud unknowingly. With a pang in my stomach, I forward Grace the email, *please see to this today*, holding my breath.

I answer as many emails as I can, and forward the rest to Grace for follow up on reorders, packaging and requests for marketing materials from Vermont, Nevada, New Mexico, California, Colorado and Washington. Prior to boarding, I emailed everyone we knew that might be attending the conference, not one email inquiry has been answered. I am not surprised as the conference is in full swing, and everyone has their phone on silence or off.

Parking across the street from the conference center, which is a complete bustle, Laddington uses a handicap pass as well as a city pass, he hangs from his dash to park, so we are not driving around for an hour looking for a spot. *Must have been a perk from retirement.*

The building is not as assuming as most conference centers, it's pink to start with, and looks more like a Spanish mission than a nondescript convention center. Its large rounded windows are inviting rather than humbling. Dozens of people with plastic name tags hanging from their necks are mulling about, I recognize several people instantly. Since the conference is still in session and we have 20 minutes before our meeting with the coordinator, I enlist Mr. Laddington to question attendees about anything unusual and if they recognize Remy's picture, if they didn't know him already. I casually chat with colleagues and ask if they have seen Remy, to no avail.

I have known many of these attendees for ten years or more, all of us pioneers of the Cannabis Industry, we have been through all the hoops, the rings of fire that seldom other industries endure. This type of stamina breeds bonds in lieu of competition, we are all survivors, the last man standing. Everyone I speak to asks about Remy, mentioning they had been looking forward to his lecture. For good reason, Remy is not the typical stodgy speaker at a conference. His personality is large although his voice is calm and quiet, he commands a room. Remy's idiosyncrasies are flagrant and entertaining, combine that with a very dry sense of humor that has no boundaries for social etiquette, and you have one hell of an entertaining front man.

As I speak with people, I notice I feel as if I'm floating, *this cannot be happening.* I close my eyes momentarily with the hopes I will wake from this nightmare and Remy will walk out to meet me, only to greet the unbearable

California sunshine and an overwhelming sense of loss.

Turning to walk into the building, someone touches my arm.
"Stephanie?"

"Miles?" I answer startled.

"We should talk, I was worried when they postponed Remy's lecture that I would miss you both."

My mind a whirlwind, the look of surprise on my face unconcealable. "Miles, I'm a little confused," I admit candidly, thinking to myself, *where the hell were you? Why did you stand us up?*

"With good cause." He states sheepishly and follows with a long pause. Miles is an attractive sixty something, his eyes are soft and his grin is a little askew, giving him the look of understanding, unpretentious gentleman. But his behavior was wholly questionable.

I snap out of my haze. "We thought you had changed your mind? What happened?" I blurt out, the strain of sensory overload taking control. At this point I realize, Miles is flanked by two men, large men.

"When will you be free today?" Miles asks while taking my hand, there is a calming factor in his actions, but he is in a rush.

Against my better judgement I respond, "I'm not sure yet, my schedule is a bit hairy, why don't you call Grace later." I manage stifling a current of nerves, removing my hand from his grasp. Miles cocks his head and responds, "Are you alright?"

My eyes begin to fill with tears as I choke back a wave of emotion. Quickly I turn my head a way, "Yes, of course." I manage before slipping through the door. Taking two breaths, and a moment to regain my composure. *I have to be stronger than this.*

Being stood up is one thing. Killing innovation that our nascent industry relies on to progress and compete with the big business that is slowly moving in on our territory, is quite a different story. In my wildest dreams, I could not have imagined Miles with this intention, but the cannabis industry has shown me people are capable of anything. Our small company has to expand. Expand or die. I am struck by a thought, *we are swimming in an ocean completely unknown to us and suddenly I am aware we are being circled.*

The interior of the conference hall is a bright reflection of the daylight outside. High heels clicking in all directions. Reminds me that the cannabis industry is one of the few industries in the U.S. that is led by 40 percent female CEO's, "The Green Queen's", we are called, and we come in all ages, shapes, and sizes. Like so many of my colleagues, I have taken the spotlight in print and editorial. Glamorizing the trenches of each phase of growth our companies achieve against most odds. I wave to several gals I have been on panels with and or met in the past. Thinking to myself, if only I had come for the conference today. Everyone I see becomes suspect to me. *Could someone here be responsible for Remy's disappearance? Remy, where are you?*

I continue to walk, unsteadily toward the main hall as a stridency of sound hits me like a wall. I notice the same hawkers manning their tables as most of the conferences we attend; security companies, marketing companies, lighting companies, extraction services, packaging purveyors… the usual crew. I grab a map of the main floor, the event is set up in six rows, with a main corridor straight down the middle, dividing it into two sections of three rows, the press room to the far left and the food concession to the far right. There are four break- out rooms, directly facing me at the main entrance. One of those rooms is where Remy should have spoken today.

Out of habit, I count how many infused edible companies are in attendance. Baba Chocolates, a very popular infused chocolatier that quickly covered the market but treated everyone like a corporate franchise and pissed everyone off early on, I think to myself with the tiniest bit of pleasure. Renegade Drinks, a monster of a company, funded early, grew exponentially, only a few of us know what's really going on there. They looked like they were poised for unparalleled greatness but the CEO, Randy Howell, is in hock up to his triple chin. Too big too fast, making it hard to deliver a quality product and most importantly, they are finding it hard to cultivate loyal retailers, especially after their sugary fizzy drinks started exploding on the shelves.

There are three other edible attendees, I know one very well. We had licensed our products to BB Edibles in Colorado, the Mecca of marijuana, for three years. Working under their license, manufacturing our products with our own teams in their kitchen. I oversaw sales and distribution.

BB Edibles is a family run business, they started out with candy, gummies and tootsie rolls. When we met them, they were beginning to branch out into more baked goods and granola. We had a connection, all of us had been in the industry prior to 2009, a landmark for any edible company. Everyone we had asked about them at the time, spoke highly, which can be needless to say, unique.

We basically paid them a monthly fee for use of their facility and to produce products under their "Marijuana Infused Products" or "MIP", license, required by the state. After three years, they saw the growth potential of our gourmet organic beverage line and offered to license our brand exclusively in Colorado. I recall being stunned at their offer, we had intended to terminate our relationship at that very same meeting. Remy and I had started feeling our brand was being treated like a step child, it was difficult to have anyone at the facility follow up on anything, our needs were placed on the bottom of the pile. We were being ignored and our brand was suffering from it. When they approached us for licensing, we considered they just weren't making enough money perhaps with our monthly payment to make it worth their while. If they bought the license and had to pay a unit price fee, we were sure things would change.

That was not the case. Barbara and Michele, the owners of BB Edibles had been together for quite a long time. They couldn't be more opposite. Barbara, a total control freak, shortish and squattish, suffers from hair loss and bad diet. In a good mood, she can actually be pleasant, but they are far and few in between, I recall with a bad taste in my mouth. She doesn't work with women well, we watched as many talented female employees were thrown under the bus.

Michele, is down to earth, calm, slower to react to a situation than her counterpart, takes things in stride. When we needed to discuss any issues, we called Michele. They had married and adopted a boy and a girl, prior to starting their cannabis company of course. "Who would let a lesbian couple in the marijuana industry adopt in this uptight, in the box country?", I recall Remy declaring, never at a loss to point out the inescapable. Michele and Barbara were divorced by the time we met them but continued to work together and raise their children together. That was profound for me, I admired both of them for their commitment.

After our license agreement was signed, they didn't launch for six months. That left us out of the holiday season, a huge season for us. Against our better judgement, they launched in January, a soft launch at that. I had a bad feeling that was growing, intuition should never be ignored. We politely disagreed with Barbara that cutting our menu by two thirds was not a good idea, she insisted she could still sell three times our numbers. So, we went with it.

The writing was on the wall, and it was our fault. We knew better, we had taken our company from infancy to thirty -six products. "You don't fix it if it's not broken," Remy reminded me, "No one knows our product better than we do, next time that needs to be impressed. Our menu cannot be altered, by anyone, I don't care who they are or what they say they are capable of." I nodded in agreement. One of our biggest lessons learned the hard way. Our termination from BB Edibles was not pleasant, and although I will say hello to Michele and ask about her kids, I try to avoid Barbara. Remy has a different approach, I can remember cringing the last time he walked right up to Barbara and asked her, "Monopolize anyone lately?" To my surprise, she laughed.

Barbara may not be very nice, but she would not hurt anyone physically or deign to conspire against Remy, few would. Besides, I shake my head thinking, she has her own house of cards to worry about, *not a suspect.*

As I walk into the entrance of the main hall a security guard stops me. "Can I see your badge please, Ma'am?" The tall handsome African American young man interrupts my thoughts with his bright smile.

"Oh, my badge, shit! I don't have a badge," *because I never thought I would be here, I'm sure not here to attend the conference.*

"It's ok Devon, she's with me, please be sure she has access to anywhere she needs to go in the building." A voice behind me states very clearly,

"Yes, Ms. Holland," Devon replies standing up from his chair.

Ms. Holland, a short emphatic woman with small eyes and a round face, walks up to me, Laddington at her side, smiling triumphantly. In her late 50's, her fashion sense lends itself entirely too much to Jackie O, especially since although this conference is directed at health practitioners, it's focus is cannabis as a natural solution. She seems sincere enough though, leading us through the main hall to a break- out room, usually reserved for lectures.

Laddington insists he will handle the questioning of Evelyn Holland, with the assumption it would upset me to ask questions myself. I don't agree but acquiesce to his experience in the field and check my controlling tendencies, for the moment.

We are sitting in a small conference room off the main conference hall, it consists of four moveable walls painted battleship gray, not my favorite color and a single door leading to the main entrance hall in the middle of the largest wall. We are surrounded by half a dozen eight- foot round folding tables with blue linen table cloths on them and an array of folding chairs holding imprints of the people that sat in them recently and left abruptly.

After ten minutes of excruciating self- control listening to Laddington's questions, I learn; Remy never physically checked in with the organizer but had called as he was getting out of his car to notify her, he had arrived, and to ask her where he should check in to go over the schedule for his lecture.

"What did Mr. Beroe's voice sound like to you, did he sound peculiar in any way? Incoherent or slurring?"

What? That, sounds leading.

Evelyn responds, "I had never spoken to him before, so it's difficult to say what his normal voice would sound like. I didn't arrange for him to speak, that would have been Miss Carter. I simply keep the event running smoothly based on the schedule I receive."

I Interject before she can continue. "Yes, I understand," I say calmly to comfort her, she seems uncomfortable. "Could you tell me what his voice did sound like?"

"Well, he was very loud and I guess you could say, direct."

I think to myself, Remy doesn't have a soft voice at the most desired times while travelling, his voice is low and deep, almost a growl, just thinking of it sends chills through my body. I love his voice it's effectual, you simply can't ignore him. Directness is another virtue of his, a true Scorpio, don't ask if you don't really want to know. He has little patience for inefficiency and should really travel with an assistant to keep the ball rolling at his very eager pace.

"Anything besides that? Umm, could you hear anything else? In the background, while he was talking?" I ask, with the hopes of hearing a clue as to where he was when he called. Laddington looks utterly miffed.

Evelyn is truly disheveled at this point and breathlessly answers, "No. Well actually there was something, it seemed funny to me at the time, as he stated he had just gotten out of his car."

"Yes." Leaning forward in my chair, I inquire encouragingly.

"It's difficult to describe, it was a sort of grumbling sound, metallic but not high end metallic, perhaps metal, like wheels."

"Perhaps a plane?" Laddington interjects.

"I don't know. I don't think so, maybe."

"How long did you wait, to call our assistant, after my husband did not appear?" I ask as calmly as I can manage.

"Well, I had asked him to meet me in the lower level green room. I was taking the stairs down as we spoke. I got there and although I chatted with several other people on the way, I waited fifteen minutes, then called him back. It went to voicemail, so I continued to look around. I waited another ten minutes, thinking perhaps he needed the bathroom, then I had to go back up to the conference floor to walk the next speaker to room b, we have 4 lectures rotating at once. I texted Mr. Beroe while walking back down the main stairs about 40 minutes later, I started getting worried as I still had not heard from him. He was scheduled to go on in half an hour in the main room, as you know although he is not the keynote speaker, his lecture was an anchor in the program today." She adds, looking directly at me.

"Yes." I answer barely moving my lips, "I know. So approximately an hour and five minutes has gone by, what did you do next?" I ask while Laddington does not take his eyes off her.

"I asked one of the security guards to check the men's rooms, sometimes people get nervous, you never know. A little over ten minutes later, he reported he was not in the bathrooms. At this point I texted Mr. Beroe that he was to be in the Main lecture room, at five minutes till eleven latest, I would meet him there. When I did not receive a reply to my text, I texted Jean."

"Jean Carter?" I ask with familiarity.

"Yes, I was concerned and wanted to let her know we may have a problem with the itinerary. Of course, that is exactly what happened, I had to cancel the lecture as he never turned up!" She commits somewhat irritated.

"What did Jean say?" I ask quietly.

"She said she would try him and look for him herself."

I know Jean, her company Cannabis Today, had been one of the first, if not the first company to produce and promote insider conferences. When they first started out ten years ago, the conferences were vetted. You had to be invited to attend, based on the recognition of your company within your region. Remy and I had both been guest speakers at dozens of such conferences over the years. This type of networking was a catalyst to our national brand. We were able to meet a network of industry people from all over the country. I enjoyed these conferences, small and intimate, never more than 100 or 200 people. Structured as "Think Tanks" instead of just meet and greets. The host Jeremy, is the original cannabis game show host, in fact, he is now on network T.V. with his own show on the cannabis network.

Ten years ago, this industry was small, we had known everyone, certainly every edible company. Although we were competitors, we were also family, standing against the man, together as a coalition with the ideals of the innocent. Maybe not all of us, but for the most part, it was all about the patient back then. A means to ail the dying, to promote and educate the masses on the benefits of a natural plant, that seemingly had the answers to sickness and wellbeing. As I had reminded people so many times, this industry was created from compassion. The Lynn and Erin Compassionate Use Act of 1996, allowed the legal use of cannabis for medical purposes. This act of compassion gave us a chance to act for the people, for the patients, and our business models and practices should reflect that. This is what sets us apart from any other industry in America, this industry is founded on compassion, not bottom line. These round table events accentuated our bonds. Not one person in the room of an event had not lost someone dear to cancer, AIDS, Alzheimer's, MS. We were bound by our pain, and desire to release the chains of pharma as the only choice for salvation.

"Where is Jean?"

"She is on the main floor. Would you like me to call her?"

I nod my head. Jean is not only a pioneer in this industry she is also a friend, she and her partner Sophia have spent several vacations with Remy and I in Costa Rica at our retreat shack, a little house we rent out in a fishing village. We have dined in each other's homes, disagreed, laughed and cried with one another. She is not a confidant, but she is a good friend. While Evelyn Holland is texting, I notice that my private detective has been very quiet, perhaps he is not wanting to step on my toes? I tend to take over a situation with an authority and direction that is difficult to undermine. *Should I give him space to deduct?* With that in mind, I turn toward him, "What do you think Laddington?"

"I think we need to talk to some people before the event is over." He says as he changes the position he is sitting in with a grunt. His face has taken a turn for the darker, the sparkling eyes and blinding smile are now lost. That worries me.

Checking my phone waiting for Jean, it is now 4:20, I snigger, the quintessential happy hour of the cannabis world. Most people don't know where that little tradition comes from. Originally and oddly enough in the 1970's a group of high school kids in California, called the Waldo's used the term 4:20 as the code to sneak off for a bong load. Most people think it is the police code for possession of marijuana, illegal possession of course. It is not. From there the term became synonymous with cannabis. Our industry celebrates itself on April 20th – 4-20. Remy is in the habit of calling out, "It's 4:20!" During our workday, not that we would stop to load up a dab, neither of us really consume cannabis on a regular basis. I certainly don't even like smoking it. But the occasional infused tea or coffee definitely realigns my sense of fun and desire for less stress. Both of us use topicals for unknown blemishes or odd skin disorders that age seems to incubate. Remy always says, "You cannot be a stoner in this business, it will eat you up and spit you out." *Where are you, my love?*

I can hear Jean before I see her, Christian Louboutain shoes, indenting the linoleum along the corridor she careens outside the hall door, she is living proof that petite women should never be underestimated. Asian, slight of figure, dressed to kill she pushes the 10- foot door open with the look of Alice, coming through the looking glass.

"Stephanie? How are you?" she asks while moving swiftly to embrace me. "Is there anything I can do?"

Containing my composure, "I don't know."

"Do you need anything, water? Are you hungry? You look exhausted." She whips out her walkie talky and orders a tray of food and drinks, with an efficiency that is beyond contestation. "Stephanie, could he have gotten side tracked, a big idea or opportunity?" She asks taking me aside.

Although Remy can be decidedly distracted and considers public "pas mures", he would never not appear when scheduled, *not unless....* "No, he hasn't contacted me since his plane landed. This is your event Jean, if something had come up, he would have contacted you, he would have called me."

"Have you called the police?"

"No. Standard procedure is 24 hours after the person has been discovered missing." Laddington inserts.

"Oh my God girl, what can I do?"

A man in a white serving jacket brings in a cart with the requested platter of sandwiches and a bucket of random healthy choice drinks. Absentmindedly, I walk over to the cart and grab a Hansen's soda. Popping the top, I drink three quarters of it, before turning around, all eyes on me. "Ok," I say rallying my wits, "I would like a list of all personnel working this event, including the caterers, and would like to talk with them as a group before they go home today. Everyone Jean. AV, attendees, speakers, photographers, if you have them on a list, I want to meet them." I fix my eyes on Jean, "I would like five people to help us ask attendees questions while people are milling or leaving. I will need a couple of copies of this." Handing Jean a snap shot of Remy, she looks at it and looks back up at me blinking.

"He will be ok, Steph. Remy is tough."

I smile, "Yes". *Yes, he is.*

16

LE SOLEIL EST PRES DE MOI

At 5:30 cocktails are sponsored by Chromo labs, a laboratory for testing weed for pesticides, solvents, mold and cannabinoid content, in the main hall. After a long day of conventioneer collective thinking and networking, it is highly attended. I send Laddington and the five volunteers Jean rounded up for my use, outside of the facility, two in back and three out front armed with Remy's picture, although I doubt that was necessary, everyone it seems knows him.

I stay in the hall, mingling with colleagues, feeling it best not to state Remy is missing. Tactfully, maneuvering from one to the other, I don't have to ask if anyone has seen Remy, upon approach they ask me where he is? Why his lecture had been canceled? I make up a tale that he had to fly to the east coast for a meeting at the last minute and that I had attempted to arrive on time for the lecture, but it just didn't work out, plane got delayed. This seems to appease everyone, as I tick people off my list at an astonishing rate.

I texted Grace to contact me immediately if she had heard anything, she was checking hospitals and upon my suggestion, the police stations here in San

Francisco. It is not completely out of the question that Remy could have offended a police officer, looking for a reason to bust someone at a cannabis event.

This is not a High Times Cannabis Cup, I remind myself, with scores of stoners dabbing until their knees give out and all sense of coherence deleted. This is an insider industry event, and there are definitely pot friendly personnel inside, attendees know better than to light up outside the venue. Discretion is imperative, hotel rooms, rental cars are the preference. With the discussion of passing recreational cannabis use in California recently, they still haven't worked out where one may consume the product. Public spaces are a no- no, same with parks, federal buildings, federally funded buildings or institutions, bars, restaurants. Cannabis consumption is still being demonized. Colorado is pushing for much needed cannabis friendly business legislation. But with everything else in this industry, the process is slow. That is one of the reasons edibles are so popular, they are so damned discreet.

I spot Tyler from across the room, smiling he waves with the anticipation of speaking to me. Tyler is the assistant to H.S. the CEO of DBS, the other large corporation we had negotiated with before Miles. He is tall, handsome and early thirty something, impeccably dressed today donning a Tom Ford suit, that's light gray and sets off his green hued, well endowed …eyes.

Walking over to me with a drink in each hand and handing me one, he salutes, "Stephanie, how are you? I didn't know YOU would be here. I missed Remy's lecture, I got pulled into the press room."

"Tyler. My appearance is …last minute."

"Hey, you know we were really thrown when we couldn't work out a deal with you two. We are still very interested, how long are you in town, maybe we could meet for drinks? You haven't signed anything with ole Miles yet, have you?"

There is a genuine note of hope to his voice, but I have no intentions of rekindling a deal. Truthfully, I have nothing against Tyler, he seems hardworking and accommodating. Incapable of knowing why, I just don't trust him. His good looks and dark complexion do not completely veil an underlying darkness. Knowing his boss and how difficult he must be to work with, it is dismissible but keeps me on guard.

The opportunity offered by his company DBS seemed a dream come true,

"And it usually is." Remy reminded me. With our ideals on our sleeves, we had been very close to being wooed by the promise of large figures, large returns, and unlimited access to marketing, sales, and promotional teams as well as total artistic control over our brand and company initiatives. But they stepped over the line of wooing, my eyes were opened to a whole new insight.

I can feel the cloak of guilt covering me as I reply, "I will be here for a couple of days, with meetings." Thinking it will take me several days to talk with all the employees if Remy doesn't turn up in the meantime. "Send me an email tomorrow and we can work something out." *Am I really saying this? What is wrong with me?* The last thing in the world I want to do is entertain Tyler, H.S. and their conglomerate. So why do my impulses present invitation?

"Wonderful, I will be in touch." Tyler walks away and before I can shake my head at my behavior, a warm hand touches my back. I turn and see Laure. No longer capable of holding my composure any longer, I embrace my College friend.

"Stephanie, honey what's wrong? Come with me, let's get out of here." She urges feeling my body shutter.

Laure Giovani is my oldest friend. We grew up together in college, dating the same boys, cutting each other's hair, listening to the same music and reading the same books. We had lived together for several years, on and off as roommates, during our formidable years. As true friendships do, we stretched its limits with distance, growth, love, and pain. Several years ago, Remy and I brought Laure on to oversee social media and marketing, she is a natural. Always hip to the latest trends, she has landed us many a national and global editorial spread. Unable to afford her deserving services full time, we introduced her to other cannabis companies looking for a dedicated promoter. It did not occur to me that she would be here. I had not called any friends or family to ask if they had known where Remy was, *if I didn't know, no one did.*

Laure quickly pulls me into the ladies' room, still imbued by the lingering aroma of hash, "Tell me what's wrong?" she inquires in a comforting motherly tone. Always straight to the point, she retrieves a box of tissues from the sink counter and hands them to me.

"Remy is missing!" There, I finally said it out loud, maybe too loud, it took on the sound of crowing, reverberating from the tiled walls and floor. Laure is physically taken aback, as I lose total control, my breathing becoming awkward.

Drawing her eyebrows together, she repeats, "Missing?" Laure looks at me in utter disbelief.

"He was scheduled to lecture at eleven, he never showed. He made it to the building and then nothing, I haven't heard from him since a little after 9:30, no one has!" There is no controlling my tears, as I focus on my breath to get every word out before the crushing pressure in my chest devours me.

Laure has known Remy almost as long as I have, as Remy and I met about four and half years after I met laure. She understands our unique connection.

"Shit." She whispers, hugging me to her.

That brings a smile to my face.

"What do we do next?"

Feeling stronger than I had upon my arrival, I text Laddington, that I will meet him at the entrance to the conference center and that he should round up the volunteers, so I can question them as to what they have found out. Having filled Laure in with all the details I had, which are not a lot. She begins to promptly cancel meetings and clear her calendar, this gives me strength. I arrange for Jean to also meet us, it is now eight pm the event is over for the day. All of the attendees have left for a shower and dinner meetings. Grace has not been in contact, which means she hasn't found anything, I assume and with me gone, she is handling a big work load.

It is finally dark outside, the fluorescent overhead lights, make everything look a shade of gray, what a contrast I think, from the searing blue sky of today, as I walk up to the front doors. The small group that awaits me inside the entrance hall, is visibly tired. Laddington has his pad out and is taking notes on it with one finger typing, as Laure and I approach.

"Here." I say as I hand Laddington my phone, I turn on voice notes, "Record their statements instead it's faster and I can listen to them later."

"Good idea."

Introducing Laure to Laddington, I notice he is taking inventory of my support group, catching his eye he smiles.

By the time, we record everyone's reports it's close to ten. I retrieve my phone from Laddington. "I will see you tomorrow, I have the names of all of the employees and I think it's best to start interviewing them one at a time tomorrow."

"I can do that," he offers, "send me the list and I will get on it first thing in the morning."

"No, we will break the list up in thirds, each of us will take a portion." I state looking between Laure and Laddington, "That way we will get through the list faster and hopefully have something to tell the police. Perhaps you could follow up on the car agencies and cabs, you can also enlist Grace for phone calls, just send her names of places to look up or ideas of names of places and she will coordinate with you." I suggest to Laddington.

"Sounds good Mrs. Beroe, where will you be staying?"

"With me." Laure resounds.

"Thank you, Laure but I think I need a little alone time. Grace set up a room in the Haight District."

"Ok, if you're sure? At least let me drive you there."

I say my goodbyes and thank you's to my makeshift staff. Jean wants to meet around nine thirty AM and tells me the center staff should arrive around seven thirty AM.

"We should all return here in the morning around seven, I will bring the coffee." I offer.

"Don't bring your coffee," Laure jokes, "we will never get anything done!"

"Actually, that is exactly what I could use right now," I say with as much humor as I can muster. *There are no clues, no witnesses, and no motives so far. Most importantly there is no Remy.*

17

A THOUSAND KISSES DEEP

Grace found an air bnb room about three miles away. In the passenger seat of Laure's car, I silently watch the world around me, blurry and distant.

"Do you need anything? Food, drinks, clothing? Laure is treating me like a beloved child in need of coddling.

"I'm good, maybe, just stop at that liquor store. I would like to get a bottle of wine."

"Sure, no prob honey. Listen Steph, I can feel it in my heart Remy is ok. You would feel it, if it were otherwise, right?"

"I hope so." *Would I?* She is looking over at me in the passenger seat, but I am unable to make eye contact without breaking. *People die every day without their loved ones having any idea, brutal deaths, and peaceful deaths. Would I know?* "Yeah, I would know."

"What's the schedule for tomorrow, what time do you want me to pick you up?"

"You don't have to. I can get a cab."

"Get- out… your just lucky I am letting you stay alone tonight, tomorrow is another story, besides I am sure we will find him, I mean, he will turn up…Damn." She slaps the steering wheel. "I am so sorry."

"It's nice to be wanted. Can you pick me up at six fifteen?"

"Sure."

"I intend to speak with every employee at the conference center that had been working a shift at the time Remy disappeared."

"Got it, good plan. Hey, have you tried looking at his phone itinerary and emails to see if there are any messages or meetings that came through?"

"That is a great idea! *I will do that at the hotel.* Laure?"

"Yeah Hun?"

"Why would anyone want to hurt Remy?" I ask still afraid to look into her eyes.

"Who says anyone has? I'm sure it's just a mix up, you know things happen!"

"Not like this," I say turning my face to the window.

More patiently than I would have imagined, I wait for the conference centers' Managing Director to email me a list of employees and schedules for the following days, so I can arrange to meet with them one at a time, feeling this is the last stone left unturned. I thank Laure for the ride and walk up to my lodgings for the night.

The lovely little Victorian is in the center of the Haight District. It's adorable but the filigree and gingerbread facia mock me as I walk up to the door. Perched on a hill, a story book San Francisco Victorian, painted purple, pink, and the saddest shade of baby blue. My room is small but well appointed, clean and in the morning, would be bright with California sunshine. The sheets are linen and the bed spread a natural cotton. Remy and I despise synthetic coverlets that are common in hotels. Travelling at least two weeks out of every month, and attempting to find suitable places to stay that are not ridiculously priced is a difficult task. A main task I bequeath to Grace. No; sterile, never ending hallways, no in room heaters without thermostats, no non- opening windows… the list goes on. I have no idea how the 70's and 80's travelling sales personnel survived all those sick building Holiday Inns.

I unpack my large purse containing a clean shirt, undies, and my toothbrush. I should have stopped at a store, but frankly, I just don't give a damn about how I look or what I wear. Opening my lap top I connect to the WIFI, resynching our calendars, and then downloading Remy's calendar and emails. There is one email from an old acquaintance that is an extractor. The subject strikes me as off color, I open it;

Subject: glass houses

"Remy, what up? Saw this in the NCI newsletter. Doesn't sound like your girl, but I thought I would send it to you."

I scan down to the quote from the article.

Stephanie Beroe, CEO of The Mad Hatter Coffee & Tea Co., openly states their new infusion method is not ideal and has several draw backs.

My eyes blink. "What!" I yell openly, scanning for the reporter's name, and quickly jumping online to read the whole article. It's just a blurb, in an infusion with extracted oil article. But it is a quote I never made, and would never make. "Damn it!" Sitting on the bed I exhale, shaking the bed posts. I notice the email was sent today and it had been read at nine am. Surely, Remy would ignore this as confused somewhat intentional slander. He would never believe I would say something so detrimental, not to mention untrue. Looking through the list of emails, I realize there were at least five more "acquaintances", bringing this slur to Remy's attention. *Why didn't anyone bring it to my attention?* I look at the clock before dialing Grace, it's now a little after midnight, too late to call her.

Remy was right, there is something else at work here, too many coincidental mis-quotes.

I stop thinking and breathing for a moment. *Could this have been a last straw? Maybe he needed to disappear to figure this all out? Maybe he is pissed off at me?* I lean back on the bed, "Maybe..." Staring at the ceiling, a tear falls down my cheek.

"Pull it together Steph." Attempting a final rally for the day, having already divided up the lists for tomorrow, I decide to take a shower, change my energy and clear a new perspective. The water cannot be hot enough, my tears flowing down my face mingle with the searing stream. Bracing myself with my hands against the cold tiled walls, unsure now of the one thing I have always been so sure of.

Once the water runs cold, I dry off, not daring to look at myself in the mirror, not bothering to wipe the fog from the glass. Wrapping the large soft towel around me, the sound of silence overtakes me. *I have to get out this room!* Changing back into my dirty clothes, layering my clean shirt underneath the long sleeve linen top I can smell from across the room and my jeans. I Make a note to wash out the top before I go to bed. Grabbing the now open bottle of wine, the glass from the bathroom and my jacket, I quietly find the stairs for the deck I had seen on the internet.

The house is cheerful, flowers brighten the landings of all three floors. Perhaps a little too much striped wall paper, but overall the vibe is secure and welcoming. The deck had been obviously built between the 80's and present day. Although its design is plain compared to the thoughtful embellishments of the turn of the century architecture the house reflects, it encourages a lovely view of a city edged by the night's fathomless black sea.

Sitting there nursing a glass of white Sonoma Valley Pinot Grigio between my legs, the cool breeze brushes sadness across my face as I remember a phrase from the tombstone of the Lady Taimhotep, a mother entombed in ancient Egypt; *The West is a land of sleep where darkness weighs on the dwelling place. Those who live there, sleep as mummies. They do not wake to see their brothers and cannot see their fathers or mothers. Their hearts forget their wives and children…turn my face to the north wind at the edge of the water. Perhaps then my heart will be cooled in its grief.*

18

SPINNING

Looking around the small group surrounding her, all of them frightened, Delta knows they are all depending on her to keep them alive, she has, after all, been there the longest. Almost a year she has survived this grueling test of survival. Remembering how scared she was when she first arrived, fills her with compassion for the others, especially the new ones. It felt like only yesterday, waking up on the hard jungle ground, oblivious to what had happened and where she was.

The day had started out like any other day, drinking coffee on the ferry from her Staten island condo, while she read the Inquirer and the New York Times on her phone. The imminent presidential election blanketing the headlines. She had been so excited about Bernie, he broke all the boundaries; free college tuition, corporate transparency, higher minimum wages, decent vacation, and maternity leave, most importantly the dismantling of big banks. He was a man for the people. This had excited her, and it seemed the majority of the registered voters for the democratic party. But the DNC just wouldn't go there. She exhaled into the chilled morning air crossing the New York Bay, looking at the luminescent phone screen before her with a picture of Donald Trump looming like a bad omen.

Arriving at the office on 53rd and Lexington an hour early, as usual, to give herself plenty of time to prepare for her boss, Richard Bannock, CEO of Bannock Industries, arrival.

The Elevator opened on to the receiving room on the 38th floor, a large now empty desk at the end of the elevator corridor is where the floor Assistant sits and checks in visitors. This is the Executive floor, Senior Executives to the right and Department Heads to the left. She was the only personnel in the office that early except for security. Heading down the familiar wood paneled corridor broken by opaque glass walls extending into doorways for private offices with views, she noted the corralled area hidden in the center of the building, designated for assistants. No windows, just the light permeating through the glass panels of the executive offices, accompanied by the artificial lighting from above. Of course, at this time of the morning, only the artificial lighting was apparent. The maze of individual cubby desks always hidden from view by a second layer of conference rooms and presentation spaces, conceals the work force no one wants to see, obscured by luxury. After turning right at the end of the hall, a set of large ornate double carved doors loomed over the long passage, dotted with lifeless artwork.

Unlocking the doors made of some exotic wood she cannot remember the name of, the lights turned on automatically to the interior office space. The anti-chamber. Her desk a slab of cold gray stone for looks, not comfort, strategically blocked the next set of double doors that led into Bannock's private sanctuary. There was a private guest bathroom located next to the custom exotic leather chairs across from her desk. A large window to her right that overlooked the city still in darkness and an opaque glass wall that permeated light to her left. The wall separating Bannock's office from hers was designed with built in filing cabinets and closets, that blended into the wall exterior not visible to visitors. She need only push in and the storage space revealed itself from the wood paneled wall. After placing her purse and coat in the designated coat storage cabinet, she sat down.

This was a solitary position. Alone in a room for most of the day, only the muted city to keep her company. Bannock Industries was a web of consulting firms for real estate management and acquisition, that spanned the globe. They originally began as an investment consultation firm in the late 1800's as Bannock and Brier. Through the years, they expanded into contracting firms that built roads, bridges and utility infrastructure globally, while purchasing key buildings and potential building sites in developing countries. After World War II, they began purchasing wide tracks of undeveloped and decimated land throughout Europe. She was just beginning to understand the expansive reach of the company she worked for. Heads of state were in direct contact with Bannock, her boss a demanding, impatient man was used to the world coming to him.

Eight AM like clockwork, he bounded down the executive corridor, all of the doors to all of the offices he navigated were always open and prevailing to the boss man.

Without so much as a hello, she was greeted with demands for breakfast as he scanned his palm for entry into his dominion, dropping his coat on her desk. She remembers hanging his camel hair coat in the cedar lined closet and waiting for the obligatory summons to run over his schedule for the day.

"Good morning Mr. Bannock," her greeting ever warm and cheery.

"Let's get this over with, I want to eat my breakfast in peace this morning."

"Absolutely," she replied and proceeded to list the day's events without time for rumination. At the conclusion of this unaffable exchange, she turned on her heel to leave as Bannock reached for his phone.

"Wait."

"Yes, Sir?"

Without any further discussion, she was handed a piece of paper with a list of errands to run. No explanation, as usual. Cursing herself for being inveigled by a paycheck, she returned to her desk.

Most of the list was shopped out to messengers. The personal items were her responsibility. Town car waiting outside the building, grabbing her coat, she set out for what should have been three hours of running around, with traffic. The driver was friendly, spoke English and knew his way around town.

Having worked for Bannock for a year, she was getting to know her boss. The money was very good, but he, was an animal. Being a Personal Assistant is not un like being a priest, she reminded herself. You get to know all the little idiosyncrasies and bad habits of the person you work for. Your job is to keep them happy and keep their secrets. She had kept those secrets, the call girls to the office. The call girls to his suite at the Ritz Carlton kept for his interludes. It did not go unnoticed that all of the women she procured for him were African American, and not unlike herself in looks. Never the same gal twice. The balding, seventy- year old that she worked for, was a handful. His midlife crisis was twenty years in the making. His language foul, a raging racist against; Jews, Europeans, blue bloods, college grads, the un educated, gays, heterosexuals, immigrants, the list was endless. In retrospect, there wasn't anyone he really did like or respect. He had no friends until he started communicating with Warren Bazel, another wealthy CEO. Based on the fact that he answered to no one, he was never challenged. Although many a time she wished she had given him a good slap. The lesson here, being a billionaire doesn't buy you intelligence, class, taste or morals.

Laughing to herself she remembers his terrible suits, with all that money, she recalls shaking her head. Having developed a maternal responsibility for a brief moment, in the beginning for her boss, she thought she could encourage him to wear clothing that wasn't made in the 90's. He just didn't get it, not that he wasn't vain, he was just oblivious to anyone else's thoughts but his own. She was sure, had he not been born with a kazillion dollars, he would have been on the street or murdered by someone.

Delta remembers his chasing her around his desk as a common nuisance. Then there was the event in the Caymans he had asked her to attend. It was not unusual for her to accompany him on trips, but she always had her own room safely located on a different floor from his preying hands. This time she didn't make the arrangements and found herself in an adjoining room from his palatial suite. Her immediate response was a poke at humor, "Well, this should make midnight letter taking easier."

His response, a solicitous glare, sent chills down her spine. She unpacked and attempted to text her friend and neighbor but had no service and could not find a password for the WIFI. *I can handle this*, she told herself.

That evening, she recalls, they dined on their suite's private patio together, going over details of the next day's events. Everything seemed above board, the small boutique hotel frequented only by the very wealthy and or famous, restricted access by large airplanes, so they flew in on his private jet. She wasn't even sure where she was as private security took care of their passports.

After dinner, she went for a night swim in the pool adjacent to their cabana. The drone of laps acting as a cleanser, clearing her mind of questionable thoughts. Returning to their suite, she remembers saying goodnight to her boss, somewhat engrossed in documents, closing the lockless door and going to bed, hoping for the best.

The next day she followed him around the small conference taking notes on people he met and collecting contact information, feeding him with information about the people he was meeting, running errands for him and fielding his emails and phone calls. It was a spectacular day and the meeting room was a columned roofless patio surrounded by flowering trees that overlooked the Caribbean Sea. Perhaps thirty men were in attendance with their P.A.'s, all women. The day was a success and they were both happy with each other's behavior, perhaps influenced by the setting.

The consortium was scheduled for the mornings, leaving the rest of the day off, she decided to sunbathe. While setting up on a scalloped shaped wicker chaise facing the ocean, slathering her legs with cocoa butter a familiar voice behind her offered, "Allow me." As Bannock scooped up some cocoa butter and began rubbing it into her back and shoulders.

Frozen she kicked herself for being silent, *is he being helpful or is he being a lech?* As his hands started working their way down to the top of her bikini bottoms the question was answered. She forced her back against the chair to terminate the incident, something she had developed a proficiency for.

There were several other people on the beach as she looked around, all of them more intimate than most job criteria should include. Bannock sat down in the chaise next to hers.

"It's beautiful here, don't you think?" He asked with complete candor as if he was not just slipping his fingers down her crack.

"Yes," She replied stiffly. Afraid to really say what she was thinking, as the butler who had been designated for their suite, trudged over at that moment through the sand, "Is there anything you would like?"

Yes, a ticket out of here. "I would like a glass of ice water."

"Bring us two mojitos and make them strong." Her boss demanded of the young frightened man, that left quickly.

Bannock turned around on his seat facing his back to her, and then asked, "Would you do the honors?"

Dumbfounded, like a mechanical remote- controlled toy she began to rub oil on his back as if that weren't really screwed up!

"Hmm, that feels great. Yes, keep rubbing like that really hard on my left shoulder. Hmm, that's good."

Trying to disguise the ick expression from her face as another couple walked by them on the shoreline, she quickly filtered through her options. *Yell for help? Run back to the room and bar the door with furniture? Try to fly the private jet home?* She removed her hands, "There you go."

Bannock turned around, incredibly agile for a slump of unexercised man, to face her. "You're a beautiful woman Danielle, your smart and beautiful." He said in a creepy voice as he grabbed her bare foot and started massaging it in his hands.

She looked around the beach, couples, swimming together, kissing. It looked like a honeymoon resort. But she knew all of these people were not married, everyone was attending the consortium.

"Are you propositioning me?"

"I will do whatever you want me to do." He replied placing her tenderized foot over his dick while proceeding to rub it with her foot.

She looked around to see if anyone was watching this, completely confused and overcome by guilt at the same time. The butler returned with the drinks, she hoped his presence would end the intercourse. To her horror, it did not. The drinks were placed on the table and the young man retreated silently back to the sand.

She felt Bannock getting hard, his breath heavy, and just as she pulled her foot away, he climaxed in front of her. Sitting back in her chair thinking of the bobble headed tween he was married to and felt sorry for her for the first time, before she became outraged. His lack of respect for women was intolerable, but *who would believe this, and who would care, if I told them?* she asked herself.

Almost a year later, her last day of civility, now sears her memory. The first stop on her list of errands was the Chrysler Building, to pick up a large package from her boss's new bestie. Terry the assistant met her at the door with a box about three and half feet long wrapped in brown paper and tied with string. It seemed very old fashioned at the time, and it was quite heavy.

"Good morning Danielle." That was the last time anyone called her Danielle, she remembers this humiliating scene like it was yesterday while moving rocks around on the jungle floor with a stick.

"Hi Terry, how is your day?"

"Busy, but good. I was told this had to be delivered into your hands. Y voila!"

"Yes, valuable merchandise." They both smiled.

"Don't work too hard."

"You took the words right out of my mouth." Smiling and turning back to the hallway she carried the package back to the elevator bank. Life was good, for the past week since their trip, she had managed to stay out of the office running errands.

The second stop on her list was written out by hand on note paper that was printed on the top with, "Because I'm the Boss." It gave an address with the directions; *Enter through the service entrance, should be marked. Tell them you are from Bannock.*

The car stopped at 387 in between the block just after sixth Ave. The streets were bustling, the sidewalk packed, just another day in the Big Apple. Getting out and walking to the address, the service door was up a small flight of stairs. It was a metal door with a small glass window in it. The door was locked. After a knock or two, a baldish head came to the window, without opening the door.

"Yeah?"

"I'm from Bannock."

"Wait a minute." The bald man curtly replied.

After a minute, there was a buzzing sound unlocking the door. She walked into the small gray corridor with a desk in it and everything went black. That was it, the last memory she retained of her former life.

Rocking back and forth on her heels, squatting at the small fire lit for comfort on a warm sunny day, Delta wipes her eyes without drawing attention to herself. Suddenly aware of a large sound about twenty yards from their camp, she wakes everyone quietly. All of the women begin to exit in the other direction, when they hear dogs, and not far enough away. As they turn back, they can now see the outline of a male, a large male heading directly for them. They are trapped! Taking an attack position, the women spread out in a crescent formation waiting, as the sound of dogs moves closer from behind.

Surrounded. How could I have let this happen? She prostrates, sweat dripping from every pore, muscles tense with apprehension, now straining to hear the footsteps in the leaves. *Whoever it is they are not in a hurry. That could be a problem.*

The dogs are now a hundred yards away if that. The brush in front of her breaks, and a man, a smiling man comes walking towards them.

"Who the hell are you?" Delta all but screams. "Never mind, no time for that!" Grabbing his arm, they all run.

19

I WEAR YOUR RING

Unlocking the front door of the Beroe town home with her copy key, it seems strange walking in without either of them home working. This place is always such a beehive, Grace thinks to herself, turning on the mp3 player. The Pretender's Chrissy Hynde is spelling O-H-I-O in the back-round now, "That's better."

Having brought the mail in as a habit and tossing it onto the large middle table that stands between the Beroe's work stations, she becomes aware of an unerring feeling that takes hold of her looking from one desk to the other. Her phone rings, startling her.

"Hey."

"Morning Stephanie, how are you today?"

"That's a loaded question."

"Yeah, I'm sorry."

"I only have a minute, before Laure picks me up."

"What happened to Laddington?"

"Oh, he's on the scene, I am meeting him at the conference center this morning to question the staff. I sent you an email late last night, with an update."

"Oh, sorry, I just got here at six to get a head start on a couple of things."

"Did you find anything?"

"No, I checked all the hospitals and police stations in that area. There is just no sign of him, but that could be a good thing, right?"

"Right. I am going to need you to check all taxi's, oh and find the driver that dropped Remy off. I want to talk to him or her."

"Got it."

"Let me know immediately if anything turns up and text me the driver's info when you have it? Also, please get the Colorado blend estimate to me ASAP for approval so they can order, and I sent you an email about Illinois last night, please make that a priority?"

"I will."

"Thanks Grace, really thank you. Gotta go." Trying not to let my voice crack, I hang up. I've got less than seven hours to figure out a lead before I can report this to the police. Laying back on the bed, fully clothed as I have been awake since four. Numbed by physical exhaustion weighing me down, my eyes close.

The sun is bright and warm, I feel the heat penetrating my bones, opening my eyes to the most marvelous view of the sea. Remy stands next to me; his long blonde and gray streaked mane reach out into the nether like tentacles blowing in the breeze. We are at peace, hand in hand, standing on a deck in perfect harmony with ourselves and the nature that surrounds us. The wooden deck built above the shoreline, is similar to the boardwalk at Jenkinson's pier in New Jersey. No one else is sharing the view with us, and we cannot draw our attention away from the sea, so blue it's mesmerizing. There are dozens of people below us, playing in the surf and on the shoreline. Children running after each other. Parents pushing their little ones around on rafts in the calm water. Lover's swimming nose to nose a little past the break water. Playful laughter mixed with the call of sea gulls intertwines the gentle rhythm of the sea. The salt air so thick, I can taste it on my lips as I draw my tongue across them.

Suddenly, the ocean rhythm stops. Silence followed by a shadow so large, I look up to see what cloud has blotted out the sun. But the sky is clear. Dread creeps up through the very surface of the decking, pouring into my body. I clasp

Remy's hand and squeeze, unable to speak or even utter a sound. Remy is standing there, still looking at the water, as if under a spell. I turn my head, to follow his gaze, toward a turmoil of giant 30-foot waves. One after another lined up and now breaking directly on the shore, churning the bodies of all the people below like rag dolls. Their black silhouettes enhanced ominously through the backlit water. I am consumed by the deafening roar of the sea muting their screams.

My eyes shoot open, breath, heavy and fast, sweat running down my neck, as I stare at the ceiling above me in my rental room. Desperately attempting to clear the images from my mind, I take off all of my clothes, turn the hot water on full, and force myself back in the shower. The hot water simmers my thoughts, *where did all of this start going wrong?*

I don't know how long I am in the shower, but the cold water stings me back to the claw foot tub I am standing in. Stepping out, shivering grabbing for a towel, I sit back on the rim of the tub, taking a moment to absorb the moisture in the room. *Both companies wanted us, both still do, even to my surprise. How could that have anything to do with Remy disappearing? People just don't kid nap someone and force them to sign a contract. Especially when it's Remy, he can be incredibly stubborn, dangerous even. Besides, I would have to sign the contract too.* Tossing the whole idea like a crinkled piece of paper, I wipe off the fogged mirror, "Get a grip Steph." My phone buzzes on the bed.

"Hey, Laure," I answer.

"Hey Girlie, you ready? I 'm outside."

"Great, I'll be right down."

Laure and I pick up a dozen coffees and an assortment of bagels at a small deli. My stomach is cramping from hunger. I realize I haven't eaten anything since yesterday afternoon.

Giving me the once over, Laure asks, "Are those the only clothes you brought?"

"What? Oh, yeah. I was in a hurry to catch my flight yesterday."

"Would you like me to stop at my place and pick up a couple of things?"

"Maybe later. I'm a little one track minded right now, I manage while devouring a bagel."

"Got it."

Laure is dressed impeccably, a smart two- tone brown, tailored pant suit, her silk top is barely purple. Sexy but intelligent. It shows off her big brown eyes. A runner now, she is in better shape than she was in college. Toned but still shapely, a real woman's figure. Her cork screw curly black hair has been cut just below her ears, its punky and clean at the same time. Since she has moved out to San Francisco she has blossomed. Another Jersey Girl, that finally escaped, I'm happy for her.

The car ride is unusually quiet but the city around us is already bustling with joggers, dog walkers, and bicyclers everywhere. The traffic is grave. A small layer of fog being forced to retreat from the marbled blue sky above. *It's going to be another beautiful fucking California day, for Christ's sake.* "Doesn't it ever rain here?"

Placing her hand over mine Laure looks at me, "Hey, it's going to be ok. We are going to find Remy."

I look back and just nod.

"Let's turn on some music," scrolling through her phone, masterfully directing the device without lifting her finger from the screen. Goldfrapp breaks the silence. My phone is vibrating, I scramble to check the screen with the continual hope that it's Remy. It's Grace, forwarding emails from Tyler wishing to confirm drinks for tonight at The Wilson Bar on Jones street, and Miles hoping to meet with me at four o'clock at the Fairmont Hotel in Knob Hill. Illinois has also checked in, requesting the original high res files again in a malleable format so they themselves can create the labels they need. Pretty safe to say if they can't create a logo on their own, creating our labels is out of their league, but I acquiesce and send a second request to Grace.

Laddington also emailed, "I'll meet you at six at the conference center. No leads so far." I read the last sentence twice, my belly churning.

I reply to Tyler first, *six thirty will work tonight, I am bringing a colleague.* I'll talk Laure into coming later. I also confirm with Miles at the Laurel Court Bar at the Fairmont Hotel, copying Grace. My instincts are telling me to poke around a bit.

Tactfully, I reply to Illinois, that I have sent a request to my layout guy to send them the Illustrator file with layers so they can manipulate the file, while we park. Jean has also sent a text, *I'm here, have morning staff from yesterday, same break out room.*

We are ten minutes away. I text back, I am not a traditional texter, I use it like email, with punctuation and full sentences. Modern technology is no excuse for poor grammar. Remy would laugh at that thought. *Remy. Where are you?*

The morning air is chilly, "Remind me to borrow a warmer jacket from you later." I say to Laure as she puts her arm through mine and we walk across the street to the conference center.

20

DAS MALEFITZ

W here the fuck am I?" Directing his question to the scantily dressed women, observing him with caution and definite malice, Remy's confusion is harboring on irrepressible anger.

"As far as we can make out, we are on an Island or a very remote region of land." The tall woman that just dragged him through the jungle at a heroic speed answers with a hint of laughter in her voice, "Somewhere between the Tropic of Cancer and Capricorn, based on the behavior of the sun and lack of storm patterns." The obvious leader replies, sincerely out of breath, leaning over her knees. "How long have you been here?" Her tone turns serious.

"I woke up about two hours ago, smelled smoke and walked towards it. Who are you?"

"How many others were with you." She asks ignoring his question.

"What do you mean?"

"I mean how many other people were with you when you woke up?"

"None."

"No one spoke to you? Did you see anyone?"

"No."

"That's new." Standing to her impressive height of at least six feet, she offers her hand, "They call me Delta, and you may want to sit down."

Protocol would demand he be brought back to the camp for the men to question him. But protocol was becoming a form of oppression for the women, with this in mind, she doesn't hesitate.

"What's your name?"

"Remy, Remy Beroe."

While Delta explains that all of them had woken there on the island, without any memory of being abducted, he searches his mind for the last details he can remember while following her narrative. Everything so hazy, he feels stoned. The flora is hyper in color, the smell of moisture, salt and wet soil overpowering his senses, he can almost taste it, he is high, on what he has no idea. Head pounding with his heart beat from running. The woman in front of him is tall and lithe, her chocolate skin is set off by golden eyes. Her hair has been woven into corn rows that unravel in the back, just past her shoulder blades. She is striking.

The five other women, staring at him are a curious mix of primitive steam punk, all of them wearing fragments of clothing from… *office life?* The leader is donning what may have been a white linen shirt, with the sleeves ripped off, tied in a knot under her breasts. The skirt, or what's left of it is macro, with makeshift slits up the sides to her hips. A cell phone is strapped to her thigh, he notices they all have phones attached to their clothing if you can call rags clothing.

"Do you get service here?" He interrupts her litany of experiences, obviously not the only one she has debriefed.

"Do you?" She asks with such sincerity, he believes he might. Checking his pocket for his phone oddly, for it's the first time he's thought of it. *No service* is clearly written at the top corner. Noting that today is the sixteenth he realizes he has been incoherent for an entire day? Glancing his inbox, he sees Steph has emailed a dozen times. They all ask the same thing in the subject, *where are you?*

"Steph." Remy whispers, thinking, *she must think I'm dead.* "No, no service." He says turning off the phone to save the battery. "What were we running from and how long have you all been here?"

"Dogs and men. I have been here the longest, a year maybe, not really sure."

"A year? There's no way off? What do you mean dogs and men?"

"You haven't heard the worst of it."

That is an understatement while picking up a stick from the ground and squatting to her knees Delta explains the gruesome details, "There are, from what we can determine, twenty- four of us at a time on the island." We have split into two factions, our family, and the Others. "

That sounds a bit ominous. "Men?"

"Yes, eight men and sixteen women. Always."

"Ok." He notices three of the women have their backs to him, they look like they are on look out, either that or bored with the conversation.

"The island is patrolled by armed guards, they have dogs, flame throwers, lots of other neat tricks to drive us like cattle into the open. We have managed to kill a few, but they are tougher than hell."

Remy blinks.

"The Others, are at war with us."

"Why?" Remy asks incredulously.

"Because they believe, if they kill us, *they* will be able to go home."

"What? How do you know this?"

"We have interrogated a few and we were all told the same thing." Her eyes look away with an expression of distaste. "The worst part of this, however-"

"You mean there's more?" He can feel his eyebrows raising involuntarily.

"B-O-H-I-C-A." A gal with beautiful dark skin and really long legs calls out to the group with a snigger.

Delta stares her down as the rest of the group quiets their laughter.

"What does she mean, what the hell is bohica?"

In mumbled response, Delta says, "Bend Over Here It Comes Again." before changing the subject and continuing, "You will notice throughout the terrain, about twenty- twenty-five feet above us, is a train track," Using her stick as a pointer she points up and to the left, where a large cement infrastructure hovers over the basin of trees, they are mired in.

Ignoring the cotton mouth erupting, Remy cannot, however, ignore his knees buckling from some unknown strain and squats down before he falls to the ground. "Train tracks? Have you followed them?"

Delta nods her head in complicity, "They lead to several caves in the sides of some really steep rocky cliffs."

"Are they accessible?"

"No." She states emphatically, "Even if you could climb them, they are all electrified, the tracks, the pylons, all of it, at all times. They are either well above the canopy or the trees have been cleared. You can't climb the pylons, it's suicide."

"What's the train used for?"

All six women turn their eyes toward him filled with fear and anger. Almost in a growl, Delta replies, her eyes impassible. "Hunting."

If her voice had not been filled with dead calm, he may have laughed. Standing back up to shake off this new reality, Remy walks several feet to a small clearing filled with mottled light. "Let me get this straight, a train comes through here, and people shoot at you?"

"Men. They're too far away to identify them, but they are all men."

21

VIOLINSONATEN NUMMER EINS

S tepping out of the **Dornbacht Sensory Sky shower** cursing, as he can
never remember which button works the temperature controls for the head
and mistakenly activates the jasmine perfumed mist instead. He rinses off the
flower scent for hopefully the last time, recalling his itinerary for the day; lunch
and then drinks with Stephanie. *Stephanie. Is she the good cop or the bad cop in Mad
Hatter?* He has never been able to distinguish that. Most people are so simple,
within minutes he can size them up, she is different. He understands her
husband Remy, they have a lot in common actually; they are both driven,
intelligent men, he thinks to himself toweling off, his favorite kind of opponent.
Admiring himself in the mirror, assessing the more than twenty years difference
between them, "That cannot be helped." he murmurs. "Besides" soothing
himself with his towel, "I have other assets."

Surveying the empty bedroom that leads off of the marble walled bath, he
throws his towel on the carpet of the very large open space dipped in neutral
colors with burgundy accents. The bed commands the room, displayed on a

platform of marble, above it hangs a Peter Beard photograph of a large elephant bull charging, the dust below the bull's feet create a cloud of ferocity. Smiling he regards the image with reverence, he is positive he can win her over. *I will ingratiate myself, with humility and sincerity,* he laughs, *sounds like one of their tea products. All of the pieces are in place.* Having dressed to kill, his phone dings from across the room. Scanning the texts, he finds the one he is looking for and her timing couldn't be more perfect, *Drinks are confirmed for this evening.* Smiling to himself, he murmurs, "Let the hunt begin".

22

STOPWATCH HEARTS

The conference center is empty except for the security guard at the main entrance and the small cleanup crew busily vacuuming the pamphlet strewn carpet, the incredible amount of wasted resources is apparent at any convention: post cards, flyers, endless business cards, stickers no one wants, cheap plastic giveaways that have no use outside the building, *Remy would be disgusted.*

He is the one of the biggest proponents for single exit bags for Marijuana products, "Instead of placing every bud of flower and every 10 mg edible, in its own child proof plastic container," I can hear his calm, definitive voice commanding the conference hall at the Native Nations event in San Diego, "Everything purchased should go home in **one** child proof bag. If **we** are a **recreational product**, why are we not being treated like alcohol? Which, according to the CDC, by the way, kills more people a year then heroine and prescription drugs **combined.** Furthermore," he continued while pulling out a small fifth of Johnny Walker, cracking the top and taking a swig, "The last time I checked my scotch bottle, I didn't see a tamper proof top." The room filled with laughter as Remy's eyes scanned the rows of attendees, looking like a fisherman that just set the hook. "Standardize our industry before the feds get a hold of it, we can implement sensible safety regulations for our own industry, no one knows it better than we do. We are already the most regulated legal recreational product on the market. Let us determine positive environmental impact choices from inception." The lecture concluded with a standing ovation. I was sitting in the back row watching him, absorbing the riveted eyes of everyone in the room.

Shaking the vision from my mind and looking back at the littered layers around me, it literally looks like a ticker tape parade had occurred. "I hope they're all using recycled paper and earth friendly inks," I say looking over at Laure.

"Yeah, right."

Opening the door to the conference room, I am paralyzed by a faint rumbling sound coming towards us from down the hallway. I cannot see it as there is a corner blocking the bathrooms, strategically placed not to draw attention to themselves. I stop, waiting silently and perfectly still. "Do you hear that?"

"What?" Laure reacts, bumping into me.

"That, that rumbling sound, it's almost like a small earthquake or", *a plane taking off!* I start running for the corner, leaving Laure at the door with the coffees, confused. The sound growing louder, I pull out my phone while I am running and turn on voice notes. The sound is now reverberating in the empty hall of the conference center, as I round the corner, trying to run quietly, to not ruin the recording. Blind, I hit with a smack, into a metal food carrier rack loaded with trays of food, managing to put one hand out, but bumping it with my head. Setting my back against the wall, I brace myself. The forty something year old caterer that was pushing the damn thing, is aghast.

"I am so sorry, are you ok?" he squeaks.

With what must seem like a sardonic smile, I ignore him, pressing stop and replay. Only until I actually hear the metal rumbling sound playback from my phone, do I look up and reply, "I'm fine."

Laure is now taking the corner, "Steph are you ok?" She offers her hand to help me up, "Your head is bleeding a little, hang on." Dashing into the nearest restroom, which happens to be the men's room, she returns with a wad of tissues. Dabbing my head and meeting my eyes with hers, I notice a look of real concern, she asks, "What were you doing?" almost on the verge of tears.

"I have a lead!" I respond with a new surge of strength coursing through my body.

"Sweetie, I'm lost." Laure looks at me as if I have completed gone out for drinks.

"Don't worry, I'll explain later." I get up and turn to the caterer, "Were you working yesterday morning between nine and eleven?" I ask attempting to catch my breath.

"Yes." His eyes nervously react to my direct tone.

"Where were you between those times?"

"Serving breakfast over there." He says, pointing to the open commissary to the left of the main hall of the conference center. "Setting up and breaking down breakfast."

"You use these racks to bring the food in and out?"

"Yes," he answers, now looking very uncomfortable.

"Show me where you load and unload the food from outside." This comes out as more of a command then I had wished, but I achieve the correct result.

"Oh.. ok." He concedes turning around to walk back down the hall he initially came from.

"Steph?"

"Laure, when I spoke with the event coordinator yesterday, she said she had heard a sound behind Remy's voice, a low rumbling sound, while he checked in with her. He was getting out or had just gotten out of his car and was walking into the building. He called her to ask which way he should come in and where to meet her to check in for his lecture."

"Holy shit, you think this rack made that sound?"

"She said it sounded like a plane taking off, or metal wheels on concrete."

"Oh, My Fucking God!"

"Exactly." Turning back to the caterer, "I'm sorry, what's your name?", I calmly ask the man, obviously weary of two seemingly crazy women.

"Penton." He stops and turns around to look at us.

"Could you bring the cart with you, I would like to try something Penton."

"I don't know lady, I'm supposed to be working."

From behind me, a voice resonates with the authority of a bull horn, "Penton you are to do whatever this woman asks." I turn around to see Jean standing behind me.

"I figured when you were late to the conference room, you must have found something on your way."

"I think so, listen to this," I say leading both women into the kitchen, with Penton following us pushing the seven foot- high, metal multi tray rack on casters rumbling down the corridor. The entire tray is covered with a heat proof bag with a large Velcro seal on the outside. I bring Jean up to speed. Once we reach the kitchen load in area, the scene around us changes completely. Bustling like an ant hill, dozens of cooks are heating and prepping food for the 1500 conference attendees, press, and panelists. Accustomed to strangers walking in and out of the kitchen, we go unnoticed. The loading dock allows for trucks to unload at kitchen floor level, which is about three and half feet higher than the street level, from the back of the trucks. My brief moment of triumph bursting before my eyes, this area is far too busy for any type of abduction.

"Is this the only place you unload?" I turn my attention to Penton, attempting to feign my disappointment.

"Yes." He replies, eager to take his leave.

I look around, there are several doors leading to the outside from the kitchen, the first has stairs, leading to it from the outside. The second is at street level without stairs, it is on the west side of the building and leads to the street. The third door on the East side of the kitchen has a ramp leading up from the sidewalk. I open the door and walk out on the ramp, I can actually see the walkway leading to the main entrance hall from this vantage point, there is a traffic light on the corner. "Bingo! Jean, call the kitchen manager please, or head caterer, whoever is in charge of the kitchen."

Jean, whips out her walkie talkie, calls a name I don't catch and within 30 seconds a very tall man is standing in front of her, he is unbearably thin, with unusually long fingers. His head is a long accentuated, rectangle, set off by painfully white skin and jet -black hair. My guestimate is late 30's?

"Stephanie, this is Richard." Jean pronounces the CH as an SH.

Richard's hands are clasped in front of his belt as if he is going to sing a song, he is definitely peculiar, but not sinister, I note.

"Hello," I state with as little notice to his appearance as I can manage, we are after all in San Francisco.

"Madame."

"Can you tell me, under what circumstances these food trays would be unloaded through either of these doors instead of the loading dock?" I ask all hopes in one basket.

"They would not." His voice pronouncing every last letter of every word precisely, like a dagger.

"All of the food comes in through the bays?"

"Yes." He pauses…. Unless… something had been forgotten in the morning delivery, perhaps?"

"Was anything missing yesterday?" I gasp.

Richard pulls out his phone and texts someone. "Let me check with the kitchen coordinator."

Once he looks up, I ask, "Where do all the carts get stored?"

"They are returned to our main kitchen, to be prepped and refilled for the next meal." He confirms as I am watching the trays being removed from the carts. Once all the large baker's trays are removed by sliding them out of the one-inch tracks they rest on, the entire seven-foot-tall by three-and-a-half-foot square metal enclosure is open, like a cage without bars on one side. My mind is reeling, I can feel perspiration on my forehead and under my eyes.

"Steph, what is the connection?" Laure interjects.

"Just let me think a minute."

Richard's phone dings like a dinner bell, he looks up and states, "Yesterday two racks of bread were brought here at eight forty- five."

"Where would the racks have been left after you unloaded the bread?" I ask tripping over every word.

"The bay doors would have been closed for safety, so over there against the wall." He declares pensively, pointing toward the door with the ramp.

I turn to Jean and Laure, "It's time to talk to the staff."

23

BLACK COFFEE

The Fairmont Hotel is already bustling at 6 am, as he leaves his suite for a cup of coffee in the cafe. The two large men in dark suits join him on the elevator.

Not a stranger to travelling, he prefers the public to a quiet room, even a room as stately as the Buckingham Suite, the original Presidential suite from the 30's, it's cigar room décor akin to his palatial estate in Nob Hill.

The waiter a man of late sixties, in white livery approaches with finesse.

"Anything for you this morning sir?"

"Yes, two poached eggs over sautéed greens with light toast, jam, and black coffee, please."

His wife had argued ceaselessly, that black coffee was common and vulgar. He laughs to himself at the thought, *who is not common and vulgar today?*

"Yes, Sir." The waiter totters off, with such regal air, as to profess he is not common, causing a droll smile while he observes the other patrons in the café. It's easy to tell who is on vacation and who is there to work. Times were changing though, the business man's uniform had changed too, he notes with disdain. Instead of a brief case, a hand- held device. Jacket and tie are substituted for an open collared long sleeve shirt. He prefers his suits, they offer a sense of pageantry, a ceremony to the dawn of the day, and the endless possibilities it contains.

That possibility today is Stephanie Beroe. It is the only reason he is in San Francisco. The chance to ally and dominate cutting edge technology with global food grade and pharmaceutical applications for the cannabis industry. A chance to steer his company into a new era and ensure its future. This is his dream and his passion, he will not fail.

The last foray with the Beroe's was a disaster. Even with Remy out of the way, how could he win Stephanie over without offending her by his previous behavior. He couldn't tell her the truth, she is smart and intuitive, she will see right through him. That would be a deal breaker, he sits back cursing his weakness. Why hadn't he reached out to smooth things over, bridge the gap he created?

Sitting back in his chair observing the rhythm of the waiters, clearing his mind. It had been a month of close quarters and board meetings. Meetings upon meetings actually, *I use to enjoy this*, he thinks to himself, placing his napkin on his lap. His concern turning again towards Stephanie. He hasn't desired something this strongly in a long time. It is his only focus of late, consuming his conscious. *Failure is not an option.*

24

MAD WORLD

The walk through the jungle, gives Remy time to calm a jumble of thoughts; *Who could have dreamed this shit up? Why would anyone kid nap all these beautiful women and then shoot them like wild animals? I could see a couple of people wanting me dead,* he admits to himself. *I 'm an asshole. I've had to be an asshole, to survive and to protect Steph. In fact, my New Year's resolution is to be a bigger asshole! But why the game? The train? The abduction? Why not just shoot me?*

At a normal pace, he looks around at *the family* as Delta called her cohorts, behind their feral eyes, he can imagine each of these women in modern life. The smallest gal, a tough looking blonde, that definitely worked out in a gym, has stopped mid stride. In silence, everyone stops. Raising a hand widdled stick she's palming that looks like a javelin, she walks four steps into the brush. Remy can barely see her, when he hears a thump and then a rustling, she returns to the group with an animal that is a cross between a raccoon and an ant eater, sporting the longish furry coated animal over her shoulder, quite dead, she returns to the group as if nothing has happened. This act of heroinism does not even draw a response from anyone in the group, they just continue as one, in the same direction. Remy is silently impressed.

There is no path, the area is heavily treed by a labyrinth of vines connecting each tree. The branches and bushes block the way every step. The only clear space opens to a ravine. The small river is clear and cool, with parched lips, Remy stops to take a drink and the whole group stops, like they heard him think. In turn, each of them refreshes themselves, their eyes continually scanning the periphery.

This is a scene out of Planet of the Apes, he thinks to himself as the terrain begins to incline, it's has been a good two hours since they started walking and nothing has been said, no verbal interaction at all. Their energy is high pitched, they are fine- tuned, tapped into a primitive world, not a sound goes un noticed.

A tall, long legged woman in her early thirties if that, walks up close to him. Remy turns his head toward her, nodding to her in acknowledgment, before realizing; *she's checking me out!*

A snort escapes unintentionally as she looks away and drops back in step with her friend as she declares, "FNG number four", to the seriously buff African American gal walking next to her with the biggest eyes and longest lashes Remy has ever seen, neither of the women look friendly.

'FN- what?

"Pitt," Delta reprimands them, "Keep it to yourself."

Continuing up a steeper incline, Remy becomes bored with his new silent team members but the fire ahead and the smell of roasting meat draws him forward, fatigue setting in and his stomach growling so loudly, one of the gals laughs. She's average height, mousy brown hair but her eyes are remarkable, almost a white gray. Smiling at her, she blushes and quickly turns her head.

Suddenly they approach a large clearing, perched about 500 feet above the jungle floor, the view of the coast is awesome, breaks rolling in to a very small crescent beach.

There is actually a left break off the point north of the camp, Remy becomes momentarily excited, before realizing where he is.

Small huts have been made in haste with branches and palm frongs, under the canopy of a huge tree, its trunk is truly incredible in size with thorns covering the bark, it looks more like the leg of a gargantuan animal than a tree trunk. A small fire burns in the middle of the clearing and he sees a barbeque has been made with rocks, it's three- sided rock walls hold up a larger rock lintel that the fire sits under, meat is resting over lava rocks above the fire, searing itself to the rock, with a hiss. The aroma is antagonizing, he can barely stop himself from grabbing a piece.

Everyone is sitting silently in a circle, Remy does the same, ignoring his stomach. Delta gives him a nod and then looks toward the last hut, obscured by the shadow of the sun, while she picks up a stick from the ground and settles on a large tree trunk. The light is incredibly bright reflecting off the sea. Remy curses under his breath, whomever left him here that didn't leave his sunglasses.

Just as he is about to suggest someone turn the meat over, a figure emerges from the hut. This guy is a little taller than Remy, lean with a mass of brown hair that suggests he may be crazy, then upon seeing the man's eyes Remy realizes, *he IS crazy*.

Delta breaks the silence, her voice like a herald, "This is Packard."

None of the women move, they are frozen. Packard limps toward the center of the group, a makeshift bandage of torn cloth and leaves over his left shoulder, his psychotic eyes on Remy. "Who is this?"

"We found him in the flats," Delta responds perfunctorily.

Remy looks at her with regard to her statement. Her eyes darting to him with a silent message to be quiet.

"Hey man, who are you?" Remy is tired of games.

"I am the leader of this family and you will learn to respect me."

"That sounds ominous."

Three other men have now joined the circle. Two, look tough and dumb, the third is a boy, of eighteen fear in his eyes, a teeny bopper, fidgeting constantly.

Remy knows he can take Packard, but he would have a hard time fending off the Marx brothers **and** the women, although his instincts are telling him the women are not a hundred percent behind Packard. *It's time to play nice.* "So, what's next?" Mustering as much humility as he can. *Steph would be proud, "Temper sweetie."* he can hear her voice in the back of his head, his Nemertes.

"Feed him, then we have some questions to ask!" Packard barks but obviously weak. All of the women quickly disperse, some begin to eat, long legs and her unfriendly side kick attend Packard, sitting him down and checking his wounds, he is visibly weak. Delta takes a large portion of meat over to Packard and the other men, once they have been served, she walks over to Remy with a couple of strips.

Afraid to ask what kind of meat, he doesn't want to know, he's starving, he could eat teeny bopper at this point.

Delta looks down at him and smiles, there is a message there, holding each other's gaze for a moment, lingering before she turns to sit back down by the fire to eat.

While hacking through lunch with his incisors, Remy takes time to study the scene around him. Blondie, the small blonde, is now cleaning her kill, it looked like a meal when it had its fur, but it's about the size of a house cat now and she doesn't seem to be enjoying herself.

The only conversation, is the small group of attendees around Packard, all obvious sycophants. It becomes clear to Remy that *the family* is in two factions, Pro Packard and No Packard. Delta and the other five women, as well as baby face teeny bopper, are all hangin' together. Packard, legs (the gal that checked him out whom he over hears as being called Pitt), the buff black chic they are calling Freeman and the Marx Brothers (the two big dumb guys) are all very comfortable together. *What a fucking nightmare!*

While Pitt and Freeman re-bandage Packard's shoulder, Remy clearly sees the bullet wound and loses his appetite.

Now that he has stopped moving, with his ass firmly planted on the rocky ground and fed, he notices the sweat pouring off him like a pig. Still, in the jeans and the long sleeve button up, Steph had picked out for him yesterday morning. *I've been gone a whole day, she must be freaking out!* He thinks to himself taking his shirt off and mopping his head with it. Rolling it up he sets it to one side. Luckily, he has his high tops on with light socks, he takes them off, in the hopes they'll dry next to the fire. His feet are pruned, *I've got to come up with a plan! Whatever game is going on here between the factions of men and women, is not hospitable.* He is the only male that is a challenge to Packard, and he has no intentions of getting stuck in some kind of alpha male war. *I just want to take a look around, scout out the cave the train goes into, and figure out a way out of here!* For the time being, he decides to play along with whatever fantasy is going on, maybe he can learn more about The Other family and the train.

Packard stands up and walks over to him with obvious strain, Mo and Larry directly behind him, Pitt and Freeman sit down, one on each side of him. Delta watches everything.

"Where are you from?" Packard starts off, brusquely, with a tone of sarcasm in his voice, his bearded face gives him the look of primitive man.

"California," Remy replies, thinking how odd it is he didn't ask his name.

"Aha." Non plussed, Packard drones on, "What's the last thing you remember?"

"I was walking into a building in San Francisco, I had just put my phone away and as I went to grab for the door…. nothing."

"Nothing? No sounds, voices, shadows?"

Packard is mansplaining now so Remy stands up. He remembers a lot of strange sounds, and a shadow against the wall of the building, but because he just doesn't like this guy, he takes the fifth. "Nothing," Remy repeats eyes steady, attempting to ease his body's tension.

Packard nods, looking over at the gals now standing next to Remy. "How do we know The Other family didn't send you over?"

"You don't."

Packard steps toward him, his nose is so close, Remy can see the clogged pores at the end of it, "What's to keep me from killing you, right now?"

"Besides bad manners? I would say, you need all the help you can get. This little rag tag group you have here, doesn't account for much. But your welcome to take your best shot." Remy takes a step closer as he speaks, removing all the space between them, in his grill.

Packard blinks. Remy can clearly see the sweat gathered at the sides of his weakened, feverish eyes.

"You realize if we don't take you in," Packard states attempting to regain face, "you'll be dead before the sun rises?" An amused smile spreads across his warped face while his posse laughs, but Packard backs up one step. Remy notices, so do the women, with an unbroken stare, he closes the gap, "I wouldn't be too sure of that."

25

DISSOLVED GIRL

Why am I questioning this list of tasks I *was handed two months ago?* "Am I suffering a moral dilemma?" A wince appears on his face as he mumbles the words aloud in his lavishly appointed hotel suite.

He is a bright man, ambitious to a fault, well-bred, affluently educated. Remembering the words of his mentor he questions the times, and purpose of it all, *"Real finance, has no place for conscience, true moguls tread the gray lines."* When asked by that same idol to do several questionable things, in secrecy, of course, he never hesitated. It was all business, he had witnessed situations like this before, surely. *So why the hesitation now?*

The answer traverses the universe before landing in his lap… *I KNOW these people. Even worse, I like them.* With that revelation, the large suite he is expensing becomes small and inescapable, as a wave of guilt courses his nervous system. Suddenly he feels small and inconsequential, perhaps even used, sitting on the bed, a bath sheet wrapped around his waist. Propelling himself into the bathroom he looks into the wall sized mirror in the marbled cavern, he has come to a crossroads. *Do I continue down this path that has been laid out before me for the taking? Or do all of my dreams come to an end because I can't control my conscience?* Turning away from the mirror to read a text confirming drinks with Stephanie Beroe, he opens the closet door to an array of custom-tailored suits. "It's all about choice."

26

JIGSAW FALLING INTO PIECES

On the way back through the now bustling corridors of the convention hall to interview the staff, I text Grace. Any word on the Uber car? Please go online and download Remy's phone calls from yesterday, text the list over to me, please?

Jean is ahead of us, her heals beating out a rhythm on the floor. I turn toward Laure, "I know how he was taken." I whisper to my oldest friend. "We just don't know who, why or where he is."

"Do we really know?" She asks me with a layer of incredulism, I am not prepared for. I stop on a dime.

"Yes, I do!" I say with as much conviction as I can muster. "Jean?" Jean pivots around instantly. "When is Ms. Holland expected?" I ask not able to look at Laure for the moment.

"She will be here at eight, we have a fifteen- minute staff meeting before the day begins." She says with great empathy.

"Ok, listen ladies, I know this may seem a bit off, but my instincts are telling me that the pieces of this puzzle are falling together."

Silently they stare back at me. Jean finally breaks in, "Do you think this is Industry oriented?" Standing there like a doll, perfectly coiffed, her pretty face set in a grim expression, she is holding her phone in one hand and a walkie talky in the other. Laure, shifts uneasily from one foot to the next in her own rhythm, waiting for my reply.

"Yes, I do. The next step is finding out who." I say with determination I didn't know I possessed. Grabbing another bagel, I drink all of my hot chocolate in one never ending gulp. It's not safe for me to drink coffee, "*You mean it's not safe for the world, for you to drink coffee, Sweetie.*" I can hear Remy poking me. "*We don't have to worry about you drinking the profits.*" Looking at me with those amused eyes, as if I could possibly continue to be amusing after 15 years together. *Hold on Sweetie.*

There's a dozen or so people staring at me in the conference room, I look over to Jean, madly texting. She answers without my asking, "They're all not here yet. Early birds." She walks out, texting as she maneuvers the conference doors and leaves Laure and I standing in front of eager eyes.

"Let's break up and talk to each of them, one at a time. Can you record each interview on your phone?" I ask Laure.

"Sure," Laure responds moving to the first person in the front row.

By the time I am finished with my first victim, a Hispanic woman in her late fifties that spent the entire previous day tending the ladies room and maintaining the entrance hall, who emphatically tells me she did not hear or see anything suspicious, I see Laddington walk in. He gives me a nod, I look down at my phone, it's now seven forty-five, *mental note taken.* Walking over to him I ask, "Can you interview these last five?"

"Sure." He says taking off his jacket and brushing it off with a preoccupation for lint that is almost compulsive. I look over at Laure, who hasn't missed a beat. "Please record the interviews, so I can listen to them later. Here, show me your phone, I'll turn on your voice notes." He hands me his phone and unlocks it, it is in his email app, and I notice before I swipe the screen to open notes, that he has several emails from Grace. *Good, she is on him, we may need to double team.*

I just finished interviewing the other four staff members to no avail, when seven more people walk in. Mostly security guards, two of them look like they work at the registration desk. *Very good, maybe some of the security guards can be enlisted.* I approach a woman in her forties, she is African American, average height, which is about 3 inches shorter than I am. She has an ingratiating smile, dressed in a dark blue uniform, with a large utility belt, but no gun.

"Hi, I'm Stephanie Beroe, do you mind if I ask you a couple of questions about yesterday?" I lead her over to a chair and sit down next to her. I notice her brass plated name tag that reads, Michelle Giverrs.

"Not at all Sweetie, what's going on?" She asks while placing her walkie talkie on the table.

"I believe my husband was taken yesterday, while he was approaching the building from the west side kitchen entrance. He has completely disappeared." No beating around the bush, I figure she's a security guard, she can handle it.

Obviously taken aback, Michelle looks at me with surprise, "Are you kidding me, nothing like that has ever happened here! You poor little thing. Have you checked the tapes?"

"Tapes?"

"Yeah, the security tapes."

I look at her in utter amazement. *Why didn't I think of that? Why didn't laddington think of that? This is what he is supposed to be good at!"* I turn to look at him, like Laure he has stopped mid- sentence and waiting for my reaction. "Jesus!" I explode. "Where is the security room?"

"I'll take you honey, just come with me."

Michelle gets up and adjusts her belt, this is a woman that takes pride in her work, unlike my questionable detective. *Mental note taken.* I turn to Laure on my way out, "Just keep questioning everyone as they come in. Text me anything that seems important."

"Ok." She says nodding her head, looking a little frightened.

Michelle takes me through a staff door, off the main lobby. There is a small stair way, it's well lit, now I notice the cameras.

"You should have come to us right away. This is what we do, honey."

She is absolutely right. I suppose, I just assumed that the security guards were for show, a public stand to impose order, like an empty police car placed on the side of the road at rush hour.

"Were you here yesterday, Michelle?"

"I sure was." There is a hint of Texas or Florida in her response.

"Do you have posts, or do you all just walk around?"

Cocking her head to one side, she says, "We have routes and specific areas to patrol."

"Makes sense," I confirm as we reach the top of the stairs. At level two, she opens the stairwell door and we head down a small ambulatory without windows. The second door on the left says "Security" in big black letters on a white sign. I follow Michelle into the room, not much bigger than my kitchen. A man of about sixty is sitting in front of a desk with a flat screen t.v., the screen is split into twenty split screens, all about 6"x6". *This is no Fort Knox.* The security room doubles as a break room, there is a large table strewn with to-go coffee cups, newspapers and random personal items. A pod of small lockers, as well as a sink and mirror, are on the wall to the left of the t.v. monitors.

"Hey, Martin." Michelle addresses her co- worker with great familiarity. "This lady would like to see the tapes from yesterday."

"No one sees the tapes without approval from the main office." The baseball capped white man drones while tapping his pen, on the desk his feet are resting upon.

"Come on Martin, something big time went down yesterday. You want to be responsible for obstruction?" Michelle works him playfully.

"Michelle, what are you talking about?" Martin responds, obviously annoyed, but concerned he may have bundled a job.

"Hi, my name is Stephanie Beroe, Martin." I intercede "I believe my husband was taken while approaching the building yesterday." I say with torturous calm but have his full attention as I work my way over to his desk slowly. "I need to see the tapes from yesterday between 8 am and 11 am."

"Holy shit, really?" Martin's body is now rigid, with concern. "Ok, let me make a call, and we'll get you what you need. Ma'am."

I can barely control myself and feel my hands shaking, as I notice the split screens are divided into ten interior angles, 8 exterior angles, and 2 angles of the roof, while Martin is looking on a clip board for a number to call, I ask, "Are these the only angles the camera's cover?"

"Yes, Ma'am."

The front of the building has very little activity as the conference doesn't start for another hour and twenty minutes. The cameras on the sides of the building are just recording traffic, as no one walks in California. I can see both side kitchen doors, on two different cameras. The back of the building has two camera angles pointing in that cover the corners of the building toward the loading bay entrance and rear parking area. *Those are the angles I want to see.*

Martin hangs up his phone, "There's no answer." He says, looking at me in despair.

"By eleven o'clock, the police will be here." I state matter of fact, "I am trying to gather as much information as I can to give them." I pause looking down at my hands, "My husband is missing, Martin. Do you understand that?"

"Shit! Hang on." He grunts, sitting back down in his swivel chair before taking up the key board with one finger typing. "What time did you want to see again?"

27

ROAD, RIVER, RAIL

The private jet was waiting on the tarmac for us at 10 am, we were picked up by a private car earlier and driven out to the runway. We were running a little late, I had a difficult time deciding what to pack, so I packed everything. It had been a while since Remy and I had been on a trip that was not work related, of course, this was also work related, but it was the Cayman Islands and the trip was free, palm trees and rum punch awaited us, I was giddy.

Remy was not as effervescent; his stoic demeanor reflected the conflict within. Cayman Islands – tax shelters – corporate transparency or lack of, having been the top three topics of conversation for the last week. I, of course, got it. The question, "How much money does a corporation need to make while strangling the workers and community it feeds from?" had passed my lips too many times to count. I was purposely choosing the rosie colored glasses for this trip, if only for a well- deserved diversion.

The month and a half prior to this trip, I had spent my time redesigning our Oregon packaging for the brand-new recreational regulations, that had of course been decided at an emergency meeting. Giving all manufacturers 30 days to comply, 30 days! "If state regulators told the twenty- five coal plants in the United States that are responsible for one third of the toxic mercury emissions, while only supplying eight percent of our nation's electricity, that they needed to upgrade their plant efficiency ratings to prevent the second- hand poisoning of the local population, water and lands as well as being the major contributors to global warming. Oh, and it had to be done in 30 days? What do you think the response would be?" I had asked this to a convention floor, just shortly after the regs were placed into effect. "Exactly," I continued to their silent response, "We are not the coal industry, we are helping people have better quality lives without the risks of big pharma side effects. On average three children, a year under the age of six have been hospitalized for taking marijuana since 2009. None of these cases were fatal or caused permanent health issues. Are you aware that over 17,000 children were hospitalized for eating laundry pods in one year? Seven percent of those were fatal? The manufacturers have a warning symbol on the box, but they are not mandated to place them in child proof boxes, despite the fact they are a common household item that children are exposed to, and they look like a candy?" The diatribe went on for several more minutes before we all reached the conclusion that Marijuana was still being treated like a taboo, and we had to seriously lobby if things were going to change. Yada yada yada, it's the same old conclusion.

As Remy and I walked up the stairs to the Boeing jet door, waiting on the tarmac, I was ready for a vacation, I could feel the weight of the constant fight lifting from my shoulders. I was not, however, ready for the overwhelming luxury that enveloped us. The aroma and quantity of stephanotis used in the dozens of bouquets dotting the impeccably furnished main lounge was astonishing. Dark rare hard wood for wainscoting mixed with fine soft leather in neutral tones and perhaps the highest quality carpet I had ever witnessed rendered this custom aircraft, who's worth I could only guestimate.

I recall suddenly becoming aware and concerned that I was perhaps not dressed as stylishly as protocol demanded. The inflight stewardess was considerably more coiffed than I was.

I had only to look over at my ever- casual spouse to come to my senses. Remy gave me a wink in his converse high tops and vintage bright yellow and white hibiscus flowered linen pants, with a purple t shirt from weedmaps, exclaiming; *Excuse me while I kiss the sky,* written across the front, gave me no cause to dread, so I held my head high.

We both ordered mojitos, for our preflight cocktail. The aircraft was truly a scene from a Jason Bourne film. I felt as if I were in the CIA flying to some exotic scene of intrigue. *Little did I know.*

Heather our in- flight attendant, tended to our every need as if she had been with us for years, busying herself with lavish finger food. We preferred music to the 80- inch flat screen television spewing bad news about shameless presidential candidates. We were the only passengers on the flight as she closed the door. Remy waited for Heather to slip into the galley with takeoff preparations before he spoke. "What do you think of all this?"

Wondering why he was lowering his voice I replied, "I'm impressed." Although I was thinking, for the amount of money spent on this aircraft, a lot of lives down on earth could be changed for the better.

Nodding his head, he distractedly commented, "I suppose it would be easy to get used to, it just doesn't feel…natural." Remy countered, swiveling in his chair like a child at an ice cream counter.

"Let's just try to enjoy ourselves."

"Let's just hope it's not a bunch of assholes comparing golf clubs."

Shaking my head yes, but knowing, that was exactly what this was going to be, I resigned myself. We had been there before, the freaks in the room. The only non- ivy league personnel other than the help. No pin stripped button-down collars, or polo shirts or designer hand bags, for us. No stratus network of friends or family to amortize, we were working class.

Back in the days of our music and art careers, we had been entertained by many members of the elite wealth. We were the color added to the dining table, the dinner show, sort to speak. Wild, young, handsome and without barriers. We would discuss anything and in Remy's case, without any fear of insulting someone while voicing a strong informed opinion. I was more of a listener back then. *I think my husband would agree that has changed now.*

Trying not to allow my disappointment to show, I settled back in my leather lounger, grasping Remy's hand like a tether to a world that was slowly becoming obscured.

"Are you ready mam?" Michael the security guard repeats sitting next to me at his control panel waking me from my reverie.

"What, oh yes. Absolutely." I respond, bitterly forcing Remy's impression from my mind, "Play it."

The tape is time coded at the bottom. The time reads 08.00.00 every single camera angle is playing simultaneously from that start point. At eight am, not much is happening, although it is the first day of the event. As usual, all of the installation and prep was completed the night before. There are three caterer trucks in the loading docks and as Richard had detailed the food from the trucks was being unloaded, wheeled off the trucks in the large towering castored racks with insulated jackets. The trucks are backed up with their payload facing the loading dock.

The kitchen staff could be estimated at around twenty personnel. I note there are four security guards visible, two near the front doors that were being unlocked and two others walking around through the main hall. "How many guards are on duty?" I ask looking at Michelle briefly.

"During the event, there are seven of us. Two at the entrance, two at the hall entrance checking badges and two walking the floor of the hall and Martin." She responds with an air of efficiency. I nod continuing to watch the sped- up version of life as seen from above.

By eight- thirty several vendors at the show are straggling in, taking out their badges stowing their gear behind their tables and heading for the breakfast bar. Traffic on the street is pretty consistent, bicycles, cars, and trucks stopping at the two traffic lights on each corner of the building. By eight forty-five the front door is mobbed, the registration desk is backed up, all booths are manned by their hawkers. My concentration is on the loading dock.

Richard had said the bread was delivered at nine. The time code now reads 09.00.00, but no new trucks, I am starting to sweat and fidget. Everyone in the office with me has their eyes glued to the screens. The main hall floor is now packed, it's difficult to see the carpet through the bodies. The entire center is a bustle. Finally, at nine- thirty a truck pulls up to the loading dock, unlike the previous trucks he parks with the engine facing the kitchen, as the bay loading doors are closed, not taking my eyes off the screen, I wait. The driver gets out and walks to the back of the truck while a caterer, a small man in white kitchen grubs also walks to the kitchen door at the ramp entrance before disappearing behind the catering truck. They both emerge after a moment with a covered castored rack each and wheel them into the kitchen, through the side door with the ramp. The driver returns to the truck and leaves, as the caterers grabs hold of the castored racks, and begins opening the heat bag coverings by pulling on the Velcro attachment at the top. He proceeds to pull out each tray in turn and hands them to anxious staff members that then walk out of my line of vision, into the dissonance of activity in the kitchen. Three minutes later both of the racks are emptied of their trays and stand open like empty boxes, their contents having been carried out to replenish the ranks at the buffet table. The breakfast bar is open until ten, Joan had told me. The empty racks are then wheeled over to the wall next to the kitchen ramp exit door, their heat proof jackets open without trays in them. They look like a Houdini device.

I readjust my chair without allowing my eyes to leave the screen as two very large caterers, definitely men, football player sized men with their backs to the camera move the second rack outside through the exit door. They do not return.

"Who is that?" I screech. "Who are those guys?"

"I have no idea. They use different caterers all the time here." Michelle responds.

Scanning all of the cameras for a glimpse of the men, the time code is ticking like a countdown to my own personal doom, 09.35.16 no changes. "Why can't we see them outside?"

"The cameras are angled to see approaching fields, people leaving or coming if you are up against the building you are out of vision, it's where everyone goes to have their cigarette break," Martin adds with defeat in his voice.

09.38.52 a light- colored hybrid pulls up to the curb near the corner to the traffic light and stops.

"Stop the tape!" I blurt out, "Play it real time. Please." For one whole minute, nothing happens. Then the rear passenger door opens and Remy emerges. My heart feints, tears well in my eyes, blurring my only vision of my husband for over 24 hours. Removing my hands that are bracing the desk, I wipe my eyes quickly making a note of the time code. Remy is talking on his phone as he gets out of the car and starts walking towards the kitchen door with the ramp. Backpack in his left hand, holding his phone with his right, his walk is unmistakable, casual, confident and focused. He is still on the phone as he approaches the building, I am assuming he is talking with Ms. Holland and will check her phone to be sure. My throat is constricted with tension as I watch, I want to yell at the screen, touch it. The path my husband is on, will cross over the view point shared by the two cameras as he rounds the corner of the building from the walkway. As he disappears from view of camera angle six, I turn my focus to camera seven. Nothing. I wait.

"Where did he go?" I ask no one in particular, searching all the cameras, panic now taking over. "Where did he go?"

28

EDGE HILL

After a less than friendly exchange, Freeman and her pal escort their leader back to his hut. All is not well and it's obvious. The two stooges go back to eating, as Remy turns toward Delta, she nods directing him to an area where clothes are laid out in the sun for drying or whatever. Picking up his sneaks and socks he joins her. She throws him another piece of meat, "You are going to need this, eat as much as you can at camp. Look around there is fruit everywhere." Taking a moment to do just that, he hadn't stopped to notice before, but she was right, they are in the middle of a mango grove, mixed with some kind of almonds, bananas, and guava that are plenty.

We could be in Costa Rica, how ironic is that? Birds are everywhere and making a lot of noise. Between the birds and the sound of the sea, even from this distance, there is no silence. *No wonder they are all crazy.*

As Remy gnaws into the mystery meat, Delta flashes him a brilliant smile, "You've got everything it takes, it's just a matter of time and he knows it."

Not going for the bait, Remy changes the subject, "You don't like him very much, do you?"

A smirk is her reply.

"By my count, you out- number the men, what gives?"

"We are so divided, constantly fighting with each other over men and food," She spits out with a look of great distaste while readjusting the jungle vines used to hang the… laundry, if torn rags and remnants of clothes can be called that. Her large golden eyes imploring, as he shakes his head.

"I don't want any part of this. I don't know how I got here, or why, but I am going to get the hell out of here, if I have to tear that god damn train down to do it." Remy claims while standing up.

Delta reaches out and stops him with her hand, "Be careful. If you don't play by their rules, they'll make you pay and they enjoy being brutal."

"You mean Mo and Larry?"

Delta cracks up, a burst of laughter escaping her lips before she can control herself, and it's obvious, she hasn't laughed in a while. "That's great, but yes." Gaining her composure, back to warrior drone.

"You up for scouting?"

"Anything is better than hangin' around here." She replies throwing a large mango skin into the fire.

"Let me get my sneaks on, I don't trust any of these guys."

Without too much notice they leave the camp, neither of them speaking until they are sure they are not being followed and are well out of car shot of the camp.

Leading off, Remy goes for the back story, "Alright so tell me what's really going on here."

"What you see, is what you get. It's like the Island of Misfit Toys. We were all thrown together by some crazy sleight of hand. Torn from our families and lives, stripped down too little more than primitive men and women, look at us! In the time I have been here, I have witnessed unimaginable things, I can't even speak of." Her body language is closed and pressed as she continues fervently, "I myself have killed and now that I have broken the taboo, there's no going back."

Noticing she has not looked up once while talking, her voice full of emotion, Remy says nothing as they continue the steep descent to the flat lands of canopied trees below. Growing up with sisters has ingrained listening skills into his genetics, he is thankful to know when to stay quiet.

Following a creek, iguanas are everywhere, he is on high alert for snakes as the under- brush is about as high as his calf, Remy attempts cool and nonchalant.

"Do you think we were all picked up randomly?" He asks changing the subject to something more constructive.

"I don't know. Packard doesn't allow any of us to talk about our previous lives. He says it's detrimental to our morale. That's why he changed our names, named us after where we lived.

"Delta?"

"Pennsylvania."

"What do you think?" Remy replies, feeling her out, knowing exactly what she thinks, but awaiting the confirmation.

"I think it's a bunch of bullshit, just one more way for him to control us, by not finding common ground. I am so tired of being manipulated." Her eyes are glowing with anger and fear.

Not having any answers for this woman Remy doesn't intend to be the target for her anxiety, so he keeps to his objective. "Where's the lowest elevation of the tram?"

Startled she looks over before answering, as if she's measuring him up, "It's about a half a mile from here." while cutting at a wall of vines with a flat edged piece of wood like a crazed Celt on a battle field.

Packard's belligerent leadership coming to mind, Remy ventures, "Do you think he will survive that bullet wound?" while noticing the temperature is rising at a considerable rate as the day moves on.

"I hope not." She answers out of breath. "But it's going to get messy, you can see the power struggles. Freeman has had her eyes on the power prize ever since Packard dragged himself back to the camp wounded and vulnerable for the first time. He is merciless, you can't imagine the things he has done." Her golden eyes level with his, the inference of determination behind them is unmistakable, yet there is a hint of amusement in her voice.

Mental note, don't piss off Delta.

When they have finally levelled out into a small clearing, the jungle that surrounds them in a hollow so thick he can only see about two feet beyond the perimeter in front of him and its broad daylight. The jungle is amazing, wild, dangerous and alluring all at once. The amount of life force exuded from every plant, twig, flower, and creature in his vision is overwhelming, *I must still be high.*

It's like a form of magic humans have forgotten how to tap into, even if I weren't high this would be amazing.

Delta is unaffected by all of it and swats at the jungle like a fly annoying her at a picnic. "We don't have far to go."

"Where were you before you came here?"

"I was in New York City, just living my life, running errands for my boss and whammo!" Her vocal crescendo matching the thrust of her swing.

"You notice any links between the people here, similarities, connections?"

"No, I just have bits and pieces from the few that trust me.

Without another word and without his noticing, they are now standing in front of a twenty-five-foot-tall pylon of cement. There are no trees near it, just small full brush and tall grass.

Remy sizes up the pylon, "Looks like they ran electric wiring right into the cement, layering it with metal. It's a monorail, the kind you take at an airport between terminals, but …different. The guys with the dogs, are they the same ones that shoot at you?"

"Hard to say, they're pretty far away, and I'm usually moving in the opposite direction."

"Yeah, I get it. Has anyone staked out the train? Checked out how many are on board, schedule…?"

"No." She answers shaking her head. "It's random, there's no discernable pattern. It can come three times in a day and not come at all. It can go backwards too." Delta answers, her big eyes looking up at him.

Definitely lost puppy. "I guess you guys are so busy with your social lives, you're too busy to sit and watch a train for a day or two." The smile on his face parries her response. "I am going to need food and water, a couple of days-worth." She nods silently understanding his intentions and splits.

Looking up to the rocky cliff face that opposes the tracks above, splattered with vines and some type of thorny saplings, he can see the vantage point he's looking for and starts climbing. The rock face is pretty damn steep from the bottom. If he hadn't had his high tops on, he wouldn't have even attempted it. There's some type of small spring coming off the rocks, making them green with moss and super slippery.

Glad he sent Delta back to get some supplies, he takes a moment to get his thoughts together, consider options and plan. *How could none of them have scouted out this train? I have been here for a day and it's all I can think about!*

Once past the slippery rock, the climb is not as hard as expected. The thorny shrub brush is a pain in the ass though, tearing his favorite pants that Steph bought him and getting stuck in his hair. Now, just a little higher than the tree tops from the ground below, he needs something to hang onto, the rock face is incredibly vertical. He looks for a crevice or a ledge, something he can hold up in for a couple of days. There are bright green tree snakes everywhere. Luckily, they don't bother him and he doesn't bother them, making a point not to look them in the eye.

About even with the monorail now, he is looking for a ledge or overhang, the rock is a little loose under his feat, as he struggles to move in an upward direction. Using the base of the small thorny tree trunks as grab holds, they're now cutting the shit out of his hands. Wedging his ass on the slope side of a larger tree trunk he rips off the pockets of his pants, wraps them around his hands to staunch the bleeding and give them a cushion from the thorns. The jungle is so dense, he really can't see much on the ground now but has a good view of the monorail. *If I could get just four feet higher, I would have a bird's eye view of the rail.* Un wedging his ass continuing to move, the brush thins and he can see a small rocky ledge. It has a bunch of brown bedding on the bottom, as he moves closer, he realizes it must have been some birds nest. Flipping the nest over, and sitting down, it's nice to have something soft to sit on.

He's going to have to sleep in fetal position, but at least there are no snakes nearby. Catching his breath and calming the adrenaline from the climb, he can make the ledge work, but the bright yellow and white flower pants may be problem.

Dropping back down the cliff side Remy starts breaking off small thorny branches with leaves until there is enough to weave a makeshift blind. Good thing Steph's brother always has the hunting channel on when we are visiting, or he would be screwed. He ties the branches in a bundle with a small thin sapling branch and slings them over his shoulder before climbing back up. That's when he hears a funny noise, so do all the animals. It's a faint high pitch, constant tone. The only thing that makes it noticeable is the consistency of it. The monkeys start calling out first, like an audience at a Bruce Springsteen concert, low and droning, all consuming. Sitting tight, using his hands to hold himself up, leveraging both feet in the dirt and resting his ass on the incline, the bundle on his back acts like a pillow. Level with the rail, the cliff is about fifteen feet from him. Eyes staring down the track, he can see about twenty meters, before it turns away into a tunnel carved out of another steep rock face. Sweat, stinging his back as it drips down into the waist of his pants, mopping his forehead with the blood- soaked pocket on his right hand. He is glad Stephanie is not here, closing his eyes for a second, he can see her face, her smile, her laugh, her peace of mind, when a new smell forces his eyes open, metallic, man- made.

Coming right at him from around the corner, is the train.

29

SEE YOU ON THE OTHER SIDE

The doors of the conference opened at 9 to the public, all the vendors have already taken their posts. Carpets are cleaned of all the debris and the trash cans have been emptied and are now ready to be refilled with more vendor swag. I walk back to the break out room, through the main hall detouring to the bathroom first. I don't have to go, I just want a moment alone. I pick the same stall I chose yesterday, a little habit of mine. No matter where I am if I've been in the bathroom before, I always choose the same stall as the previous time, even if it's been years. *What the hell is the name for that psychosis?*

Most public toilets don't have lids now a-days, so I just sit down. I take a big long breath and attempt pushing it through the tips of my fingers, toes, and head…the tears just start running silently down my face, uncontrollably. The last image of Remy from the security tape, replaying over and over in my mind; He is walking around the corner of the building as if nothing were wrong.

I know what I need to do next, check Ms. Holland's phone for time comparisons, find the lyft or Uber driver, question all the kitchen staff, but I can't move! Seeing Remy walk around a corner and disappear is just too much!

I've blanked out! Numb and empty headed, I sit there for a moment, my head resting on the cold metal stall wall, vision blurred and the taste of salty tears on my lips.

I see Remy coming out of the aqua marine colored water, tanned and wet. He's caught me surveying his inventory and responds with the smallest of grins.

"How is it?" I asked.

"It sucks!"

"Yeah right."

He plopped down with rigor onto the lounge chair next to me, little droplets of water spraying my face, relieving the sequestered heat of the island sun, temporarily.

"No really, it sucks! There is NO surf here!"

I looked at him severely over my people magazine. "It's the Caribbean."

"The brochure said there was surf."

I manage to smack him with my magazine before he pulled me over and gave me a kiss, wet and salty, just the way I like them.

It was late in the day, having arrived late with the time change, flying east. We unpacked enough to grab our suits and hit the beach, before we were expected to meet up with H.S and his assistant for drinks, prior to dinner with the executives of DBS. They had invited us to their yearly executives' meeting, a fancy name for a bonus vacation, but I was not complaining.

The sun had diminished to a golden glow, of course, we were on the east side of the island so the sunset was over land, a bit unnerving for west coasters. We regarded its deficiency as a minor detail to the exquisite scenery. The view of the horizon in front of us was mired by a goliath ship, I could not take my eyes off. I had never seen a boat that big before so close. "That boat is ridiculous."

"It's a ship, yeah it's crazy. I read about it, it belongs to H.S. You'll like the name, Jove's Gift."

From the shore, I could see the ship had five jet skis, a banana boat and something that looked like a bouncy house roped to a deck at water level on the back with no less than four patio tables and eight lounge chairs set up. A large glass door that opened onto the deck, could accommodate a mac truck. Even more incredible, on the left side of the boat was an opening in the boat itself, a crew of six men in what seemed like a small thirty- foot boat, were coordinating the exhumation of a ship twice its size from Jove's Gift's belly, via hydraulic ramp. To top it off a helicopter pad, crowned the top of five tiers of decks. It's was a personal cruise ship. "How big do you think that boat is?" I asked Remy shaking my head.

"It's a ship. Four hundred feet long, it has a disco bigger than our house and one of the swimming pools has a glass bottom as a ceiling to one of the formal dining halls. Oh, and a theatre, and indoor shooting range."

"Seriously?"

"Seriously sweetie, that is what we are dealing with. This kind of wealth, it's over the top."

"Yeah," I replied having found a taste in my mouth I didn't quite care for.

The Caribbean Club, an incredibly exclusive beach resort on Grand Cayman, was quite a surprise. Our stand- alone ocean suite, that looked out to the bay, was twice the size of our town house and all on one floor. Looking back to the balconies from our lounge chairs, the hotel had maybe forty rooms, all of which were booked for this event, the manager informed us upon check in. Designed in a series of three floored balcony buildings, each floor contained a three thousand square foot suite, that sat majestically on the white sand beach.

"This place looks familiar to me." I kept saying to Remy.

"Really? You were here with your other boyfriend?"

"Yeah, I can't quite put my finger on it." I remember replying distracted and then laughed, as Remy stood up and threatened me with his wound- up towel prompting me from my utter and total relaxed state, "Come on we better get a move on." He snapped his towel at my legs like a school boy.

"Hey." I swatted at him playfully as we walked back to the room, bumping each other.

Our porch was right on the beach, it had the most, lovely x shaped woodworking for railings. "I know! This is the villa they used for that James Bond film."

"What bond film?"

"The one with Daniel Craig, where the girl rides the horse down the beach and he comes out of the water like a Chippendale dancer."

"Holy shit, you're right, that's cool."

"Imagine Daniel Craig on the floor of our suite, frolicking with some young hot Venezuelan."

"I've got a better idea." Glean in his eye, Remy closed the patio door and whipped me with the towel into the bedroom.

By six-thirty we were dressing, Remy had chosen a tan linen short sleeve button up shirt, with a vintage print of a hula girl, placing a flower in her hair on the back. The image is in black and white tones that match his black draw string linen pants. He carried the air of yogi, peaceful, comfortable calm. I noted his hair was spectacular. Honestly, it didn't seem fair that he could just hop out of the water and shake his mane out into the perfect do. In that humidity, my hair was a perfect example of mop head, regardless of the deluge of argon oil I had slathered on endlessly. I slipped on a silk crepe backless halter dress with green, blue and black abstract watercolor flowers. I don't often wear heels but managed to squeeze into a black strappy pair. The dress was low cut in the front, and backless, a bra was not an option. I wore the simple pear- shaped abalone pendant on a black silk cord that Remy had given me for our anniversary. Checking myself in the mirror, Remy directly behind me, he purred, "You look ravishing."

"I Look ravished."

He laughed, "Are you ready?"

I nodded as he took my hand and led me out the door.

H.S. was waiting for us at the bar with his young assistant Tyler. They were both in pleated tan linen shorts and polo shirts. Tyler's was an odd shade of emerald green. They both stood when we arrived, to greet us.

"Stephanie, Remy, nice to see you both. Thank you for coming." H.S. led off, "I hope your flight was enjoyable?" He inquired, taking my hand as if to kiss it but deciding to shake it gently at the last minute.

"Yes, everything has been very first rate." Remy replied before continuing, "Tyler, hey man, nice to see you."

"While you are here, charge all of your expenses to your room; food, rentals, massage… you are our honored guests." Tyler announced with a warm smile.

"Lovely, thank you," I replied to the dark- haired young man, who was difficult to read. His outwardly expression sincere but there was a hint of underlining conflict, I could not put my finger on this incredibly handsome man and made a point not to linger.

Remy ordered drinks, spiced rum with coconut water on the rocks, for him and a glass of pinot grigio for me with lots of ice. Our hosts led us over to a table overlooking the sea. There were several other couples in the bar, all of them acknowledged H.S. with adoring eyes. The line between H.S. and his work force was obvious, they regarded him with equal measures of respect and fear.

"Tyler will send you a copy of the itinerary, we have a coordinator organizing day trip excursions, meals, and golf rounds to entertain everyone. Give you a chance to mingle with the department heads." H.S. continued engaging Remy, "I will introduce you to Sly, the head of Research and Development during dinner tonight. I think you will be quite pleased with our menu for this evening."

"Sounds good." Remy added, "All of the heads of your departments are here?"

"Yes, and their wives," H.S. replied.

"Very nice." Remy nodded while looking around, his long lashes always a surprise.

"Do you like sport fishing?" H.S. asked with a glint in his eye.

"Yeah, I did a little tuna fishing and sail fishing in Mexico."

"Wonderful, the day after tomorrow we leave at dawn with a handful of colleagues, why don't you join us? H.S. proffered.

"Sounds great."

"I will be working on my tan. Maybe find someone to snorkel with." I remember replying to the small circle of men.

"We will be sure you are introduced to the other wives." I cringed as H.S. finished his sentence.

"Lovely," I responded with a glance to my husband. It was at that point, I decided to take a head count as to how many female executives were attending this extravagant affair. H.S. was brilliant there was no doubt, confident perhaps to a fault and filling a room where ever he went. Most importantly he was smart enough to surround himself with the best people in the industry. I recall thinking, how unsure of his true talent I was, I didn't think it was managing people, he's too narcissistic for that. Not the creative type in the classical sense, it was a question for sure. I made a point to focus on that during our trip.

Knowing if our partnership was going to succeed, we needed to understand each other.

As the moon began to rise, the bar began to filled up, most of the guests, DBS executives were a good fifteen to twenty years, older than Remy and I. Sadly, our premonition had come true, we were the least conservative couple in this large group. I spotted several duck belts and way too much pastel. Restraining myself from judgements, I mingled and kept a positive outlook.

"Sly," H.S. called over to a rather tall man with black hair, his skin was smooth and beautiful, he was Eastern Indian, his wife beside him was as lovely, they were by far the handsomest couple in the bar and were completely unassuming. Sly looked awkward, however, in his loafers and pleated pants.

"I want you to meet the Beroe's," H.S. stated very clearly.

"I have heard many things about you Mr. Beroe." Sly acknowledged Remy with a hint of accent.

"Please, call me Remy."

Inclining his head, sly continued, "I believe, I have an appointment to show you our facility next week?"

"Yes, we're looking forward to it."

Sly looked to me with Remy's comment. "Mrs. Beroe, it is a pleasure, this is my wife Amrita."

I reached out my hand, "Beautiful name."

"Thank you it means…"

"Immortal." I interceded.

"Yes, that is right." Her dark eyes were curious, her accent heavier than her husband's, was very sexy.

"Mythology is Steph's hobby." Remy volunteered, "She is a sculptress and a successful song writer, she weaves the stories of the Gods into her work."

I blushed.

"Beautiful **and** talented, a dangerous combination." H.S. mused, raising his glass to me, as another couple approached our small party.

"Hello, Dean." H.S. graciously invited another colleague into our circle.

"Won-der-ful pa-rty H.S." The Connecticut top drawer drawl, immediately brought to mind a Katherine Hepburn film. Collar up on his pastel pink polo shirt, sear suckers, and penny loafers to boot, a real dandy. His wife, a pretty, fit blond was being strangled by nautical stripes.

"Dean is head of marketing." I cringed, not because I assumed, he could not fulfill his job criteria, but because I had nothing in common with this guy, and never would, the realization that Mad Hatter would likely be a subsidiary of DBS and would most certainly have me reporting to Dean. *Times they were a changin.*

"Nice to meet you," I offered my hand," Stephanie Beroe."

"Steph- an- ie what a plea-sure. I've heard a-lot a-bout you. You have done an amaz-ing job with Mad Hat-ter." His affable demeanor was very charming, I turned down to defcon two.

"Thank you."

"This is my wife Car-o-line."

"Good evening." She responded with a nod. I followed suit.

As I turned back to Remy, he was replacing my glass with a fresh wine, I recall smiling as his warm hand braced my back.

The wives gathered around me within seconds.

"Where do you live?" was Caroline's opening question.

"Southern California," I replied noticing she was surveying the room intensely with no intention to engage while we chatted.

"So, what do you do in California Stephanie?" She continued still measuring the room, with the distraction of boredom.

Taken aback by the question, I inaugurated conference mode. "Remy and I own and operate a cannabis infusion company, we design beverages for medical and recreational patients throughout the country." Both of their mouths closed after some unintended hang time, after a slight pause and obvious recovery, Amrita responded with a hushed voice, "That must be very interesting."

"Yes, it has been, to say the least." As I finished my sentence, I noticed Caroline staring off behind me with a look of fear. As I turned to follow her gaze, I easily spotted the culprit. A six- foot tall, early thirties, red headed bombshell, steering toward H.S. through the crowded bar as if parting the Caribbean Sea. Strappy Ga Ga heels, a micro red dress, and an overabundance of…confidence. Both of the women I had been talking with, demurred instantly.

"Hi Ya'll, is this a party or what?"

"Trudy!" Both H.S and Dean greeted the southern amazon in unison.

Remy's expression was priceless.

"Now who do we have here?" Spotting Remy for the first- time Trudy cozied up like a gargantuan magnolia to my tree.

"Remy Beroe." My husband responded with the perfect amount of charm.

"Remy and his wife, are The Mad Hatters," H.S. added, as Trudy drew her attention to me.

"How wonderful. I 've heard all about you of course." The Texas twang was sing song and sprite.

"Trudy handles public relations for us." H.S stated matter of fact. Which left me wondering what her job criteria was.

As we all moved out to the moonlit courtyard between the villas and the bar, I was enchanted by the lawn bedecked with white linen table clothes and white satin covered chairs. Miniature crystal chandeliers hung from invisible cords over every table creating a very Cocteau- esque effect. Votive flower arrangements inferred a romantic glow from the latticed woodwork of the surrounding bougainvillea draped balconies. The low murmur of the sea, a heartbeat, it was all quite lovely. A small band had set up and started their set off with a muzak version of Roar. As the guests started moving towards the dining area, Remy and I hung back.

There wasn't enough time or privacy to comment on the events we had just witnessed, our silent intuition took over as I clasped his hand and we walked into the garden. Noticing the painted gold leaf scallop shell on each plate, we searched for our names. Tyler signaled us, to come over to his table, we were sitting on either side of him.

"The rose between two thorns," I said to Tyler as we sat down. Tyler's smile was very charming, with the slightest dimple at the side of his mouth. His heavily lashed oddly green eyes were startling up close. He could be dreamy, except for the feeling of unease that popped through occasionally. I realized looking around the room, he was the youngest attendee by maybe twenty- five years. No wonder he seemed uneasy. This would be a difficult crowd to be around ad continuum and reminded myself, he must be incredibly sharp to be hangin with the big boys.

"You are in for a rare treat tonight, H.S has flown in a renowned chef from Japan."

"Sounds marv-e-lous." I let a little southern twang fall out, but got the response I was looking for, a flash of perfectly aligned teeth. Remy was seated next to Sly and was chatting away on the other side of Tyler. I was seated purposefully next to Amrita, who as lovely as she was, was quiet as a mouse.

The waiter, dressed in white setting off his incredibly handsome dark skin was an elderly man, perhaps from the island. With a brilliant smile, he poured an exceptional white wine with his white gloved hands. Each table designated its own waiter in attendance. After each guest was served the first course our waiter announced with quiet reserve slightly accented by Caribbean flair, "Sake steamed abalone."

"Abalone? Isn't that endangered in the U.S?" I asked Tyler conversationally.

"This abalone was flown in from Japan, and we are not in the U.S."

"Ah." *As if that makes a difference.*

In between the Pufferfish course and the Toro course, I realized Tyler and I had been talking nonstop about Ancient Greek and Egyptian philosophy and caught myself. "Where did you acquire your interest in the Ancients?" I asked wondering how someone with an obvious business degree had time for a double major so off track.

"My Mom is or was Egyptian. My family in Egypt are associated with the Cairo Museum, in fact."

"How wonderful, where did you go to school?"

"Oxford."

I could feel Remy's gaze and averted my eyes from my gracious host to my sexy husband, feeling a blush wash over me as he smiled.

Wiping my tears from my cheek, there is a gentle tap on my bathroom stall. "Sweetie, are you ok?"

One more deep breath, "Yeah, yeah I'm fine." Flushing the toilet for good measure I open the door to Laure waiting for me.

"What happened?"

"I saw the footage, of Remy entering the building, he turns a corner and…" The tears begin again.

"Ok, it's ok. Everything is going to work out." Laure soothes me with a loving embrace. But the look on her face is unmistakable. After a moment, she braces me. "The police are here."

"Shit. I haven't finished interviewing everyone yet." I mop my eyes with toilet tissue. *I should have invested in waterproof mascara, I look like Ozzie Osbourne.*

"Will you interview the kitchen staff for me, while I talk to them?"

"Of course, is there anything, in particular, you are looking for?"

"Strangers, two large male caterers that don't belong, food trays missing from the racks, unknown vehicles… let's start there." I don't bother to look in the mirror as we exit the bathroom, but take a moment to text Grace as I walk the hall; *The police are here, have you found Remy's ride yet?*

The breakout room is eerily quiet upon my return. Jean is standing next to a very short man, I assume to be the officer. I am not sure as he is in civilian clothes.

"Mrs. Beroe?" His voice is deep and assertive.

"Yes."

"I am Detective Brennan."

Despite his size, there is nothing slight about this man. His personality, voice, and command exude confidence, I am instantly relieved by this.

"It's nice to meet you, Detective."

Surveying the room, and my army of interrogators, he adds, "You have quite an investigation going on here." Jean's eyebrows raise in alarm as he continues. "Not the normal protocol."

"Detective, there is no doubt my husband is missing. He did not leave of his own accord. I could not let 24 hours go by without turning over every stone I could find. Time is of the essence, I'm sure you'll agree."

"Why don't we start from the beginning." Brennan holds out a chair for me. I sit down and face him as he takes out a notepad, not unlike Columbo.

"Need a pencil?"

"No, I'm good, thanks." He ignores my joke. "When was the last time you saw your husband?"

Sobered by my situation, two hours later I have gone over all of the details I can remember. The presence of this no- nonsense man, keeping me from emotional breakdown.

"You should write everything down." He looks at me square adding, "As you find it out, and then your thoughts after you have thought about it. I would like to see all the names and notes from everyone you have questioned." His voice is sincere.

I nod. *That makes sense.*

"Do you have any questions for me?" He asks calmly.

"I would like to know what you think after you've checked everything out," I state matter of fact.

"Well, one thing's for sure, I don't think you did it."

"Why do you think that? Women kill their husbands all the time. Don't they?"

"Actually, the statistics state that 34% of homicide fatalities are perpetrated on wives by their spouses, whereas only three percent are committed by wives."

I shake my head, "Wow, I had no idea."

"No, of course you wouldn't." He pulls out a business card, "You can reach me anytime, please feel free. I am going to talk with everyone in this room and then start on the rest of the staff you have talked with. I also want to see the tapes."

"Ok, I was going to talk with the caterers next." I realize I am looking for permission and change my tactic, "Everyone else, keep working down your lists, please." My volunteers all nod, the arrival of the police officer re-emphasizing the gravity of the situation, is apparent on all their faces.

"One last question, Mrs. Beroe."

I turn back to the well shaven detective.

"Do you know of anyone that might wish your husband harm?"

30

NO REGRETS

The driver that was hired for the day, is waiting outside the hotel at valet parking. The plan is to attend the conference for a couple of hours then come back for a refresher at the hotel, before his meeting with Stephanie. Driving through the hills of San Francisco always brings back memories of the first time, what seemed like a sleepy town 45 years ago, versus the high- tech luxe city San Francisco has become.

He was just seventeen then and travelling with his parents. His Father's company was sponsoring their first conference for pharmaceutical and food technologies. They stayed at the very same hotel, and although it has been kept in a luxurious manner, it seems to have lost the glamour he recalls from his youth. The conference held at the original San Francisco conference center, attracted a collection of men from all over the world either selling or buying technologies, was not remarkable. The singular memory of that trip that has stayed with him, the vision of a girl he caught a glimpse of in a car, pulling up to the hotel as his family was leaving.

She was perhaps sixteen, dark haired and dark eyed with an olive complexion, exotic compared to the ivy league mistresses he had conquered. By coincidence, their parents knew one another. Her father was a well- known lawyer that had worked for their industry on occasion and to great success.

Watching her approach his small group, he recalls the consumption of her melancholy, oblivious to her own beauty and innocence, she seemed lost between both worlds of child and adult, not quite one or the other. *"It was love at first sight, at last sight, at ever and ever sight."* The words of Vladimir Nabokov caressing his lips. He was ruined. There were no sights, conversations or realizations that could temper his desire.

Enduring the rest of the day's events, upon returning to the hotel, driven to distraction, he had hoped was not visible to his parents, he found himself searching the hallways and restaurants for another glimpse, he recalls, finally finding the nerve to tempt fate. "Father, would it be appropriate to invite your colleague's daughter for lunch tomorrow?"

"Hmm? Which colleague?"

"Mr. Corvani's, Dear." His mother interjected, without prompting. The natural preoccupation for work his father encumbered, eschewing the day's facts. His mother, Margaret always there to step in, "The young lady we met this afternoon? I should think you would both crave a couple of moments away from your parents." His mother always intuitive if not snobbish, looking up from her letter writing continued, "Your father and I already have a luncheon appointment tomorrow, you would have to be on your own anyway. She did seem a bit young?" He recalls his mother's eyebrows raising over her diamond pave' reading glasses.

"Dead on Mother, as usual. We could meet for lunch here at the hotel, I am sure there is nothing improper to that?"

"Wonderful my boy, Corvani is a powerful man, his partner in law has become the Attorney General for State of New York." His father added over the Times morning edition.

With that blessing, instructing the concierge to connect their rooms was next, remembering his palms sweating while waiting for an answer, but no one picked up. Deciding to write a note instead on the hotel stationery, he was determined, the message had to get through.

Dear Mr. and Mrs. Corvani,
I would consider it an honor to receive your daughter, as a guest for luncheon here at the

hotel tomorrow the twenty- first of May at One P.M.
Yours Sincerely,

Giving this note to the concierge with a gracious tip to ensure its delivery, every minute became endless. He was obsessed and could think of nothing else.

The blur of the passing world outside the car window is the perfect back drop for his memory. At nine AM he recalls a tap on the door of their family suite, pulling him from his forlorn depression. The only bill in his pocket for a tip, was a ten- dollar bill, eagerly he handed it over to the bearer of his dream. Tearing open the personally embossed envelope, he greedily absorbed each word with haste.

Our Daughter Julia, would be delighted to luncheon with you today at
One P.M.
Regards,
Mrs. Constansie Corvani

Remembering, exhaling as if it were the first time, closing his eyes to savor the exquisiteness of the moment. With no memory of the rest of the day, his obsession growing exponentially. His thoughts commandeered with questions; What does her voice sound like? What makes her laugh? The hours seemed eternal.

By ten A.M. that day, he was dressed and waiting, having said good bye to his parents, pacing the shared suite, enraptured by the unknown. By twelve thirty, he could stand it no more.

Having palmed the maître 'd twenty dollars, he was seated in the center of the room, with large vases of flowers behind the table, he still recalls the overwhelming aroma of stephanotis. Ordering a glass of club soda, he broke out the French cigarettes he had been hiding from his parents. Time stood still. Several pretty girls walked in and subsequently joined other tables. Women of breeding did not dine alone in hotels.

At exactly ten till one, she was a vision. Standing in the entrance of the restaurant, in a simple but smart blue dress with a large white belt. Her hair, short in the style of Audrey Hepburn, accentuating her large almond eyes. Rising to meet her, at first, she hadn't noticed his approach, and then the sweetest smile graced her lips.

"Julia?" Reaching out an arm to her.

"My chivalrous date? Thank you for asking me to luncheon." Her voice was a song.

Leading her to the table, all heads turned to watch them promenade across the room. He doesn't remember what they ate, he couldn't tear his eyes away. Conversation was forced, he stumbled and mumbled. She didn't seem to mind. At one point, she asked him if he was enjoying the conference. He replied honestly, "What conference?" She understood him at that moment and her smile lit up the room. Julia was sixteen, attending private school in Connecticut. Loved poetry, Tennyson her hero.

After Lunch, they walked around the hotel grounds, it was all very innocent, he never even kissed her, his only regret.

The motion of the car stopping at a traffic light derails his memory, *I will have no regrets today.*

31

BREATHE

It's now one-thirty, I think to myself, looking at my phone with absolutely no idea what to do next. Bits and pieces of information are swirling around me like nargles. I decide to check in with Grace. She should be at the office and running down some things for me, including keeping Mad Hatter on schedule during our absence. *Not that I care, without Remy,* **none** *of this matters, but it wouldn't be right to let our licensee's down, regardless of my personal situation.*

"Hey," my voice a bit lack luster.

"Hi Steph, how is it going?" Grace's voice is sincere.

"I just met with the Police Detective, it's good to have an expert to look at this." While my lips are moving, I am thinking, I just can't fit the pieces together. "Ok, so what have you run down?"

"I 've checked all the local hospitals and cab companies... nothing. I have also checked with the police stations too."

"What about Uber and Lyft?"

"They won't release any information to me."

"Maybe Brennan can jostle them."

"Who?"

"Detective Brennan."

"Oh."

Changing the subject, "What about the Vermont blend? Are the numbers finished?"

"Yes, I sent them over for approval."

"Before you sent them to me?"

"I can send them to you now Steph, the numbers are right, I figured you had your hands full."

The retreat in her voice snaps me out of whatever hole I was going down.

"No, no, of course, their right, I'm sorry Grace. I think I'm a little tired. I apologize for being snippy."

"Of course, you're tired, I can't even imagine!"

"So, what's on the schedule next? Combine Remy's schedule to mine please, so I can make sure no one is forgotten."

"Well, today you have the meetings with Tyler and Miles back to back. Tomorrow, you have a conference call with the new group from California." I wince, Remy needs to be on this call.

"Postpone the meeting for next week please, and send me an agenda for next week, anything I should know about that's pending on both of our calendars.?"

"Ok, that's it on my side, will do."

"Sounds good." As Grace disconnects, I think to myself there is something I am forgetting, but I can't put my finger on it.

Laure walks over to me, "It's lunch time sweetie, what do feel like?"

I just look at her, not hearing what she is saying. "Hmm? Oh, whatever you're having, I can't make a decision right now."

"You got it. Are you Ok?"

I fill Laure in on my conversation with Grace, which boils down to no leads. "Can you do me a favor? Can you contact Lyft and Uber and try to get them to confirm if Remy hired one of their cars? Grace wasn't able to get anywhere with them."

"Sure sweetie, no prob. Hey, it's going to be ok."

While Laure is on her phone, I am remembering how odd Remy had been about secrecy the other day. He never told me why, I didn't think to ask. *What did he know, that I didn't?* I turn back around to the group of strangers sitting at the conference tables waiting for me, wondering why they are here in this room. Before reality hits me like a dart. *Just breathe.*

32

The phone rings twice before he picks up.

"Yes?"

"I just spoke with her, she doesn't know a thing. There is a police detective now, a guy named Brennan."

"Anything else?" She pauses, the silence alerts him. "What is it?" he inquires slowly and calmly.

"The Uber car, there is no way to hide it."

"We don't need to hide it, stalling is good enough. You're doing great. Just stay calm, don't let her rattle you and remember whatever task she gives you, just do it slowly."

"When will I see you again?"

"Soon, if you can get time off work?" She laughs, precisely what he was going for, a distraction. "I'll see you soon? Call me if anything else comes up."

"What about Landon?"

"Get rid of him. She trusts you. Convince her she doesn't need him, or the expense, since she has a police detective now."

"You aren't worried about the police?"
"No, not at all, and neither should you."

33

CLUBBED TO DEATH

Had there been a train conductor, he would have been screwed. Yanking the branches in front of him and reminding himself to never wear a loud colored t shirt or pants again. Even at this proximity, he can barely hear the engine, a low hum but the wind is the giveaway. The train pushes a good amount of wind in front of it, like a whiney whisper, not a natural sound. The monkeys are literally going ape shit, the sound must bother them. Once the train takes the curve around the rock face, he has a clear level view of the cars.

"Holy shit!" *This thing has been custom made. Those fuckers!*

The entire side of two of the cars have special doors that lower by retracting, exposing the whole side of the car to the jungle. There are gun mounts spread out evenly, maybe six per car side. As the second car approaches, he counts two men with rifles on mounts, they don't see him, they're looking down, not up.

From this distance, if I could get enough leverage, I could jump on that god damn train! His mind is reeling.

The next three cars are all enclosed without windows.

Remy's body is rigid with tension as he hears shots, the jungle goes crazy, especially the monkeys.

So, this is it, we are the entertainment for some gun crazy yahoos! "God Damn it!"

Taking off his shirt, he starts rubbing it against the ground to muddle the colors, when he realizes he is grinding his teeth with anger, as the hullabaloo subsides.

Sitting and waiting, swatting mosquitoes, it's hot. Sweat is rolling down his back, behind his curled- up knees, even his head is sweating while he is sitting still. The group of monkeys move in below him on an almond tree, they are completely oblivious to the situation. Watching them dangle from their tails to pick a nut, take a bite and drop it. The young are on their mother's backs, chasing each other around thin bending branches comfortable in the safety of their canopy. *Steph would love this.*

A brutal thought hit's him, more frightening than a couple of guys with guns. *If I am here, where is she? This is not some random abduction. This is methodical, someone wanted me out of the way. I've got to get out of here!*

Ten minutes later he recognizes the whiney wind sound again, the jungle does too and holds its breath with him. In reverse, the cars are coming back around the rock face towards him. First the enclosed cars, one – two- three, then the open cars. Grabbing his branches, as the monkeys are scrambling and howling like lions, he sees the same two guys posted in the open cars, as they go by, they open fire on the monkeys. Dropping like discarded fruit to the ground, some with young still clinging to their backs.

The train moves out of view around the cliff face, as the monkeys lament for their fallen, its crushing; clambering down to the lower branches, they continue calling to their troop to get off the ground, to no avail. The sound is onerous. He doesn't have a clear view of the ground but can guess that ten or so bodies are strewn down there. Their grieving goes on for a good fifteen to twenty minutes before the tribe moves on, the only sound as they disperse into the canopy are the cries of the orphaned young. Like strange whimpering dogs, the sound is haunting, as tears sting his eyes.

Remy spends the rest of the afternoon collecting more branches for the blind. Just before sunset, there is a whistle from below, a bird like sound, two sharp tones low then one high. Scanning through the canopy he can see movement but can't make out the shapes. He sits tight. Five minutes later, Delta is crawling up the side of the cliff face. Signaling back to her Remy descends. She has three of her family with her, Ora with her golden hair and the stout but fierce, gray eyed Arona that killed the unknown animal they all ate, as well as teeny bopper. All of them have figure eight shaped gourdes around their necks fastened with a twine made from jungle vines. Teeny bopper has a whole dried fish wrapped in a banana leaf and a cloth sac made from clothing, full of mangoes and bananas. They look pleased with themselves. Remy feels like he's on a survival show.

"This is all we could sneak out of the camp. It should last you two days." Delta looks visibly shaken.

"What happened?" Remy asks.

"One of our gals is missing. She was out gathering food when the train came by, it doesn't look good."

"Have you sent anyone out to look for her?"

"Packard won't do it, he thinks she was ambushed and doesn't want to lose anyone else."

"Where does he think you are?"

"Patrol. We're supposed to be looking for you."

"Why?"

"In all of his wisdom, Packard thinks you took Camden."

"Who?"

Camden, the red head at camp, she's really passive, one of Packard's favorites. The whole camp is looking for **you** now."

"Great," Remy adds with a touch of sarcasm.

"We scouted out the area she should have been in, on our way here. There were no signs of her. Did you see the train?"

"Yeah, I saw it. What do you think happened to her?"

"I think it could have been the other family or she was shot, or both." Delta's voice becomes noticeably quieter.

"The guys on the train, have they ever…"

"No," Delta answers quickly, with tired eyes as she continues, "To our knowledge, they have never taken anyone. There aren't any predators big enough to worry about either since there is so much food. It has to be the other family."

Everyone in the small group sits on the jungle floor.

Now seems a good a time as any to cross reference an idea. Remy turns to teeny bopper, "What's your name, buddy?" The kid looks at him then to Delta, she nods encouragingly.

"Haven."

Delta interrupts, "I think he means your real name."

"Real name? Oh right, Packard." Remy responds naturally, "What an asshole!" Everyone laughs. *A good sign.*

"My real name is Marcus Handel. I lived in Connecticut, New Haven with my parents." The young man blurts out, inspired by Remy's bravado.

Marcus has got to be in his early twenties but looks a lot younger. Thin, not the outdoorsy type with a wild head of blonde curls. A good-looking kid, but a kid. "Hey Marcus, I'm Remy Beroe. I live in Laguna beach California with my wife Stephanie. We own a marijuana infusion and technology company, called Mad Hatter Coffee and Tea."

Remy waits to see if anyone recognizes anything he just said. Nothing. *Shit.*

"That's cool. My family's been in the banking industry for generations." Marcus adds with disdain, "I am the first NOT to be a banker. I hate numbers and spreadsheets." He's mumbling now.

"So does my wife!" Remy adds as Marcus smiles.

Looking to gray eyed Arona, he asks, "How about you?" matter of fact. She is buff, terminator buff. Maybe five feet four tops but you would not mess with her. Although the clothes she is wearing are tattered, Remy notices they were stylish before they were shredded into jungle wear.

"My name is Tracy Mueller, everyone here calls me Arona, I lived in Arona, Pittsburg, I was an assistant for the Chairman of the oldest private bank in the U.S., Baggard Brothers and Harris."

Charles Baggard the surviving brother of the ancient firm is well known to Remy, a conservative, right wing benefactor. Baggard's entitled political views of marijuana, gay and women's rights and anti-social programs are notorious, verging on extremist. *He is no friend of mine but then again, I have never met him,* Remy thinks about that, "Did you learn to hunt in Pennsylvania?" He inquires, smiling into her gray eyes, remembering her skinning the small mammal.

"I learned to hunt here."

Remy doesn't push. *That's two banks, or is it just a coincidence?*

Turning to Ora, he nods encouragingly.

"I'm from a little town outside the city. My real name is," she pauses looking around like a tween making sure their parents can't hear them," Katherine Beaumont, my friends called me Kat. I worked for the second largest private company in the U.S." The thirty- year old, fit woman sitting next to him blurts out as a confessional.

We have a couple of people that worked for or are related to impressive banks and wealthy private companies. All east coast, close to New York, "Where did you work?" Her hair looks like it's made of gold, Remy has never seen anything like it.

"I worked in the New York offices but the home office is based in Wichita. I lived in New Jersey outside of the city in West Orange. They call me Ora here." Her Jersey accent is a dead giveaway and reminds Remy of his own Jersey girl. "I'm sure you know my employer." She continues.

Remy looks at her, waiting. Hoping this is it, the link to why and who.

"Brendan Steele." Ora continues, with more than pride, as her hair breathtakingly catches the light of the sun.

Of course, Remy knows of Brendan Steele, who didn't? Brendan Steele and his brother Adam are infamous billionaires. Infamous for their archaic, warped views of the world they wish to create by unabashedly buying politicians and policy. They have spent the last three decades attempting to reform the GOP into their weapon. The only positive note is in this past election they loathed Trump more than Clinton and kept their wallets in their pockets. Regardless of the Billionaire brothers' distaste for legalizing marijuana, there is no connection between Mad Hatter and Steele. No, the only real connection here so far are wealth and position.

"How long did you work for him?" Remy asks, trying to understand why a woman would want to work for the Steele's, without judgement.

"A year in Wichita before I was transferred to New York," Ora replies with a slightly pursed lip that perhaps only Remy notices.

"And you?" Remy pushes on looking over at Delta. Her golden eyes starting to connect the dots.

"I worked for Bannock Industries. I was the assistant to the CEO Richard Bannock in New York City. I was actually abducted while I was on an errand for my boss." She pauses, throws her head back, looking up to the canopy above, "That son of a…" Snapping the stick she was using to scribble in the sand.

"Well," Remy surmises rubbing his face with two hands wiping the sweat off, "we do have a couple of patterns." Leaning back on his heels, everyone is looking over, the looks on their faces can only be described as, pissed. Remy considers: *They are all wondering why they hadn't shared their back rounds before. So am I.* "Banking is the most obvious, the east coast, either related to or worked for a C.E.O., and may I add," he pauses for drama, "you are all strikingly beautiful." Marcus raises his eyebrows, the women blush, except Ora.

A flock of disorderly parrots encumber a mango tree close enough to silence the group, caught in reverie, memories of family, work, mortgages, happiness and love that once were bombard them. Closing his eyes, waiting out the birds, all Remy sees is Stephanie's face; The morning light on her hair, her gentle whisper in his ear, her soft hand inside his calloused mitt. Her laugh.

"I'm going to get out of here," He announces to the group, "and you're either with me," opening his eyes and levelling them, "or you're against me."

For the next hour, Remy informs the new loyal squad what he learned about the train. They're all stunned, none of them had ever gotten a good look at the train apparently, they are always running from it. Once he tells them his plan, he notices a renewed energy they are getting pumped.

"Remy you have to be very careful, basically everyone on this island is looking for you, except us." Delta reminds him.

"Yeah, I know. Is there anyone else at camp that wants to leave, that you trust? We could use a couple more people."

"Maybe two tops. It's risky to ask, I'm not really sure what they're thinking." Delta shakes her head in reply.

Ora offers, "I know Galax, I know she has no loyalty to Packard. She's no fighter, though."

Remy recalls Galax as the woman tending the food back at camp. *Definitely not a fighter.* "What about the other family?" His question is met with immediate surprise, and no reply. "Look, if you want to get off this island, we have to have as many people on our side as possible." Looking each one in the eye before he continues emphatically, "We don't have guns, we have the element of surprise, and we outnumber them. I'm going to watch the train for one more day, then I'm going to find the other family's camp. I'm new, maybe they'll think I just got here. Who knows maybe we are all thinking the same thing, but no one wants to say it out loud?"

"Maybe," Ora remarks, shaking her golden head in what is taken to be agreement.

"We'll keep our family away from you, for the next day. The other family are perched on the backside of that second rolling hill." Delta points out behind them, "You better have a weapon."

"No, I think it's best if I look like I just fell off a truck and wandered in."

"It's ballsy, I'll give him that," Blondie adds to no one in particular as she stands up and throws a twig to the ground.

Remy smiles to himself thinking, *that's why my wife married me.*

34

GOLDEN -VEIN

On my way back to the kitchen, to interview the five employees left on my list, I feel the weight of impending time, hurling me down the corridor.

"Steph!" Laure yells.

I turn around, still in a daze.

"You have to hear this! Come with me!" Her voice is so excited, it draws me in. My legs are jelly, I need to eat something my focus is wearing. We open the door to the breakout room and sitting in front of me is a young woman about twenty, with dark hair and eyes, her face a mixture of concern and boredom. Laure directs me to the chair next to her.

"Can you repeat what you just said to me?" Laure prods her gently.

"Sure, well, I was unloading bread from the bread racks, and I noticed two big guys in chef scrubs wheeling a rack outside."

"Can you tell me why you thought that was unusual?" I ask with timidity.

"Yeah. They were really big, like football player big. Oh, and have you ever seen a chef doing grunt work?"

I stare back at her blankly.

"Exactly. They DON'T." She snaps sardonically.

Holding back a laugh as to not distract her, my heart is lightened. "Can you describe the men?"

"Yeah, sure."

I take out Detective Brennan's card, while Landon makes his way across the room towards me.

"You get anything good?" He asks.

"Yes, I think so." *With no help from you.*

Laure brings him up to speed. "How about you? Have you gotten anything interesting?" She inquires as my phone connects.

"Nothing." He states plaintively and walks back across the room.

"You're paying this guy?"

"Yeah."

"I think you're wasting your money Steph."

"Detective Brennan." His deep voice resounds, in my ear.

"This is Stephanie Beroe, I think we have a witness." I notice my hands are shaking, so does Laure.

"Are you in the conference room?"

"Yes."

"I'll be right there, don't move."

Brennan is in front of me in two minutes true to his word, he initiates a series of questions to Karen Ferring from Rockford Illinois with such proficiency, that I can see the image of the person she is describing, his tactic is impressive.

At twenty minutes to three, the door to the conference center room opens and an older man in his sixties walks in with a large sketch book. He introduces himself as Lieutenant Casey. Acknowledging Brennan with a nod, Casey sits down and opens his book as Brennan starts over with his questioning.

Laure finally orders food, sandwiches, and drinks for everyone in the room, and is plying our young witness with healthy snacks to keep up her momentum. I can barely unwrap my sandwich, I am so hungry.

Landon grabs a sandwich and sits next to me quietly. We are all intently following to the interrogation;

"How tall would you say he was?"

"About six foot three or four, they were both tall."

"Let's just concentrate on one at a time, just picture the one you remember the most."

"Ok."

"Can you describe his face? What shape was it?"

"His face was sort of long and rectangular."

"Good. Any marks on his face? Birthmarks, scars acne…"

"No, but his hand had a very dark tattoo on it."

"Can you describe it?"

"It was round and purplish, very dark. The whole circle was filled in."

"Are you sure it was a tattoo and not a burn?"

"No, I'm not sure. I guess I thought it was a tattoo because it was centered on his hand like it was deliberately put there."

"Which hand?"

"The right. On the top of his hand."

"Great, let's go back to his face. What color eyes did he have?"

"Dark brown eyes and hair. His hair was cut like a military guy."

"Large eyes?"

"No, they were kind of small, considering his head was so big and rectangular."

Brennan's voice is calm and gentle as he coaxes our only witness. "Anything else stand out about his features? Ears, nose, mouth…"

"Yeah, his nose was long and his nostrils were big, kind of piggish."

"A real Romeo?"

"Yeah, I guess." Karen laughs, and I notice her shoulders relaxing.

Laure sits down next to me and places a hand over mine, that I now notice I had been clenching. I whisper in her ear, "At 3:20 I have to meet someone. Would you come with me?"

"Of course. Do you want to change before? You can borrow some of my clothes?"

"I won't have time. Laure, but thank you, for everything."

She pats my hand.

Brennan continues his interrogation as the page in front of Lieutenant

Casey comes to life. Now that he has a basic sketch, he shows it to Karen.

"Yeah, that's right! That's amazing!" She pauses staring at the image. "His mouth is a bit off, I think it was crooked, lower on the right side then the left, kinda curled down."

Casey adjusts the sketch, "That's it!" She exclaims.

"Great Karen, you are doing a fine job. Let's concentrate on the second man now?"

"Sure." She replies with an endless amount of energy, I remember having at some point in my life.

I walk over to Brennan and whisper that I have to go to an appointment. He looks at me with consternation, before speaking. "Does this face look familiar?"

"No."

"Don't go alone. Where are you going?" He demands before adding, "If you don't mind my asking."

"No, not at all, we're meeting a colleague at four at the Laurel Court Bar in the Fairmont Hotel, I have a second meeting at The Wilson Bar on Jones St. at six-thirty. Laure is coming with me."

Looking over to Laure he simply states, "I don't like it."

"Neither do I." I interject like a child being spoken about by her parents while she is standing next to them, "Believe me, but my instincts are telling me to go." Fatigue washes through me, as I look at this man.

"I've called in the FBI." He retorts, snapping me out of my lassitude. My eyes are now wide open and tears are starting to well. Laure grabs my arm steadying me. "They will be here tomorrow morning Mrs. Beroe. There is something going on here and it may be more complicated than we think."

Turning my head away quickly to hide my tears, I see Laddington staring at the wall across from him as if he is having a conversation with it.

"Go to your meetings but be careful. Tomorrow is going to be a busy day. Oh, and text me the names of the colleagues you are meeting. I'll be in touch with any progress we make here." With that Brennan turns around to re-engage our witness.

Signaling Laddington to follow me out the door while Laure collects our bags, my private detective asks me from behind, "Looks like you have things under control here. Is there anything else you need me for?" His voice is even, suddenly I know the answer to this.

"Yes, I do. I don't want the detective to know, I need you to follow me tonight."

Laddington's eyes light up at my request. "Ok!"

"I want you to act as my body guard, be in the room, but no contact. Can you do that?"

"Yes!"

"Great, we are on our way to The Fairmont Hotel, follow us over but stay close."

"You got it."

Laure and I head out of the building silently. The sandwich is kicking in. Feeling my thoughts clear as I get in the car, I am mesmerized by the dazzling blue sky overhead banded with golden veined clouds, and curse whichever God thinks this is amusing.

"What's with Laddington?" Laure asks as soon as the car doors are closed.

"For some reason, I think it's a good idea to keep him busy and close."

"Steph, it's your money." Her brown eyes staring at the key chain in her lap, "I've watched him all day, if this guy is a detective, I'm Angela Lansbury."

"You could be Mrs. Columbo." I add, "You have the accent."

"What? I don't have an accent."

I laugh.

As we pull out of parking space she asks, "Do I have an accent?"

The car ride is soothing. My thoughts are of Remy, Brennan's words echoing in my head. I look down at the tear that's hit my hand. I'm numb but I've gone beyond sadness and concern. I'm angry. Angry at the thought that someone we know may be have caused this, someone we know may have taken Remy away from me! *So much for taking the higher path!*

Our conscience decision to not confront or engage in crazy was our personal endeavor to sustain peace and contentment in our daily lives. It cost us money, it may also have cost us jaundiced opinions from outsiders, misconstruing our silence as culpability. "I don't care what they think," Remy's words barraging my thoughts, "We don't owe an explanation of our actions to anyone. As long as we can live with the decisions we make, fuck them!" His gruff words were unable to hide the purity of his intent heart from me. While

Remy is always throwing himself out in the milieu, as the innovator and entrepreneur that the position projects, it's easy to presume he's callous. This could not be further from the truth. His capacity for empathy is his greatest strength. It is what drew me to him so many years ago and keeps me by his side.

A wave of rage rushes through me, I can feel my jaw tighten. Images are flashing through my closed eyes; Laguna, New York, Connecticut, Vermont, the Caribbean, San Diego, Los Angeles, Colorado, Illinois. All of the places we have been in the last six months and all of the faces of the people we interacted with. Nothing stands out. A moment goes by and suddenly I am back in the Caymans; The sunrise is glorious as the salt air lay heavy on our sheets. Remy sat up in the hotel suite's king size bed barely draped. Scarlet and crimson mists heralding the eternal birth of day, the sea before us, a calm exquisite reflection of the ethos.

"They say that Eos had an un-satiable appetite for handsome men." I purred.

"Oh, really?"

"Yes, the Goddess of dawn ravished armies of Gods and men, hypnotizing them with her rose-colored fingers." I continued moving with the stealth of Artemis, my face now directly above his.

"Are you sure those were fingers?" Remy's dazzling blue eyes, smiled with mischief as our passion consumed us.

We decided on a late breakfast, as we were on a quasi-vacation after-all, alone in the sun kissed courtyard, it seemed the DBS crowd was very type A, with everyone engaged in some sort of activity or another, almost afraid to stop moving.

"What do you want to do today?" My attentive spouse inquired over his scrambled eggs with caviar, that he pushed onto his toast. He could make a sandwich out of soup, I thought to myself with a giggle. I was about to suggest we look around for options, when H.S. and Tyler came bounding into the garden, in much the same attire as the night before.

"Good Morning. Here is the itinerary for today." Tyler announced handing us both a black leather-bound book. Our itinerary was written out by hand in calligraphy, like a wedding invitation, I recall staring at it my eyes blinking.

Remy never at a loss for words tossed the ball to H.S., "I was speaking with Sly last night and he mentioned your lab has had minimal exposure to cannabis research."

"Well, our laboratory is in Connecticut, where unfortunately the medical program has not…"

"Rolled out yet." Remy finished H.S' sentence while chewing.

"We are not concerned." H.S. added with irritated confidence, "You will also find we are very well connected, our affiliates will be awarded the majority of licenses from Connecticut as well as the surrounding states."

Remy nodded raising one eyebrow, without comment.

"We are looking to you, to bring **your** innovation and expertise to our group." H.S plied with an ingratiating smile.

"Not to talk shop, but where would I conduct my research until Connecticut comes around?"

"Anywhere you see fit. Your wish is our command. You tell us what you need and where you want it, and we will create a lab, to the likes of which you have never seen."

"I've seen quite a bit."

Laughing, H.S. placed his hand on Remy's shoulder, "That's why YOU are so valuable."

Again, no comment from my husband. I watched this exchange with a mixture of pleasantry and confusion. It is not like Remy to throw curve balls, Sly must have told him something else that got his hair up. I recall wondering why he neglected to share it with me.

"I expect to see you tomorrow at the fishing boat?" H.S. prompts with comradric persuasion before moving on to another table.

"Absolutely, I am looking forward to It." Remy nodded as both men turned to head off toward the main lobby.

I waited in silence, my fork and knife at the ready.

"What?" Remy asked after a moment.

"What are you really thinking?"

"I'm not sure yet." This little disclosure was expelled in- between bites, "It's a beautiful day, what do you want to do"?

"I saw a couple of SUP's down by the beach cabana, maybe we could paddle around while it's cool?"

"Great idea, let's get changed and go before we get recruited for water polo."

As we made our way back to the room to change and coat ourselves with sunscreen, I noticed a group of men with golf clubs amassing near the lobby. Sly was there as well as Dean and several other men we had been introduced to the night before. Tyler was talking to Sly as we walked through, the conversation did not look pleasant.

"You don't want to try your hand at golf?" I asked teasingly and somewhat distracted.

"I don't believe I have the appropriate attire," Remy said with a smirk, placing his hand on my back as he escorted me through the commotion.

In our suite, I turned on him, "Ok, what's going on?"

From the overstuffed chair in the living room that looked out to the Caribbean Sea, he acquiesced, "Look Steph, you don't need to be a rocket scientist to know we have very little in common with these people. In fact, that may be a good thing, as we are both bringing things to the table the other lacks. My concern is whether we will be able to communicate with each other on a long- term basis."

I recognized the look on his face as deep concern. My Zen Master is uncommonly neutral most of the time, the furrowed brow was a dead giveaway. "So, you're not concerned about the lab and where it goes?"

"I'm concerned. In fact, it may be a deal breaker. It will cost millions to build."

"They seem pretty enamored of you my dear, I think he will give you exactly what you want." Straddling his chair, I stroked a stray hair out of his face. "You know what happened to the boy that got everything?" I asked him feeling a little like Charlie in the Chocolate Factory.

Remy replied while removing my blouse adeptly, "He lived happily ever after."

I let out an exhale, perhaps louder than normal.

"Hey, are you alright?" Laure asks, like my surrogate sister.

"Yeah, I'm good. Thanks for coming with me." I reply as our eyes connect.

"It's going to be ok, Steph."

"I know." I say wiping my face, "I've got a plan."

35

TAKE MY BREATH AWAY

The jungle is calm as if approving of their decision. Delta sends the others ahead, they've gone over a couple of different strategies. She turns to Remy for support, "Do you really think we can do this?" She asks, with a glance towards the women she has become responsible for.

"With a small dedicated group of well- organized people, anything can be accomplished." One of his favorite lines from the movie RED, falls out of his mouth.

"I'm a secretary." She says flatly.

Looking at this woman standing in front of him, she gives new meaning to the title secretary. Fierce, loyal and having been driven beyond the routine band width for survival, he replies, "I'd say you're a lethal cocktail. You are so much more than a secretary." Placing his hand on her shoulder. "Look at you. You are adaptive, intuitive, a natural born leader. I wouldn't mess with you!" Delta smiles as he continues, "We are going to get out of here. All of us."

She nods her head in silence.

Remy believes he is seeing a side to this incredible woman no one else is privy to, she can't afford to show vulnerability. He can relate to that.

Placing her hand on his chest, her eyes locked to his, she whispers, "Thank you, Remy." And she turns and walks into the trees.

His hands ache from the thorn wounds, as he hides the water gourds in the brush. The fruit can be easily eaten by any animal so he eats as much as he can before heading back up the steep cliffside for the night. Pushing the wet musky earth with his feet, he is able to scrape out a good foot or so of space into the cliff side, at least he will be able to lay down in fetal position to sleep. The night is coming on strong, now the sun has gone down. The jungle is going to bed, at least the daytime creatures. Within an hour of sunset, he can't see his hand in front of him. Pressing his back up against the cliff side, he turns his concentration inward to the other Family. It is remarkable to him, that people sharing the same fate, can't find cause to unite. His sales pitch will need to be dead on, he knows he is walking into a hornet's nest, but what choice does he have? Eyes closing, taking comfort in creating his own darkness, his mind is all over the place before he finally rests on Steph. Remembering the smell of her hair, the softness of her skin, her wicked sense of humor and eternal bond of loyalty.

A song she wrote years ago, he can't remember the name, comes to him through the sky-less night. The story of Odysseus returning home to his ever-faithful wife, a declaration of love after being gone for twenty years. Remy feels like he has been gone for twenty years, disconnected, isolated, wanted. Can he get these people out of here? Will, he ever see Steph again? He mutes his questions with the melody in his head as he hears Stephanie's sweet voice, "*At night I lie alone. I hear your voice as it calls, I lie awake, my lady in mind. For you I'd grasp the sky, a million stars in my eyes could never disway my ladies love.*"

36

A FUOCO

Walking back through the jungle to the family camp site, Delta feels the exhilaration of hope she had found momentarily, diminish. The further she walks away from Remy, the more vulnerable she feels. Confused, she questions herself. He's good looking and strong, why shouldn't she trust him? For the last year, she had learned not to trust any man while managing to deter all uninvited sexual assails from the men in her "family".

Packard was the most difficult, she remembers his first assault. He was the new guy, couldn't have been there for more than a few days and she was tired of being strong. Scared and confused, he was relentless and persuasive, little did she know he was just testing the waters, deciphering who he could control. She trusted him and he used that power to take control of their family. So many faces have come and gone since then, she can't even remember their names.

Everyone except Freeman and herself gave in to him, the other women have been beaten into submission when no one is around. Which is why they stay in groups now.

The look on everyone's face upon their return condemns the missing Camden to a fate unknown. Both Freeman and Pitt hover around the entrance of Packard's hut while Galax serves the remains of a poor unfortunate animal.

"Did you see any sign of her?" Galax asks anxiously.

"No."

"Do you think that new guy took her?"

"No," Delta replies, noting Galax is visibly shaken. "What's going on with Packard?"

"He's lost a lot of blood." She whispers so no one else can hear, "I don't think he's going to make it."

"That not such a bad thing."

Galax looks at her and then looks around at the group, her expression is un-readable, "What do you think will happen?"

Sensing Galax's fear and vulnerability, Delta observes the pretty young woman, worry lines have prematurely aged her. Like most of the women, she has desexed herself as a response to the male oppressions. Rarely has she seen Galax make eye contact with anyone, she has never seen her smile.

"I think Aristes and Freeman are going to slug it out," Delta whispers the most obvious answer with as little emotion as she has for the situation.

"Who do you want to win?"

"The only leader I want is one that can get me out of this place."

"That would be great, but that's not what's going to happen? Is it?"

"You never know," Delta adds getting up to walk away.

Galax tugs her arm gently before she is out of reach, "I'd like to get out of here too." Her whisper a silent scream.

Bingo. Delta thinks to herself, one more for our team. Now she just has to wait for Harli to return. It's impossible to imagine any of her family wanting to be led by anyone here, they are all such imbeciles. That thought stirs recollection of the imminent presidential election prior to her abduction. It may be the only positive to being imprisoned here.

Surprised Freeman hasn't put Packard out of his misery to claim the throne, Delta finds a place to sit down anticipating the obvious tension in the air. She recalls her attempts to befriend Freeman when she first showed up at camp. For the most part, all of the women stuck together, except Pitt and Freeman. At the time, Pitt was hangin with the girls but playing them, feeding Packard information that he could use. Delta knew it, she felt the insincerity and shallowness in her voice and shift of eyes. Pitt stayed somewhat neutral until Freeman arrived, that's when things got really interesting. The group divided once again, the men, Delta's group of women and Pitt and Freeman. Consumed with keeping all the women safe from constant sexual attacks, Delta now had to worry about Freeman and Pitt beating the women into submission if they were left alone.

If it's going to happen, it's going to happen now, Delta thinks to herself, her eyes moving slowly around the circle. Both the Marx Brothers; Aristes and Leeds are skulking over the fire.

"Where have you been?" Aristes glowers at Delta, like a huge man child, his face contorted with more confusion than normal.

She shakes her head, *such a pity so much beauty is doused in so much cruelty.* She has never witnessed him actually take anyone, but will never forget the aftermath; the bruises, black eyes, cut lips and limping. She would die before she would allow any woman in her family to be assaulted. Which is why the men pick them off when they are alone.

Cowards. "Patrol. Shouldn't you be going out now?" She incites.

"Don't tell me what to do!" Mumbling he looks over at Packard's hut.

Seeing an opening, Delta continues to push, "How's he doing?" She asks putting her best concerned face on.

"He's not," Aristes responds.

"Not what?" Delta asks confused.

"Not our leader anymore," Freeman announces, moving into the center of the circle.

Standing up to face Freeman, Aristes growls, "Then who is?"

"That all depends." Freeman insists, cocking her head.

"On what?"

"On how stupid you are."

Like a streak, Aristes is on Freeman, he is wound tight and maybe three times her size, but her long legs are fast. Rocks in both of her hands, she is using them to weight her punches, tearing the flesh from his arms and face. The result is bloody as the rest of the group backs up.

Smart enough to stay out his reach, easily feigning his swings, like a cat Freeman strikes, again and again, leaving trails of blood as witness. With each connect from Freeman, Aristes becomes angrier, his eyes bulging blood shot red.

The sound of flesh on flesh beating is enough to make Delta sick. Bones cracking, groans of pain, it takes all of her discipline to watch the spectacle. She could care less who wins, neither victor will bring an end to the brutal oppression they have all been subject to. Remy is the only hope any of them have, she becomes sure of this while Aristes goes for broke. Tired of swatting at the fly in front of him, he is now on the offensive. Freeman starts throwing rocks at him to keep his bold approach back.

Looking around at the spectators faces, a mix of fear and disgust, it's obvious only Leeds is enjoying the show. Positive he was a fan of reality tv in his other life, Delta waits.

Freeman grabs dirt with both hands and throws it in Aristes eyes. For a moment he is paralyzed, arms out flailing while he squeals like a pig. She takes that moment to kick him in the groin, knocking the neolith to his knees with a moan. Quickly picking up a fairly large sized rock she slams it on his head with a definitive thud. Aristes is completely still for one second, everyone waits. But instead of falling to the ground with his brains slithering around, he reaches out and grabs Freeman unawares by the waist throwing her to the ground with a clunk. It's as if the impact of the rock actually knocked some sense into him.

Pulling her back by her hair and pinning her shoulders down on the ground under his knees. Freeman is now immobilized. Aristes looks her in the eyes and says something in her ear, no one else can hear and she stops struggling. As if a switch has been turned off, it's over.

That can't be good. Delta thinks silently.

"Stupid, am I?" Aristes announces to the receding crowd as he opens his mouth and directs a long stream of spit in Freeman's face.

Delta is disgusted. *Who's going to argue now?*

"I make the decisions from now on!" Aristes stands up screaming at everyone within a mile radius, obviously pumped with adrenaline. "You will all do as I say!"

He leaves Freeman in a pile on the ground. Pitt moves to check on her friend.

"Leave her! She is no longer allowed to speak in our group." Pointing an accusatory finger at Freeman, assuming a Moses like pose he continues with his commands, "Does anyone else have a problem with my leadership?" Aristes demands, attempting to instigate more mutineers, looking from Delta to Leeds, there is spit dangling from his chin and blood all over his body.

"No man, that was awesome!" Leeds replies like a teenager at an X games event.

Carefully assuming her position on the tree trunk Delta sits down, Ora and Arona join her, nervously fidgeting. Ora's golden hair looks like spun gold in the fire light. Neither of them dares look up from the ground, terrified to draw attention to themselves.

Galax, brings meat over, being sure to offer it to the new alpha dog first. He takes half the plate with a sneer. They can only imagine what life under his new dictatorship will be like. Delta is thinking she shouldn't have wished Packard dead as Freeman crawls away from the fire on all fours, attempting invisibility.

"Where do you think you 're going?" Aristes gets up and pulls Freeman over by her hair as she screams.

I 've seen enough. "Do you want me to patrol?" Delta stands up and solicits the new dictator, with forced boredom on her face.

Aristes looks her in the eye, searching for a sign of challenge or weakness. She gives him nothing.

"Yeah, be back at dawn. Somebody's gotta bury him." He replies with the air of a new born king before turning his attention to Freeman.

Delta catches Haven's desperate look, shakes her head at him discreetly and he sits back down picking up a stick to play with the fire. Ora and Arona join her, they reach the perimeter of the camp, when she notices that Freeman's buddy Pitt has joined them. *This should make for an interesting night,* she thinks to herself thanking her stars she is not Freeman. She feels sorry for her and had Freeman not beaten the other women into obedience, she would have helped her. At this point, she just wants to get as far away from the camp as possible, the honest fact is whatever fate awaits Freeman, is her own karma.

Once they are out of ear shot of the camp, Pitt begins and endless diatribe. "That slime ball will have us all as slaves if we don't do something." Her voice is strong and angry but controlled.

Delta remains silent, so does everyone else. They walk about a mile or two, no one is actually looking for anyone or thing, not that they could, the forest is thick with leaves and getting darker by the minute. They are all preoccupied with the scene they just witnessed, while the jungle is in the middle of a shift change. Delta feels the breath of the jungle still hot from the day, they have not had any rains for over four months now.

She likes this time of year, less bugs but more heat. Hopefully, the rains will begin soon, replenishing and cleansing as it pours. In another hour, they will have their first respite from the heat as the sea breeze finally turns towards the shore but it takes time for the jungle to cool. Delta stops and so does everyone else, except Pitt. In her stupor, Pitt walks right up Delta's back. Catching herself, she blinks. "Why are we stopping?" Pitt asks, obviously annoyed she didn't make the decision to do so.

"We need an intention."

"A what?"

"An intention, our purpose," Delta offers. The other women know the routine. They believe in destiny as well as the choice to change their fate. In teaching them to become the hunters they are, she had to create a mind set to go with it, or they would have all died. None of them had served in the military or police force. Most of them had been secretaries, consultants, bank officers, one was a hair dresser for Christ's sake! After Freeman and Packard had gotten to them, there was nothing left. Delta rebuilt their sense of purpose and belonging, creating a family worth fighting for. *Give them hope, that is my purpose*, she thinks to herself.

It took some doing and a lot of trust on their part. These lionesses are now a pack. With intention and purpose, they think as one and act as one. Delta is proud of them, pushing buttons on a keyboard one day and widdling weapons the next.

"Oh," Pitt replies lamely and closes her mouth.

Clueless. Delta begins as everyone huddles around her in the dark that overshadows them, "Our bond is more important than ever now." Delta looks at each woman including Pitt, their faces so close they are practically touching. "The line between survival and oppression has never been more fragile. The time for action is coming soon, for now, we must stay focused on the big picture. Stay safe and let fate lend a hand." Purposely she does not mention Remy, by the looks on their faces her gals know what she is talking about. She cannot trust Pitt with any of their plans and wishes she had had the foresight to tell them the same. "Safety and Patience." All of the women repeat, "Safety and Patience." As they do, she can sense Pitt's alienation.

"Pitt? Stay with me in the rear. Arona take the lead."

"Ok." Pitt waits with her while the others move ahead. They don't need to be told, they know the formation.

As the women start to move, Delta hears footsteps to their left. Crouching instinctively and pulling Pitt down with her, they wait. Arona has doubled back and zeroed in. In one fail swoop, she has tripped their new guest. A woman falls into the center of their diamond, going down with a harrumph. Arona can tell instantly it's Harli, hair in her face and wide eyed, even in the dark.

"What happened to you?" Arona asks picking her up.

"I got lost. It is so damned dark, I couldn't figure out where I was after 10 minutes of walking in one direction." She replies, shaken up.

"Did you see anyone? Did you see Camden?" Delta asks.

"Yes and no. I found someone, a woman, she looked like a marshmallow. Burned. No Camden, and it's very quiet out there."

"Did you recognize her?"

"The marshmallow? Her own mother couldn't have recognized her."

Squatting down to digest this and make a plan for safety and patience Delta closes her eyes and clears her mind, after a moment, she decides to run a perimeter around the area Remy is held up.

It takes them a good hour to get into position. Maneuvering through the night jungle is a chore, once they've reached the outer perimeter, they all rest. The air is noticeably thinner, cooler as they huddle under the canopy of the trees, finally a reprieve.

"Where are we?" Pitt asks, her voice obviously skeptical.

"We are North of our camp, just East of the hill from the other family," Delta replies matter of fact.

"Why? Aren't we supposed to be patrolling our camp perimeters?"

"I think the other family is moving camp, my guess is they will do it at night. This is the best chance we have of keeping tabs, without being discovered." *I hope she falls for this.*

37

WATCHING THE DETECTIVE

Laure has preemptively stopped at her apartment to force a change of clothes on me. I am grateful. Thank goodness, she is a clothes whore. I choose a black Ula Johnson sleeveless, georgette silk dress she had tucked away for a rainy day. It's simple with a touch of dare, my black demi bra just visible. I also borrow a pair of wedge shoes with black satin wrap around straps, similar to French milk maid shoes. *I feel like we are in college again, just girls going out for the night, if only that were true.* Laure insists I wear her Stella McCartney Jacket with flared sleeves, I take it but it's not the effect I'm going for.

After a quick but luxurious shower, I flip my head over and just shake out my hair, a brush cannot help at this point. Using bobby pins to hold in place three strands of hair from the top of my head that I twist and then criss- cross over, (I call it Greek braids), I let the rest of my hair fall to my shoulders. *Shaken but not stirred.*

Laure is in a shark skin suit, "It's reflecting how I feel tonight, we're on a mission. Right?"

I nod, gathering my thoughts as I apply my makeup, for a moment the shower has cleansed my soul and I feel as if I am preparing for some mischief before the gravity of my life snaps me in the face.

Looking anywhere but in the mirror, attempting to keep the tears from ruining my mascara, I look around the apartment, it's small but in a great little neighborhood. A large pudgy cat is staring at me from the hall of the bathroom with an unapproving glare. His name is Simon, and although he adores his mommy, he is not partial to strangers, hence the peculiar sounds arising from his throat.

Laure has a great eye for detail. Her home is comfortable yet chic, familiar somehow. With one last sip of wine and a glance below the neck in the mirror, we head out the door.

Upon arrival to the Fairmont Hotel, the valet's take our car, Laure comes around to me and I hook her arm, noticing Laddington in line behind us. "How do I look?" I ask my dearest friend.

"Girl, I wouldn't mess with you."

"That's saying something. Let's go."

We are ten minutes late, but I consider since Miles stood Remy and I up without any cause or apology, he can deal with it. Promenading through the front entrance, I feel as if I have been summoned to the Pantheon itself. The space is tremendous. Gilded pillars, vaulted gold leaf paneled ceilings dimpled with exquisite chandeliers. The marble floor is cavernous under my wedges as we navigate several potted palm trees working our way to the Laurel Court Bar, both of us silenced in awe, move involuntarily. I am focused on the hand I am about to play. Laure is a rock of support. I can see laddington following us, for once following directions. *Everything seems to be in its place.*

The bar is a show stopper, numerous sections of marble pillars form perfect circles supporting a round series of domed ceilings that compel us forward. The hotel has been modernized and the effect is classic and humbling at the same time. I am prepared for the offering.

Miles occupies a chair that commands the center of the first ring of pillars facing the door. A round divan couch, the centerpiece of the ring stands between us. Rising, he acknowledges our entrance, I notice he is surprised I am with Laure, ever gracious he takes my hand. "Stephanie, thank you for joining me."

"Miles. This is a colleague of mine, Laure Giovanni."

"A pleasure Miss Giovanni. Please take a seat."

I sit on the blue and gray brocade monster of a divan directly across from Miles. Looking toward the door I notice Laddington taking a seat to my left three tables over. Laure occupies a chair across from Me.

"I wasn't sure you would come."

"Neither was I," I respond with a coquettish smile looking over the menu that has been placed before me by a handsome young waiter. For such an enormous room, the sound is incredibly contained. A trio of piano, cello, and violin are softly playing midway through the chamber, I feel the sweep of their melody release the tension in my body. The waiter is hovering so I order, the celery root prawn salad and a glass of Pinot Grigio, as the words come out of my mouth, I feel my stomach lurch. Laure orders the butternut squash soup and a martini. *Love that gal.*

Once the waiter disappears, Miles continues, "First you are owed an explanation."

I fold my hands under my chin in reply.

"The story I am about to tell you sounds incredulous I know but please believe it is the truth."

Interest peeked I nod back, Miles looks around the room seemingly checking to see if he is being overheard. I can't help noticing he looks nervous.

"I arrived and checked into the Casa de Camino Hotel the evening before our meeting, as planned.

"Yes, the desk clerk told us that."

Miles resumes his tale without comment to my remark, "The mission style hacienda in Laguna Beach, was certainly a welcome change from the formal anonymity of the Four Seasons, my usual stand by. You must understand a routine schedule of travel over the past 45 years allows me a certain level of status that is recognized by sight. Having to brandish a credit card upon checking in on this night, was almost charming."

I quickly glance over at Laure, and catch her eyeroll, before Miles continues, "The clientele in the lobby mostly in their sixties, was sprinkled with a few young couples, mingling about. I wondered what my wife would think of the hotel, would she find it romantic or common? She can be such a snob sometimes." Miles looks over to Laure, "I find it entertaining. Laure nods back at him, obviously wondering why he is telling us this story. *She is not alone.*

Miles shifts in his chair and continues, "I checked in and the porter carried my luggage to my suite. A young man of twenty or so, dark brown hair under an old-fashioned porter cap that brought back memories of menial jobs from my own youth. I recalled being struck by the memory of my father insisting I work in every department of his company to learn how it breathed from its source. Lowering his voice to channel his father and then sustain his digression he continues, "It was good advice, it had opened my eyes. I had led a sheltered and privileged life, private schools, Ivy League. It did not give me the chance to mingle in different social and economic classes. Working in the mail room did, as well as the cleaning crew. At the time, I was humiliated and angry with my father, I even changed my name, and took my mother's maiden name, to avoid pity for the rich boy. Following the footsteps of the Porter, I recalled the resentment I had held for my father at the time. None of my friends had been put to a test like that. They were all offered office work, or apprentice jobs with powerful companies and even more powerful men, at the time I did not understand how powerful my own father was. Such a shame you never truly appreciate someone until it's too late.

Laure has drained her cocktail glass and is desperately looking for the waiter. I don't blame her! I nod at Miles hopefully encouraging him to get to some point.

"I handed the porter the key and noted the pride at which this young man held his position. He was proud to work there, to carry luggage and open doors for the more fortunate, he was no beach bum. I followed the Porter into the room and paused to take in a deep inhale, a resignation of sorts. The young man looked back over his shoulder while opening the terrace window that looked out to the auburn horizon reflecting on the sea, it was the last light of day. The young man then asked if he could get me anything, a sincere solicitation. I asked for a glass of scotch."

Thank goodness the waiter has arrived with refills, I am restraining the urge to jump across the table and scream GET TO THE POINT! Before it dawns on me, this is just how Miles is, old fashioned, so I suppress my impatience.

Miles unceasingly continues, "The porter stated, yes, of course, your bar is stocked, would you like that on the rocks or neat?" I thought to myself, I like this young man as I sat down in a denim covered club chair facing the sea. Neat please, I requested, as usual, loosening my tie, I took out my phone and turned it off, the day was done. I had reached my destination and thought, tomorrow I will consider my plan of action, thinking resolutely over the months questionable events." Miles nods in acknowledgement of the news articles in question and continues, "The young man crossed the expansive room and handed me the crystal glass with amber liquid in it the color of twilight's sun. He asked if I would like to order room service and feeling suddenly sleepy, I thought that was a good idea. I had heard the lobster meatballs were not to be missed and ordered them and asked him his name, he told me it was Henry."

As Miles pauses to take a sip of his drink, the look in his eye is that of someone that should be taken seriously, I can also tell from his physical language, he is uncomfortable so, I place my hand on his gently coaxing, "Thankyou miles for sharing this with me."

Reaching out he squeezes my hand, delicately but personally before continuing, "Henry asked me if I would like a refill, I acquiesced as the whitewashed room filled with salty ocean air. The sound of the sea was hypnotizing, the weight of fatigue overwhelming. I Reached into my wallet and pulled out a hundred- dollar bill and handed it to the young man while retracting the beverage.

"Thank you, Sir, enjoy your rest. Please let me know if you require anything else. Taking the first empty glass from the end table, he closed the door quietly. Fine young man, I remember saying, before losing consciousness."

I am silent for a moment, digesting this. Many things are swirling about, none of which I really feel at liberty to discuss with miles at this point. "That's it?" I reply almost angrily, not being able to process all of this quickly enough as I drain my glass.

"In a nut shell, as the saying goes." He retorts while retracting his arm.

"That doesn't make sense, what were you drinking?"

"Scotch, and not a very good year I might add." Smacking his lips, eyebrows raised in his own disbelief.

"So, you just fell asleep?"

"Yes, and I didn't wake up for two days."

"Two days? Did you call the police?"

"No. I have… personnel working on it." His dramatic pause leads me to believe that's true.

"So, what do YOU think happened?" I ask somewhat impatiently.

"I really have no idea."

His nonchalance is aggravating my confusion. I look to Laure and she is having a difficult time staying silent as well. Lots of threads are connecting between the both of us. *Am I being played, yet again?* "Do you think you were drugged?" I ask lowering my voice.

"Most definitely."

Of all the things I had considered I would hear as an excuse to blow us off, this was not one of them. The temptation to tell Miles that Remy has been abducted is uncontrollable. While our waiter dances around the table, silencing our conversation, I look around the room. Mostly couples and a couple of business people filling the other tables, but now this massive room has suddenly become oppressive and confining, the marble gaudy and ridiculous, as I contain my grief and confusion. *If Miles had told us this sooner, maybe Remy could have been saved, it's a big maybe, but it's a maybe!* I take a sip of wine, reigning in my control while extracting a prawn. Chewing, will hopefully give me the time I need to compose myself. Laure has become irritatingly interested in her soup. Reaching for my wine glass, the table over Miles' right shoulder has caught my attention abruptly. Two large men with army style haircuts are sitting together. They are dressed impeccably, but something is off. They are too… stiff. Uncomfortable in their clothes. I also notice they are not talking, nor are they eating the food in front of them.

Pulling myself back into the moment, and not a bit happy that Miles didn't give us a heads up, I finally respond, "Why didn't you call us? Why didn't you tell us what happened?" In a hushed voice.

"Would you have believed me?"

Probably not. We really don't know Miles well, having conversed mostly by phone or email, as we occupy different coasts. I have always liked him, but the only way to draw out a wolf is to play dumb. Is he a wolf? "It's not so unbelievable now," I reply getting his attention.

"How do you mean?"

Laying my cards on the table along with my fork I concede, "Miles, Remy was abducted over twenty- four hours ago."

Miles looks from me to Laure, who has stopped eating and is sitting with her hands in her lap, watching our discourse like a tennis match. "Abducted? Are you sure?" Miles responds, taken aback for a moment.

"Yes. Yes, I am sure." My eyes don't leave his for a moment. Miles is truly stunned. I continue watching him for any incriminating response, "No one knows, except my inner circle, the authorities and now you." I am bracing myself, saying this out loud is taking more strength than I anticipated.

"Stephanie, I am at your disposal, if there is anything you need or anything, I can do to help you, anything at all." His eyes and voice seem sincere.

"You realize our situations are connected." I throw this on the table like a wild card.

He blinks, "Why would you think so?"

"Prior to our meeting with you, there had been a series of bad press releases for our company and yours. At the time, I didn't connect them. Remy did. He was on to something, he had a theory he was working out just before he was …taken." I close my mouth hoping to still its quiver. Looking back over Miles' shoulder, the two men continue to derail my attention. "Someone has been setting us up," I whisper.

Miles closes his eyes for a moment, hands raised in prayer under his nose, "Let my people work on this for twenty- four hours?" He responds with absolute calm, I can appreciate.

"The FBI comes in tomorrow morning. I have been working with the local authorities but I don't know what the feds will be like."

"The FBI? I understand. I may know some people that can help."

I look Miles in the eyes, the only thing I think to say, "Thank you," Is barely audible. I fill Miles in with all of the details I have gathered, at this point, I want to believe he wants to help.

Miles leaves soon after his discovery. One of the men at the table I had been watching leaves shortly after his departure.

I text Miles, *I think you're being followed.*

I know, He replies instantly. Inhaling deeply, I'm not sure what to think.

"So, what's next?" Laure asks, pulling my attention from his text.

Tyler. This should be interesting.

"Why didn't you tell me about the bad press?" Laure looks wounded, as we gather our gear to head over to The Wilson Bar on Jones Street.

"Honestly? I hadn't thought about it until today. Brennan is right I need a notebook, I hate typing on my phone and now the details are inundating me."

"Anything else I should know about?" She is sincere, but a little guarded.

"Now that you mention it," I say with a beguiling smile. "We have another meeting."

"Spill it, girl."

I give her the low down; her eyebrows ascend as I describe Tyler's looks.

"Would you like me to pump him for information?" She asks, putting her arm through mine as we navigate the palatial interior.

I just laugh. "You're a riot Alice, a real riot!" I do my best impersonation of Jackie Gleason as we walk out of the lobby fit for a God.

En route to The Wilson Bar, my phone starts imploding with email notifications. A mixture of fear and hope that there is news of Remy strikes my core as I unlock my phone with my thumbprint and scan the inbox. Nothing from Brennan, several emails from Grace and our licensee in the mid-west. They hold several licenses in 3 states including Illinois, Michigan, and Minnesota. Their funding for start-up is impressive, but they come from the plumbing industry and they don't imbibe. I start with the most recent of the six emails from my assistant-

Michael is off the wall. Complaining the packaging is taking too long and angry about the travel expenses he has to pay for your training. He does not want to talk to me, he wants you or Remy.

I go down to the last email from Michael that Grace has forwarded to me, from yesterday.

Stephanie,

I have been trying to reach you without any communication. (It has been a couple of hours, sorry I haven't told you, my husband has been abducted.)

Where is the packaging? (I can't print until the proofs I sent you two weeks ago, are approved through your state compliancy board, I think to myself.)

Where are the proofs? (They were sent 2 weeks ago.)

Why is this taking so long? (Because you changed the format of the packaging after we templated all 33 products. I am now murmuring to myself feeling my temper rise. Oh, and you also forgot that every product package and label had to be approved by your state and the one state employee they designated for compliancy approval is inundated.)

This shouldn't be this difficult? (Actually, in my experience in the cannabis industry, nothing has been easy or efficient, absolutely nothing.)

I type my actual responses back with a cajoling hilt and of course great deliberation. Every single one of our licensee's needs their hands held. It's not uncommon or unwelcome, it's just bad timing. My post script also reminds him he hasn't paid his second installment of $25,000 and it's thirty days overdue, without a mention.

Laure hears my sighs and asks, "Bad News?"

"No. No, just business."

It's six-fifteen and I receive a text from Tyler that is a bit confusing – *A bushel of crabs.*

That's all it says. *Ok, that's weird.* I text back, *we are on our way.* Scanning my in box, I see a couple of texts I can ignore until tomorrow and one from our licensee in Oregon. *Call me ASAP!*

Probably not a good idea to ignore that one. I bring the phone up to my ear, in anticipated despair, "Shannon?"

"Stephanie, thank goodness. Are you sitting down?"

"Yes." Laure looks over with dread, I nod to her that it's not about Remy.

"There was an emergency meeting with the OLC today."

"Ok." *Christ, not another emergency meeting at the Marijuana Regulatory board. We just reconfigured all the packaging at an incredible expense from their last emergency meeting requirements demanding a thirty- day time limit to comply. Most of the product hasn't even been distributed yet.*

"They have just decided that all packaging rules are the same for Medical as Recreational with a whole new set of packaging and labelling requirements."

Shit! "How long do we have?" *I don't know, how much more of this, I can take.*

"Thirty days."

"What?" My voice is so loud, Laure impulsively pulls over and stops.

I am dumfounded. My usual stance of, *there is a work around for everything*, has just forsaken me.

After a moments silence, "Stephanie, you there?"

"Yes, I'm here." Quickly, I organize my thoughts, "Alright send over the new specs for the labelling. What about the packaging, are we still good? The bags themselves?

"For a one- time use, single serving we are good if you have certification that the bags are child resistant."

"Ok." My mind is in overdrive, *our bags are 4.5 mil thick, a child under the age of 7 or an adult for that matter cannot tear open these bags, they are 1.5 mil thicker than the certified bags. BUT THEY ARE NOT CERTIFIED! I am screaming inside my head.*

Since we print directly onto the material, this is a BIG PROBLEM. However, as the licensor of a national brand, I cannot allow my licensee to feel anything less than – we can handle this, it isn't a problem! "Alright, that's a pain in the ass, but we can figure something out in thirty days for new product."

"That's the thing, it's not just for the new product."

"WHAT?"

"I know, it is RIDICULOUS." I can hear her taping a pen on her desk, usually a sign of going over to the dark side. "The new rules are for ALL PRODUCTS."

"Products on the shelves already?"

"Yup"

"How can that be? They want you to recall all of our products that met last month's NEW REGULATIONS, and re package them?"

"Yup."

Gasping, "Mother Fuckers!", just slips out.

"Tell me about it, I'm surprised the OLC rep they had at the meeting got out alive, it was touch and go there for a minute. I even asked her if they had any idea of the burden of cost to our companies their NEW INSTANTLY, in place regulations were going to cause? She just repeated "You have to meet compliancy within thirty days. Did I mention, the all new packaging and labelling has to be reviewed by the OLC before you can distribute ANYTHING?"

"It's a Goddam witch hunt!"

"You got that right."

"How do you plan on getting the inventory out there, back? I ask feeling another world crumbling before me.

"Don't worry about that, you just work your magic on the artwork and packaging, I'll take care of all the distribution logistics."

"Sounds good, hang in there. It should only get better." *That I truly mean.*

"Please, don't curse it." She says and hangs up.

I sit there staring at my phone, like it holds some mystery to the world, I no longer wish to unlock.

"Hooo hoo? Steph, you're scaring me." Laure whispers, waking me from my state of incomprehension.

"Sorry. Throwing my phone in my bag, punishing the messenger, I run my hands over my face before I answer. "Regulatory bullshit," I squeeze between creased lips.

"What is it this time? Do you have to accompany the patient home and administer the tea personally?"

I let out a sigh and a tinsie-insie giggle, "Practically."

"Who?"

"Oregon," I reply while madly texting Grace, to get on this ASAP. I will need proofs in three days, and to immediately call our printer, and if they cannot certify our bags as child resistant, we move on to child resistant packaging with child proof zippers for our multi packs from another company, which will mean retemplating, EVERYTHING!

"I would have thought Oregon would have rolled out their program correctly, they've had illegal cannabis as big industry for decades there." Laure condemns after I give her an overview of our latest request at piety.

"There is no logic to any of this. If this is a recreational drug, why are they treating it like a pharmaceutical? It doesn't matter what color a bottle of gin uses on its label, or if it uses a cartoon character, an illustration or a grape to denote its wine. Who is coming up with all this nonsense? Most importantly, why are we sucking it up? Why don't we tell them to go screw themselves? Enough is enough! This is a multi- billion-dollar business!" My hands are shaking as Chris Isaacs croons about trouble going down. Resting my head back I whisper, "You have no idea."

38

DON'T LOOK BACK

Upon our arrival to **Jones and O'Farrell street**, I notice a line of patrons desperate to enter a bar called Bourbon & Branch. I'm glad we're not going there, although I look good in my borrowed designer couture, Laure and I are at least ten years older than the oldest in line and frankly, I am in no mood to proffer myself to a doorman.

"Wow, this place is hopping. Did they send you a password?" Laure asks.

"A what?"

"A password, this is one of those speakeasy bars, you know, looks like and feels like the 1920's. You can't get in without a password. I think it's silly, but with the right guy it could be romantic."

Instantly understanding the cryptic text Tyler sent me about crabs, I realize I have the password, and I decide to try and look as cool and hip as this place assumes. There is a paid lot a block down, so we park and I take care of the fee, then we walk arm in arm down the block.

"Sort of a strange place for a business meeting." Laure offers.

"Yeah, he is a bit strange."

"Life is strange."

We walk up to the door, as a small, very white hostess comes out through the crowd with a clip board. She has the straightest jet- black hair I have ever seen, it's blue it's so black, cut in a baby doll style with a pin curl above her left eye, drawing attention to a beauty mark on her chin below it. Her crimson lips and dragon lady nails, make me very afraid. She could be a star in a Woody Allen film and she's young enough to date him.

I catch her eye and whisper, "A bushel of crabs", into her ear, somewhat self -consciously.

"Follow me, please." She replies, checking us out. I am pleased we pass her scrutiny, skirting the crowd and walking into another time, the era of prohibition, *I can relate.* The walls are covered in book shelves stuffed with books. Behind the bar the nude brick walls are lined with carved niche's containing old bottles, it's dimly lit and wall to wall. *There is some serious mixocology going on here.* The place is packed and it's six-thirty.

We walk the entire length of the bar to a door with a small square closed window. The hostess with the mostess knocks twice and the window slides open. She whispers the password I assume as the metal door opens and a new reality greets us. *This place is over the top!* "Have you been here before?" I ask Laure from the side of my mouth.

"No, it's great. But weird."

It sure is.

The room is much the same as the Bourbon & Branch bar, however, you are meant to feel as if the store front of the speak easy is a private detective agency called Wilson & Wilson. Cage bars silhouette the reverse lettering of the feint agency storefront from the street lights outside. There's a hand full of tables and Tyler is sitting at the only four- top. I steer Laure over to his table.

"Stephanie, looking beautiful as ever." Standing he pulls out my chair, sounding eerily like his boss.

"Tyler," I nod my head, "this is Laure she is on my team." There is no room for error in that statement.

"Laure, it's nice to meet you."

Laure takes the seat to the other side of Tyler. I notice his eyes catch her for a moment.

"The rose between two thorns." He mimics me, but his smile is genuine.

"This is some place."

"Yes, not your average bar." He adds after a pause "The cocktails are amazing."

A Barman comes over and places a linen napkin in front of us all, I glance quickly at the menu, an enormous book of perfectly concocted drinks, a liquid diet lover's dream.

I order the Red scarab – a sparkling wine with apple brandy tinged with brown sugar syrup and hibiscus. Laure orders the Pulp Fiction, in my opinion, a gruesome mixture of cacao-infused Campari and herbed vermouth. Oddly enough Tyler chooses a Truth Serum – scotch, bitters, and sarsaparilla.

Cleansing my mind of the era inspired Disney park I have forayed into, I turn to Tyler. "So, what's up?" I attempt familiarity.

"Putting all the B.S. aside Steph, you are both known for that. I love it."

I just look at him waiting for a real response.

"Ok, we were so close to a deal. DBS would really like a chance to prove to you that we are the only choice for Mad Hatter globally."

The libations are delivered, giving me time to figure out a plan of attack. Surveying the room, I feel like I am on a T.V. show as an extra, plus it's displacing and eerily macabre that Tyler chose this place, a detective agency speakeasy to meet. Laure is right, it is an odd place for a business meeting. You would meet a heavy date here or go with girlfriends. No one in this room is talking business of any kind, but personal. *What is he up to?* Attempting to shake off my surroundings, I flash him a brilliant smile. Immediately he is drawn- in, like a fly to a web. "I'm all ears."

"Connecticut has turned, and our subsidiaries have secured six licenses between them including the only two lab licenses for the state."

As my stomach turns, my smile remains constant.

"In six months, we can break ground on the first lab facility, following the specs your husband designs. We have the capability to take the technology to every legal state, as well as covering Canada, Europe, and Central America."

I sip my concoction, meeting those green eyes of his with every inch of intent I own.

"We can patent the technology that is developed and dominate the market. Every edible company out there will be knocking on our doors."

For a moment, I think I am talking to Dr. E-vil, his voice is so out there, and the scene so slapstick. The look in Tyler's eyes is disturbing, I have a difficult time not placing my hand over his as a calming note. Laure is obviously affected by his tone as well.

"World dominance is certainly something we have fantasized about." I am purposefully flirting now, Laure is confused. "Look Tyler, your energy is", *unaccountable and creepy*, "spot on, but both Remy and I have been concerned about the innate cronyism imbedded in your ranks." I am channeling Remy now and, on a roll, however, as I finish my sentence his attention is drawn behind me, not the reaction I would have expected. I continue none the less, "How would H.S. feel about all new teams for Mad Hatter to interact with, a new generation of teams, hand- picked by Mad Hatter?" I add, with the hopes of drawing more information out of him.

From behind me, a familiar voice replies," I think it would be quite appropriate, if that is what you desire."

A wave of nausea courses my very core as the hair stands up on my arms, my face has gone pale. Laure is trying to keep up, her eyes search mine imploringly for a sign as I close mine for a necessary second to reconvene with my inner strength. I was not expecting this, and from the momentary look on Tyler's face neither did he. *Who knew it was a surprise party in reverse?*

Placing a hand on my shoulder H.S., Tyler's boss the CEO of DBS, is standing directly behind me, I can feel the front of his jacket against my back. *Ick, too close*, I swallow.

Laure has sensed my discomfort and takes the reigns as good friends do.

"I'm Laure Giovanni, you are?"

"Call me H.S., it's a pleasure."

"Ah", she rises to the occasion as if on that ridiculous "Bachelor" show. All systems on.

"Your timing couldn't be more affective. Won't you join us?" She continues enticingly.

That's an understatement. I brood, but outwardly I am chin up and smile on, inside *I am* **screaming**!

"Stephanie, always a pleasure."

"H.S." I reply as my hand is kissed and a little too wet for my liking, I restrain my instinct to wipe it off as dulled blue eyes wash over me.

Stuffed in a suit, the power shift at the table is obvious, "Where is that brilliant husband of yours? I was hoping to catch him off guard."

Before yesterday I would have never though that possible. "Remy had to leave early during the conference for an impromptu meeting on the East coast. I flew up to take his place." *At least that sounds true.*

"I had wondered why he did not make his lecture, quite a few people were disappointed. I hope it's nothing serious?" An awkward silence overcomes our group as we sample our drinks. The barman with impeccable timing saves me from myself. H.S. waves him away dismissively, surveying the party, "I prefer my drinks, uncomplicated."

I am beginning to sweat in my little black dress, time for a little girl's room visit. Eyeing Laure I grab my bag and stand up, "If you will excuse us, we are going to freshen up?"

"I hope I didn't scare you off?"

"If there is one thing the cannabis industry has taught me, it's to never be afraid." Smiling, we turn on a dime and saunter off.

Once we are safely in a stall together, Laure very quietly mouths, "What the fuck is going on? First this crazy bar and drinks with Mr. Green eyes gone over the edge and then this guy. Who the hell is he? Why are we here?"

"I have some CBD oil; do you want some?" *Now, I really feel like I'm in college.*

"I will take whatever you have at this point! I feel like I'm having a fucking heart attack!" She squirts three drops of the golden oil onto her tongue then unwraps a mint. "That tastes horrible."

"It's a sample, unrefined and unflavored. But it should calm you." I do the same then I squarely look Laure in the eye and take her arm as the bitter oil melts in my mouth. "Relax, I'm playing them. H.S. was a surprise for everyone. Did you see Tyler's face when H.S. came in?"

"Yeah, almost frightened, do they work with each other."

"Tyler works for H.S., his right- hand man, H.S. is the CEO of DBS Industries, they courted us heavily for a while remember and we called it off. Not a good fit."

"Ya think? I mean there are some strange cats in this industry, but something bat shit crazy is going on out there. Should we call Brennan and where the hell is laddington?"

"I neglected to give him a password. No, I think we can handle it."

"Great, I feel so safe now. What's you plan Steph?" She's serious and I sense impatience in her tone.

"Make them think we want back in the fold and see what happens. You take Tyler and I'll take H.S." I say after a quick pee.

"You're the boss."

After a look in the mirror, we walk back to the table. Both men seem to be giving each other back. Laure has placed herself directly in front of Tyler and she starts shaking him down. I notice Tyler checking her out, and there is a lot to check out. They would actually be a great couple, I could ship them. Laure has a bit of dark side to her as well, I remember the demons she fought during college. The bouts of depression and the brush with heroine. She is in a much better place now. In control of her life, I envy her.

Turning to my opponent, I begin, "So H.S. it's been awhile. Tyler told me about Connecticut. Congratulations."

Taking a moment to inhale my entire being without any conscious, he finally says, "You look ravishing, as always." Then breaks his stare to look off into the dark bar room as my skin crawls. "They should allow smoking in bars, don't you think?"

Looking around following his gaze, I add, "This room would be more believable with smoke." As I look back H.S. is staring at me with a look I cannot explain. Determined to stand my ground and play his little game, I smile back.

"You have had a difficult last couple of months." He states this a little too matter of fact for my taste.

"Yes, I'm sure you've read the papers. This industry is quite a challenge."

"Are you alright Stephanie?" He responds like a guy at his best friend's funeral.

"Yes, of course. I just realized I haven't really eaten today."

"Do you have plans for dinner? This place is lost on me." Reaching across the table H.S covers my hand with his. The difference in our age is obvious as his hand covers mine. Every ounce of discipline I own is being called upon to not pull away, not to flinch and not to look at Laure or Tyler. Forcing myself to look him in the eyes, *I can beat you.* "No, no plans." Before carelessly removing my hand to sip my drink.

Pulling out his cell phone H.S. arranges his car to meet us outside. "Let's go then, everyone."

Laure and I take the lead exiting the bar, once we are through to the street, I let the coolness of the night air replenish my strength. I suddenly feel liberated, *the oil must be kicking in.*

"Shall we take my car?" H.S. offers as a large black Bentley pulls up on que.

"We will meet you, what did you have in mind?"

"Venison. I can't resist wild game." He replies speaking into his phone before I realize he is requesting specific foods for dinner from someone on the other end of the line. "Tyler will text you the address, we have a stop to make on the way, the reservation will be under DBS." He closes the door and the Bentley drives off instantly. The air of authority at which H.S. commandeered the evening is absolute and a humbling sign of his power. Both the drinks and his arrogance have left a bitter taste on my lips. *Damn, it would be nice to know where they are going,* I scold myself as Laure and I walk to her car in a haze. Once inside with the doors locked, she turns on me.

"Ok, what the hell is going on?" Laure's voice is level but loud, her dark brown eyes are fired up.

"H.S. likes me. A lot."

"I can see that."

"Does he like me enough to hurt Remy, is the question?"

"Steph, that sounds crazy."

"Yeah, well my life is pretty fucking crazy right now!" My phone dings. *Saison, 178 Townsend St, China Basin area.* "We're going to Saison. You know it?" Her expression changes from pissed off to pacified.

"Really? Wow. Glad I made you change. I know it, I've never been there. It's ridiculously expensive, maybe the best restaurant in California."

"Always one to impress," I mumble as we push ourselves into traffic. The movement of the car is familiar and comforting, maybe because it's a small impenetrable space.

Remy is in front of me as if he never left, and this was all a dream. Waxing his board in shorts that are falling off, no shirt or shoes. Hair dripping down his back. Magnificent. The sinews of his lean body capturing the light. I can feel his warmth and succumb to my vision, as I close my eyes. Turning around he senses me, the light behind him golden, splashing sunlight in his eyes.

"Hey, sweetie."

Just hearing his voice soothes me. I say nothing but reach out and place my arms around his neck, our bodies barely touching. We kiss, slowly. His hands working their way up my back, bracing me against the world. Our kisses, warm and wet, my entire body starts to tingle. Lifting me onto the board, supported by wooden saw horses, I run my hands and tongue over his chest. Firm and taught with specs of salt water teasing me, like an offering of candy. Slipping my bathing suit bottom off, I'm burning, for him, his love, his safety, his strength. Laying me back on the board, we are one. Our bodies rising and falling in rhythm. Slowly at first, softly whispering our sighs. His beautiful face above me, surrounded by golden strands of hair, deep blue eyes mirroring mine, both of us wrapped in a desire that closes our entire world into another space and time.

"Steph are you alright?"

My eyes open, I am breathing a little hard. "Yeah, I think I fell asleep there for a moment." I turn my head toward my reflection in the passenger window and watch another tear fall down my cheek.

39

SPELLBOUND

The Bohemian Club is not a club for the feint hearted or small
inheritanced. A familiar face attends the door as he walks in.
"Renfry, nice to see you."

"You too Sir."

As a matter of family tradition, he continues to hold memberships in five of
the most prestigious and exclusive private men's clubs in the world. During his
fathers' day, men's clubs were necessary. It was common place for men and
women to socialize separately. Husbands and wives dining together on the
obligatory Friday night, leaving the rest of the week for "The Club", socializing
and networking.

Remembering well as a child the informality of it all, once you got past the
door. Men yelling obscene retorts and witticisms back and forth to each other in
the lounge. The unusual cross- dressing parties, famous musicians playing the
piano for man to man dancing and compulsory cigars. It was always in good fun
and a psychological challenge of the wits.

The burning of "The Care", the original burning man, where old woes and worries are burned to ash, still a yearly event. The two- week long camp- outs on the Russian River at The Grove, his family's cabin being one of the oldest at the club camp. *Times have certainly changed.*

Having finally attained "Old Guard" status after being a member for over forty years. He is a God among members now, they all know him by sight, if not reputation.

The six- story brick building in Nob Hill does not have the same behemoth weight it did when he was a child. Today the building covered in Ivy vines is obscured by the towering skyscrapers that surround it on the corner of Post and Taylor streets. Originally created by journalists and artists, it has enjoyed over one hundred and thirty years of exclusivity. The motto; "*Weaving spiders come not here,*" a Shakespearean echo in his mind. For that is precisely why he has come this evening, for information. Of course, no one gives information without receiving. But the brotherhood ensures it cannot be used against you, and that is uncommon in today's world and worth it's price of membership fee.

The door to the men's lounge is opened for him and he uses that time to quickly assess the room for advantageous cohorts. Wood paneling and book shelves always a respite from the modern world, it still feels like the turn of the century in here. Time has stood still, although he reminds himself, he is on a time schedule and cannot linger.

Spotting the Governor immediately both men acknowledge each other with a nod. Governor Vernon Macintosh has been good to California. He is no nonsense and has ears and eyes everywhere. Invests heavily in ground breaking pharmaceuticals and innovative tech. Both are insider's games, when you are dealing with fortunes, very little is left to chance.

Fording a path over to the Governor, several youngsters stand up to greet him. He is gracious to his admirers, with two thousand members, however it's not possible to remember all of their names.

"Vernon, how are you this evening?"

"Fine, fine and you? We haven't seen you for a while." The older Governor replies, extending his generously long legs out from under the clothed table.

"Yes, I've been travelling." Noting to himself, he still manages to attend a week out of the month while being based on the East coast.

"The cannabis industry seems to be luring you away." The Governor adds with a look of deprecation.

"That's an understatement, care for another?" Noticing the empty glass and nodding to the bar man.

"Yes, thanks."

"Vernon, you read the industry rags?"

"I like to keep my fingers in all the pies, yes." He is shifting in his chair as he replies with candor.

"I know you do. It's your strength, I admire that."

A humble nod is given. "What's on your mind?"

"Have you heard of anything unusual that might be relevant for me to be aware of?"

The valet sets their drinks in front of them on a linen napkin. Again, the Governor shifts in his chair, picks up his leaded glass and rattles his ice around with the appearance of a man deciding something. After a long pause, he responds dramatically.

"Maybe."

"Ah, very good." Placing his now empty glass on the table, he sets the bait, "Such a shame about Epi pen."

The Governor's large eyes look up intently. "EpiPen? How so?"

"Haven't you heard? Their patent is up this January it seems." This information is exchanged with the innocence of critiquing a film, "Looks like someone else will get to heal the masses."

"You don't say?" Vernon replies brushing off his slacks. "By the way, did you hear about the NEW club?"

"Hmm, no I don't think I have." He maintains neutral calm.

"No? From what I understand, it wouldn't be to your tastes."

It's not a lot but it's enough to go on. "Vernon, to your good health." Lifting his refilled glass to toast his brother in arms.

"Will you be joining us at the Grove this year?" The Governor asks.

"I wouldn't miss it."

Rising and walking into the bar, he notes the room is full, Cards are being played, chess, backgammon, darts. Holding court is a prominent comedian. *Must be a guest of a member, he looks too young to wait out the twenty-five-year waiting list for membership.* Time is of the essence, he must be on time for his rendezvous.

As an only child raised in fortressed mansions, sometimes the only comfort from what seemed like abandonment was found in the arms of the staff. *The secrets of the world are privy to the silent by standers.* Scanning the dining room, on route to the men's changing lounge, he follows the cavernous hall and becomes well aware of those bystanders. Circumventing a wave of members preoccupied with their conversational gossip, the club attendants stand aside to clear a path. Silent and stealth, eyes forward as their backs press against the wall, their priceless packages of newly buffed shoes, fresh towels and newspapers locked in their unyielding grasps.

The men's lounge is his best bet, and he is not disappointed. Among the Corinthian leather arm chairs, Dyson stands like a sworn praetorian. Without missing a beat, the burgeoning octogenarian crosses the room to greet him upon sight.

"Good evening sir, it's been awhile." The slightest hilt, of a southern accent still present in this man's infamous docile manner.

"Dyson, I only come here to visit with you, you know that." Gifting him five hundred dollars by carefully palming it to him while they shake hands.

Pocketing the cash, Dyson walks his honored guest over to an unoccupied club chair. The club has its rules, a member is welcome anywhere in the club at any time, however no one sits in the Men's lounge without Dyson's permission.

He feel's sorry for the jack asses that have insulted Dyson. *Every place has its hierarchy.*

Feeling the pang of mortality every-time he checks in with Dyson, as his once robust stout form has become fragile, now bent by the weight of wannabies. The smiling electrifying eyes of mischief he once knew, are paled and clouded over, but Dyson's spirit is commendable as always.

At the last board meeting, Dyson's employment was questioned, by newbies of course. He himself and the remnants of the Old Guard, squashed their pandering immediately.

"Let them sit out in the bar if they can't figure it out." Was the response of an elderly former Vice President of the United States. "This would be like any other club without Dyson," and that was that. No one questions the old guard, one of the perks of impending death.

Taking a moment to absorb his surroundings. Wood paneling, flocked wall paper, billows of cigar effluence. Bankers, politicians, remnants of the industrial age and creatures of the pregnant technological age, sitting side by side. They are all here. No one takes new money seriously unless you are a member. For some, it is all they have, families broken or gone, enveloped by frenemies, just the club and the indentured staff at home. It's quite sad, and a future he wishes terribly to avoid.

Dyson returns with a chilled glass of water and a glass of scotch on a silver tray, the finest the club offers. Turning on the Tiffany lamp beside his guest, he places the evening edition of the Times, another sad victim of technology, on his lap.

"Tell me, Dyson, what's been going on while I've been loitering around the East Coast."

"I don't know how you do it, Sir, my knees hurt just thinking about the winters out there."

"You my friend, will out- live us all."

Dyson laughs, his eyes playful and glowing, then he becomes very serious, lowering his voice to a murmur. "I hope not Sir, I don't think I'd be too comfortable here with all the newcomers."

"Nonsense, they need someone to keep them in line." He replies absent mindedly thumbing the paper.

"That's right! Couldn't have said it better myself." Dyson quietly chuckles, well practiced in the art of not drawing attention to himself.

Putting the paper aside and encouraging a shine, their eyes lock. "Maybe you can help me, Dyson?" He states, as his loyal friend sets up his shine station.

"Whatever you need Sir, you know that."

Looking around, he is familiar with everyone in the room, no one here is a threat that he knows of. Most of the men he is in company with, he has known for over 40 years, including Dyson, they were all young men initiated together. In a hushed voice he continues, "Some strange things have been happening lately."

Dyson looks up at this and very quietly replies, "There are definitely some strange conversations going on."

"How so?"

"Well, Mr. G had some guests from the Union Club a couple of weeks ago. You know, I don't play the status game Sir, but the gentlemen of that their club, are just not up to par in my opinion."

"Yes, I've heard that." Feeding his will to spy, "Go on Dyson."

"I only caught pieces of their conversation, but what I heard was enough to make me think."

"What would that be?" He asks, leaning in to his conspirator.

"They were talking about a hunting club, which is no new news, everyone here seems to shoot at poor innocent creatures they have no intentions of eatin. Ya'll need a lesson in bible study, my late wife's favorite song by St. Francis Assisi, *teach us to see your design in all of creation.* It's just lost on you folks."

Anyone who knows Dyson, understands, tolerates and to some degree admires the level of contempt he holds for the bad behavior of the entitled. Ironically, it is the reason he is so highly revered.

Pausing from his shine, Dyson looks up. "No Sir, they ain't hunting elk."

40

BEYOND RAGING WAVES

Paddling out into the whitewater, it's a big day with an even bigger beach break. The hammer sound of the crashing waves is primordial and sends a warning right down to his sphincter. Toe curling. Keeping his eyes on the horizon line when he can see it over the face of the never- ending washing machine of whitewater. The sky grows dark and brooding, but there is a promise of sunshine pushing him along though the break is unfamiliar and he is the only person out, two big no- no's.

Shaking the water out of his eyes on his board, he digs. The burn in his shoulders is deep, teeth grinding, his breathing is heavy and rhythmic, fighting the awesome power of the sea. Duck diving under the turmoil of wave face after wave face, he pops up to see the outside set forming, big and heavy. He has never seen waves this big from his belly. Scared for the first time in the water, really scared but muscle memory takes over as he paddles out through the abyss in defiance. Looking for a safe channel that doesn't exist on a beach break. Anticipating when the first monster will break, calculating where he should be, to not be engulfed. It continues to grow, a creature from the depths. A test. A punishment.

Keep paddling, he can't even look up for fear of what's in front of him but knows it's there. The enormous shadow now looms above him, a dark omen of death rushing toward the tide line. It sends shivers to his core. Looking back to the land over his shoulder in the attempt to line himself up with his marker. There's no beach! The endless sea in kaos surrounds him. Now he hears the suck, all encompassing, it's all he can hear, stomach caving as he sees the lip of a titan poised to drop with the finality of time.

Remy wakes abruptly, the infinite black of his surroundings cause him to recoil from the reality he had hoped to escape his dream to. *Am I still dreaming, is this a tsunami?* Eyes deluding his reality. In the complete dark, every one of his pores sweating, he is disoriented and can't remember where he is. Thankfully his other senses kick in, dense laborious air pressing on his skin as if at the bottom of a deep pool.

The birds of the night as maniacal as they sound, wash him in welcome comfort. At last, he exhales, gratefully leaning against the hillside he has burrowed into, like a wild animal desperate for shelter.

"Holy Shit!" Now he knows why all these people have gone crazy. Being thrown into the food chain, with nothing but the clothes on your back and a worthless cell phone is enough to make anyone crack! He pulls his cell phone out of his pocket and turns it on, for just a taste of his life, a light of hope, a reminder of who he is. The screen illuminates while performing a clever montage. His home screen is a picture of Steph he took lying on the beach in the Caribbean without her knowing. Her eyes are closed, she is lying on her back, the outline of her body, a soft landscape against the blue water. *She is so beautiful,* he closes his eyes. "Mother Fucker!"

Everything makes senses to him! As if all of a sudden, the lights are on! He knows WHO, he knows WHY and he knows HOW. *Taking the higher path, just went out the Mother Fucking window!* Turning off his phone with one last look at his woman, the screen goes dark, when an idea comes like a rushing tide, *maybe our phones aren't so useless after all?*

The jungle is alive and busy around him, rustling, digging, hanging, eating, killing. Remy is cooking up a plan, going over it a couple of times when he hears a big sound below. Not an average animal, he closes his eyes as if he could be any less distracted by more darkness and hears voices. *Human. Women.*

Magically, his eyes track immediately to flickering firelight below, faint at first but they are coming towards him. The branches below are too thick to make out any shapes in particular.

Quietly he climbs down about ten feet, using his ass and feet like some kind of genetically modified crab, digging into the soft musty earth just below the canopy, completely blind in every direction except towards the fire.

Taking up behind a large boulder, he sees a group of four women, much like Delta and friends, squabbling. The smallest woman seems to be the leader, she's Asian very petite and not looking happy. A rather long-legged, Cleopatra type is arguing with her loudly, the other two women are watching intently. One of them is older maybe in her fifties with gray-streaked hair, fit but remarkably older and larger than everyone else. The other is a toe head, almost six foot, definitely Scandinavian, she is model attractive in her twenties, very serious.

"Manaya, YOU are NO leader, you don't even care about tracking the OTHER WOMEN!" The fierceness in her voice is awesome, almost a growl.

"No, I'm not Sam. I am more interested in saving the women I live with than causing harm to someone I don't know." Her Eastern Indian accent is thick, Remy can tell she is choosing her words carefully while controlling her emotions. The two other women are standing behind her in solidarity as the firelight eerily shadows their faces.

"If we can get RID of the others, we can go HOME!" Cleopatra Sam spits out.

"Do you really BELIEVE that Sam? Do you really BELIEVE the words of someone who abducted you? Left you for dead and SHOOTS at you? Now keep your voice down, you're making us all targets." Manaya lowers her voice looking at the two women by her side, "Besides, we would be stronger if we banded together." They nod in agreement. The older woman makes a comment, Remy cannot discern, signaling the end of the argument.

From his vantage point, he can see that Delta and company have surrounded the squabbling group while they've been engrossed. Sam sees them now too.

"Fuck!" Cleopatra Sam spits out.

"Keep your voice down or I'll gag you." Manaya condemns, Remy likes her style.

"Too late for that." Delta's voice silences everyone. All four of Manaya's troupe assume a defensive stance in response.

Delta with Pitt at her side reveal themselves. Standing there like Hippolyta herself. *Impressive for a secretary.* Remy decides to wait this one out, it may be best if he is not on a side. Watching silently Arona, Ora and a woman he had not seen before slip out of the jungle and into view of the torch that is jammed into a rock crevice. No one speaks, the jungle becomes uncannily loud, he can feel the intensity of the unknown before him, the calm before the storm. Pitt looks like a top that has been wound too tight and is mirroring the energy of Sam. Delta turns to Pitt attempting to redirect her energy, for a moment, it looks like Pitt will stand down.

"WE out number THEM and THEY are NOT armed." Pitt harangues, ready to blow her top.

"That's not a reason to attack." Delta scolds, not taking her eyes off Manaya.

It is obvious to Remy, they have never met before. This is the kind of break they all need if it doesn't fall apart.

Manaya walks over to Delta. "We need to talk." She demands.

"Yes, we do."

They both walk near the torch and face each other. Sizing each other up, they sit in profile to Remy's position, which makes it difficult to hear their conversation.

All of the women are wearing fragments of their previous life, without shoes, it makes Remy really reconsider the uniform of the modern worker; The new gal from Delta's lot is actually wearing a vest made from a woman's gray pin-stripped suit. No sleeves, no collar, buttoned up the front without a shirt on underneath. Everyone has a phone, either strapped to their upper arm or thigh. *That makes nine.*

Pitt and Cleopatra, come back into focus. They are silently taunting each other, but perhaps they won't engage without their leader's direction. Both of them seem to be on the skids with their leaders and their insecurities inflate in front of Remy's eyes. It amazes him how women can be so like men and yet, so different at the same time.

This peaceful pow wow, goes on for about five minutes, when Pitt launches herself onto Sam, who had been shaking her fingers at the earth with anticipation. Both leaders, look at one another, Delta shakes her head with a scowl. They both stand, but neither attempts to break up the dust kicking brawl by firelight. The scene is ridiculous. The worst of man or in this case, womankind. Both families are standing side by side watching the spectacle. No one is pleased, no one is shouting or egging on a winner. They are all standing with dead eyes and tired hearts in the shadows of fire, like unearthly demons spreading discontent. Several minutes go by, head banging, hair pulling, knee kicking, vicious scratching as the two women curse uncontrollably at one another. At one point, Pitt moves to pick up a rock and notices, no one cares. She stops for a moment to look at their faces, they are frozen with disdain. This gives Sam the perfect opportunity to kick out Pitt's incredibly long legs and drop on her like a Sumo, knocking the torch to the ground and out. The pitch darkness takes them all, silencing everyone. That's when Remy hears it. The train is coming and they are ALL in its path!

41

RIPPLES

The wood-paneled room is seeping with color, large Tiffany chandeliers and period table side lamps illuminate the crevices of patrons as well as the first edition books that line the walls of this 150 year- old exclusive club.

Garrison Levitt the CEO of Global Bank has just arrived. *He is a pompous ass, from a bloodline of pompous asses.* He thinks to himself, remembering they studied together in the same class at Oxford and were not the best of friends even then. *He cheats, he steals and he lies. The perfect profile for international banking.*

Cheating at the club, is grounds for expulsion. In fear of disappointing his forefathers, Levitt chooses to be a sore loser, rather than tempt fate within the brethren. His resounding, whining complaints can sometimes be heard echoing throughout the halls.

With that in mind directing intentions on his prospect, he walks across the room purposefully. Just before catching Levitt's attention, he intentionally adds a small stagger to his gait and spills scotch on his hand, manifestly aware of his plan.

"Garrison?" A slight slur has been added for effect. Within seconds it is obvious the bait has been taken.

"Hello, old friend." The pompous English accent comes down hard on the D. "I haven't seen you, in some time. How are you?"

"Fine, fine… but I must say, Garrison, I'm a little disappointed with the newbies. I can't get a game of rummy going to save my life." Displaying his best look of condescension.

"Well, I always aim to please." Levitt replies, "Shall we go into the game room then?" He replies, pleased as a school boy with his good fortune, and his unexpected opponent's seemingly handicapped condition.

"That's the spirit, lead the way." Our provocateur entices as they make their way into the handsomely appointed game room with numerous card tables, billiards, and dart games. Opportunity is taken to reiterate his play at drunkenness, by knocking into another club member, a newbie and draining his drink on the young victim.

"I am so sorry sir, are you ok?" The youngster inquires as he makes a grab for the elder man's shoulder to steady him.

"Yes, quite," Is the corte reply to the fresh- eyed, bewildered and frightened forty– something as he recognizes his assailant as a tenured member.

Garrison Levitt capitalizing on his old friend's handicap, ignores the exchange and leads him to a dark table in the corner, "How's this ole boy?"

"Fine, who's dealing?"

"I will take the honor; would you like another drink? You seemed to have lost a bit on the way over?"

"Damn newbies they're a nuisance!"

"Anything wild?"

Pleased his opponent is already focused on the game, he spurts, "Ace of spades and queen of hearts." They play in silence for the first thirty minutes.

Losing two straight hands in a row to Garrison, he has now succeeded in cultivating a positively enigmatic mood for his host.

Time, for conversation. "Levitt?"

"Yes, ole boy?"

"Don't you ever get tired of the same old routine?" He solicits while vacantly staring around the room.

"Whatever do you mean?" Levitt Garrison replies, looking around to be sure no one is judging his lack of moral conduct before turning back to his pigeon.

"You know." He continues swishing his glass around like a tankard. "There comes a time when you've done it all… what's left?"

"It's your turn to discard."

Dropping an obvious feeder card onto the pile in the middle of the table and watching Levitt pick it up and lay all his cards on the table in triumph he professes, "Christ you got me again!" Simulating a whine, throwing down his cards, "Let's up the ante a bit? Give me something to work towards. Let's say ten thousand a hand?"

"Lovely, I'm meeting a friend at nine thirty, two hands, winner takes all?" Levitt replies with glee, his eyes infused with greed.

Now is the time to get what I came for. "Sounds good. I'll deal." Shuffling the deck, he realizes why he belongs to the club, but keeps participation down to a minimum, while likening himself to a gay friend, that is homophobic and throws the best card in his hand. "Seriously Garrison, what do you do for real fun, these days?" Touting a look of genuine discernment.

"Well now that you mention it," Garrison Levitt's eyes are zeroing in like a hawk about to strike, "Did you know one of our subsidiaries just claimed the patent for pharmaceutical synthetic cannabis?"

"Is that one of your new past times now?" He asks with humor, waving his hand in dismissal, "Yes we have been aware, of the backround presence of big banking in marijuana, funding research in alternative countries, while denying banking access to startups here in the U.S. Although, I must say you have done a good job keeping it from growing beyond your grasp by not lending or participating out in the open. Well played my friend." The last comment is said with respect to the card his opponent just picked up, but they both know the hidden meaning.

"I do tell you this as a friend, get out while you can." Levitt's voice is sing-song, he is really enjoying this, "Once our friends in the fed de-schedule, your new past time will be obsolete, just like all of those ridiculous mom and pops out there." He is absolutely gloating.

"That's probably why I'm looking for something new? Any ideas?" Ignoring taunts and staying focused, while repeatedly throwing down feeder cards, he wipes his hand clean.

"That depends on what you're looking for."

"A little danger would be good, everything is so God damn tame and watered down. Including this SCOTCH!" Heckling out to the barman he continues, "Sometimes I wonder why I get up in the morning."

Having finished his third drink, riding the wave of victory Garrison Levitt's usually pursed lips are noticeably more pliable, his uncommonly large hands easily holding his spread of cards. "What exactly are you looking for? Women? Drugs?", he lowers his voice, "Boys?" His voice just above audible, but a bit impatient.

"I don't know, maybe something out of the ordinary. The boredom is killing me!"

"This isn't the place or time, but… maybe I can help you."

Wonderful, he thinks to himself and loses the last hand.

42

BITTERSWEET FAITH

S aison is difficult to find for all its review hub bub on social media. Laure
parks on the main street outside the small alley it inhabits. The large brick
warehouse from the industrial age supports an obscene modernized glass
protrusion from the seam of bricks that previously shouldered the roof, it's an
abomination. Once inside, the casual atmosphere I am disoriented. "I thought
you said this was one of the best restaurants in town?" I ask Laure to confirm
we are at the correct destination.

"It is. Also, THE most expensive."

"Ok." *For San Francisco, that's saying something.* A woman greets us at the door,
again casually.

"We're with the DBS party this evening." I offer, feeling a headache
approaching that only one of our tea's or a good romp in bed could cure.
Having neither available the runner up is wine.

"Wonderful, please follow me." The denim clad millennial, drives us
forward.

We walk through the restaurant. The walls are lined with wood for wood ovens and made of brick and corrugated steel. Not what I would have imagined for a restaurant with this cache, it feels more like a low-end winery or an Urban Outfitters retail shop than a high- end restaurant. We are led passed a pair of impressively large and genuinely old, open barn doors that guard a kitchen stage, the pinnacle of the space. Upon stepping into the kitchen, the heat and energy created from culinary practice becomes contagious. I feel a lift.

We are sat at the only table in the kitchen with a bird's eye view of the chef himself and his minions. Lifting his head for only a moment to appreciate his newest devotees, who, unbeknownst to him have no idea who he is or what he does. I feel my attitude becoming brittle and edgy with each new wave of pressure in my head.

"A bottle of Domaine Weinbach 2008 Altenbourg Pinot Gris has been chilled for you." The average looking hostess posts like the weather.

The only thing I understand is Pinot Gris, so I nod, gratefully. Within seconds our glasses are filled by a poised waiter in white. I drain half of my water and at least that of my glass of wine.

"Easy girl." Laure playfully warns me, with due cause. I am perilously skimming the edge, she sees the warning signs. "What's next? How are you going to play this?" Prompting me, perhaps even a tactic of redirection.

"I have no fucking idea." I mean it. I'm lost, untethered and floating dangerously. Laure looks away, trying to conceal a smile in an attempt not to encourage my adolescent inspired mood.

The waiter comes back with a small plate of somethings, they look abstract and sculptural, *not sure about edible.*

"Amuse Bouche." The waiter announces placing the white plates with what now seems to be several oysters in front of me and a couple of red round balls, in a perfect French accent.

Once he recedes, I ask Laure, "Are you kidding me?"

"It does look like a mouth." She adds wryly.

"Good thing you lived in Paris, I can see you really picked up on the culture."
She laughs, so do I. The second plate contains something red, raddishy red, with nasturtiums.

"I guess they figure we ordered it by phone so there's no sense in telling us what it is?" I am playing, of course, an Amuse Bouche are simple little plates of lovelies to please the mouth. The food is amazing, Alice Water's -esque in its creation, Boulee' in conveyance. My headache is gone with the return of my focus after a few amused mouthfuls.

"Where do you think they went?" I ask Laure who is making a yum sound.

"I have no idea."

I could see Laddington sitting in his car as we walked in. I would hope he would have sense enough to call Detective Brennan if in the event something happens. I am wondering why he chose not to cozy up to the bar for a better view of our tableaux.

Taking a deep breath, I ask the inevitably hard to stomach question, "Laure, I may get, friendly with H.S. I need you to…" I can't think of the words, completely at a loss, my mind goes blank.

"To not freak out?" She asks, raising an eyebrow. "I can see the obvious tactic here, just one thing though? Do you really think it's safe to put yourself in his path, if he really is behind this?"

"If it's the only path to Remy?"

She stares at me for a moment silently. "Sweetie, I will do whatever you ask, but don't you think we should call the detective and let him know what's going on?"

"What would I tell Brennan? I'm just chumming the waters. Please keep Tyler occupied."

"I can do that." A smirk crosses her face as a second plate of modern art is placed in front of us.

43

COMFORT ZONE

The lights of the city flash in the Bentley windshield, casting shadows like a screening film in the backseat over his mentor's face. The same questions resurfacing, like pesky bugs that won't go away regardless of the time of day and how many stops are made, to distract him.

Who is this man? How far will he go? Fear alone keeps these questions locked up tight. Fear of failure, rejection, isolation, abandonment. For a grown man, these are difficult fears to wrestle with and it sits with him like a stone.

I could leave, he thinks to himself, *stop right now and just disappear. Go back to Egypt, blend in and most importantly, forget all of this.* Deep down, however, knowing there is no escape from *him* or the world he is now drowning in, he succumbs. The weight on his shoulders unbearable as he inquires, "Where are we going now?" feeling the inadequacies of his inability to predict the intentions of his mentor.

"Be still I'm thinking."

Turning to face the window, shamed, wondering if his game at the Wilson Bar was perceived. Not having enough time alone with Stephanie to allow her to glean the appropriate information from him, he is concerned now that the only person that understood his elaborate scheme, is sitting next to him.

After several minutes of guilty silence, realizing where they are, a small wave of temporary immobility claims him. The black car lumbers to a halt in front of one of the only mansions to survive both the earthquake and fires of 1906, The Union Pacific Club. A monster of late 1800's stone architecture that dominates Knob Hill. Attaining membership through birth has not eased the oppressive distaste he nurtures for this place or its members.

"Come in and be quiet." The icy stare is familiar, Tyler nods and follows.

At 8:30 in the evening, this place should look like a warm, welcoming English Manor, instead, the lamps glowing in the windows are wide unrelenting eyes against the stark building and are anything but welcoming.

Once inside the enormous lounge with gilded ceilings, crystal chandeliers and portraits lining the walls, they are encumbered by pretentious eyes following their path. His mentor is well known in this circle. Well known, unfortunately for ruinous actions. Several men previously thrown to the wayside turn their backs as they proceed into the luxuriant institution.

There was once a time, this was attractive. The thrill of power, so exciting. Knowing people were afraid of them was a kick. Now? Now he feels dirty. Closing his eyes at the bar to the realization, he has become one of them, Tyler's thoughts move inward. Drinks are provided, orders given. He is to, "Stay here, out of trouble." *That's a laugh,* he thinks to himself, *Oh no. The trouble father, has just begun.*

Turning his back toward the bartender and his drink, with the intent to form an invisible barrier in his mind to avoid eye contact with anyone, and at all cost avoid conversation, is futile. Waddling over like a gigantic walrus is the prodigal son of the former president of a prestigious investment firm. Obviously, not an athlete he is known for his exotic safari expeditions.

"Walter."

"Tyler? I didn't even think you were a member anymore. "Then he adds, "You're never here. I'm confused."

"Well we wouldn't want that now, would we?" Tyler mumbles lifting his glass silently for a refill. Purposefully turning his back on the glut.

Oblivious to any repulsion, the walrus squeezes in next to him. "That was s-ome bet." A forced Connecticut drawl slithers through his pinched lips.

Having no idea what he is talking about, Tyler utters a response barely audible, trying to ignore the bumbling intruder.

"My Fa- ther told me." Walter is thrilled he is privy to this information and cannot stop himself, "What d-id it cost you?"

Looking at him with zero comprehension, *a bloated khinzir,* now swaying to the emotionless muzak continually pumped into this relic of a place, Tyler just stares incoherently.

"Your b-oat, I mean y-acht."

"Jove's Gift?" Tyler responds surprised.

"It's going to be h-ard to give th-at up. Of course, I w-ould have given him a r-un for his money, had I been there. I'm an ex-cellent sh-ot."

"So, I hear," Tyler answers with a little more interest now, as this is news. Thinking it is not well known that he is the heir to his Father's fortune. In fact, he took his Mother's last name at a young age, to avoid social repartee.

No one at DBS and most people in their inner circles don't know, they assume he is an Executive Assistant, the grandson of a wealthy railroad magnet. His Mother an Egyptian heiress, bequeathed her dark complexion and Macedonian stature to him, both a blessing and a curse. A blessing because it allows him to meld into the back-round when necessary. A curse because he was the ONLY dark child in a parade of private higher education institutions, and never allowed to forget that he was the outsider.

Walter knows him from the club, both of them being dragged into the mire of status with their initiation into it, he is securely wrapped in avariciousness. Tyler has never felt comfortable. Mistaken as the help or an errand boy frequently, his foreign customs always apparent. They assumed inclusivity was unnecessary, as he offered no national networking, the basis to club's like these.

Having lived in Egypt most winters when home from school with his Grandfather, he was taught Arabic, Ancient Greek, and Coptic by the old man. Treating Tyler like his favorite Son.

Their family had somehow inherited the rights of the railway systems throughout Egypt, although the British built them. The story is fuzzy at best, they were never wanting for anything and lived like royalty.

Tyler's Mother Bahiti, the only Daughter of thirteen was the light of his Grandfather's life, his true "Fortune". She met his father at Harvard while she was studying ancient languages, he was a law student. She was strikingly beautiful, large almond shaped green eyes with the darkest lashes framing them,

Like his Grandfather, she was kind and loving, graceful, her movements that of a dancer and her gentle laugh contagious.

The day she died, his father blocked the last of the little contact he had endeavored with his only child. Schooled abroad, warehoused with his Mother's family, sent to camp or summer school. Presents were mailed and cards were exchanged unceremoniously.

After graduating from Oxford top of his class, H.S. finally sent for him, having remarried three times by then, the memory of Tyler's Mother surviving only in his own heart. Impressed by spectacular academic prowess, he was offered an internship at DBS while attending business school at Harvard. Mortality in question, Tyler could see it in his father's eyes, this was not about blood bonds, it was about inheritance, at least he knew where he stood.

The desperate need for his Father's attention, approval, and love drew him in like a rat to a trap. *Why do we seek that which we can never attain?*

Tyler did everything asked, without question, for *him*. Not out of love or loyalty, but the need to be accepted, always the inevitable dangling carrot.

His Grandfather died before he graduated from Harvard, his Uncles inherited the fortune but he inherited his Grandfather's homes in Cairo and Armana, as well as his dahabeeyah, beautifully restored. Gifts full of treasures from ancient pasts. A refuge from the world.

The words of his Grandfather ringing now like a bell, "Our choices decide our happiness. That is why no choice is simple."

Looking at Walter, also the product of a twisted society of megalomaniacs, continually engaged in a boundless attempt to dominate everything, he orders another round and purrs, "Tell me Walter, what did you hear exactly?"

44

MONEY GO ROUND

Friedland Beckett is a heartless son of a bitch. Continually tracing blue blood back to the May Flower is his favorite pastime, if he's not talking about himself, it's because he's eating. That thought brings a noticeably rare smile to his lips, remembering that the only reason Beckett is Chairman of The Park, is because *he* himself, didn't want to be.

Catching Friedland's eye, they silently move to a quiet table in the far corner of the club's main bar, filled with the usual suspects, loitering about the men's club.

Looking around he considers how outdated this scene is, one would expect men to be wearing evening kit. Questioning why so many people feel the need to fill their lives with pointless nostalgia? Nostalgia, as he understands it, is for people without imaginations, he quietly concludes, his smile replaced with obvious contempt as the world now freshly judged, seems right again.

"This *is* a surprise," Beckett states with guarded interest, and settles into the leather club chair.

"Yes, well I'm full of surprises."

"I know that look, what are you up to?" Beckett cuts to the quick.

"Just following protocol, Friedland."

"Hmm, what protocol would that be?" Eyebrow cocked he prepares himself for anything.

"I'm surprised you are so ill informed." Smile simmering as a 50 year- old Speyside scotch is deposited in front of him, thinking, it's British and a bit too traditional, but it's the best they have here at The Union Pacific Club.

Beckett's eyes narrow with scorn. "I'm listening."

Purposefully pausing to control the power in the conversation, he confirms his belief that people become slack and useless once they're comfortable in your presence. Then only after a long draught of scotch does he continue, "It seems I've lost someone dear."

"Hmm, yes, that I know." Friedland's eyes sparkle with delight to have plundered the news on his own, "Have you delivered your yacht yet?" Beckett adds with amusement while folding a linen napkin into a tent absentmindedly.

"I have made all the arrangements." He confirms inconsequentially before adding, "And some others too." Just to see if Beckett takes the bait.

"Hmm, really? Do tell?"

"Let's just say I will be prepared for open season tomorrow."

Beckett's response is silent, just a raise of the eyebrows while he sips his ghastly gin and tonic.

"A real dandy too." He adds before getting up to leave.

"Before you go." Beckett implores somewhat confused.

"Yes."

"You should know, there have been inquiries for membership." His large lips straddling a huge cigar. The obstruction causes him to mumble.

"It's a closed club Beckett, until death do we part." His temper rises with impatience.

"Yes, I know. But all the same, there have been, inquiries."

"Who?"

"Of all people." Beckett replies slowly with no attempt to hide his amusement, before settling back into the comfort of his chair and continuing, "Miles Venery."

45

SENTIMIENTOS

The phone rings only once. "Horace? I know it's late but I have something that might interest you."

"I never sleep you know that. I'm all ears." The baritone voice full of warmth and amusement has through the years been a grounding device for him.

"Can you meet me at the club in an hour?"

"This must be good."

He says nothing knowing silence excites him.

"I'm on my way."

Horace Mendell, a man as large as his reputation, owns one of the largest conglomerations of news agencies in the world. Magazines, newspapers, online editorial sites, history channels, as well as radio and television news networks. Some people collect stamps, Horace collects news organizations.

Sitting in the lounge of the Bohemian, an institution created by newsmen, recalling with particular relish when Horace's parent corporation Global Diversities went head to head with a subsidiary of DBS, ironically. There were clear lines drawn; A subsidiary of DBS was lobbying to own and regulate all solar collection.

The bill they were trying to impose in key states to first gain momentum, clearly included regulating solar panel systems already in use and all subsequent systems installed. Literally, anyone who had in the past paid or in the future intended to harness the sun through solar collection would be a built- in client base.

It was the same old shake down, the backers of the bill, were to be trustees and stock holders, collecting money on the backs of the voiceless. What would be next, air? Someone had to point out the absurdity of this ruse to the public, so actions could be taken. Horace Mendell took that role seriously, assigning teams of reporters to investigate the purpose, implications and the outcome this bill would have on society.

Lighting a cigar, he nods to familiar faces, contemplating the fact that most large corporations would fail ethics and morality tests under a microscope, whether a corporation is public or private, laws are in place to promote their long- standing prosperity. Loopholes exist for tax, finance and organizational purposes, guaranteeing their proliferation. The same cannot be said for the individual. The in-balance in society is now at an obvious tipping point.

An insatiable evening at this very club with Noam Chomsky over brandy, what seems like eons ago, changed his disposition forever. Eloquently Noam argued, "The current political-economic system is a form of plutocracy, diverging sharply from democracy if by that concept we mean political arrangements in which policy is significantly influenced by the public will." He recalls Chomsky continuing to site John Dewey, "Gentlemen, short of industrial workers being masters of their own fate, and all private and public institutions coming under public control, politics will remain the shadow cast on society by big business."

Thirty minutes later, Horace strides in at least a head higher than anyone in the bar, wearing an open, custom made Brooks Brothers overcoat as easily as a bathrobe. His imposing size a forewarning to his mental acumen, at his most calm, he can be frightening.

They went to school together abroad as boys, their childhood tribulations and victories bonding them for life.

With a wave to the bar- tender, Horace embraces his old friend. "Why didn't you tell me you were in town?" Horace complains immediately, taking a chair.

"Initially I had planned to stay for only two days, I didn't even open the house." Referring to his family home in Nob Hill.

"Not acceptable!" Horace's voice booms filling the cavernous room, chiding his friend smiling, over a glass of Glenmorangie scotch that he supplies the club with personally. "What is it, Miles? Although it fits you, you are not normally so… mysterious."

"We have suffered several damaging editorials this last six months." Miles begins matter of fact.

"It wasn't me, old friend," Horace replies with raised brows.

"Yes, I know. It goes further. A company we have been attempting to acquire has suffered the same. This can, of course, be expected while a merger is in process."

Horace nods, wondering why Miles is bothering him with these tedious details.

"I flew to California to meet with the principals of a small cannabis company several weeks ago, they are small but their potential is unequivocal. I arrived the night before the planned meeting. Enjoyed a sunset drink in my suite and didn't wake up for two days." *That got his attention.*

Staying his drink mid- sip, and stiffening his broad back, Horace demands, "You were drugged?"

"It would seem so. A day and a half ago, one of the principals disappeared."

"They are linked?" Horace asks.

"Definitely. Coincidently, an old friend of yours was negotiating with them a year ago as well. Oddly enough with all the bad press, they are still attempting to do so."

Eyes twinkling with excitement like Father Christmas, Horace steers his glass to the table, the dim light of the room hiding signs of his age. "Send me everything you have, don't leave out any details, names, times, places, and most importantly your instincts. Do you understand?"

"Yes, with pleasure my friend." Chuckling at Horace's new found concern, before continuing, Oh, I almost forgot, have you heard of the new club?"

"I hear it is very exclusive, with a life pact at initiation."

"Really, what type of club is worth your life at initiation? I think it's a ruse."

"Who said it was the member's life?"

Eyes widening with intrigue. Miles is struck speechless.

"These are crazy times. Just send the details." Horace rises to his full height with a stretch. "I have some calls to make, send me everything within the hour, by messenger not by email."

"Horace?" Miles calls out, but when the Maverick turns back, Miles can't think of a thing to say. Horace nods and resumes his departure.

Texting his driver to pick him up outside, Miles then sends a short text to Stephanie Beroe, *Are you available for a phone call? Important.*

46

THEY MOVE ON THE TRACKS OF NEVER ENDING LIGHT

While the waiter pours water into my glass, the inevitability of what I need to do becomes apparent. Before I can verbalize this to Laure, H.S. and Tyler saunter through the doors of La Saison, I ready myself.

"Smiles on," I say to Laure, drawing her attention to the two men that have suddenly filled the room to capacity.

"Ladies, so sorry to have kept you waiting. How is the wine, Stephanie?"

"It's lovely H.S. thank you," I reply, the curtain is up and the show has begun.

With a nod to the chef, our companions for the evening sit down as waiters place napkins on the men's laps.

Tyler is curiously staring at me when Laure opens the conversation about France and food as the third array of dishes are deposited. This time the waiter clarifies the chef's culinary intentions, "Lapin tenderloins infused with truffles, and ris d'maison, our house specialty."

Laure mouths rab-bit, to me silently from across the table. I can make out the rabbit all by myself thank you, but sweet breads are really not my favorite. I am sure they taste delectable but animal pancreas? It's just not my thing. H.S. on the other hand, has not taken his eyes off the plates, this is definitely HIS thing. What a surprise? I place one of the small helpless rabbit morsels on my plate so I can push it around to keep up appearances.

Noticing Laure's empty plate with a momentary lapse of concern, H.S. turns on her, "Not hungry?" His tone is that of an offended parent.

"I am a vegetarian." She replies without apology.

After a millisecond of scrutiny, H.S. calls the ever, attending waiter over, "Have the chef create a vegetarian menu for my guest."

"Yes, sir."

"My apologies, I did not know." He offers, smiting Tyler from across the table as if it's his fault Laure is a vegetarian.

"The rabbit is delicious H.S," I add to keep the ball rolling. "So, you have my undivided attention, **woo me.**" Both Laure and Tyler look at me, but I have made my point and now have his undivided attention.

"Hmm, yes." H.S. replies with a smirk at the corner of his rabbit filled mouth. "We have begun construction on the extraction lab in Connecticut already, and we have just secured a property here to cover the west coast operations, with intentions of breaking ground within ninety days."

"You have begun construction? Based on Remy's specs?" I inquire innocently, concealing my anger. Knowing Remy had no idea this was happening.

"Yes, of course."

"You are very sure of yourself," I state, all too comprehending my double entendre. I am fully aware that the state of California, having just legalized recreational Marijuana, is a flurry of pro marijuana organizations and anti-marijuana organizations brawling in the dirt for control over local input on regulations. From what I understand, if a city or county had not regulated by March 1st, (2 months ago) the state would regulate them blanket style. This fear of state regulation caused most cities and municipalities to place a rash ban on growing, selling and distributing MMJ by patients and organizations. The local police have only been too helpful in enforcing the ban, shutting down companies and caregivers that have been in business for years, as well as confiscating and arresting individual patients. It's a tumultuous hotbed and the reasoning behind our staving off licensing our products in California. I would not be investing in property until a decisive map of allowable areas and restricted areas has been defined. I am sure he knows something I don't.

"Yes. Very sure." He replies devouring me with soulless eyes.

I reach for my wine glass and continue. "Where is the property here?" I inquire, while as gracefully as possible, pull my legs out from under the table and cross them in front of H.S.

Involuntarily his mouth stops chewing as he consumes my new stance before he continues, "It's near market, not far from here. I can drive you by after dinner if you would like to see it?"

"Perhaps tomorrow?" I reply off handed. Knowing full well what his true intention is.

"Unfortunately, tomorrow I leave early in the morning."

"That should be some hunting trip?" Tyler interjects disrupting his employer's rhythm.

H.S. says nothing, calling the waiter over, "Another bottle of wine." He demands.

"Yes, sir."

The waiter leaves taking the utterly vacant plates with him as Tyler persists, "Where exactly is your hunting club meeting this time, H.S.?" There is an air of cat and mouse legible on Tyler's handsome face.

"If I told you, dear boy, I would have to kill you." H.S. replies with a smile that terminates the conversation instantly, dropping his napkin on the floor as the plates are brought out for round four.

I excuse myself, glancing over to Laure for her to remain. In-perceivably she acquiesces as I leave the table to her, now sensing eyes following me out of what seems now like Hell's kitchen. I am a model on a runway sensing prying eyes determined to violate my person and start hyperventilating.

I only see the door in front of me, my hand pushing it open, I hear only my breath, no sounds of clinking silver, or extraneous chatter. Finding the same stall, I just visited, I sit down and close the door. Gripping my borrowed designer bag, clinging to it like worry beads. *Now what? Are you going to go home with this monster?* I start rubbing my face as a tear escapes. *Don't you dare!* I take a deep breath, letting the exhale channel through my toes, fingers, and head as if I was in a yoga class. Closing my eyes for strength, "Ok I can do this." I say as a reinforcement to myself, my head resting on the cold stall.

I see Remy in his yellow surf trunks with white hibiscus flowers, leaning over an open drawer of the dresser in our room at the Grand Cayman suite. Just seeing him, his form and weight, gives me inner peace and resolve. My body relaxes;

"Try not to miss me too much." He said playfully, noticing I was following his every move.

"Do none of these women like to fish? I asked, like a child not invited to a birthday party.

"I don't know what these women do. If you don't want me to go, I won't. I'm just playing along here."

"I know. You should go, it will hone your killer instincts." I encouraged, feeling every bit as trite as I sounded. The early morning light had yet to make a seam in the curtains next to the bed of our suite.

"You want to braid my hair for me?" He asked as I felt the indent his body made sitting on the bed next to me.

"Sure," I grabbed a hair bungee from the side of the bed and sat on my knees as I finger combed his hair back in comforting silence. I was just wrapping the bungee around his golden braid, Remy turned around and looked at me.

"You know if this deal goes through, we would be able to afford this kind of luxury." He said, his intent hazel eyes fathomless.

"Yes, I know."

He kissed me long and steady, then he pulled away, moving the hair gently off my face, "I love you."

I could feel his words molecularly absorbing into my marrow, "I love you too." I whispered back with a tear falling from my cheek as he walked out the door. Dropping back into bed on my tummy, feeling grateful for this incredible man I had dared to love.

I could not have been asleep for more than twenty minutes when I was awakened by the feel of his hand running along the nave of my back. The sun now creating a wedge of light onto the floor of our room.

"You missed me." I managed, barely waking from a dream still on my tummy. Not caring why he came back, but glad he did. I melted into the bed as he gently folded the sheets back and continued down the length of my body, the break in the curtains now creating a blue glow on the floor, heat growing rapidly in my body with every caress. My skin reacting to the slightest nuance of his touch, as I became fully awakened. A gentle groan escaped my lips as he slid his hands between my legs. Tenderly arousing me, I began to move in rhythm to his touch. Inserting his fingers, I was taken to a nether world, moaning with each push, gripping the sheets below me. Unaware of my surroundings, a captive. My breath became heavy as I was driven to glorious climax, writhing on the bed like an oracle before premonition. Feeling the heat of Remy's body moving in behind me, now beginning to rub up against my back, matching my rhythm. The touch of his absolute hardness behind me further propelled titillating waves through my body. Lowering himself for penetration, I had all I could do to control my desire, when an unfamiliar scent paralyzed me. Instantly, I scrambled out of bed and on to the floor into the light, slapped with the cold reality of my actions.

Startled back into my bathroom stall, I realize Laure is knocking. I recognize her shoes below the draped cloth privacy curtain.

"I'll be right out."

Quickly gathering my thoughts and things I walk out to the mirror facing me, in shame. Laure is reapplying lipstick, one eye on me.

"You ok?"

"Yes, I'm fine."

47

START SHOOTIN'

Th**ese freakin flood lights, rock this carnival ride!"** Chris yells over to him on the train like a tween at his first coed dance, it's embarrassing.

"Whatever guy, just remember no casualties today. We're hired to scare them, no kills."

"Yeah right."

"No seriously, the big wigs come in tomorrow and they want everyone available for their opening day. Crazy mother fuckers. Just don't give'em any reason to replace us."

"What's that supposed to mean?"

That gets his attention, he ignores Chris and feigns reloading, but the writing is on the wall for the peones, he thinks to himself as the newly installed infra-red on the tracks below them continue to systematically illuminate the night time jungle in their headgear without alarming anyone below in the park of their arrival. It's the latest black operative technology, creating the affect that the train is coming out of nowhere in the dark. They get to test all of the good shit out before it goes to the field for testing. It's a perk. What the rest of his team is not aware of, is word came down from the top that brand new biped drones have been shipped.

His crew has already been downsized by half and the remainder will be trained in controller operations. *We are being replaced by machines. They don't want us on the ground anymore, too many accidental shootings, fires, traps. What the hell! What do they expect? Give a dozen guys serious hardware and leave them on their own, shit's gonna happen.*

There is enough track to cover most of the captive area below, however, some nooks and crannies of underbrush and rock overhangs still exist, that is what the dogs are for. His team is forbidden to engage one on one with the feeders. Drones don't think, like his buddy Chris but, drones can be programmed not to kill and his men get so damn jacked up on adrenaline, the only way back, is to kill. The last week had been a disaster, three losses, and he has to answer for these assholes.

His job is to keep the targets alive for the big wigs but keep them scared and divided. Having completed two tours in Iraq, three tours in Afghanistan, and numerous operations he could only guess as to where his squad had been inserted, Jo has pretty much seen it all. That's why he likes this job, little to no direct contact. Some roughing up, threats and good old fashion containment, that justifies the hefty salary without guilt.

Being a soldier is all he knows, it was the only thing he was ever good at. Failing school miserably, socially inept, adolescence was brutal. The best day of his life was the day he walked into the recruit office; his mother's suggestion. She loved him, he knew that, but she didn't understand him. They had always been on their own, he was her "little man". Moving from place to place, never settling in or belonging anywhere, changing apartments to stay ahead of rent due. Life had been unpredictable and insecure.

Unable to save his mother from a stray bullet at a movie theatre in Colorado while he was on a tour, that was a turning point for him. It didn't matter what he did or where he went after that, as long as he could maintain glorious isolation. Alone is better, no attachments, no expectations.

The eleven guys he lives with and has command of on the island, are a bag of nuts. Half can follow orders, the other half are trouble, he has learned to distance himself from all of them.

It's a good gig, he has more money than he has time for. The train is his detail, as well as coordinating ground coverage, no drone can do that. The view from above makes him feel renewed and clean, the responsibility he carries is important, regardless of his directives. Let's face it a guy his age, with no skills for civilian life, would find himself with a bullet hole in the side of his head.

"I don't see a god damn thing, do you, Jo?" Chris whines from behind.

Jo presses the DE -celerator of the train with a finger on the tablet screen, "We've got something up ahead. Not sure what I see."

"Yee ha! I see em! Looks like we got ourselves a little party. Have to do something about that."

Jo com-links to the base station, the exact GPS location of the group they have spotted. Within minutes five men are dispatched to the area, three men with dogs, and two others armed with flame throwers.

"I say we just blast the area over their heads!"

"Alright on three, two, one…" The sound is incredible. Both of them filling with adrenaline and the maniacal behavior it breeds, like junkies. The rifles they are using are AR-15's, the epidemic of bullets draw a line in the canopy, cutting and tearing small trees and brush in half like a divine wrath.

The small group of women below the objective line are scrambling for any cover on hands and knees. Hiding behind trees and rocks from their covert captors. The only light discernable from the ground is the detonation of the gun powder from the train.

"This is going to be good," Jo says out loud to himself.

The sound of the oncoming dogs, barely audible from the East as they watch the pack of women below carefully starting to move away, like a group of ants they have just thrown water on.

A drip of saliva is caught at the corner of Chris's mouth, his excitement levels are so high the euphoria can only be quenched by one thing. *Who will it be this time?* He set's his sight and peers around at the frightened captives, all women, barely clothed. With the loss of canopy, he can see their eyes, *terrified and fuckin beautiful! The tall dark one with dreads behind the tree*, "She looks so fuckin proud."

Delta, as silently as possible, directs the women to scatter in different directions with hand signals. All of the women working as a group, against an unknown enemy. It would be easy for a stranger to perceive her calm reserve as pride. She's not even sure where she picked up these survival skills. Certainly, her up- bringing could not be credited. It was important not to lose contact with Manaya. The last women standing, face each other.

"Where can we meet next?" Delta calls out from her behind a tree, risking everything for a hope, yelling over the onslaught of fire.

"The river mouth, the mango trees. Dawn." Manaya yells back, before stealing off into the brush.

Delta stands there for a moment watching her potential ally disappear. A little too exposed, more concerned with their future than her safety. The dogs are getting closer she needs to pick a direction. For one excruciating moment, fear grips her. Indecision manifests itself. She is frozen.

Unable to see the infra- red mark made by the rifle on her back, standing there in the darkness presumably alone, she couldn't imagine why anyone would want to kill her. Unable to act, she grips the tree she begs protection from, like a child unable to let go of their parent in a strange crowd. Time is standing still, seconds are an eternity when a horrifying scream breaks the night.

Oh my god, which way is it coming from? She thinks to herself while wiping tears from her vision. An agonizing sound accompanied by the familiar smell of burning flesh. *I have to help her!* is the last thought she has when without warning the mark on her back moves up to her head, the silent knock of death.

The shot rings out, "You, crazy asshole! No casualties remember?" Jo screams at Chris while accelerating the train to see what the hell happened with the fire brigade.

What part of NO CASUALITIES, don't these morons understand? "God Damn it! I have to answer for your shit!", he cracks his neck, rolling it from side to side.

"Listen, Stevie Wonder, there was someone else there, and I want a piece, go back!"

"You are an adrenaline junkie," Jo states, rising from his seat in front of Chris, "**and** you are letting it cloud your vision." This is stated while walking the four steps over to where Chris is sitting, the look on the underling's face changes quickly from anger to intimidated. Jo continues, "We are NOT members of this club!"

The train car slightly glows in infrared mode as the tram lurches forward,

Chris can feel the ominous weight of Jo, who is now standing behind him. Removing his hands from the gun locked into the mount in front of him Chris holds them up in surrender.

"Don't forget your place." Jo ends the conversation through gritted teeth, desperately attempting to control his own anger, as the train engages in autopilot, a default protocol, moving slowly out of the clearing towards the glow of burning trees.

Jo immediately sees two men casting shadows from a small burning mound on the ground that can clearly be seen from above. The underbrush and several trees are also on fire.

"God damn it!" He spits out, grabbing the com-link. "What the hell happened here?" The smell of flesh fills the train.

"I dun-no," Jerry replies from below through the monitor, his rectangular head in shadow of the flames. "She just stopped running away and started running AT me. Crazy bitch! By the time I took my finger off the trigger of the flame thrower, she was toast."

The charred remains of the women curled on the ground, looks like something from Hiroshima.

"You idiot, that's four in two days. Tomorrow is open season!" Jo reminds them. "Two club members are going to be pissed! SHIT! Who was she?"

"That's the thing, they were ALL here," Jerry complains.

"Are you sure? All of the women?"

"Well not all of them, but both sides."

"That's interesting. Who was she?"

"The older one with gray hair."

"Yeah, the one we took outside that bar." The other merc adds.

"Wrap it up, you morons."

48

PEOPLE JUST AIN'T NO GOOD

While Laure excuses herself, Tyler's eyes follow her lean body out of the kitchen and into the restaurant. Ignoring the tension between himself and his mentor-father, while he ventures a look around the institutionalized eatery, he realizes the craving signs of genuine humanity; Real people in real places, eating REAL food. The ten-thousand-dollar suit begins to feel confining, as he loosens his tie. *It's all a trap.*

"You want to tell me what's going on in that pretty little head of yours?" The foreboding tone matches the look of disgust on H.S.'s face.

"I have no idea what you're talking about."

"Don't tempt me Tyler. I am in no mood."

Tyler has seen this look before, actually, he has seen it so much, it has no effect. *I am not one of the office boys you enjoy frightening into submission on a daily basis, I don't give a damn.*

"Your little game at that bar did not go unnoticed," H.S. replies while scraping the last morsel of duck from the plate with his fork with the determination of a starved prisoner. "**You** are no match for **me**. Be careful boy, you're testing my limits of progenation."

Tyler, sits back in his chair, surveying this man, they do not look alike, H.S. is a bloated younger version of Jimmy Swaggert, stuffed in a suit, his cologne overpowering and rude.

Together they have taken down monopolies. Countries themselves lying barren in their wake of unquenchable greed. Conscience stowed, he played the role of freedom fighter, waving the flag of avarice and corruption. Ignoring consequences, excited by the rumination and fallout, feigning invincibility. Striking forcibly, all in the name of conquest. Years of anger well inside him, rising in his constricting throat, but he maintains outwardly calm, no stranger to the game and with nothing to lose…Tyler has learned from the best.

"When is it enough?" He asks leaning in over the table.

"Not tough enough to stick it out with the big boys?" H.S. retorts, unsurprisingly ignoring the question with port glace' dripping from his chin, eyes barely looking up from the plate, as a rare thin smile spreads over his lips.

"Is there nothing sacred to you? Love, devotion, honor?" Tyler ventures a last attempt, emotionally barre.

"You're talking nonsense, the drivellings of an old man. I shouldn't have kept you in Egypt for so long, it ruined you." H.S. replies, waving the waiter over to remove the plates as his napkin drops to the floor.

Lowering a shaking head, desire turning to resolve, Tyler stands, then notices the ladies returning to the table from behind H.S. unnoticed. For an instant, Tyler registers surprise on his father's deplorable face, as if in a million years, his father could never imagine he would walk out on him.

I've got you.

49

SANTA MARIA, DEL BUEN AYRE

The venison dish placed in front of me upon our return from the ladies room, is the only food I have recognized all night. Laure has a plate of risotto with mushrooms in front of her and seems pleased.

"Stephanie, how are things going with your expansion?" H.S. asks while placing a large piece of meat in his mouth, unaware and unconcerned with the splotches of juices littering his jacket, shirt, and tie.

"We've had a couple of set- backs this month, mostly from the press fabricating stories." I watch his response waiting for a sign of complicity to no avail, "But all in all, expansion is on schedule. Remy and I decided to not take on any new territories until our present licensee's roll out products and maintain a schedule." *Now is as good a time as any to just put it out there.* "Tell me H.S. why are you still interested in Mad Hatter? What makes us stand out over all the other edible companies out there?"

"First, I don't take no for an answer." Pausing from his bacchanalian trance for a moment, "Second, I admire your passion." He adds, leering as he sits back in his chair. "There is nothing worse than a passionless person. Don't you think?"

Did I just see him look toward Tyler with that comment? Although Laure and Tyler are deep in conversation about France in French, they are both straining to follow along. I place my fork and knife down on my plate and push it away, instantly our waiter removes it.

"Not hungry?" H.S. asks perfunctorily.

I could strangle him! What would Remy do in this situation? He WOULD strangle him! Attempting a different tactic, I'll go with ego… "What do you do H.S., when you're not ruling the world?"

A strange smile appears momentarily with his answer, "Hmm" He takes a moment considering my question while studying my face ad nauseum, before replying, "I collect wives and hunt exotic animals."

"Isn't that one and the same?" I reply. Laure almost spits out her wine.

"There it is, that passion again. That is what separates you from other edible companies."

Touché'. "Tyler how long have you been slaving for this man?" I ask with unprecedented humor, camouflaging my disgust.

Tyler is silent for a moment with a look to H.S. before he replies, "I began as an intern while I was attaining my MBA from Harvard."

His eyes are egging me on, so I go with it. "I noticed you are always the youngest executive in the room. Has that been challenging for you?"

"Yes, it has." Tyler's response is quite natural and immediate now. His reserve always insinuating a high intellect.

"That is exactly our concern," I say with dramatic pause, silencing the table.

"Nonsense, you can pick your own teams, and have your own division of personnel for integration." H.S. intercedes, grumpily, like a man child.

I have stumbled onto something. "Ultimately," I continue, "we would still need approval for budgets, marketing, development and funding for R&D from the old guard. Remy is most concerned about potential conservative, "in the box" corporate limitations. No offense, but there are a lot of stuffed shirts on your staff."

Laure's mouth is open, but I see a glimmer of amusement from Tyler. H.S. has finally wiped his dripping mouth while snuffling snot at the same time, a disgusting repetitive habit, but he is not at a loss for words.

"Those stuffed shirts have managed to develop DBS into a top 50, fortune

500 company. They may not be stoners, but they still have some tricks left."

"Don't get me wrong H.S. both of our companies have strengths and weaknesses that we bring to the table. We know what your strengths are... but what are your weaknesses?"

Sitting back like Java the Hut he announces, "I don't believe we have any."

Obliviously stating his greatest weakness, he continues with a slight raise of his brows and asks, "What are yours?"

I sit back in my chair throwing my head back with a pause before continuing honestly, "I don't think Remy and I were ever meant for the business world. We weren't born to be negotiators." Looking to Tyler I add, "We were born to be conduits of life's deepest emotions and sensations, artists nurturing our muses by isolating them from the mundane." Tears well in my eyes, mirroring the deep sadness possessing me, "We have developed the obligatory armor, social defenses and offenses as a bridge to the monotony, but our hearts and our spirits are very fragile."

Tyler comments quietly, "Your strength and your weakness."

As dessert is placed before us, a confectionary exhibition, H.S. appends with a slaverous grin, "I couldn't have said it better myself."

Feeling a bit like Alice, I pick up my fork and eat.

50

HOUSE OF CARDS

Lying on the ground just ten feet away, laying on top of Delta's limp body Remy over hears every word of the mercs exchange. Confirming all of his intuitions, his heart beating fast. Seeing Delta, a victim is almost more than he can bare. She is recovering from the impact of Remy's blow, on the ground disoriented, crumpled like a broken doll, but alive. Shaking her head as recognition registers on her face, she's heard the man near them on the ground talking before.

Remy places a finger to her lips, to be sure she doesn't make a sound, they are in shadow but the hallow of fire continues to burn, casting an unpredictable light, he cannot risk their being discovered, as their eyes follow the two-armed men intently. Waiting for an opportunity to present itself, every muscle in Remy's body is pitched with fever, knowing they may never have another chance like this.

Both men are big, they have crazy head gear, they obviously have had training. Balls to the wall, Remy picks up a large rock and chucks it to the left of the men. Delta looks at him, silently pleading for direction, a mix of fear and excitement on her face. He signals for her to stay put, knowing she is strong, but these guys are big and armed and she has taken quite a hit.

Both mercs stop. Visually scanning the area, believing they are concealed by the night and invincible.

"I'll go around, you stay here." The larger of the two men grumbles before turning away.

As the jar head starts walking into the dark brush with the stealth of Frankenstein, his cohort moves to the edge of the fire lit area. They are both making a lot of noise, assuming they are at the top of the food chain. Remy uses this as cover and moves lithely, skirting the dark edge of the brush as silently as possible, the crackle of the jungle blaze around them covering his footsteps, until he is within jumping distance. Delta picks up a rock and throws it in the opposite direction, it hits a tree with a thud before landing disruptively in a bush.

That was the distraction Remy needed, as the second merc turns away from his friend's path to question the movement, Remy lands on his target, knocking the merc to the ground, taking his head by the crew cut and slamming it into the ground. Definitely breaking the unknown man's nose with a crunch and simultaneously rendering him unconscious. Dragging the heavy body under cover quickly from the illuminated area, Delta instinctually wipes away all foot prints and tracks with a branch, like baby Hermes, and straps the merc' s gun around her shoulder. Together they grab hold of their captive's collar and start running through the jungle, dragging the lifeless man toward the river, like a fatted calve.

Following Delta's lead, he knows she will lead them to a location that is remote and yet accessible for the dead weight they are pulling around, anger welling inside both of them as they run. After a minute of full out running, they both stop. Silently, Remy removes the man's belt, rips off his pants and shirt, tearing off the pockets from the shirt, before rolling them all up and tucking them into the back of his own pant waist.

"What are you doing?"

"I may need these later. He needs to be bound." Remy adds stuffing the pocket into the unconscious bleeding man's mouth.

Delta takes the belt and ties their captive's hands behind his back with it, forcefully, before she comments, "Don't talk in front of him." Remy nods his head as they begin to drag the large limp body onward into the ceaselessly dark night.

Images of that last day in her own world, flood her memory as they navigate the pitch. The voice of this very man echoing in her mind as she tightens her grip.

"Don't talk in front of her." He had said, as they brutally dragged her down a cold metal surface and stairs, barely conscious by her hair until she felt the unforgiving rocky ground scraping her back below her. Gagged, blind folded and hog tied for what seemed like an eternity, she was left in the middle of the night in the jungle alone, hungry and petrified. His final words had been, "You're way too pretty to leave here to die." He grunted running his fingers down her neckline, "You want to go home?" She remembers nodding her head, with a muffled cry as silent tears rushed down her face. "Your only chance of leaving this place, is by picking a team and killing off the others. You got that?" He spat out before kicking her bare foot with his boot. She nodded again, not comprehending a word, but afraid to disagree. By the time, she had felt safe enough with the idea of removing the blind fold with her unbound hands, her captives had disappeared without a sound or sign.

Now pushing through the underbrush practically blind, scraping her legs and arms, the hatred for this creature, wells inside her almost uncontrollably.

On auto pilot, she finds herself at the river with an idea. As they approach the banks, Remy can both feel and smell the openness of the marshy landscape before he sees it. A welcome change to the oppressive weight of the canopy that seems forever overhead a viscous burden. Stopping in the clearing for a moment to catch their breath and get his bearings in the dark, an occasional lightning strike far up the river valley becomes their only source of illumination.

Seeing a small island just past the river in the flash of strobe, Remy nods to Delta, removing his shirt and tying it around the head of their new prisoner, obstructing his view and he will admit, issuing a little payback. Delta removes their captive's boots and shoe laces, using the latter to bind his feet, one tied at his ankles the other securing his knees. She dumps his boots in the river after securely wrapping up their almost naked package as they start for the island. The echoes of dogs are pretty far off, but the sound is a bucket of cold-water spurring both of them on, regardless of their exhaustion.

The marshy area around the river is difficult to navigate and buzzing with life even at this time of night. Remy's thoughts run back to watching that bastard on the train take sight on Delta, as he plods through the river clay in the cloudy moonlight. He ran full bore while the infra- red dot, moved without conscious to her head, not knowing what came over him. The full body tackle it took to clear her from the rifle sight, as he landed on top of her, holding his hand over her mouth, was worth it.

Once they reach the rivers' edge, the thought occurs to him that the water may wake up their prisoner. So, he headlocks the merc in his left arm just in case. The river isn't running very fast, but it's wide and his toes start to curl thinking about crocodiles. "Wish I had my longboard."

"What?" Delta grunts in between pants.

"Nothing." He laughs, *Steph would have loved that, hang on baby*.

They wade in slowly on a diagonal moving up the river in case anyone is following them. The overhead moonlight is dimmed by increasing storm clouds, just a faint glowing sliver, but it helps. Listening intently, he can faintly hear the sound of the waves upon the shore. Once they are in middle of the river, a view of the sky opens up and he can see up stream. There is a storm building, lightening amassing, and now the smell of rain washes over them. Ears straining for sounds of men among nature, careful not to dunk his passenger's head, so he doesn't wake him. Remy tightens his grip, following Delta up the river a good thousand meters, until she starts for the island. They head left, it's an eerie vision of silhouetted tree tops that merge into a blanket of absolute ink black midway down.

Purposefully trying not to make any sound, but the sounds he is making, seem extremely loud in the darkness. The water is chest high before it recedes. Excited to finally be moving out of the pitch black water, they are both moving faster now that their feet are no longer mired in sludge, Remy's grip remains steadfast.

The lightening is more frequent and dangerously horizontal. By the time they make it to the shore of the small isthmus, the thunder is all consuming. Dropping his new friend face down in the sandy mud without any remorse. They both stop to get their bearings.

The storm may be a good omen, he thinks to himself. They both hook a hand under their captive's armpits and swiftly head for the safety of the trees, moving forward the ten feet into the tree line when Remy realizes they are in a mangrove. "We need a machete," Remy says out loud before realizing he has just broken the code of silence.

Delta goes over to a young sapling and snaps the trunk off by standing on the young top and bouncing, it's about three feet long.

"Take him. I'll clear the way." She commands, then turns whipping the jungle in front of them into submission.

The air around them is growing thicker with the anticipation of rain. Creepy amounts of sweat are collecting between Remy's body and the dude's over his shoulder. It's slow going, but they are moving forward, as the storm makes its way down the lumbering river. Great flashes of light strobe every couple of seconds. The sudden and constant illumination is disorienting and ominous; One roll of thunder after another seemingly creates a never- ending low rumble. They both stop when a crack of lightening splits the sky just above them, the hair on Remy's body stands on end. Pointing to the only big tree he can decipher through the pyrotechnics, Delta climbs up first then reaches down to grab hold of their new friend, wrapping him around a branch. Remy climbs up and around her attempting to look around the tree, it is enormous.

"Let's go up." He says pulling one arm of their guest with one hand and himself with the other.

They are a good twenty feet off the ground before they stop climbing. The marsh below has disappeared. Remy turns their prisoner to face the main trunk of the tree, then unties his legs. Delta helps push all six feet of him up against the smooth trunk, her back against the mercs, so he looks like he's hugging it. Tying both shoe laces together, they attempt to tie him to the tree but the laces are not long enough, the tree is too big.

Frustrated, she starts climbing back down, "I'll be right back."

Using a shoe lace, Remy fortifies the pocket gag in their prisoner's mouth then leans up against his captive, pushing the hulk of a man into the tree with his body weight, squeezing out all of the space between him and the tree. Sitting there he runs over in his head what he over- heard in the clearing until Delta returns a couple minutes later with a large quantity of jungle vine around her neck. They secure their captive's waist first, then the back of his neck, turning his face to one side, before they untie his hands and tie each one individually with the knotted vine on the other side of the tree. *This asshole isn't going anywhere.*

Once they've checked all of the bonds, they climb to the branches just below their guest, as the sky opens up without warning. No drizzle or little spray just a deluge of water, an unseen hand has turned the faucet on full. They sit silently against the tree, the rain and thunder so loud, it's not possible to talk. The only sound they can hear is the force of the storm. Through closed eyes, flashes of lightening are alarming. All they can do is wait.

51

SEA GREEN

The bill for our culinary gesticulation never arrives, he must be running a tab for his ceaseless exotic meat addiction, Laure thinks to herself, trying not to judge. Every pore of her body wants to get as far away from this domineering man as possible, and she doesn't even know him. She can hear Steph's phone vibrate on the linen draped table from her borrowed purse. Steph ignores it, undoubtedly thinking it would be rude to pull her phone out at the dinner table.

"Let's go see this building, shall we?" Stephanie announces with an air of "je ne sais quois", that scares Laure.

Laure watches as her friend, collects her things. H.S. with a look of triumph stands up and pulls out Steph's chair.

"Tyler, it was nice to see you, Laure I will catch up with you tomorrow." Steph felicitates as if they were having drinks with friends.

Once recovered from Steph's departure Laure turns to Tyler, "Are you interested in a drink?"

Laure drives, they find an old neighborhood corner bar, not an easy task in a billionaire town but it's filled with real people with real jobs, she sighs with relief.

In the din light of a candle, they take off their coats and sit down, she notices how tired and how much older Tyler is than his years. Deciding, he is by no means old. He is mysterious, and youthful but with a man's body, a man's hands. She is drawn to the darkness he covets behind poised, bold sea green eyes and determines, *there is a secret there.*

"Laure, how long have you known the Beroes?" The light tone of Tyler's voice does not match the concern on his face.

"Steph and I went to college together." She explains, noting the waitress in skin tight, no, Ramones tight pants and a "Born to be Wild" tank top that is taking their order. Not an unusual ensemble except that she is about sixty. She continues, trying not to stare, "We both lived in New York City together when she met Remy, in fact, she had asked me to join them on their first date, but I had made other plans for the evening." Memories of their twenties come rushing forward pushing tears into her eyes. "We are more than friends, we are the sisters neither of us had."

An unusual silence engulfs both of them, Laure's is caused by the fear of what type of compromising position her dearest friend has placed herself in. But she wonders, why is Tyler silent.

"Yes, I can see that, you look like sisters as well, both beautiful women."

For a moment, a smile graces his lips, and things don't seem so bad after all. "Tyler, I'm not really sure what's going on here. But I think Steph does, and," her mouth just stops working.

"And what?" Tyler's eyes are so intent with his response, they seem charged by some super natural force, it's both alarming and magnetic.

"I think you do too?" She adds softly. His eyes close for a second silently agreeing with her. "That bar you took us to, you were trying to send her a message, weren't you?"

"Laure," as he says her name slowly and takes her left hand gently, she feels a twinge of excitement, "I have done questionable things for all the wrong reasons," Tyler confesses.

Slowly and definitively she asks the most obvious question, "Do you have anything to do with Remy's disappearance?" The tone in her voice is unmistakably unforgiving.

"Remy disappeared?"

"Yes. Yesterday."

"No, I had no idea. No!" His head shaking a repeat of his statement as if talking himself into it.

Laure retracts her hand thinking, he is obviously torn and although she barely knows this man, her concern for his well- being is overwhelming.

Tyler's eyes follow from her hand, cautiously moving up her body to meet her eyes. "I think I know who did, though." He finally responds.

At that moment, her phone dings as if to punctuate his statement. "Excuse me, I just need to be sure it isn't Steph."

A text from Detective Brennan; *Where are you both? I have news.* With lightning speed, she texts back, *I am at the Ave bar in Ingleside. Steph went off on her own with H.S. from DBS.* She looks around the bar at the hulky customers while waiting for a response.

Where did they go? Brennan texts back immediately.

"Do you know where Steph went with your boss?" She quickly asks Tyler, before texting the address of the warehouse he gives her.

Brennan replies immediately, don't go anywhere without telling me.

An ominous feeling of doom sobers Laure instantly. "Tyler, please tell me what you know. I think Steph is in danger."

52

CARNIVAL

The stinging warm rain punishing their bare skin with welts, creates a visceral curtain, between them and the jungle. Dizzying, macabre vignettes of twisted branches and silhouetted leaves flash into focus every couple of seconds blindingly. Remy now understands why man has been afraid of lightning and thunder, its power is absolutely frightening. His life, troubles, and worries as they are, are insignificant to natures metamorphosis before him, he is awed.

For an hour or more it rains like he has never seen rain. At the climax of a torrent, he is amazed that water can fall so heavily from the sky and not be a wave of water, when another clap of lightning and thunder surrounds them, pushing with it yet another thrust of water, so loud and onerous, he is deeply concerned the tree will be swept away. Delta huddles into a ball on the branch beside him, the sound of the storm is like screaming angels falling from the sky.

He hopes a positive to this, is their tracks will be washed away, he hopes it has given them time. Remy wraps his arms around his legs and tucks his body in too, rain flowing off of his forehead like a gutter as he silently goes over a plan.

They meet with the other leader at dawn at the river mouth. Hopefully, they can cross it. He considers the train tracks are minimal, just two independent cement rails with a surface of about twenty inches per rail. The pylons are shaped like some kind of Egyptian monument, tapered at the top and steeply slanted on two sides, too steep to climb. The train itself is locked on by overlapping the train tracks. The wheels of the train must be underneath, concealed for stealth, weather, corrosion and other obvious reasons. He hopes his plan will work, it has to.

The deluge finally begins to wane, taking the thunder out to sea. Without the lightning, however dark closes in again as the tempest leaves her mark on the jungle, ions charging it with life. He feels invigorated, cleansed, energized.

Delta lifts her head and looks over toward him, concerned about a new sound that has replaced the down pour. The river that surrounds the island is roaring. They have chosen an ancient tree, that has seen thousands of storms. They have to believe it will weather this one as well.

"Are you ok?" Remy yells over the clamor of the rushing effusion.

She nods.

Reaching out to take her hand he states clearly, "I'm going to tie you to the tree, so you can sleep." She nods again. Wrapping the vine cord around her waist and securing it close to her, in case she wants to get down in a hurry. Remy then secures the last cord around the branch he is sitting on and wraps it around his waist before tying it down, leaning his back up against the main trunk for stability.

"We need sleep, tomorrow the hunters arrive." Closing his eyes, trying to force rest, visions of the Cayman Islands interfere with his attempt at calm.

Returning from the fishing trip that H.S. so desperately wanted him to be a part of, he knew there was something wrong.

Tyler had explained to everyone, once they were on board and heading out to sea, his boss sent his regrets, due to an unavoidable conference call. Something didn't feel right. Remy took the bait, it was a beautiful boat, and a beautiful day, he went with it. There were eight company men on the boat, all of which he had met the night before plus Tyler and himself. Staying above deck, he watched the island diminish as they headed out to sea. The ship's captain and mates all crew from Jove's gift were busy with preparations. Dawn just breaking as they laid wake through the calm water, the entire morning sky gray with the anticipation of blue.

About an hour out to sea, the cabin doors opened to reveal Trudy, in barely a bikini with a flimsy transparent robe. The rest of the party didn't find this peculiar. Remy ignored the situation and turned back to the sea, always a sense of strength for him, not surprised that Trudy not only handled public but also private relations. This was exactly the kind of corporate bullshit he detested. All of these guys except Tyler were married and their wives were within two miles.

Tyler walked over to him after getting the long lines out, having been assigned as his handler. "You enjoy big game fishing?" Tyler asked handing him a beer.

"No thanks, too early. I like the fight in the water, but the bludgeoning, I can live without."

"Yeah, I know what you mean but, I do love sushi, and it doesn't get fresher than this."

Not sure if he was referring to their concubine or the actual fish, Remy just nodded, containing his distaste.

"Are you hungry? Breakfast is being served in the cabin."

"Sounds good."

The ship "Minerva", was impressive, over one hundred feet of luxury, the trailing boat for Jove's Gift that stores in the belly of its' father. A chef was preparing custom omelets. Bloody Marys and Long Island ice teas lined a silver tray at seven-thirty in the morning.

Remy remembers sitting next to Sly, "Hey, morning how's it going?" he asked.

"I love these fishing trips." Sly proclaimed, barely taking his eyes off of the Amazon, his voice actually cracking. Remy got up disgusted, with the intention to move out to the upper deck with his china plated meal, as he headed out the door, Trudy, who seemed engrossed in conversation with Milton Davis the head of accounting, reached out for Remy's arm. He stopped, looking down at her hand before he looked back at her for an instant. She very intuitively removed her hand. Once above deck, he put his hat on and ate, trying not to think too much about the bullshit surrounding him.

Tyler followed him up on que. "Great day."

"This is NOT my scene man."

"My apologies."

"No worries, let's just fish." Remy took pity on him because, in all this, he seemed innocent. *What was I thinking?*

After spending an hour reeling in a heroic sail fish, that propelled itself out of the water for a view of its captor, his arms ached. He had let it run for some time, just to experience its power, he envied that fish, master of its universe, the gorgeous big blue it's domain. For a moment, Remy became addicted to harnessing the wild creature. Then it dawned on him, *Steph and I are the fish!*

Just as they pulled the gaffs out to hook him, he cut the line.

They returned with mahi mahi from the long lines and a sunburn. All but two of the others were stumbling drunk when they docked.

"You're a peculiar man, Remy," Tyler commented almost absent mindedly as they walked up the dock.

"Yeah? Why is that?"

"You're not trapped by the confines of manhood."

"Well, I was raised by six sisters."

"It's more than that." Tyler smiled at Remy, "You remind me of someone I had almost forgotten. Let's all meet for drinks later."

"Sounds good, how about sunset? Down at the beach by our suite? We'll bring the drinks."

"Ok." Tyler walked off, Remy remembers thinking he liked him, appreciating his European upbringing. Not in a rush to grow up, life is about experiences for them. *We should move*, he remembers thinking to himself, *we should definitely move.*

Stopping at the pool on his way back to his room, he took off his "Got Weed?" t-shirt, slipped off his vans and threw himself in. The cool clean water reviving him from the blistering heat of midday. Only the professional sun bathers were out now, everyone else had taken shelter until cocktail hour.

Swimming a couple of laps to stretch out his body and release the muscles in his arms, his sunburn stung like hell in the pool water. Popping his head up and turning on his back, he looked up at the wispy blue sky outlining the trees that surrounded the pool courtyard. That was when he noticed Trudy at the end of the pool. She took off her robe, like a pole stripper and dove in. Sly's wife, who had been sitting under an umbrella reading, packed up her things and left hastily. Remy continued his laps and found Trudy waiting for him at the opposite end.

"Hey."

"You didn't e-ven talk with m-ee on the boawt." She simpered in a drawled twang.

"I'm not interested." Getting out of the pool, he picked up his clothes, grabbed a towel from the man who guards the towels all day, and walked away. There was nothing else to be said.

The suite was full of light when he returned, the maid had been in, but it was empty and vapid, a lot like the company they were keeping. Wrapped in a towel, he walked into the bedroom and sat on the edge of the bed facing the sea, wondering what the hell they were doing there? Seeing Steph in a lounge chair out on the beach under an umbrella at the shores edge, he grabbed a beer and a glass of wine from the fridge and headed out to her. The sand was extremely hot, having forgotten his flip flops, he practically danced his way down to her. "Hey, sweetie." Approaching her chair from the side, that's when he noticed, there was something wrong. Steph's face was marked by stress, she had her big ole movie star glasses on she was so well known for so he couldn't see her eyes, but the rest of her body language told a story. *Why didn't I see it?*

Startled, she whispered his name.

"Are you ok?" He asked.

"You're sunburn." She responded, not hearing his question.

"Yeah, you ok?" Remy knelt down in the painfully hot sand next to her as she checked over his body like a mother checking for wounds, "Hmm?"

"Steph, are you ok? Are you sick?"

"Yes, yes I don't feel well."

"Something you ate?"

"Probably." Her voice so rarely lackluster, he figured, she must not be feeling well at all.

"Do you need anything? Kaopectate, Pepto-Bismol?" Touching her fore head, she was burning up but, it was also 95 degrees outside under an umbrella. Then he noticed she had goose bumps in the heat. "Are you cold Sweetie?"

"A little."

"Let's get you back to our room."

"No! No, I want to stay out here!"

That was alarming, "Alright, scooch up so I can sit behind you," *and save my screaming toes.* Squeezing in he wrapped his body around hers, she took his arms and crossed them over her chest.

Feeling the tension releasing from her body as she leaned her head back against his chest, Remy remembers thinking very clearly, there isn't anything he wouldn't do for this woman.

About an hour later, Tyler approached, "Hey, you two? Am I interrupting? Are you alright Stephanie, you look pale?"

She cleared her throat and leaned back, "Food poisoning I think."

"I am so sorry to hear that. There is a doctor here at the hotel if you need anything just call the concierge. We'll catch up another time."

"Thanks, Tyler. I think it's an early night for us."

Remy watched the sun go down in silence. The tide was coming back in, almost unperceptively.

"Alright my lazy sunbather, let's go in and take a shower." There was no reply. Steph's breathing was steady and rhythmic; she was out cold. Slipping out of the chair carefully, he took a moment to study her face in the fading light. So beautiful, so strong. How did I get so lucky? He asked himself before picking her up and carrying her back to their room.

After taking off her bathing suit he gently laid her in bed. Turning to take his suit off, she bolted upright, her face pale as she rushed into the bathroom, where she spent all night and most of the next day.

Ordering meals in, once she had finished heaving, he kept a wet cloth on her head and a trash can next to her, rubbing her back while she slept. The next day she slept peacefully. Remy ordered room service, dry toast and ginger ale for her and mahi- mahi for himself.

"Sweetie, I am going to go for a quick swim before the sun goes down," he whispered in her ear, giving her a kiss, before heading out the patio door for the sea before the food arrived. She nodded her head, but her eyes were not open.

It's beautiful here, that is undeniable, he thought to himself walking down to the Caribbean crystal-clear water. But I need waves, he recalls thinking while walking into the surf-less, almost lifeless water as warm as a bath. *This is for old people.* He just floated.

"Remy!" Barely audible he heard his name. Looking back towards the beach he saw Steph dragging herself out of the room and toward him, panic struck. Running towards her, tears running down her face, she had the sheet from the bed wrapped around her and she looked like she was running from a ghost.

"What's wrong? What is it?" He asked reaching for her as she clung to him in terror, unable to speak, her face contorted. Looking back to the open patio door he saw a bellman, just as panicked, coming out of the sliding door of their room running towards them. His white gloves and jacket, a complete contrast to his skin as he ran up to them.

"I am so sorry! I did not mean ta scare da Miss! No one answered, so I let myself in ta deliver your dinner! Please Sir, is there anything I can do? I am so sorry."

"Steph, is that all that happened? Are you ok?"

She nodded her head silently after a minute, "Yes."

A group of lookie loos had gathered on their balconies to see what the commotion was all about.

"Sorry man, just a misunderstanding," Remy responded to the prostrate bellman, walking Steph back into their room. After locking the door, he laid down next to her on the bed, she was huddled up like a beaten dog. "It's ok," he whispered as he wrapped his body around her, stroking her hair. "You just need to sleep, I'm right here." Thinking the fever was giving her nightmares and hoping this would pass, as her incapacitation was scaring the shit out of him.

Waking the next day, he was afraid to leave the room. In all the years they had been together, he had never seen Steph delusional.

Just before dawn, he made coffee in their oversized vacation kitchen and reheated her toast.

"Hey Sweetie, how are you feeling?"

"I am SO hungry."

"That's a good sign." He laughed, handing her the toast and ginger ale from the previous night. "I think you gave the bellman a heart attack."

"Oh my god!"

"Don't worry about it."

She ate her toast in three seconds, then looked around for more.

"Let me call room service."

"I'd like scrambled eggs and more toast and ginger ale."

After ordering the food he sat on the bed next to her, "What did you eat? What do you think made you sick?"

"I don't know, I don't want to think about it. I feel better, just weak. I need food. I'm sorry I ruined your vacation." Remy remembers she looked up at him with those crazy brown eyes.

"Listen numb skull, this place means nothing to me. You didn't ruin anything. Besides seeing the look on that bellman's face was priceless." She smiled for the first time in two days. The world was right again.

He can still feel the warmth of her skin against his lips as he opens his eyes to the moonlight finally breaking overhead, the storm lighting the distant sea. *That was not food poisoning, something happened to her. Something so bad, she couldn't tell me.* After that trip, her attitude towards DBS had changed dramatically. They were no longer in the running as potential partners. Which was fine with Remy, he absolutely believed they were better off alone then saddling up to their brand of dysfunction. What bothered him was that Steph wouldn't have a real conversation about it. *Now I know why.*

Tears stinging his eyes as he thinks of how he failed her. Sitting on a branch in a god damn tree, the reality of their situation smacking him in the face. *If I am here, where the hell is she?* Reaching over, he shakes Delta, "We have to talk."

53

PARALYZED

The dark Bentley is waiting for us outside the restaurant in the chilly night air, exiting one door and entering the other so quickly, I forget to go to the bathroom. H.S. whispers something to the driver, as he walks around the car, I take a moment to review my emails.

Grace; Forwarding this from Vermont – We are exercising our right to terminate our contract. Effectively Immediately. I close my eyes for a brief moment holding in a wave of expletives.

"Anything wrong?"

"No, everything's fine," I answer ignoring the pit in my stomach. I can't even go there right now. Next, Detective Brennan - *Please check in.*

He will have to wait until I get some privacy. Next, Miles Venery – *It is imperative that you call me. You may be in danger.*

No kidding. He will have to wait as well. *Damn.*

I sit back on the heated leather seat and as I do the hem of my dress slips well above my knee. I feel larcenous eyes upon me, *some men are so simple.* H.S.

pours a scotch from the mini bar for both of us. I don't like scotch, *but that's not the point, is it?*

"So, tell me, where is your genius of a husband really?" he asks while unapologetically drooling scotch on his pants.

Taking a sip from the crystal glass, I draw power from the heat now coursing through my body like fire. *Perhaps you can tell me that?* I look over to his unerringly expressionless face. "He had a meeting back East, last minute, very time sensitive."

"Not with Miles Venery I hope?"

"Now why would you say a thing like that?"

"I've been following the editorials. I wouldn't think that type of match would suit you at all. It seems the writing is on the wall."

So it seems.

His phone lights up. "Yes." There is more than a note of annoyance in his voice. I cannot hear the caller.

"You are as inept as you are over- paid. Notify them immediately you imbecile." H.S. stares at his phone for a second after ending the call. Then looks back over to me, with an effort to decline an elevated state of anger.

"Something wrong?" I ask with the slightest smidge of glee.

"I'm growing tired of the working class."

Did he actually just say that to me?

The car comes to a slow stop in an industrial area, after a thirty- minute drive on abandoned streets. A large fenced- in expanse of land with an old- style brick factory standing on the left of the property is in my direct view. The vintage single pane windows are lash-less eyes looking out to the modernized street, in fear for its future. Sodium street lamps cast an eerie aura over the area as if the light were coming from within the structure. I have no intentions of getting out of the car.

"Leave us." H.S. orders his driver out into the night before turning his attention to me, "As I mentioned before, no expense spared. Prime location, the finest of architects and engineers at your disposal. We will monopolize this industry. I already have patent staff creating applications."

The tone of his voice has changed, it's more unnatural than usual. My skin crawls, and I am beginning to breathe fast.

"We can do this together." He all but whispers in my ear while moving closer to me, his body completely against the left side of mine, I feel his weight and recognize his smell.

I'm paralyzed and losing sense of time. "What do you want?" I ask afraid to move.

"I – want- it- all!" He growls throwing his weight on top of me while capturing my face in his hands, pushing the back of my head against the bottom of the window as he pins my arms down one under me, the other in between us. His hot breath foul as he tries to stick his tongue in my mouth.

"Why are you doing this!" I scream.

"Because I can. Be still!" He orders straddling my body with his weight, "I want you to enjoy this!" His moan is maniacal and connected to a trickle of drool that falls from his mouth onto my cheek.

I can feel my arm beneath me tearing at the shoulder, the pain causes me to violently turn toward the front of the car, catching him off balance while unzipping his pants inches from my face. Feeling his body fall forward into the seats, the removal of his weight on mine gives me a heightened sense of mobility. I kick him wildly, hitting him in the face and throat with my heels unrelenting, as I fumble for the car door handle. Pulling at it, with no success, *God damn child locks!* Throwing myself into the front seat. H.S. grips my ankle and twists my leg in the opposite direction of my body. My scream is futile.

"Don't make me hurt you!" His groan echoes in the confinement of the car.

I grab onto the steering wheel allowing my lower half to twist in his grip without resistance, kicking him with my free foot, causing enough damage to draw blood. Taking a breath, I let myself be reeled in intentionally then push forcibly off of the steering wheel to accelerate the impact of my body, it throws him off guard and back into the seat behind him, he releases my foot. Quickly grappling for the door and hitting all of the buttons at once, the door opens and I fall between it and the car abruptly. My legs tangled I scramble to my feet, using the door as leverage, I pull myself up deciding which direction to run.

54

Part III

DAY AND AGE

The Bohemian Club is clearing out, only the alcohol infirmed widowers are left now, embedded in their club chairs in the men's lounge. Miles knows them well and is grateful to not be counted among them as he surveys the room.

Worried, he wonders where Stephanie is and why she hasn't contacted him. He needs details only she would know for Horace. Upon thinking his name, Miles' phone illuminates. "Horace?"

"Miles, have you contacted your friend Mrs. Beroe yet?"

"I have, she is not replying. I do not believe this is benign Horace."

"It may not matter, I've got someone working with the Detective handling her case now. I have all the details she would have been privy to. But the big news is the FBI has been called in."

"Really?"

"Yes, my sources inform me that several unusual abductions have been linked to an undisclosed group under investigation."

"Anyone, I know?"

"Anyone you don't know is more like it. This thing is huge Miles, affecting the largest fortunes in the country."

"Abductors or abductees?"

"Both."

"So, what's next?" Miles asks now titillated by his friend's excitement.

"Where are you?"

"I'm at the club."

"Stay put, see if you can find anything else out. Notify me immediately, I don't care how small of a detail."

"Yes, of course."

"I will update you by three, no matter what." Horace states as he hangs up.

Feeling as if a whirlwind just passed through the room, Miles' mind is in a flurry. At any time of the day, some of the country's largest fortunes are in this club. Everyone is now suspect, he decides to take an overview, traversing the appointed hallway, he passes a heated conversation between John Jameson, a lifer, and Brendan Steele.

Miles' history with Jameson is more relevant to John's father John Jameson Senior, an Industrialist who died about ten years ago, they traveled in the same social circles. As for Steele, he is not a member although he and his brother Adam are members of several clubs including the Olympic. Oil magnates, they own a good majority of refineries in the U.S and a flagrant percentage of pipelines in the world. The Steele's inherited hundreds of millions in the 1960's and have turned them into hundreds of billions. Miles finds the brothers annoying men at the best of circumstances and doesn't agree with their purchase powering politics or their radically blinded social views. He is surprised Brendan is in the club without handlers.

Brendan had run for political office in the 1980's unsuccessfully, his aberrant Libertarian agenda was fraught with Anarcho-Totalitarianism. Under the auspices of terminating all corporate and personal tax, (which in an illusory world would sound attractive, if all men were born equal), the grand scheme to abolish all federal oversight agencies, including the FBI, CIA, SEC, Social Security and the Department of Energy, was the true hidden agenda, thankfully public opinion was not willing to embrace either of them.

Corpocracy their real goal and the hundreds of millions of dollars both brothers advocate to political parties yearly, lobbying, and most importantly underwriting special interest organizations used to manipulate scientific facts and public opinion, is in his opinion the biggest danger to the welfare of the commonwealth. Miles silently remembers Brendan's son William is being groomed for politics, *very curious*. He slows his pace to catch a bit of their conversation.

"You don't want to mess with me, Jameson."

"You don't scare me, there is no escape clause." Jameson's voice is ominous.

Both men pause as Miles passes them, simulating working on his phone to avoid eye contact as he proceeds into the game room at a snail's pace. Finding a stool at the bar, he immediately forwards this unusual exchange to Horace, his eyes scanning the expansive room while a glass of scotch is placed in front of him. Looking up the barman announces, "From Mr. Sterling, Sir."

Benedict Sterling is an accomplished writer, his family *was* the publishing industry, now fraught by internet piracy, a paper man for generations. Sterling made his reputation when news men found stories instead of creating them. Except for a full head of white hair, he is un-assuming, average height, the same age as Miles, impeccably groomed and notoriously un-married. Always one to quote Wilde, an asset to any party, quite entertaining when he wants to be. *I have always like him.* "Benedict, how are you?" Miles raises the glass in salute.

"Well Miles, well. Surprised to see you."

"Yes, well, a one- day meeting has turned into a lifestyle it seems."

"I bumped into Levitt tonight, he seemed pleased to have relieved you of a small fortune." The amusement in Benedict's eyes is playful.

"Yes, I bet he was."

"Anyway, he is off to some big game hunt tomorrow. Can you imagine in this day and age?" Benedict looks down at his glass shaking his head, "Such a cliché."

Without regard for anyone's opinion Miles comments almost in a trance, "There are so many who refuse to see the changes necessary for all of this to work."

"It used to be a good thing for life to imitate art Miles, you remember? Space travel, brain transplants, technological gadgets, scientific achievements, architecture. So many of the greats were tapped into the future like Oracles heralding our path through literature, music, painting, poetry, design. What do we have today?" Benedict's shocking head of hair shakes disapprovingly while he queries out loud, spreading his arms as if to encompass the entire building and all of its contents with his embrace as well as his theory. "This place is swarming with tech gurus." Sterling's tone is imbued with disdain, "Have their achievements enlightened our society? I ask you, has their technological genius united us as a world conscious on a global, regional or even local level?" Silence overcomes him, retreating, placing his drink on the bar. "No." He continues, turning his head towards Miles, "Do you know why?"

Miles garners himself, knowing Benedict is not drunk, he is simply empathetic, as Benedict places a hand on his shoulder and continues unhindered, "Because we have allowed accountants and paper pushers to rule our world! We have become the heretics of old, worshipping the dollar. There is no heart, there is no spirit. There is no love. I fear it is the beginning of the end, my friend." Benedict's usually playful eyes are full of tears, too frightened to fall.

Chilled by an ensuing flux of hair now standing up on his arms, Miles reflects upon Benedict's emotional distress. It is real, Miles knows this. These concepts are so relevant he is afraid to confront them, never mind speak them aloud.

Resting his weight against the bar, Benedict continues adjunctly, "My own Nephew told his parents he was pursuing a Ph.D. in philosophy, do you know what they told him? They told him he was wasting his time. Wasting his time, Miles." Benedict pauses only to take a sip, "I guess we don't need thinkers or problem solvers anymore."

55

FOUR THREE

Watching the Bentley pull out of the abandoned lot, Laddington drags his E cigarette from the safety of his car, parked behind a large commercial dumpster, his hands shake. *"I didn't sign up for this!"* He tells the smoke infused mirror. His part was to obscure, slow down the process, he was paid well, but not well enough to be an accomplice.

"Now what? Fuck!"

As the smoke in the car begins to dissipate his mind clears too. *Ok, it's a good idea for me to take a vacation,* he considers options while running through the list of incriminating circumstances he has been involved in. All of the staff he questioned at the conference center can I.D. him. Laure has his number and she didn't trust him from the beginning. His texts to Stephanie are traceable.

Slamming the steering wheel, he thinks, he could say she went back to her hotel, who knows, maybe she's on her way home now? Waiting for the car to turn itself on, remunerating; *What if I just walk away? I could go anywhere, start over. A new name, new paperwork that's not the problem. So, what's the problem?* The fear of this reality punches him with a reminder, the last time he stuck his neck out for someone, he almost paid with his life, and lost everything. It's taken years to recover financially, physically, mentally. Why should he stick his neck out for her? Plus, he has no idea who these people are, where they can reach. All he does know is this is some serious shit! Taking another hit, his image in the mirror disappears in a cloud of smoke.

56

PARADISE CIRCUS

Before dawn in the darkest of night, grunting sounds erupt. Having only been asleep for a couple of hours, Remy feels the weight of exhaustion pulling on him. Delta unties the safety rope and they both climb up to the branch the merc is parasitically appended to, slowly approaching the groaning man from behind. Remy slips the T-shirt he had stored in his pant waist over their victim's head.

Delta assertively smacks the now bagged man on the back of his head with the stick she used to clear their path. Surprised but not disturbed by this, a small smile crosses Remy's lips. *She got his undivided.*

"You will tell us what we want to know or you will die a very painful death." She whispers in the jar heads ear, like a malevolent angel.

The grunt he replies sounds an awful lot like *"Fuck You!"*.

Delta smacks him again, then looks to Remy with her face in shadow, hands him the stick and then heads down the tree without so much as a boo.

Ok, I am sure she has a plan, so I'll just stay put. Hoping she does, he waits.

A very long twenty minutes later, Delta climbs back up. The light is starting to change, gradually different animals are moving around.

She pulls a small wad of fabric out from under her waist band then pulls off the makeshift hood and shakes an array of bugs into it; A large black scorpion, a centipede, some very large nasty looking ants, a beetle of some kind, two smallish crabs and a thin snake. Shaking the t shirt hood thoroughly, she then places it back on the captive's head fastening the neck with his own shoelace.

Mental note, do not piss off Delta.

Within seconds, their friend goes wild, Delta waits, watching the man spasm in fear, for what must be an eternity, for him. Just before she pulls off the hood, she looks over at Remy. The whites of her eyes glowing in the morning light, the smile on her face, makes him choke back a laugh.

"You want the hood off? Answer my questions or I will fill your pants and leave you hear to be eaten alive."

"OK, OK!"

Delta pulls off the hood and begins slowly and decisively questioning the squirming man, "I am going to ask you yes or no questions. Do you understand?"

"Yes!" he groans through the wad of material in his mouth, several ants still walking around on the back of his head as a couple of welts on the back of his neck are evident. His voice still garbled due to the gag and the sheer pressure at which his body is pressed against the tree, she begins, "Do you know who you work for?"

"No."

She looks over at Remy, pissed off, and continues. "Did you abduct any of the people here?" She knows the answer to this but wants to see if Remy registers this guy in any way.

"Yes!"

"Are there less than twenty of you?"

"Yes!"

Are there less than ten of you?"

"No."

Are there less than fifteen of you?"

"Yes."

Looking at Delta Remy mouths, "Where are we?"

"Are we in the Central America?" The ants are moving quickly down his back now.

"Yes!"

Are we on an Island?"

"Yes!"

Delta looks at Remy blankly, then puts the hood back on him, he goes crazy. Scootching up to Remy's ear, she states quietly, "We need real answers, I have to take his gag out."

Remy thinks, who am I to argue? She is giving a whole new meaning to entomophobia, he nods his head in absolute compliance.

"Stay quiet, it's best if he doesn't know how many of us there are." She adds grazing his ear with her lip while turning back to their victim.

"I am going to remove your gag, if you make any sudden sounds, I will shoot you, it won't be fatal either, just enough to attract critters. Do I make myself clear?"

"Yes!" The merc grunts showing a little more restraint.

Removing the hood, then untying his gag Delta sits as close to him from behind as possible without touching his body. "Who hired you?"

"I don't know, I just get instructions and money wired into my account, I have never met anyone except the guys here on the island, the other guards." He explains, unable to move his head in their direction. His voice is low and resonant, he must be about forty. He's fit but not obsessed.

"Please, take them off!" He implores, referring to the ants still crawling around on his back, Delta takes no notice.

"Who shoots at us from the train?"

"We're paid to keep you scared and moving around as soon as the hunters arrive, we are quarantined to our lodgings unless they need ground support, to flush out the feeders. I 've never seen them."

"What the hell is a feeder?"

After a pause, he replies, "You."

Delta looks over at Remy, she is ready to throw this guy from the tree. He holds her arm back and asks very slowly and calmly, "What's the schedule for tomorrow?"

Clearly alerted by a male voice the merc' s back goes rigid before he replies, "I don't know." Delta pokes him with the stick, "They usually get in around noon or later, they keep their hunting on a random basis."

"How many are there? Remy asks soberly.

"Twenty- four, same as you."

"How do they get here?"

"Plane, and boat!"

"What's inside the train cars without windows?" Remy asks.

"One car is a bar, with books and fancy guns on the wall." The merc concedes as the centipede crawls over the top of his head and stops on his forehead, sending a shutter down his body, "The second is a locker room, for changing clothes. The third is an armory, the gun car! Please get it off me!"

"How do I drive the train?" Remy growls.

The merc is silent for a moment before continuing, "There is an iPad station at the front and rear of the shooting gallery! You just hit the button!"

"No password?"

"No."

Delta smacks him on the head with the stick for assurance.

The merc closes his eyes and tries to shake the bug off his head unsuccessfully.

Mouthing to Delta, *we gotta go*, Remy takes the gun and hits the captive in the head with it, knocking him out instantly. They put the gag back on and shake out the hood, and put that back on too, checking all of the restraints they head down the tree to the river for their meeting with Manaya's family, in silence.

The sky is on the other side of darkness now, as they fumble through the sludge left behind by the storm. Thoughts of all the assholes in his life with Steph, flood his mind, as he literally wallows through the mud. Faces and words a ceaseless montage, from step- fathers to industry associates stealing IP, all of them taking advantage of their tolerance and need to please nature, or at least Steph's. *Fuckin thieves*, he growls to himself remembering how intensely full of anger he was at the time, to be taken advantage of by people they trusted, that he thought were colleagues and even friends.

At the time, visions of revenge were a form of therapy for him; Some he told Steph about, some he didn't. He never acted on any of them, they were a form of release, just thoughts, but evil thoughts. Sort of like filling a shopping cart and leaving it at the store, he felt satiated. The situation now, takes this to whole new level. It's going to take a lot to satiate him. Walking through knee high mud, Remy feels something change inside him, something hard and dark, he is unfamiliar with but for the moment it feels right.

Making their way to the river, the lightness of dawn cleanses their brooding thoughts temporarily. Approaching the water's edge of the river they crossed the night before, they witness the sheer power of nature before them. The force of the flooding rain waters has completely denuded ten- foot sided canyons in its path. The new canyons are steep with wet walls of sand that give way easily. There is about a six- foot easement between the torrent of water still pushing its way to the sea and the edge of the new canyon. Delta picks a place to go down while grabbing a long stick scattered among the wreckage of huge trees, bushes, and rocks that have been scattered like tickertape. The sand is so incredibly saturated, it makes a "Glop" sound with every foot step as it swallows her foot up to her ankle. Not an ideal situation for crossing, not to mention the floating debris, whole palm trees are careening the current like leaves of grass.

"Remy, we are running out of time."

Standing side by side, Delta wraps the machine gun they took from the merc, diagonally across her back and presses the stick into the river bottom, testing for depth. The water is dark and visibly un-penetrable. Following her stick in, she is now up to her waist but only a quarter of the way across, a firm current surrounds her exposed body, without turning around she just keeps going, as the sun is rising fast.

Remy also grabs a stick, a little thicker than the one Delta chose and follows her out. Once his feet are covered with water, they don't sink anymore, which he may have preferred as he realizes the current may be too strong for them to swim across if they are not anchored.

Remy is three feet away from Delta, as her shoulders submerge in the middle of the river, looking up stream he sees a large tree trunk heading towards them. Using the stick, he holds it out vertically, leveraging his feet against the weight of it, nudging the trunk to the left of them, barely enough for it to pass without colliding.

Now using their sticks as anchors against the current, both of their bodies are lifting off their feet involuntarily in the river's pull.

"We have to swim for it!" Remy yells above the rushing sound. Consumed with swimming across the current, he hadn't noticed Delta being taken down stream until she yells out his name.

"Shit!"

He has no choice but to let himself be taken, leading with his head, closing his arms against the side of his body, hoping for hydrodynamics. Within a couple of seconds, his body is moving really fast in the current, uncontrollably. The sides of the canyon flying by out of focus is disorienting, he sees Delta bobbing up and down ahead of him and heads right for her. Arms flailing around for each other as he gets close, both of their bodies slippery and invisible in the chocolate colored water. Finally managing to grab hold of her upper arm and draw her in as tight as he can, "Got you! Try to get on my back, and kick with your legs! Hold on tight!"

She climbs around him as they are whirring down the river. Once he feels her grasp around his neck tightly, he starts digging again, swimming with all his might diagonally attempting to get as close to the shallow water as he can.

They have to get out of the center of the current or they will wind up out at sea, or worse in a water fall. Pushing with all the strength he possesses, they finally start heading in a quasi-lateral direction. A large branch with leaves hits Remy in the shoulder, as he sees the side of the river within reach and feels the ground with his toes.

"Shit! Kick!"

"Remy, faster!"

Turning his head from focusing on the canyon wall, he is alarmed at a log jam they are now on a direct course for. Large boulders protruding from the sand canyon on either side have caught the bulk of the tree trunk debris from the storm. The force of the water is hitting the pileup creating a rooster tail wave rising at least twenty feet in the air.

Swimming as hard as they can, Delta on Remy's back kicking furiously, they continue to move laterally, but not fast enough. The blockade is now only about thirty feet in front of them. The sound of the rooster wave cresting is absolutely frightening.

"Dig! Swim Hard!" He yells, engaging every muscle in his body, but it's still not enough. "Shit!" They brace for the impact. "Hold on!" Remy yells.

Picking up speed, his hands and feet are out with the hope of latching on to something. Delta has wrapped her body around him from behind as they hit the dam, catching themselves on the pile of logs. The force of the river smacks both of them with such an impact against the fallen trees, they wince in pain. The bottleneck of the water is now creating a crested wave on their backs, pushing them toward the pile, they hold on with everything they have.

"We have to move up and out!" Remy yells not able to turn his head into the oncoming water.

Like crabs climbing up a wall, they start moving very slowly, the logs are not slippery but the force of the water on them is strong, he pauses in between every movement to take a breath and then holds his breath again as he moves, the water makes their movements unpredictable. It's slow going but he finally manages to pull them both up onto a well jammed log.

When they finally reach the sand, they both drop, exhausted and gasping. Once he catches his breath, Remy asks, "How far are we?"

"About two miles."

"Let's go." Willing himself up he grabs Delta's arm and pulls her up.

"Remy?"

"Yea."

"Thank you. Again."

"Your welcome, again. Come on, we have a date with destiny."

"I thought her name was Manaya?" She smiles at him.

Twenty minutes later, they approach the designated meeting place, Delta is on alert. Taking cover behind a tree with enormous vines that drape down from its branches, like loose skin. She quietly scouts out the small clearing that is just before the open expanse of the large river mouth. The sound of the rain's night time cleanse, continues to consume the day with droplets of water falling out of rhythm, leaf to leaf before smattering the ground, coupled with the white noise of the continual draining currents.

Remy takes a look around the tree as a green snake slithers up from the ground climbing the vines effortlessly. To his surprise he sees, Galax next to Haven, shy Arona, Ora with her golden hair and Harli and Freeman from the back. What concerns him is why Pitt is there, sitting in between Aristes and Leeds and why no one is moving.

Delta turns back to him with definitive concern on her face.

"What do you think?" he asks, trusting her instincts.

"I think it's a trap!" She whispers.

"Ok. Now what? We can't take them all." Remy resides looking at the drenched gun resting against the tree next to her.

"I don't think we have to."

"What do you mean?"

"Just follow me, follow my lead." She whispers giving him a light kiss on the lips.

As she gets up and starts walking towards the clearing Remy grabs the biggest stick he can find and follows her, leaving the gun behind reluctantly. They will need the bullets for the big boys, besides he has no idea if the gun will even work after being submerged in the river, as the saying goes don't throw a gun on the table if you're not going to use it.

Once they are in view, the expressions on the groups faces reveal the gravity of the situation. Galax is completely panicked; the rest of the women and Haven are expressionless. Pitt doesn't lift her eyes from the ground as they walk to the edge of the circle the group has formed.

"So, you have a plan, do you?" Aristes begins in a mocking tone as he rises but curiously doesn't move towards them. "You have been here all of two days and you are our savior?" Aristes continues bellowing as Leeds sneers, like an untrained dog at his side.

Delta steps forward at his accusation, "Yes we have a plan. A good plan. Tell me Aristes, how long have you been here and haven't thought up a plan?" She continues to his silent surprise, "So happy to oppress and rule, first Packard then you! Little dictators, running the world for yourselves! Taking the women and men that are too afraid to stand up to you! I have nothing to say to your pathetic soul." She moves closer to the group, Remy steps up with her. "The rest of you **must** listen. Make your own choice but listen." Delta makes eye contact with every one of her family as she maintains even pragmatic calm, "We have a plan, that can stop the train long enough for us to attack. They have guns, but we have the element of surprise and numbers. We can get out of here! We don't need to live like this any longer, subjected to the whims of perverse infantile men and women. This is the best chance we have and it's worth fighting for!"

"You want a fight?" Aristes howls.

Within seconds he is on Delta but she's ready for him, out maneuvering him as he runs past her in a miserable attempt to jump her. Falling to a crouch Remy loses sight of them from the corner of his eye, at the same time Leeds and Pitt, jump him. He hits Pitt hard in the throat with the edge of his stick sending her to the ground crippled and gasping for air.

Leeds comes at him swinging, he is big but dumb, it's going to take some time to bring him down. With an upper cut, Remy sends him back a couple of feet but renders his own hand almost useless. Everyone is up and in motion as

Aristes picks Delta up and throws her like a rag doll. Remy watches in horror as her spine and head impact the large tree behind her. She crumples to the ground motionless. Something inside him snaps, simultaneously a wave of bodies rushes forward, grabbing Leeds, swarming him like killer bees. It's a pile up!

Remy only sees Aristes at the end of a tunnel green with anger. Running at full speed, tackling him to the ground, forcibly sitting on his chest, he grabs Aristes by the hair beating his head against the ground. He is no longer Remy Beroe, he has become someone else, something else. Uncontrollable. Wild. Dangerous.

The liquid on his hands feels funny, as he acknowledges the ghostly white eyes from the face below him, drained of all its human physical being. *It's done.*

Dragging himself off the Neanderthal and stumbling in an adrenaline stupor he walks over to Delta, he is immediately thankful her body is warm, she has a pulse and he can see her chest rising with breath. There is no sign of blood, but he is afraid to move her.

In a state of hyper awareness, he realizes they are not alone, there are human shapes just past the tree line. Harli, Arona, and Ora also at Delta's side, stand to look at what has caught his attention. The entire family falls into formation next to and behind him, creating a protective shield around Delta. They wait in silence for what seems like a long minute, prepared for whatever comes next, panting. Sounds of twigs breaking confirm the closeness of the intruders. Out of the bushes, the other women appear. Manaya passes the heap of Leeds who is actually curled in a ball now and simpering, she walks straight towards Remy. Without saying a word, she kneels down and checks Delta's pulse as Remy's group watch in baited silence.

"It's strong, I think she'll be ok. Let's not move her until she's conscious."

"Her name is Danielle," Remy responds involuntarily, protectively.

Manaya looks at him with tremendous determination, "What's this plan of yours?"

57

BLACK MILK

Leaving the bar together, Laure hears the phone in Tyler's pocket vibrate. It's actually chilly, Laure is cold and hurrying to her car on the desolate street outside the bar. Once inside, Tyler checks his messages. "It's him, he has a task for me."

… *Get rid of the P.I.* Tyler shows Laure the text, and she looks up at him with concern. She is no fan of Landon but this is not right.

Tyler calls the number from the text on speaker phone, while keeping his finger to his lips for Laure to be quiet.

"What?" The gruff voice scowls through the speaker.

"How exactly would you suggest I get rid of that?" Tyler asks with an amused tone.

"Use that half a million- dollar degree of yours and figure it out!"

"I'm in the middle of something right now," Tyler adds, playing devil's advocate.

"Don't toy with me Tyler, you can be disposed of as easily as anyone else."

"Yes, yes I can." He says looking out the window at the street lamp across from Laure's car, "Remember Father, our bodies are just wax and wick for flame when the candle burns out, the light shines somewhere else."

"Don't give me any of your mumbo jumbo, you have until noon." Silence terminates the call.

"FATHER?" Laure repeats with a look of confusion.

After a moment's pause, Tyler admits, "Yes. Not in a traditional sense, but yes." He confirms honestly for the first time to an outsider, with more shame than he thought possible.

"Does Steph know that?"

"No one knows that."

"So, you have been working against Steph this whole time?" Laure asks in complete control of her anger now anxious she is in the car alone with him.

"No, not the whole time. I fed the journals and papers false information when it looked like they were going to sign with someone else." Pausing he looks at Laure and continues, "I am not proud of my actions. I like Remy and Stephanie."

"That's one hell of a way to show it." Laure doesn't bother to hide her anger.

"I planned on telling her everything. Please believe I had no idea Remy was missing." Tyler replies looking into Laure's eyes, imploring her to believe him.

"Ok, so now I'm just supposed to trust you? After you've deceived my friends, and are some kind of accessory to kidnapping?"

"No, just give me a chance to earn it back and I am not an accessory."

She nods while her eyebrows raise involuntarily looking at him, sizing him up. "Can I drop you at your hotel?" She adds turning the ignition.

"Laure, there is something else you should know."

"What about?"

"Grace."

58

2 WICKY

Dropping Tyler off at his hotel after what seems like the most surreal evening Laure has ever encountered, he gets out of her car and she is both relieved and torn. His last words, and the look on his face searing her memory, *"If you can find a way to forgive me, I can prove to you that I have cause to be an honorable man."*

"I was right. My instincts were right!" She discourses with herself in the empty car. *He is full of secrets. I am not sure I can work around his sleeping with Steph's assistant to get information out of her.* As those words escape her subconscious, she looks in the rearview mirror at herself. "Who am I kidding? I was supposed to be pumping him for information, and here I am getting sucked in. unbelievable!"

Hey, you awake? She texts Steph before heading home. *Let me know what happened with Tyler's Father. I have ALOT to tell you.*

Looking at the text she hopes that will get her attention! "Damn, I know how to pick em." *Engaged in corporate espionage to basically trap my closest friends and take control of their company and IP.* "Un freakin believable!"

She runs over everything Tyler had confessed to her while gripping the wheel so tightly, her hands cramp.

It's four am she is exhausted, over stimulated and frightened. It's all so hard to believe. Corporate espionage is one thing, but Remy missing? Tyler feels his father could be behind it, but he denies knowing anything about it. How can she trust someone that has been so deceitful? Laure continues to question silently to herself, at what point did his moral garner kick in? If he has been doing this type of shit for years, why stop now? Can he stop? If his father had not shown up at the bar, would he have told Steph what he told her tonight? *Oh Jesus, I have a headache and two hours before Steph will be awake. It's a little strange she didn't text me when she got back to her hotel.*

The bright side of this, she thinks to herself, is Tyler has agreed to sit down with Detective Brennan and Steph this morning and tell them what he told me. That's a start but did his father really abduct Remy or is there someone else involved? *"Fuckin Cannabis!"*

Throwing her keys into the bowl on the table next to her hall closet, Laure plugs her phone in, while hearing Simon's reproving comments from the bedroom. The bed looks good as she heads in to reassure him.

"Simon, you are so lucky you are a cat because this human life really sucks sometimes. Give momma some love."

At a quarter to five, she barely has time for a shower, and something to eat before this day begins. The shower feels so good, she is hoping the hot water will pour some sense into her. Pulling herself begrudgingly out of the warm solitude after fifteen minutes, wrapped in a towel she sits down on her bed for a moment with her furry buddy, head swarming with motives, thoughts, and emotions. She is so tired nothing makes sense. Laying down with Simon curled up, purring sweet unconditional nothings in her ear. *Just five minutes, five minutes of peace and quiet.*

With a start, eyes open, the light from the windows is alarming. *Shit! It must be eight o'clock! Why didn't Steph call me?* Leaping over to her phone, she now remembers muting it as a courtesy when Tyler had spilled the beans. There is nothing from Steph.

Tyler has called four times and texted just as many. Detective Brennan has also texted and he is definitely pissed. The surprising text, however, came in at

six from Landon.
Call me urgent

59

I'LL TAKE YOU THERE

I t's been at least five years since he visited Horace at his family estate in Russian Hill, not spending as much time as he used to on the West Coast. The old stone façade looks foreboding in the morning fog. There is a seasonal chill in the air, one can feel the weight of the impending rain destined for the day. Miles walks through the iron gate into a perfectly manicured garden, Gladstone the butler greets him at the door with a nostalgic nod reminding him that this manor was built the same year Horatio Livermore built his beacon of a home, creating this iconoclastic neighborhood.

As a child, Miles always enjoyed coming here, such a lively and loud household. On holidays, there could be twenty relatives visiting with a dozen children running in all directions. Quite the contrast to the quiet trio he inhabited in Nob Hill.

The grand interior is a compromise of old and new, once past the elegantly antiquated foyer with Tiffany torchieres, the main living room is shockingly full of T.V monitors and computer screens. An assistant's area is empty at the moment. The main focal point, a leviathan of a desk, the top of which has not seen the light of day for years, is Horace's perch.

Turning away from the monitors upon his arrival Horace bounds across the room, "Miles, sit. Have some coffee. You need debriefing."

Always one for action, Horace pours miles a cup of coffee from a serving tray as Miles sits noticing all of the windows have been blocked out by dense draperies, there is no time of day in here.

Taking a file at least four inches thick and an iPad from his desk, Horace begins, "This is quite the intrigue."

Miles places his cup on the cluttered mahogany side table, "I am all ears."

"Your Beroes, are very interesting people. Innovators, pioneers even. I can see why you would want to partner with them. The marijuana industry in no joke and the IP and branding power they represent will be worth hundreds of millions of dollars." Sitting on the arm of the chair directly across from Miles, he continues, "They have drawn a lot of attention from high rollers such as yourself. On the other side of this, they are so Mom and Pop, sort to speak, it seems that they really don't care about all of this hoopla and do what they do for their own personal reasons. Their financials reflect that. Very admirable, verging naive." Horace adds, with a lift of his eyebrows.

"I like them Horace, they are good people."

"As you know" Horace continues, "DBS courted them as well for almost a year, it is my conjecture that although H.S. is behind the disappearance of your colleague's husband, there is more to it than just corporate sabotage. Miles' is taken aback at the reality of this statement as Horace continues, "For months now, I have been aware of a private club, very restricted membership and incredibly high stakes. The members of this club are in our circles, high profilers, with several common denominators; endless finances, they all like to hunt and most importantly they all know H.S." The look on Horace's face has turned quite sober. Horace moves on, "I have a list of 20 men, all powerful in their own right, all wealthy beyond the norm, that I believe are involved in this."

He hands Miles the sheet of paper, "I know every name on this list." Noting a list of names next to each executive, Miles asks, "Who are they?"

"Those my friend, are the names of the people that each one of these men or employees of their companies have been questioned about by police or a PI in connection with their disappearance."

"You must be joking?"

"No, I am not."

"Some of these executives have three or four names next to them, why hasn't anyone put this together?"

Horace's manner lightens as he hands Miles the file. "The FBI is in the middle of an investigation as we speak. I have been led to believe due to the bearing of political and financial adiposity of those under suspicion, it's moving very carefully through shark infested waters."

"What's the next step," Miles asks ready to set the wheels of justice in motion.

"Haven't you read the morning editorials?" Horace replies raising his brows at his friend's ignorant silence. "Well, we are going to shake it up a bit?" Horace announces to the room, handing Miles an iPad.

The headline page of Horace's national news site is remarkable, "That should draw some birds out of the bush. But how did you link all of this together in so little time?" Miles wonders as he verbalizes the question.

"I haven't yet, but by ten o'clock today it will be."

"Drawing fire with fire?"

"Exactly, I have the name and number for Stephanie Beroe's friends and colleagues; Laure Giovani, Jean Carter, and Grace Hamilton do you know them?"

"Yes, I know them."

"Good, call them and ask them to meet us here at nine-thirty."

60

MAPS

Miss Giovanni? Thanks for calling me back." Laddington concedes. "I need to speak with you."

"Ok."

"In person."

"Where are you now?" Laure asks.

"I can meet you at the gas station on elm and Baxter." His request is dire, voice tense and short of breath.

Dialing Tyler after trying Steph one more time, Laure doesn't feel comfortable meeting Laddington alone.

"You're a hard lady to get a hold of." Tyler's tone is calming.

"Laddington, the detective Steph hired," Laure stops herself remembering Tyler knows exactly who Laddington is, and neglects to add, *the one you are supposed to get rid of.* "Just called me. He wants to meet three blocks from my house, he sounds unnerved."

"What's the address?"

While dressing, she has Steph on speed dial with no results. Laure is beyond worried, when her phone rings, the number is unknown.

"Hello?"

"Miss Giovani?"

"Yes."

"This is Miles Venery, I met you last night with Stephanie Beroe."

How did he get my number? "Yes Miles, how can I help you?"

"I believe your friend is in great danger. I need to speak with you. Can you meet me in Russian Hill by nine-thirty?"

"Yes, I may be a couple of minutes late, but I'll be there!" Miles gives her the address. She terminates the call, attempting Stephanie one more time without any results, her concern has turned to anxiety.

Driving over to the gas station, she decides to record the meeting with Laddington on her phone in her pocket, just in case.

There is a brand-new Saab parked at the gas station near the air hose about twenty feet from the gas pumps. It's Laddington, she recognizes him through his dash window. Parking directly next to him, she gets out of her car to walk around to his window, when a hand takes her arm, "Good morning," Tyler is freshly dressed and looks as if he has had a full night's sleep and breakfast.

She responds with a blushing smile. As they approach Laddington, Laure sees that the detective is visibly shaken Tyler is with her.

"Laddington, what's up?"

"Have you been able to contact Mrs. Beroe?"

"No, I haven't."

Tyler looks concerned as she answers.

"I followed you both last night as she requested." Laddington begins uneasily, his words rapid and confessional, "After she left the restaurant with the older man you ate with, they stopped at an industrial site. The chauffeur got out and nothing happened for a while. Then the car started shaking, and a couple of minutes later, I saw Mrs. Beroe trying to get out of the driver's side door. The rear passenger side door opened abruptly, hitting her on the head and she fell to the ground. The driver picked her up and placed her back in the car."

"And then what?" Laure yells at Laddington.

"They drove off."

Dumbstruck, she looks at Tyler, realizing he could have been in on this, and feels sick.

"Where did they go? Tyler demands gripping Laddington's forearm through the car window.

"Out to a heliport in Oakland."

"What time?" They blurt out in unison.

"Around two-thirty AM."

"Good, so you called Brennan?" *That's what Brennan wanted to tell me.*

Laddington starts shaking his head from side to side, "There's more." The look on his face is horrifying as he continues barely audibly, "I wasn't really hired to help."

"What?"

"I was hired", he looks around the parking lot and pauses, "to get in the way."

Tyler squeezes her arm.

"By whom?" Laure asks, deflecting the urge to drag his carcass out of his car and kick him in the head.

"Grace."

Unsure of her instincts at this point, Laure suggests to Tyler they take separate cars to meet Miles in Russian Hill. If anything, this gives her time to gather her thoughts. Her brain is overloading and her heart actually hurts. *While trying to play detective, I've lost Steph! She's gone! Both of them are gone!* She thinks to herself, with tears. *How much of this does Tyler really know? Did he instruct Grace to hire Laddington to get in the way? When he squeezed my arm, while Laddington was confessing, I thought I was going to throw up!* Taking a breath, she chides herself, *pull yourself together, girl.*

Laure parks, thinking they must be meeting at some kind of club, as the stone building in front of her is massive with a whole block of land surrounding it that is walled in by stone. Tyler is waiting for her at the iron gate entrance, "Any idea where we are?"

"None, Miles just said to meet here, that was it."

At the door, an ancient man asks their names and invites them in, Laure realizes, he is an honest to goodness butler with an English accent to boot. The house is something out of Downton Abby. This is the real deal. She also notes Tyler is non- plussed.

They are led to a giant room directly off the foyer and step into a new time, maybe the future. Miles is sitting in an armchair worth more than her car, talking with a huge man she does not recognize. Detective Brennan is sitting at a desk piled with paperwork, looking through a file of some sort.

They are actually announced, laure notices Miles face visibly cringe at Tyler's presence by her side. Rising to meet her, Miles comfortingly takes Laure's hand, "Ms. Giovanni, thank you for coming. You know Detective Brennan, this is Horace Mendel a friend and colleague." Horace is also looking at Tyler with a blank expression.

"I asked Tyler to join me." Laure offers, "We have information about Stephanie, and he has information that may be helpful." She says removing her coat and handing it to the butler as she moves into the room.

Detective Brennan interrupts, "I am sorry to tell you Miss Giovanni, but your friend Mrs. Beroe has also disappeared. Do you have any idea where she may have gone?"

"Yes." Laure and Tyler respond together. They tell them everything Laddington told them. Once they have all digested this, Laure continues, "There's more. It seems Tyler was... friendly with Steph's assistant to gain information as well."

The force of the room's gaze, sends Tyler back a step physically. Regaining his composure, his green eyes determined, he begins, "I am guilty of corporate sabotage, I paid Grace Dougherty, to slow things down, send out false statements to the media, and be a broken cog in the wheel for the last six months."

Finally breaking the silence, Brennan asks, "Which heliport did they leave from?"

"Oakland."

He gets on his phone and orders someone to Oakland, then calls the airport directly, demanding their flight plan.

"That's not possible!" Brennan yells into the phone before commanding, "No one leaves the heliport until after you have all been questioned, do you understand me?" Looking up from his phone he concludes, "They have no record of their flying out of there. Where is Laddington?"

"I don't know," Laure responds as Miles walks over and takes her hand leading her to a chair, away from Tyler.

"Coffee my dear?"

"Yes, please." Tears have started running down her cheek.

"There now, we are not without information ourselves," Miles says smiling at her in a comforting parental way, handing her a cup of coffee. "Horace?"

"Tyler this is a list of possible places your Father could be taking her."

Tyler's eyes blink at the mention of his lineage, Miles looks to Horace in surprise as well. Tyler takes the paper glancing at it momentarily, "Your missing a few, Switzerland, Dubai, and Panama.

"What is that?" Laure asks Tyler.

"A list of our residences." He passes the paper to her plunging himself into the chair next to hers.

"There must be over a dozen addresses listed here!" She says in disbelief, looking over the paper.

"Yes, but which one is he taking her to?" Horace asks no one in particular, turning to a map on a screen in front of them with GPS pins attached to the array of residencies in question.

"I think you are off base here," Tyler interjects.

"How so?" Horace replies turning his focus on Tyler.

"He is way too smart to take her to a known residence."

"Where then?" Brennan demands, slamming a file down on the over-burdened desk.

Just as Tyler begins to speak, three more people are led into the room by the butler; Jean Carter, Steph's friend from the conference, laure recognizes right away. The other two; a women of average height with a killer body in a dark suit, and her companion a burly tall guy, who could be a football player, also stuffed into his dark suit. Brennan immediately walks over, ushers Jean in who gives Laure a nod as she moves down the three steps into the massive room, they occupy.

The football player takes the floor with his badge, "This is Agent Navarro and I am Special Agent Spencer from the FBI."

The hair is standing up on Laure's arms, at the mention of the FBI. Tyler noticing takes her hand, she has visibly blanched.

"Mr. Mendel, thank you for debriefing us on route."

Horace nods and introduces everyone in the room, before rounding on Tyler. "So where do you think he took her?"

"I'm not sure, I have been trying to figure that out myself. However, there is something you should know, I have become aware of a private club." Tyler responds in a monotonous tone. Horace and Miles look at each other in response to his statement.

I think I am the only one in the dark here. Laure thinks to herself.

"Doesn't anyone read the news anymore?" Horace bellows from across the room.

"Let's hear him out." Agent Navarro suggests nodding toward Tyler, as she walks into the middle of the room, taking inventory.

"H.S." Tyler begins, "has acquired an unusual interest in the Beroes. For over a year he, we have attempted to partner with them, unsuccessfully. Between his unhealthy attraction for Stephanie and an unnatural desire to own a cornerstone of the cannabis industry, it has become an obsession with him. I have played my part, encouraging their assistant to behave unprofessionally and contrary to her position. I've bribed writers for cannabis newsletters, magazines, and blogs to report disparagingly about their cannabis company, Mad Hatter Coffee and Tea and you Miles." Miles' face is even and calm as Tyler continues, "It was all part of the game at the time," he pauses before continuing. "I see things very differently now."

Laure notices Tyler's voice trailing off with his last sentence, feeling his pain but very unsure if she can trust him.

"Were you aware of my business meeting with the Beroes in Laguna a couple of weeks ago?" Miles asks Tyler, with a glance toward Horace.

"Yes, I was aware you were meeting with them," Tyler replies. "About six months ago I noticed a pattern of travel, not work related for H.S. Not the norm, he doesn't usually travel unless there is a bottom line attached. The destination is unclear, but the time spent, always five days. The flare was that there were no manifests in the jet for any of these trips, even though I know he took them, saw his bags being loaded and accompanied him out to the airport on several occasions." Tyler pauses taking a moment to answer silent inquiries, "You must understand he is my father, by blood, yes, but there are no other bonds, his personal life is kept only to himself. It's always been that way." To Laure, the strain in his voice is heartbreaking.

Tyler continues, "Anyway, one thing I am sure of is, they were hunting trips, guns packed, even a very special gun he bought at auction. Last night, I ran into a child hood acquaintance at the Olympic Club," Laure notices both Miles and Horace raise their eyebrows unintentionally, "it seems my friend's father is also a member. They are both big game and rare game trophy hunters, but what struck me is when Walter said, "The game was unparalleled, nothing like the top of the food chain."

"Is his father's name on this list?" Horace asks while shoving another piece of paper in front of Tyler.

Examining the paper in front of him, Tyler responds, "Yes." Pointing to a name Laure cannot see, the feds, move in on the action.

"Wait a minute." Laure interrupts, "What are you saying? Are you saying these men are hunting…"?

"People." Horace concludes abruptly.

"Miss Carter, you were with Mrs. Beroe the two days she investigated and interrogated the facility and staff of the conference center?" Brennan picks up the ball.

"Yes, I assigned staff to her and gave her reign of the conference center in the hopes we would find Remy. They are good friends of mine. I am a bit confused, how does Remy disappearing have to do with a private hunting club?"

"Miss Carter, Stephanie is missing as well, and we have reason to believe they have both been taken to this… club. We have a good lead, but we are several hours behind them at this point and without a destination."

"Oh my god!" Jean begins to cry, as Laure moves over to comfort her.

"If you don't mind Horace, we would like to set up command from here." Agent Navarro requests.

"A good a place as any," Horace walks over to his desk, the size of a king size bed, and slides everything on it into an equally oversized trash bin.

"Let's see that map and the list of names," Brennan always one to stay on track, demands as the agents set up their gear, which is pretty impressive.

"We have pictures of the Beroes, circulating in all of the airports in California." Agent Navarro has taken the floor. Turning to Tyler, she asks, "Have you seen this man before?" Throwing an image of a curly haired man with somewhat wild eyes on to one of the large screens of the main wall of the room.

"No. Wait, yes. He looks familiar, but I can't place him. Why?"

"He was a waiter at Norma's restaurant in New York City, he disappeared about seven months ago."

"Norma's? They cater our special parties on the east coast." Tyler adds.

"Your father was listed as a regular client, but he was never questioned at the request of the owner of the restaurant."

The gasp that escapes Laure's mouth scares her.

Tell me, Ms. Giovanni, when did you decide you could trust Mr. Adom? Miles asks bitingly, with obvious contempt. She had never heard Tyler's surname before and it catches her off guard.

What else don't I know about him? "It was obvious to both Stephanie and myself, that Tyler invited us to meet him at a bar last night to tell us something. We were all surprised when his father showed up." Then it hits her the piece to the puzzle that is missing is Grace, "Hang on, where is Grace?"

Navarro and her silent sidekick take the floor. "Grace Dougherty also known as Grace Henning is missing as well. This morning at five AM we sent a field agent to pick her up for questioning, based on information provided by Mr. Mendel." Navarro looks over to Tyler, "You may want to sit down."

Tyler sits on the arm of the chair he is nearest to as she continues, "It seems she has been working for your father for the last three years. Mr. Mendel recognized her from an investigation his team engaged in during the firsts two years she was on the DBS payroll. Miss Henning was part of a lobbying group whose intentions were to change the federal regulations for public natural resources, in an attempt to garner and charge nationwide fees on private wind, solar and geothermal collection.

"I played no part in that scheme. Although, I did know about it." Tyler eyes Laure, "I never met that project group and I met Miss Henning six months ago, when I first engaged her for information, after she had been hired by the Beroes."

"Was that your idea?" Agent Navarro leads.

"No, it was my fathers."

Navarro brings up black and white photos from street camera's in a neighborhood on one of the big screens, the scene is a bit fuzzy. "Do you recognize this street?"

"No."

Navarro noticeably regards Tyler's reaction before continuing, "This intersection is the last turn before Grace Henning's house."

"Ok."

"Do you recognize this car?"

Tyler's face turns white, "Yes and the driver, it's my father's car."

"Are you aware that your father had been…visiting with Miss Henning on a regular basis for the last six months, the exact time she took residency there?"

"No," Tyler responds obviously mortified.

Eeww. Laure says nothing.

Turning their attentions to Laure the agents move on, "Miss Giovanni, could you please go over the details of the key interviews from the conference center?"

"Stephanie figured out that a food rack could be the only way they could have gotten Remy out of the conference center without anyone noticing. The name of the witness that identified the two men that must have taken Remy is Karen Ferring, she works in the kitchen." Brennan gives them an artist's rendering of the men masquerading as chefs, both agents confer.

"Run these through NSA." Navarro politely demands as her partner scans the images into a computer. "I think we are all up to speed now. Here is what we propose." Navarro announces to the group. "We have been unable to call up travel manifests for the D.B.S jet but now that we have another suspected member, we will requisite their flight plans. Agents are checking every residence on the map for signs of both Mr. and Mrs. Beroe. We have not been able to confirm any unusual movement via satellite, but we do have an all- points bulletin on Henning and Laddington, we will find both of them. Thanks to Horace, we have a list of possible suspects that allows us to cast a wider net. We'll have something soon."

Helplessness gripping her, Laure thinks to herself, *is she trying to convince us or herself?*

61

BURNING DOWN THE HOUSE

The red light of day presses on my eyelids with the weight of a splitting, headache that delays my acknowledgement of it. *Where the hell am I?*

Rolling over on my side and squinting through my eyes wincing, I don't recognize anything in this room. *Room?* I close my eyes again quickly as my body seizes in pain, but I recall the gruesome memories of last night's events. Taking a deep breath cut short by a sharp pain in my upper chest I look down at my ankle, swollen and bruised. Pulling myself up to sitting position in Laure's tattered couture, my hands firmly pressed against the sides of my head to keep it from exploding, I take stock of my confinements.

The room I am in, is enormous with huge ceilings and glass doors that lead from the bedroom I am interned, to a living room twice its size, both are flooded with light I cannot bare to behold. Once my eyes adjust to the glare, I realize this is not just sunshine, it is compounded by the reflection of a sea. *Which sea is the question?*

Willing myself to move, I attempt ignorance of my excruciating head, the compromise is I can only open one eye to do so. Hobbling around the bed, I note there is a bathroom just to the left. Everything in the room is white, the walls, the bedspread, the frames around the grotesque black and white artwork of dead animals propped up against their slayers, every nick knack, the lamps, everything, all of it adding to the terrible glare of day. *It's like being imprisoned under a sunlamp!*

The bathroom is no exception, a glass window wall extends into the shower stall, all of the walls, the sink and from what I see even the toilet is carved white marble. The wall directly opposite the bathroom door is mirrored and I am horrified at what I see! *I look like I have been beaten with a club!* Remembering I was, brings tears to my eyes. "Where am I?"

Gathering my emotions at great cost, I splash water on my face. There is a medicine cabinet to the left of the sink, hoping with all hope it's full of ibuprofen, I open it. It's full alright, Percocet, Ambien, it's a pharmaceutical show room, the containers are prescription but there are no patient names on the dozen or so bottles. At the back of the shelf, I find a bottle of ibuprofen next to nail polish remover, I snatch two and swallow them down with water from the sink with my hand. The water tastes so good on my parched lips, it's almost sweet.

Limping back out to the bedroom, I notice my purse for the first time, on a strange chair against the wall. Seeing something familiar gives me a boost, I grab the purse off the white skinned chair, with bone like arms and legs, and dump it out on the bed. Everything is in it, I grab for my phone, heart racing; *Maybe he overlooked it.* It's at 25% battery and… no service, although there is WIFI, I try jumping on, but its locked. I look everywhere in the bedroom for a password, the side table drawer, the desk in the corner, nothing. I move into the living room gingerly, again a white mess, there is a large kitchen to the right of it and a hallway that goes into another wing with a T.V. room and an additional bedroom and bath. In the middle of the hallway is the front door, I tug at what I hope is not an elephant tusk handle with no success. I am as I had guessed, locked in. With my back against the wall to freedom, I guestimate the beach below to be about four miles of jungle from here, without a clear path and steeply inclined. There are people on the beach, little black spots amidst a thriving corona. The only way anyone down there could see me, is if I lit this place on fire. *Which is not a bad idea!*

Returning to the kitchen, there is fruit on the counter, wine in the standing frig, next to the sub- zero frig, I open the door and it's full of food. My stomach lurches. I grab an avocado hungrily as well as a package of cheese. I eat both within 1 minute, tops. Then I realize there is premade food as well, the first covered dish is a roast of some kind, maybe pork, the second is a much darker meat, with a very gamey smell. I stick with the fruit and cheese.

The food has definitely helped my head, although it hasn't stopped throbbing, it's just moving around a little. Hazily remembering my purse, I go back into the bedroom noticing the only non- white element in the entire house, a woven jute screen behind the bed that runs the length of the bedroom wall, it seems like homemade twine, twisted into big loops with some kind of black shiny seed pods holding the rope in place, it looks African. I question its importance for a moment. My bottle of CBD is laying on the bed calling me. I take four squirts, ignoring the bitter taste, hoping it will relinquish my head. I also see the bottle of THC concentrate I had thrown in there, that could come in handy. My wallet, lipstick, coin purse, pen, are all in there. *I really need to rethink what I carry in my purse!*

Reaching for my phone, feeling a little bump of energy from the CBD, I review my text messages. The last received was at six thirty A.M. from Miles, the finale of a long string of texts.

Very concerned about your whereabouts and safety please contact me immediately.

There is a text from Laure, from four thirty; *Hey, you awake? Let me know what happened with Tyler's Father. I have a lot to tell ya. LOL*

'Tyler's Father, what?" *Oh my god, wow! I didn't see that coming!* Last night there seemed to be a lot of animosity between them but, they don't look alike, they have completely different sensibilities, I hope against all the odds that Tyler is not the dark angel I assume. Staring at the phone like a fallen comrade the weight of my situation slaps me. *Have I screwed up or what? What was I thinking? I was hoping to draw out information about Remy, so I could help him. I don't even know where the hell I am!*

Walking over to the glass wall overlooking the sea, I take a good look around, my hands pressed to the glass like a child oogling something they cannot possess. This is very tropical, more tropical than California, and remote. I can see only two or three buildings below, it is morning but the sun is in the opposite direction of the ocean, so Pacific Ocean is my guess. The house is cantilevered over a steep hillside that faces the sea, oddly enough there's no deck. The ground is at least sixty feet below. Just as I decide to view the ground from the other rooms, I hear the door in the hallway open. Panicking, I look around for a hiding spot before I catch myself, *it's now or never!*

Resigned, I sit down in a grotesquely taxidermized chair that once held my purse, after shoving all of my stuff back in and throwing the purse under the bed. In the moment's silence that follows, I can only hear my pulse in my head, the rhythm is strong, undulating and painful as I hold my breath.

"There you are. How are you feeling today?" Without waiting for a response, he continues, sauntering into the room, "I must apologize for last night, I lost my head." H.S. drones on as if we had a trifling argument. Sitting on the bed to face me, he asks, "Did you just wake up? Go shower, there are clothes in the closet that should fit you. You look terrible." My silence and one-eyed stare irritate him, "Don't be upset with me, this will all make sense when you have had something to eat and we discuss this like adults." His voice becomes impatient. My narrowed eye focusing on his hands, nittering, he is wringing his hands incessantly and obliviously.

"You realize you attacked me and then kidnapped me," I say very quietly. *Control is key.*

"Don't be so dramatic. This is one time your artistic sensibilities will not do you justice."

"Did you take Remy too?" I ask attempting to hold back the tears welled in my eyes.

"He is of little consequence in the big picture, you will learn this." With his reply, his tone turns angry. "Now, go clean up!"

H.S leaves the room and I run over my options. *Lighting the house on fire is looking better and better.* The reality is, I cannot over power him, not without the element of surprise anyway, I have no weapon and no plan of escape. So, I'll bide my time. Walking over to the closet with handles made from some kind of bone that have been finely polished and creepy, I find an array of clothing, from sequined dinner gowns to bathing suits. I choose the most functional items in the closet, a black halter Gucci one- piece bathing suit with three gold squares down the front and a pair of khaki yoga shorts with a man's yellow linen long sleeved top, the only long sleeve item I see. Grabbing my loot, I shower quickly, taking extra time going through the bathroom cabinets. I find a first aid kit with an ace bandage and quickly wrap my ankle; the extra support feels really good. My headache has reduced itself to a dull throb in the back of my head, where after some inspection with my hands, I can feel a small lump.

I brush my hair and tie it up in Greek knots while it's wet, looking in the mirror I take inventory. H.S is a sociopath. There is no reasoning with him. No one knows where I am. I can only hope that Laure discovers my absence and contacts Brennan. Maybe he can force Tyler to tell them where I am! Or hopefully, Landon followed us. *That's a big maybe.*

Exiting the bathroom, I smell garlic and butter and my stomach cramps with desire. I walk into the living room to see H.S. at the large white granite table that dominates the kitchen, he is sitting on the most ridiculous Lucite chair I have ever seen, the petite design is Rococo, which gives the appearance of a troll sitting on a human chair. Tucked in and waiting for me in his Ralph Lauren ensemble he is oblivious to what's really happening. As I approach the table he rises and pulls out a Lucite chair for me. *Ick.*

"Much better, don't you feel better?" His cologne is overpowering, the smell is repulsive. White saliva that is continually collecting at the corner of his lips is stomach turning.

I sit slowly in reply as this crazy person lays a napkin on my lap, then pours a glass of Pinot Grigio for both of us. I drink an entire glass of water and half of my wine as a bracer. Picking up my fork and knife. *Knife? Definitely pocketing that.*

H.S. continues with his niceties as he sits opposite me, "Try the veal, it's superb, D'artagnan - I have it flown in."

Is he quoting The Three Musketeers? Confused I realize someone had to have delivered this hot food, he sure as hell didn't cook it and all the food in the frig was cold. So, maybe I am not just in a house. I eat because this is going to be my last meal. I finish everything on my plate, the poor little baby cow and the infused mashed potatoes, I actually finish before he does, a bit heavy for breakfast, *but I'm storing carbs!*

Watching in silence as he drips madeira sauce down the front of his white buttoned up shirt without any regard. I continue to pour wine into his glass without any affect, unfortunately.

"Thank you, Stephanie. See I told you things would look better once you ate." The look on his face is calm and reserved, he has completely snapped. Which gives me an idea, *if I can get to my purse, I can dose the shit out of him! I have enough cannabis concentrate in my bag to take down the elephant that has been shot dead, in the photograph behind him.*

"Excuse me for a moment?" I innocently request.

"Of course." He rises as I stand to leave.

Grabbing my bag from under the bed en route, I go into the bathroom shutting the door behind me. The glass vial is intact. The concentrated cannabis oil, however, is congealed into a solid mass in the bottle from this air temperature- controlled environment, *I hate air conditioning!* Unscrewing the rubber dropper top and pulling it out, I tip the bottle upside down and nothing happens. *Damn!* I need to heat this up to make this work. Going over to the sink I turn on the hot water thinking I can run hot water over the bottle to encourage viscosity. But as I place the dropper back in the bottle, I realize the dropper is already full of oil. *My first break!* Slipping the bottle into the back pocket of my borrowed shorts I leave the cap on but not tightened down. Although the oil we use is very clean compared to hash oil, it still has a definitive cannabis smell and it is so dark green it is almost black. I can't just squeeze this into his cold wine, it has to go into something hot with a lot of flavor, aroma, and body for him not to suspect anything, I also need him to be preoccupied. Returning to the table, I wait.

Finally interrupting the scraping of his plate with his fork, I ask, "Where are we?" He looks up from his plate only with his eyes and smiles an unnerving smile without response, his blue eyes gleaming with malice. The hopes I had fade quickly as H.S. finishes everything on his plate and sits staring out the window.

"Coffee?" I offer gingerly.

"Yes, that would be good."

"Let me," I add getting up, clearing the plates and putting the cappuccino machine to work in no time. *This is perfect, a little cream, a little honey… he won't taste a thing.*

Once the roar of the steamer dies down, H.S. pushes back his chair and walks towards me in the kitchen. Placing his arms around me from behind, I recoil. The bottle in my back pocket, however, gives me strength.

"Now, now Stephanie, this isn't so bad, is it?"

Afraid of setting him off and losing my window for my plan, I just nod looking ahead at the cupboards maintaining calm. Then he whispers in my ear like a would-be lover, "Your husband is at my mercy. You do what I say or he dies, and I will personally skin him alive and bring it to you."

I freeze as he grabs me so tightly, I cry out in pain, then he kisses me on the side of my neck, biting me. Grabbing for the steaming coffee pot out of instinct

I throw it behind, emptying its contents.

"Ahh!" He yells letting go of me, manically looking for a towel to wipe off the boiling hot liquid. "You will be sorry for that!" For a moment I think he's going to hit me before he turns away and walks out the door.

Holding my side, I let out a primal scream kicking the marble cabinet behind me with my good foo, before returning to the ugly chair in the bedroom. Staring at the twine wall mount behind the bed in a stupor, it hits me! *Remy must be here too? Imprisoned like me? He is alive! For now, that is all I need.*

Out of the corner of my eye I notice something that had not been on the horizon before, crossing the white carpeted floor, holding my hand over my eyes as a shield, I don't need to read the name on the prow of the ship to know what it's called, Jove's Gift is moored just off the main beach with all of its toys out. Anger wells inside me and is beyond any emotion I have ever felt necessary to express. Turning around to the room, I put a plan into action. A new surge of energy overcomes my pain. I yank the white ten thousand- thread count pillow case off the bed and start filling it with all the medicine and first aid supplies in the bathroom I can find, the contents of my purse, and a good carving knife from the kitchen wrapped in another oversized man's button up shirt I find in the other closet. Seeing a pair of men's boat shoes, at the bottom of the closet I slip them on for good measure. Extracting handfuls of exotic beef jerky, bags of nuts and a large bottle of water as well from the kitchen. *I am set.* With my bag packed I march over to the wall mounting and rip it off the wall in three tugs, knocking over the white lamps on either side of the bed. *Oops.*

Using the poultry sheers from the kitchen, I start cutting the wall hanging into two- foot wide strips, the thing is at least ten feet long, so I figure it gives me almost one hundred feet of ladder, at least that's what I hope. I tie the cut ends together and roll the piece up like a sleeping bag, listening intently for any entry or sound of intrusion. After about ten minutes of tying, my fingers are raw from the twine, but I've made up my mind.

Marching over to the kitchen sink, I open the cupboard and find what I'm looking for. A bottle of bleach and Drano. Marching back to the bathroom I snatch the convenient family sized nail polish remover from the medicine chest. Once I find a spaghetti pot, I'm in business. I Pour the acetone into the pot then stand the bottle of bleach in the middle before I pour half the Drano into the bleach bottle. I saw this in the movie REDS, *Remy loves that movie, I hope it works.* For good measure, I turn on the gas stove and blow out the pilots.

Moving back towards the bedroom glass windows snagging the recently unburdened Lucite chair I take a running start, swinging the chair with all my might against the bedroom window. The sound is crushing, shards of glass are strewn everywhere, as a wave of warm humid air expresses its approval. Using one of the picture frames I rip off the wall, I clear all the jagged edges from the ground, and attach my makeshift rope ladder to the commode. Tossing the roll out the window, I stick my arms through the arm holes I had cut into the pillow case, and throw it on my back, before heading out the window without looking back.

62

SPACEMAKER

Breakfast at the clubhouse is a tradition prior to a hunt, it breeds comradery. Having already eaten, H.S. sips his coffee noting the air in the dining room this morning is obviously tainted, by what he is not sure. Bazel and Bannock are huddled together like two school girls as Jameson walks in, the young man's carefree stride is burdened as he heads for H.S. *Hope it isn't a business deal gone awry.* H.S. sniggers under his breath as the young man approaches.

"H.S. we have a problem." Jameson clatters handing him his phone across the table.

"What now?" He replies but his eyes are drawn to the page.

Private Hunting Club – Draws Federal Fire!

A private men's hunting club that has been under the suspicion for multiple abductions and murder, is being investigated by the Federal Bureau of Investigation after local authorities in no less than twenty communities exposed details linking some of the wealthiest American Chief Executive Officers to the disappearance of over a dozen people. In some cases, the missing persons are suspected family relations and or business relations of the CEO's. It is believed the victims are being used in some sort of hunting ritual.

Sargent Detective Michael Brennan of the San Francisco Police Department was quoted stating, "The scope of the investigation runs deep into the political and Financial stratus of corporate maleficence." Just before print. Names of suspects and victims are being with- held until suspects are in custody.

A.P.

Noting the original source is the Pacific Edition, a subsidiary of an old acquaintance, H.S. turns to Jameson, "They cannot touch us. This is not a problem." He concludes, handing the phone back, as he picks up his coffee cup, challenging young John with silence.

Jameson notices the red marks on the elder man's face, but says nothing, "Half of the club has left already and the other half as you can see, is panicking."

"Nonsense, this can all be handled with one phone call."

"Then I suggest you make it."

Jameson's threatening tone is admirable but laughable. Peripherally, H.S. perceives all of the members left watching their conversation, which gives him an idea. Pushing his chair back he rises and addresses the group of spoiled crybabies.

Once he finishes his pep talk, a round of applause goes up in the room. He has smoothed them over.

"What happens to the members that left?" Levitt asks unable to control his disdain for the mutineers.

Frankly H.S. is surprised Levitt is still here, Jameson replies, "They will be punished." Onerously, squelching any further desertion. Leaning in to H.S he continues so as not to be overheard, "I was informed one of our ground staff has disappeared."

"Really? In action or off island?"

"In action."

"Did you bring your new handlers?" H.S. asks the youngster.

"The bipeds? Yes, I did."

"I see a chance for you to play with your new toys, Jameson. Deploy them." H.S. orders as he places his phone to his ear.

"We haven't had time to train the men as operators."

"You have until noon."

63

BREATH ME

My body is covered in sweat, the palms of my hands are drenched and stinging, from the twine cutting small slivers into them. Climbing down the jute makeshift ladder I made is not as easy as I had imagined it would be, the twine is slack and uneven, causing me to arch my back to keep it balanced. I don't dare look down. I have to move my lower half first then my hands, it takes all of my concentration. "I can do this."

My foot is stuck. I must have pushed it in too far. Holding on for dear life, I pull with all of my might, attempting to extricate the oversized man's shoe out of the hole. But the pressure of the shoe being wedged in, is too much for my ankle. So, I yank my foot out of the shoe and continue. I move my way down slowly, coming eye to eye with the shoe, pulling it out and tossing it to the ground, without looking.

It seems like it's taking me all day to get down this thing. The house above me is, however, looking smaller and that's a good thing. Closing my eyes, I keep going, feeling my way down.

Out of nowhere, the ground is beneath me, an embraceable relief. I take a couple of minutes to look for the shoe, but the grass is four feet high, and I feel really vulnerable out in the open.

Once under the canopy of the trees, I feel safe for the first time since I woke up but it's difficult to decipher the direction of the beach, I can barely see ten feet in front of me, the underbrush is so dense. The position of the sun, my only guide. I stay with it, with one shoe and a bad ankle, I am hobbling, but at least I am not captive anymore.

Finding a long stick to use as a walking stick, my momentum picks up until I come to a large ravine, too steep to go down, too far to jump, I have to pick a direction. Left, or right? *Always go left.*

Paralleling the ravine, I notice hard fruit falling intermittently from above, but there is no breeze to be had. Then I hear them, a low deep rhythmic howl at first. It makes the hair on my arms stand up. The sound coming from every direction is consuming and terrifying, like the low growl of a hundred motorcycles. I quicken my pace to get out from underneath, for surely the dark bodies above me in the trees are the source of discord.

The yellow shirt I snatched is getting snagged on every little twig, so I tie a knot in the loose fabric around my waist. I know its morning – early afternoon, but the light is so different under the canopy, it feels like dusk and probably won't change much. Using my stick to beat back some of the herbage, I am pleasantly surprised and scared to death to find a manmade path directly in front of me. I turn left again without hesitation. A footbridge, just like the one in Indiana Jones but not so long, appears out of nowhere. Made from thick jungle vines, with wooden slats tied on top of two long vines that span the entire twenty- foot distance over a dark colored river. It's new, and well maintained, I scout out the path behind me and the other side before going out into the open. It seems clear, I don't hear anyone, so I go for it. Grabbing the rope banister, I step with my naked foot onto the first wooden slat, watching horrified, as a slat wave shoots to the opposite end of the bridge. *Ok, let's take this one step at a time.* The bridge shoots over a narrow but fast- moving river. *If I were on vacation, this would be amazing, crazy what relevant perspective will do.*

Once I get the rhythm, it's not that difficult. Crossing over to the ravine, the path splits, I turn left again, the ravine is on my left now.

Not knowing where I am going, or where I am, but determined to do something about it, I am definitely feeling braver than I am. Plus the hope of seeing Remy, gives me strength.

The path is dirt but groomed, my ankle is pulsing so I pull off the path lean up against an unfriendly, thorny tree and take two more squirts of CBD oil. Rewrapping my ankle, a little tighter I stick a piece of jerky in my mouth for good measure. The change of climate is affecting me, every pore is sweating, but my genes are on my side. *I love humidity.*

Finally, in front of me, off the path is a building in a clearing that butts up against a steep hillside. Dark natural wood, with a wraparound porch and low overhanging roof, very modern but organically designed. Instead of windows with glass, the huge openings have glass levelers, fortunately, black mosquito screens hinder any view, at least that is what I am hoping.

There is a huge tree casting shade over the building, the porch is hedged with birds of paradise and ginger. I count six, four- seater golf carts parked in a lot adjacent to the building and smell food.

Staying just off the path I get as close as I can to the building, walking around to the backside. The space between the building and the rocky cliff behind it, is narrow and in shadow of itself. A screen door is open and Latin music is coming from within. *I knew it, Central America!*

As I pass the kitchen door, I notice no one is in there, it's empty. Music blaring but no one is home. Continuing to skirt the outside of the building I walk around a little alcove covering an outdoor walk in refrigerator, "What the hell is that?"

64

MOON

While waiting for something to happen, everyone at the Mendel mansion is busying themselves looking at their computer or phone screens, the butler returns through a secret door in the wood paneling wall just to the left of the video monitors. He is pushing a cart burdened by silver platters of bagels, lox, eggs, toast, and potatoes. Laure watches as the elderly man inaugurates dishing out, in white gloves with silver tongs, a younger gentleman in actual livery, silently takes the plate from him and walks it over to a recipient in the room, with silver and linen napkin in the other hand.

It's good to be king, Laure thinks to herself, Mendel is eccentric in a genius sort of way, she notes as she is handed a plate.

"We got him!" Agent Navarro yells out, she is pointing to the large monitor on the wall in front of her.

Laure looks up, hoping to see H.S. on the screen but instead, there is a photo of the man from the police sketches, definitely military, very intimidating.

"His name is Jerry Klein, he is a known merc." Navarro continues.

Laure and Jean's oblivious response to this acronym is obvious, Navarro explains, "He is a hired private soldier for Habistram Industries."

The tone of her voice and expressions of Tyler, Horace, Miles and the agents, lead Laure to believe, she is in the dark again. Hands in the air, "And?"

"Habistram belongs to John Jameson," Tyler explains.

Now that name everyone recognizes, it's on the list of potential members in front of her on the screen, but it's also the name of one of the largest backers of the Republican Presidential campaign, now the President Elect, Horace divulges as the agents silently communicate to one another.

In the silent moment that ensues, Laure connects the dots. Not surprised, all of the pro- military corporations and organizations backed him in the election. With the rest of the sane world, she had been hoping against all odds that this freakish coo was just a bad dream, and she would wake up and life would be dependable and normal again. But it doesn't look like that is going to happen anytime soon on many fronts. "Wait a minute, you mean security? Right? Why would a corporation need soldiers?"

As soon as the words leave her mouth, Laure feels the stare of naivete, pushing on her. "Oh, right. Standing Rock."

"John Jameson's mother," Horace elaborates, "the matriarch of the family died last year from cancer, several months after her death, the youngest son of the dynasty disappeared. We investigated, of course, such a high- profile family, we found nothing but motive. Thaddius, John's brother would have inherited half of billions, without him, John took full control."

Both Agents and Horace are rapidly typing, "We've got wire taps and internet communications traces now for both Jameson and Klein. All we have to do is sift through the information." Navarro says out loud but mostly to herself in her un-creased suit.

With three screens in front of each of them, they go to work, faces glowing in the muted room.

"Would you like more coffee Miss?" The butler asks Laure, navigating the room without attracting the slightest attention.

"Yes, please." *I need some kind of crutch to get through all this,* as the entire wall of screens in front of them, now split into two fields, phone numbers on the left and email communications on the right. The phone numbers mean nothing to her, so she scans the emails. They are told that a computer is running a cross reference on the last six months of emails as well.

"We don't have any Passport activity on either of them that match in any way." Agent Spencer informs the group, breaking what seems like an oath of silence.

"Would that really matter?" Tyler responds, "I have flown dozens of times on the company jet to private fields on private islands without customs. Miles? Horace? Isn't that true?" Both men shake their heads in disagreement.

The agents look of distrust is arduous, "Just because you can do something, doesn't mean you should." Agent Spencer comments, his tone childishly judgmental.

Jean Carter, has not said a word, she is slouched in a couch that is so big, she looks like a child, with her feet barely reaching the floor. Laure walks over and sits next to her.

"Are you ok?"

"I'm here and I am hearing all of this, and I still don't believe it," Jean replies on the verge of tears.

"I see that Mr. Jerry Klein flew out of Miami Airport the first of August and into Miami airport the first of September." Horace offers. "But where did he go in between and where did he come from?"

Tyler sifts through paperwork on Horace's desk, Laure is watching him. Catching his eye, he approaches her on the sofa questioningly. "I like Stephanie and Remy, they are good people." Taking her hand Tyler comments softly, "As soon as I felt they were at risk, I started looking for answers." Shaking her head in response, unable to really express the confusion assailing her better judgement, Laure is at a loss for words. Looking into his eyes, the only thing she is truly sure of is, she shouldn't be sure of anything.

"These are manifests gathered from Jameson, DBS, and Christian Phillips jets," Tyler informs her.

"Who?"

"Christian Phillips, the father of my acquaintance from the Olympic Club, Walter Phillips."

"You grew up with all of this?"

"Yes."

"You don't seem …affected," Laure states genuinely.

"Is that a good thing or a bad thing?" Tyler replies with the softest of tone.

"It's good, it's good."

Managing a smile, Tyler continues, "Cross referencing their internet mail calendars with each other, we are able to confirm that all three men were marked for being out of town on business on the same days a month ago, as well as this week. Horace has been able to trace the internet service provider's location and found a match, all three men were using the same server for email on those days as well. This could be our break."

"How did you get that information so fast?" Spencer asks Mendel a bit put off.

"I have a friend, who knows a friend," Horace replies with a complicit smile.

Navarro plugs the IP address into her computer and a large map of the world is on the screen. Thousands of lines, as well as shaded areas and GPS coordinates, cover it in its entirety. Within seconds it has narrowed a small area off the coast of Central America in the Pacific Ocean. Everyone in the room is standing and watching with baited breath, as the computer enhances an area of the sea off the North coast of Panama. Finally, a very small island appears.

"Can you get satellite images?" Horace asks Navarro.

"No." Agent Spencer replies.

"That is where they are, right now." Horace murmurs staring at the GPS pin on the map on the screen.

The agents start packing up. "We will keep you posted." Agent Spencer tells the group.

Horace nods silently, picking up his untouched plate. The room is impregnated with silence, watching the agents unplug various devices before heading out the door, without so much as a boo.

"We will give them a twenty- minutes head start. That's sportsman like, don't you think Miles?"

"Yes Horace, that will do nicely."

65

LUCKY 13

Pausing to catch his breath, Remy counts thirteen people including himself, *lucky thirteen, two men and the rest women. Our odds are improving.* "Where are all the men?"

"They won't come, they like it here. If you can imagine?" Manaya rounds. "This is Genevieve" she points to the stunning tall blonde next to her, "Hollie", a petite gal with long red hair, "Amanda", a very fit pretty woman with a Queens accent and "Veroon", An Eastern Indian no nonsense type from the look on her face.

"Ok, listen up, I have an idea," Remy announces, "I've scouted the tracks and the train, I think we can stop the train long enough to board it."

"Then what?" Genevieve asks. She is the six- foot blonde bombshell Remy saw with Manaya before. She must be in her twenties, Scandinavian, and he is taken aback she is so striking.

"Then what? Then we kick some ass." He states coming to his senses. Several of the group look frightened, but freedom is a priceless stimulator. "I'm going to divide you into four groups, and I need all of your phones."

They all recoil, their covetous response is justifiable, the last connection to their previous life is a difficult talisman to surrender.

"I need fire makers, vine collectors, weapons gatherers, and scouts within each group to protect us all while we prepare," Remy concludes. easily.

Galax looks a little out of place, like the last kid to be picked for kick ball, but she finally settles on fire makers.

Delta looks around approvingly, as Remy kneels down beside her, "Danielle, how are you? Can you move everything?"

"I'm fine, just a little head ache." She winces, rising up, inspired by hearing her real name and their new cause.

"That was some hit you took. Ok, you stay with me," she nods in agreement, "We are going to need fire torches to set the bombs off," Remy announces.

"What bombs?" Manaya asks.

"These Bombs." Remy holds up their phones.

"Really? That's cool!" Harli injects nodding.

"We've been using rendered animal fat as fuel," Genevieve states proudly. "Can you use that?"

"Retrieve as much as you can without being noticed from your camp site? You are in charge in fire."

"Ok," Genevieve responds with light in her eyes.

Remy begins drawing a map on the ground in front of them, "This is where we'll meet in one hour." He states encouragingly while thinking, it seems hard to believe these two groups were trying to kill each other the day before yesterday. As he considers the men on the train, he feels the adrenaline stirring in his own body and notices the light changing rapidly. "Does anyone know what time it is?"

"Yes, it's about ten thirty, give or take an hour," Genevieve replies.

"Your good, have you had training?"

"No, but I attended expeditionary school as a child," No one knows what she's talking about, "You know, no walls or class room, your just outside in the summer and the winter." Genevieve looks around for support unsuccessfully at the American group, "It makes you resourceful."

"We need to be in place by noon," Remy says helping Danielle up onto her feet. "Let's go."

"You can't just leave us here?" Leeds whines, he and Pitt are tied back to back around a tree.

"You're right, good idea. Gag them both." Manaya states walking over to them while ripping off two pieces of her tattered skirt before stuffing each one of their mouths. Harli uses two small pieces of twine to secure the gags and prods Leeds, "Looks like you bit off a little more than you could chew."

The walk back to the blind is silent, Remy, Danielle, Haven, and Ora are focused on what's ahead. The jungle is purring with excitement. Birds are raucous and swarming as a real breeze, nudges them forward. The imprints of the night's landscape altering storm, mires their path but Danielle knows the way and they cover the distance quickly. Passing a huge tree with vines growing down from its branches like arms reaching for the ground bar their way, the group climbs up with little effort and saws the vines off using sharp edged rocks, gathering the vines to be used as ropes, over their shoulders before continuing to their destination.

When they reach the base of the rocky cliff of Remy's blind, he begins looking for the perfect fallen tree. *Can't be too thick, it will be too heavy for us to lift, but it has to be long enough to bridge the expanse between the cliff and the tracks or half of our group won't be able to make it across the jump, and we need everyone.* Finally, he decides on a tree with as little rot as possible and measures it off with his feet.

His thoughts begin to muddle his concentration; *Where is she? What has he done to her?* Using his frustration as an outlet for strength he heaves the tree over to the base of the cliff dragging the majority of it behind him. "Tie the vines tightly around the trunk just below a branch knob, we will need two secured one on each end."

After the trunk is stabilized, he snaps off a young, tall sapling and strips it bare of all the branches, before strapping it to his back with shirt material. Since he is the only one with shoes, Remy starts up the cliff face tying the vine to the fallen tree around his waist to keep his hands free. Haven scuttles up behind as well as the others. It's slow going as the storm has made mud of everything, it's like chocolate, his shoes are under the mud as he steps, but he was smart enough to use torn cloth from the mercs shirt to wrap his hands before he offered it around to the others, making it easier to use the small thorny saplings as grip holds to pull themselves up one tree at a time. Everyone follows suit.

Relieved to make it back to the blind on the cliff face, Remy realizes they all won't be able to fit in the small indented landing, so he starts pushing the side of the cliff away with his feet. It yields easily enough now that the soil is moist. The smell of the earth is overwhelmingly dank with mildew. Once there is enough room for everyone to gather, they focus on the tree.

Untying the vines from his waist he hands one of them to Haven and Ora, he and Danielle start pulling on the other, it takes all four of them in synchronized labor to move the tree trunk up the hill. In the cramped quarters, their arms are hitting each other as they pull.

After no small effort, the tree is several feet below them, and they secure it by wrapping the vines around a large tree close behind them, so they can all let go for a moment and take a breath. Remy shows Ora a massive branch above their heads, "Climb that tree and sit out on that branch, I'll throw the vines up to you."

"Got it." She doesn't even hesitate, climbing up the tree like a monkey.

"Let's tie the rest of the vines together, to give us enough slack." Everyone goes to work.

The branch is about fifteen feet above them, looking around Remy finds a heavy stick and ties it on the bottom of the vine before throwing it with all his might up to Ora, who ducks to avoid being hit in the face. The vine goes over the branch before it gets snagged in a tangle of branches below her. It takes a good ten minutes to untangle the vine, her golden hair lit by the sun gives her a halo.

They are moving along pretty quickly, the second vine gets secured much easier, now the hard part. Remy takes comfort that he can hear voices below, everyone organizing as planned but, they are running out of time. The sun is almost straight up.

"We need to lift this tree up and leverage it across between the blind and the tracks. Danielle, once the trunk is up high enough guide it into place, use this stick to grab it or whatever." He hands her the stick from around his shoulder. "On three- one, two, three- pull!"

"Fuck!" Remy, sees stars in front of his eyes, as he pulls. "Dragging it on the ground was easy compared to this!"

Haven and Ora are getting nowhere.

"Turn around and start walking as you pull!" Remy yells to them. Using his entire body as leverage against this monster of a tree, every pore is working overtime, his palms are dripping with slippery sweat, arms ready to give out. *I can't hold this thing any longer.*

Just as Remy relents to the weight a shadow comes up from behind him, and starts pulling, he has no idea who it is but he is thrilled, the two of them manage to get the tree to level ground with the tracks as Danielle steers the round end in a straight line, they let go and with a thunk the tree is now a bridge. Falling to the ground, arms and back aching, Remy looks back at who's behind him.

Not a familiar face, but he's thankful just the same. "Hey, man thanks."

"No problem. You must be Remy." The dark- haired man adds not quite as out of breath. Remy nods.

"I'm Thaddius." The young dark- haired man reaches out his hand.

They climb back down to the ground leaving Ora as a look out in the blind. Manaya walks up to them as Thaddius sits down against a mango tree, "I see you met Thaddius?

"He must have changed his mind?" Remy offers as Thaddius awaits instruction.

"Yeah, I guess," She doesn't sound convinced, "we have this area covered, let us know what you need?" Manaya offers as she scouts the area around them.

Each group is working on a task, Genevieve is instructing Arona and Harli to wind extra scraps of clothing around the ends of torch size sticks and roll them in fat that smells horrible. She looks up as Remy walks over, "Do you have any flint?" he asks, thinking positive.

"I can get a fire going, it will take some time though, everything is wet."

"Good, let them finish and you head up to Ora and start the fire. It can't go out."

With a sharp loud whistle, Remy gets everyone's attention, "Listen up!" We have to get all our weapons and the torches up the cliff, and you'll need both your hands to climb, so pack everything on your back and let's get a move on. Manaya, once we are all up, bring your people up too."

"Ok."

Remy removes the batteries from the phones and stuffs them in his pockets. His new best buddy Thaddius is right behind him as he trudges back up the hill. Wondering what changed Thaddius' mind, or an even better question is, why would he want to stay? And where are the other men?

Reaching the top Ora and Genevieve are working together to get the fire started, they found the remains of the nest that used to command this post and are breaking small pieces of twigs off of the underside to use as kindling when Remy looks over with probably something like panic on his face.

Genevieve replies quickly, "Don't worry we'll get it going. Don't wait for us," Serious enough to believe her.

"Everyone, grab a weapon you are comfortable with."

There are clubs with pointed knots on the ends and long staffs. Remy picks one of each and sets them aside, squatting down to prepare his battery bundles.

Once the group is armed Delta turns and faces their troupe holding her hands up for attention. "Today we fight back. Whether we make it out of here or not, THIS IS THE RIGHT THING TO DO!" Everyone is nodding their heads in mutual agreement, anger percolating behind all of their tasked faces. "These men have taken our lives from us, our FREEDOM, OUR DIGNITY, OUR HAPPINESS, our basic human instincts reduced to survival, leaving us divided and mistrusting one another. TODAY WE CLAIM OUR LIVES BACK!"

Howls go up from members of both families, now united against a mutual tyranny. Delta turns towards Remy and mouths, *thank you*. He closes his eyes with a small bow of gratitude that pierces the very essence of the moment and a silent prayer that he doesn't get everyone killed.

Stationing the majority of the group inside the tunnel against the walls for cover, Remy is hoping the tunnel is dark enough to camouflage their bodies. If they are seen, this is going to be over much sooner than expected.

Haven is the lookout for the train at the far end of the tunnel. Walking across the twenty or so feet of tree trunk suspended a good thirty feet above the ground, is not as easy as the movies make it out to be. Remy takes it like an acrobat using his spear as ballast. Everyone goes over in their own style, a couple of the gals decide to scooch on their butts, delivering giggles and catcalls from the group behind them, some go sideways one step at a time. Galax actually walks over without any hesitation, to his surprise, as she is the least athletic in the bunch if you don't count Haven.

The plan is simple, stop the train, climb on it and get into the car with the hunters as fast as possible. The element of surprise is really their only chance against guns. Everyone knows they are not all going to make it, but neither will the hunters.

Ripping strips of vine soaked in fat around each bundle of batteries, Remy ties them together into stacks planting the first stack about twenty feet from the end of the tree trunk. The second stack will be set once the train passes him. Hiding the fire is his biggest concern, how to light the batteries on fire without anyone on the train seeing a fire in the tunnel. Genevieve solved that mystery for him without even knowing it. The rendered animal fat that is on fire, is kept in a coconut shell with a small hole in the top. He hasn't tested this out, but practical science suggests the phone batteries should go up with a bang in less than 15 seconds. The only real problem is that they may need someone on the ground to distract the hunters as they pass, just in case.

"Lo and behold, look who's here?" Manaya directs Remy to Sam the Egyptian gladiator that faced off with Pitt, with a solemn look on her face.

Stopping Manaya and pulling her aside, Remy iterates, "We will need a distraction down below in case the fires take longer than I anticipate to go off."

"I can do it." Sam offers now glowing with opportunity. Remy looks to Manaya, knowing she doesn't trust Sam.

"What do you have in mind?" He asks her.

"How much of that fat do you need?" Sam asks pointing to the coconut shell between Galax and Genevieve.

"Two buckets."

"Can I have the rest?" She looks like a kid at Christmas, whatever she has in mind, she's been thinking about it for a while.

"Sure."

"Just tell me where and when."

Remy points to a spot in front of a huge tree trunk that is hollowed out. "There. You will hear me whistle."

"Done." Sam commits and climbs back down, coconuts in tow.

"That was easy." Manaya looks amused.

"It's a walk in the park," he says to her, turning back to face the train tracks, *a walk in the park.*

Manaya moves down the tracks with her team to get into position. Remy takes one more look at the little bundle in front of him. The timing has got to be perfect, once he gets the signal from Haven, he will light the first bundle of batteries at the front of the train and run to the tunnel to light the second bundle behind the train. He knows there are no windows in the front of the train, *this should work.*

Hope empowers him, then he feels the hit. Knocked to the ground Remy lands on all fours, before he can get up, he feels a blunt club reconnect between his shoulder blades, taking him to the unforgiving cement platform and racking his body with shock. Rolling quickly to the side he looks up to see Thaddius standing above him with a crazed look of madness on his hairy face. Legs moving involuntarily, Remy kicks his legs out from under him, scrambling to stand they launch themselves at each other clashing in mid- air. The look on Thaddius' face is absolute bedlam, eyes wide and void of reason, "How do you like that Fucker?" He screams.

Remy can now see all the women coming towards them on the tracks. "Stay there!" He yells, "We won't have another chance!" The one second it took to look in their direction Thaddius' fist catches Remy on the chin, addling his brains, he takes it standing up, feet planted firmly. "Genevieve, light the first fire when the train comes, Manaya light the back fire once it passes!"

Staring at the delusional dude in front of him, he yells, "I am not your enemy! Our enemy will be coming down this track any minute. Stand with us! Let's get the hell out of here!" For one second Remy thinks he reads epiphany on the crazed man's face.

"Nooooooo!" Everyone hears Thaddius scream as he runs at Remy and they both freefall off the track.

66

THE SFA

"What the hell is this thing doing in the middle of the jungle?" The train looks like a silver bullet. The platform it is on is raised, making it impossible to see in the windows. One thing is obvious, the last stop is here, this building was custom built to load passengers onto the train. I need to find out why.

Walking back around the building and up the ten steps to the double doored entry of the plantation style restaurant, I hear men arguing their voices raised, even a chair or table is moved abruptly. Between the birds, the fan on the porch above me and the muzak playing in the back-round I can't hear the entire conversation. But what I do hear, turns my blood cold.

"Do not concern yourselves with this trivial editorial, everything will be as it should. Look around you, no one can touch us." I recognize *his* voice immediately and my pulse quickens, H.S. continues, "However, in light of the mutinous situation our brothers have placed us in, we have decided to eliminate all witnesses and remove the staff. Gentlemen, you have exactly two and a half hours to tie up any personal loose ends at the park, including the dismissal of all family or friends you brought with you, send them home immediately. At noon the hunt begins."

I turn on a dime running back around to the train in an attempt to hide from the group of men now leaving the building. Crossing back over the tracks I have a perfect view of a crescent beach below, it can't be half a mile from this building and someone was nice enough to paint a sign that says beach with an arrow on the path near the carts. Jove's Gift, that monstrous boat is sitting off the shoreline like a beacon. I hobble over to a golf cart parked by the kitchen and take off down the path. *Hunt? What the hell does that mean? Where is he keeping Remy? Too many questions, not enough answers.*

Bounding down the path, I figure if someone sees me, I'll just act like a guest until I figure out what is going on here. I follow the signs and manage the beach in less than ten minutes, without seeing another person. The beach is clearing, lots of young scantily clad ladies are packing their couture beach bags, maybe it's close to lunch time, *or maybe they have just been told to leave.*

The sun is very high, I can barely open my eyes the glare of the sea abreast the white sand is unbearable. Parking the cart, attempting my most nonchalant beach- walk ever, while limping, I stop at an abandoned towel and pull off my borrowed shorts and top, walking directly into the water. Everyone seems to be on vacation, designer beach chairs, umbrellas, paddle boards, and jet skis. Dark skinned beach attendants in white uniforms are packing up the toys. *The atmosphere is very different down here than in the train house.*

Holding my breath, I reach the water's edge, expecting someone to tap me on the shoulder, I am relieved by both the temperature of the water and the immersion of my body. The weightlessness of the salt water disguises my aches and pains. Turning around to check behind me, I can see the house I was interned, sitting at the crest of the hill top. The glass of the living room window reflects the sun like a mirror, but the smashed bedroom window is now an empty dark hole. It doesn't look like my little experiment with the Drano worked, *so much for life imitating art.*

The train station to the right is juxtaposed against a fierce looking rock face that blocks the skyline of this end of the small bay, it's vertical and craggy. There are several other buildings doting the hillside, maybe twenty. A restaurant with a pool sits at the tideline with several striped cabanas, they are equipped with flat screen TV's as thin as credit cards and designer lounge furniture. I could be at a hip pool scene in a Vegas hotel. I am definitely at a resort.

The stretch of my body in the water feels good except when I lift my right arm over my head to swim, my ribs tighten in pain, so I power doggy paddle over to the boat. I'm not really sure what I am going to do, but it just feels right. If Remy isn't on the boat, I will check every single one of the buildings.

There are no tourists on the enormous decked platform off the back of the boat, several staff are storing jet skis and banana boats. I climb up the ladder next to a water slide and walk purposefully through the gaping entry into the belly of the beast, the staff turn and look but nothing is said. The darker space feels good on my eyes. A spiral Lucite staircase leads to the deck above, I walk up slowly dripping on the white ten thousand dollar a yard carpet, listening for voices. "*I got the moves like Jagger, I got the moves like Jager, I got the mo oo oo oo oo oo oo oo oooves like Jagger*", is playing in the back-round. The top of the stairs opens to a large entertaining area with a ridiculous number of couches and chairs, it looks like an asshole convention, *oh it is!*

You would not know you were on a boat, except for the horrible interior design, it reminds me of something out of a Trump building, so tacky, too much leather and gold with what is that… chintz? There is a long corridor to the left, I take that and find another larger room with floor to ceiling views to the front of the boat pointed out to sea. This is a banquet room and it has been set up for a reception or party. *How nice.* The banquet table is full of silver platters yet to be filled and crystal glasses awaiting drink next to several bottles of scotch at the bar. A dance floor covers most of the room with Saturday Night Fever multi colored floor tiles, complete with a disco ball. That's when I get an idea, *a wonderful, awful idea!*

Once I have served my purpose at the bar, I take the elevator that opens to the galley. Pretending to want coffee, I just walk over to the large vat sitting on the counter. The commercial kitchen is bustling with activity, I am not a concern to anyone. Passing a pan of melted butter, homemade pastry dough and about fifty pounds of very dark cuts of meat. My final crescendo is magnificent!

Completing my mission, pleased with myself, I head back to the entertainment area, walking out onto the deck, the beach looks very small from here. I wipe my tacky hands thoroughly on a beach towel before I slide down a two- story water slide into the sea, with a high school hoot.

Swimming back to the shore, my eyes don't move from that train house. I pick up my clothes, hop back into the cart, stick another piece of jerky in my mouth and turn the key.

I decide to park the cart about half way to the train house off the path and put my clothes on grabbing my bag, nervous I might run into some of the men. Skirting the path and walking through the trees is safest. My ankle is screaming and badly swollen, *it felt better in the water.* I have been ignoring it, but we are coming to odds now. Hearing voices, I stop behind a moss- covered tree and wait as a cart goes by. It takes all my effort to walk barefoot through the brush, the bottoms of my feet are so tender, I am pursing my lips to quell any verbal expression of pain. *I don't know how Remy does it? Walking across rocks and sticks and reef barefoot carrying a big ole board. Remy my love, where are you?*

Approaching the building again, I wait to see what kind of activity is going on, before walking out into the open. Most of the carts are gone now. I'm careful to stay in the brush and as I head towards the train, I pull my pack off, just managing to squeeze in between the train and the building that covers the first half of the last car.

My senses are peaked, listening for the slightest sound, looking for any shadow of movement. There is a platform deck with a yellow and white striped canopy and tied back matching curtains, that look deceivingly cheery. Waiting for any sound, it seems the place is empty, the hum of an air conditioning drowns out most ambient noise so I step on to the canopied deck. The train door is open and the room before me is surreal. Red carpet draws me into paneled walls in rose colored wood, with indirect lighting smoothing the ceilings curved edges, the walls are lined with large lockers, twelve on each side, a wooden rosewood bench sits in front of each row, small chandeliers hang delicately from the curved wood paneled ceiling, *this is very Orient Express.* Each locker has a number inlaid in bone or ivory, one through twelve on the left and thirteen through twenty- four on the right, *ok.* Opening the first locker that I touch, number 9, *my lucky number,* I find a man's jacket and pants, a silk scarf or ascot I guess, finely made boots, some cologne, a bottle of pills again with no patient name, a box of cigars along with a gold lighter engraved with the initials G.L and a cigar clip.

I quietly close the locker door and continue into the next car, which is something right out of The Great Gatsby. A large beautifully carved bar runs three quarters the car length on the left. Surrounding the bar are winged chairs covered in hairy animal fur I have never seen before, clustered in groups of three with standing ashtrays next to each chair. The walls are dotted with books in glass cases, torchiers dimly light the room. The floor is parquet with a hide of some sort. I recognize a Rubens painting of Hercules strangling the Nemean Lion, dramatically lit. This place is creepily luxurious. Behind the bar, there are three separate boxes hanging on the ornately patterned wall, with guns in them, spot lit, placards next to each. I read one of the cards and can't believe my eyes.

Adolph Hitler's gun? Really? Who the hell would want something like that? My hand starts shaking, this is beyond anything I could have imagined, these people are crazy! *How do Remy and I fit into all of this?*

Hobbling into the next car using the stick I had picked up as a cane, it hits me, bells goes off! My heart drops, surrounded by more wood paneled walls lined with hundreds of guns. Custom racks holding each gun like a precious object, complete with a drawer beneath each full of matching ammunition. "Jesus!" There must be two hundred guns in this room, hand guns, rifles, machine guns, all perfectly lit and shining to perverse perfection. My skin crawls, as my conscious struggles with anger and fear. I quickly move to the next car desperately needing to get away from the hateful metal.

Twice the length of the others, the same décor and the only car with windows from floor to ceiling. There is a row of club chairs scattered through the middle of the train facing the retracted windows, several inches from the opening to the jungle are metal posts with mounts on top. There are twenty-four of them, twelve on each side. In the front of the car, where a conductor would be, is another post with an iPad looking thing attached to it, there are no windows in the front of the train, just empty shelves. This room has the creep factor of an operating room with traces of death and pain emanating from its core, you can feel the malignancy within.

I turn around needing to get out of this awful place. My breath fast, I can feel my throat constricting, *I just need some air.* As I manage through the bar car into the locker room, I hear a whistling outside. Panicking as it comes closer, looking around for cover, there is nothing to hide behind!

The sound is definitely coming towards the train! Opening a locker, I wedge myself in, holding the door closed but not latched for fear of being trapped. Attempting to hold my breath in silence, the whistling is now in the train car. I can't see anyone but watch a shadow move past the crack of the locker door. Waiting in absolute silence, I listen over the overpowering sound of my beating heart, like a forest nymph encased in her tree, forever doomed to silently watch as the world outside destroys all that is precious to her. I hear glassware and an ice machine dropping ice, and cheerful whistling.

I wedged my legs in front of me, holding them close with one hand and the other on the latch of the locker door. My ankle is twisted at an unnatural angle causing severe pain, but I am petrified to move. At least the bag on my back is acting like a cushion. I smell sterno being lit, I smell garlic, butter saffron, and meat. My stomach lurches as the aroma imbues the small space I am confined. I just sit and wait.

67

EMINENCE GRISE

Walking up the platform to the train, H.S. takes a hot towel from the foreign attendant standing at the door to wipe his hands and face.

Poor bastard, if he only knew what went on, on this train, he smirks amused, *I guess we'd have to shoot him too. I still might.*

Immediately he notices the changing room doesn't have the pitch of energy it usually holds prior to a hunt, with more than half of the club members deserting, it's obvious they are still thinking about the headlines. Jameson changing next to him is steamily annoyed at the spineless mutineers, leaving him to clean up after them. "They were supposed to organize their guest's departures, not accompany them!" Jameson whines before continuing, "Oh, they will be punished."

"We have a couple of good shots among us, and if anything," H.S states, "recent circumstances adds a little spice to our norm. Between the two of us, Bannock, Bazel, Levitt, Handel, and Becket, and Dryson Pierce I'm not concerned. With your biped's as ground crew, we will round up all the feeders in one area and be done with it." He grins at Jameson, carefully admiring himself in the locker door mirror. Smiling to himself with the thought of his latest immured conquest, the anticipation of Stephanie excites him, she empowers him. The coffee fiasco, is a reminder of her high spirit, it makes her desirable, but it also makes him want to kill her. *She's mine now, and I will skin him alive.*

After the remaining handful of club members have all dressed, they walk through into the bar car, a calm reserve ensues with the usual chit chat while drinks are served. Clink, clink, clink! The sound of his ring against the glass subdues the room immediately, H.S. takes the floor. "Gentleman, are you ready?"

A murmur and raise of glasses the reply.

"The most hits wins today!"

"In fact," Jameson announces, "I will wager a million my feeder is the last to go!"

The truth is, H.S. thinks to himself, Jameson is undoubtedly the best shot in the club, it's not much of a wager, but he takes the bet in the spirit of the game.

"What if we don't get them all?" Beckett asks a look of concern on his unattractive face as the barman serves delightfully grilled mini Argentinian tenderloins stuffed with double cream brie in a complete state of oblivion.

"We have until dark, after that we send in the staff," H.S. responds, *that would be something I would like to see. Perhaps I will stay.*

Flittering back out of the gun room, Jameson adds, "Semi- automatics today, bring them with you."

The looks of the other men are challenging, automatic weapons are so… ghetto. Acknowledging this Jameson replies with boredom, "We are on a time schedule, ten hours, we may need them."

To that reasoning, the small group of men nod in agreement while choosing and loading weapons.

During a normal hunt, H.S. would probably use two to three hundred rounds with a variety of rifles. Today is different, for many reasons. As homage to the game, he is pulling out his trophy guns. Bazel walks over as H.S. rises heading for the gun car.

Swaggering Bazel proffers, "Taking out the Holland & Holland today?"

With the look of neutrality, H.S. is silent. *This Krauts insipient accent grates my nerves. He is the ugliest man I have ever seen. Of course, I know where he is going with his silly leading question.* Bazel prides himself on the Sharps Savanna double rifle.

Although it is a beauty, it is an inferior specimen to my Holland.

Without waiting for an answer, Bazel continues, mansplaining, "You know they were both designed for dangerous game in the 1800's with the ability to fire a follow up shot without needing to engage the action." Pausing a moment to catch his breath in all the excitement before he continues, "What's more dangerous than a reasoning man?"

H.S. smiles, a rare occasion.

Entering the gun car, it seems everyone else has the same idea, Jameson is going over his Baretta Imperiale Monte Carlo.

I would never say this to him, H.S. internally confesses, *but it is a marvelous shot gun. The workmanship is par none, truly a masterpiece.* In fact, he had been informed in a dealer's shop much to his chagrin that owning one would be likened to owning a masterpiece Renaissance sculpture. The hundreds of hours of engraving by master engravers is a living tradition that dates back to Dante. He has lost track of the numerous times Jameson has felt it necessary to share these tedious details with him; *"They are created in very small quantities for the world's most exclusive clientele.".* *What a bore.*

Bannock in his excitement accidently spits on Levitt as he pulls out his Barrett 82A1, a semi- automatic .50 caliber rifle. It looks like something out of a Sylvester Stallone movie, a crude weapon without any mastery, just a straight forward killer. Bannock's fat and balding stature, however, adopts a formidable quality as he checks the site. *His collection is random and competitive. Only one gun is remarkable the rest are strictly middle class.*

Levitt, in contrast, wipes the spittle off his breast with a ridiculous silk champagne cravat, a look of disgust clearly expressed, his large hands accentuating his emaciated figure while gripping his prized Howdah pistol. It looks harmless enough but was designed for self- defense against big game while hunting in Africa and India. H.S. recalls the ceaseless boasting, *"The name Howdah, is derived from the basket platforms set atop elephants for hunting expeditions that date back to the British Raj in India. My family has hunted on the royal grounds for generations."* H.S. has grown tired of the repetitive stories of Levitt's forefathers, Senior officers of the East India Company. In fact, H.S. recalls, Levitt insisting that prints of his family's lineage taken in India and Africa be placed throughout the compound. *They are not terrible, it would have been incredible to be there at that time, taking down entire herds of elephants and packs of big cats at a time.*

Continuing to take stock of his club members, as he wipes down his instruments for the day; *Jonathan Handel, feeds a cowboy complex with his collection, no one calls him on it, we all have our little quirks.* Dressed in a duster and cowboy hat from the moment he steps foot in the park, he owns over a dozen reproductions of the Sharps 1874 Creedmore rifle used in the movie Quigley Down Under, as well as three originals from the 1870's. The quintessential western gun. Every year Handel participates in The Match, a marksman competition in Montana, billed as the biggest rifle shooting event in Eastern Montana since the Custer Massacre. *For an unremarkable man, his enthusiasm for western culture is notable.*

Friedland Becket, on the other hand, is an exact mirror of his collection, bland efficiency. Having been voted in as club Chairman, he oversees the existence of the park, on my orders, of course. H.S. recollects while adjudicating, his brother in arms lack of imagination to confirm that old money begets money. Collecting guns that have been chosen in the past for standard military use at times when technology changed, is as uninteresting, as the collector. Brandishing a Peterson Rifle today, it is a common reflection of the man.

Rest assured no one in the club of twenty- four has acquired any weapon that can compare to his golden gun. Running over its provenance, *given to Hitler himself on his fiftieth birthday from Walther. It is priceless. The mystery that surrounds it, the man. There is nothing else like it in the world. It's never been shot. The blood stains just recognizable below the grip only add to the legend. I will never shoot this gun, although I keep it loaded as it was found. Bannock's trifling attempt at gifting the club Teddy Roosevelts shotgun is insignificant compared to the small pistol I have hung on the wall behind the bar. The golden hue of my pistol, emanates the awesome power of its original owner. It is my talisman, but unlike Hitler I am undefeatable. No one can touch me, with a phone call I own the press, the Presidential cabinet, the senate, and several national security agencies. That is true power. The world just the way I want it. Yes, today I will use my Holland & Holland work of art, Artemis herself emblazoned upon it and my titanium gold Desert Eagle pistol in honor of our game. After all, special days require special weapons.*

68

BLEEDING OUT

They say it's not the fall that kills you, it's the landing! Well, they got that right! Falling thirty feet before hitting the ground abruptly, Thaddius' head explodes like a pumpkin. Fortunate to be on top, Remy is smattered in blood. Straddling the decimated body, wiping pieces of brain from his eyes with his hands and present enough to shake the grasp of death from his shoulders as Sam runs over to him, "Are you ok? Holy shit, that was crazy!"

Looking up to the tracks above, he sees Danielle standing on the edge, she is yelling something he cannot understand, his senses simultaneously dulled and hyper.

Opening his mouth in a haze to reply, he sees three men coming out of the woods from behind Sam. Once they are even with her, he manages to pull himself up, standing slowly with his hands on his knees to brace his weight.

"What? Why the hell would you want to stay here?" Remy demands with as much strength as he can muster, knowing full well he cannot fight them all, not after that fall, head shaky, his knees weak now that he is standing. The looks on the men's faces are tainted by the bloody visual before them. Remy braces himself for yet another attack.

"We don't!" The blonde thin dude in the middle responds dryly. "We came to help. You need some water? That was amazing dude."

Relieved but not entirely trusting he takes the water, with a smirk. *Damn it tastes good.* Looking the group over he wipes his mouth with the back of his hand assessing the situation, before pouring the remaining water over his face to wash off the warm sticky liquid.

"I'm Manning, this is Bobby and Skylar."

Manning is thin and blonde in cut offs no shirt. Bobby looks just like a young Humphrey Bogart from The African Queen with the beard and all. Skylar is African American, hazel eyes and very fit. They all nod, Remy notes their body language is not aggressive. Again, each one of them is clearly striking to look at.

"I'm Remy. We don't have time for small talk, everybody up the cliff, we could really use you guys, if you want out of here?" He says encouragingly.

"Yeah man, we want out." Manning reiterates.

Sam turns around quietly retreating into the tree line.

"Hey Sam, I'm sorry I didn't trust you."

She smiles back.

"Do you need help down here?"

"No, I'm good. Just don't forget to whistle." She adds walking away.

Turning back to the new kids on the block, he shows them the path to the cliff and they head up the hill to the blind. Genevieve has gone over to the tunnel like everyone else as Remy hands each one of the new guys a club and a spear.

"Just follow me. Remy states before thinking twice, "On second thought you go first." They all go over the log and down the tracks to Danielle, he is careful not to lose sight of them. With a look of concern on her face, she acknowledges the new guys but voices nothing as they are introduced.

"Manning, you and Bobby stay here at the entrance of the tunnel on the left and Skylar you stay to the right just inside the tunnel, it's important you are not seen. Stay in the shadows."

"Then what?"

"I am going to blow up the tracks, the train will stop and we kick some ass."

Knowing the hunters have guns and they have sticks, the three men nod quietly, but there is a spark in their eyes. The spark of vengeance.

Walking back down the tracks away from the tunnel, getting his legs back. The sun is hot and high, casting contrasting shadows everywhere. Light thrown to the ground, white and bright, the still shadows emphasizing there is no breeze to be found. Pulling the rags off his hands, Remy notices both his elbows and knees are bleeding and badly bruised, oddly he can't feel anything, he is so pumped he barely knows how to contain himself. Sitting and waiting is a challenge as he pulls out his phone. For the last five years, he has wanted nothing more than to toss it, Stephanie always amused by his threat. Sure, it's a tether it allowed them to work virtually anywhere, but it's also a chain. Ruining their day with one email or phone call, the burden of modern man.

Pushing the side power button, squatting over his little pile of tricks next to the flaming coconut shell, he is sweating like a pig. Surprised the phone actually turns on after being dragged through a couple of rivers and rained on as the home screen pops up. *There she is, there's my girl,* touching his finger to the screen of the picture of Steph laying on the beach, "I love you, baby." Pausing for just a second, he pulls it out of its case and tosses it on the pile in front of him, promising himself, *this is the last God Damn phone I will ever own.*

69

WEIRD FISHES

As the locker room finally clears, tears roll down my cheek. I am trying to contain the wave of anguish rolling over me. The last of them is tying his bootlace before moving in to the next car probably for a drink before they begin, *how very civilized.*

I can clearly see his back through the crack in the door. The scene before me and conversation I overhear, is no less than pathological, H.S. is the leader of this group.

They are going to shoot at men, for fun. I know Remy is one of them. My heart is out of my chest, it's pumping so hard, anger and fear mixed together corroding the hope I had desperately clung to.

Once the last freak passes my locker, I hear a door quietly close and their voices become muffled. *I need a plan. I need air.*

Opening the door to the locker silently and slowly, I begin to unfold my legs while using my arms to pull my body out. My ankle is really fucked up. Grabbing hold of the pack on my back, I take stock of its inventory. Four squirts of CBD oil can't hurt. I also rub oil into the skin of my ankle biting my tongue, it's as large as a grapefruit and dark blue.

Ok, I have a knife, some unknown prescription drugs, beef jerky, a bottle of water that I slug down in one gulp and that's about it. Not exactly an arsenal. *But, there's one on the train!*

I have to stop this madness. As I stand, the train lurches forward, I don't hear the engine as you do on a commuter train, I only feel the movement. Running out of time I place my ear to the door to the bar car, pinching my other ear with my finger I can't hear a thing. They have either stopped talking or they have moved on to the other car. Thinking quickly while looking at the ivory button that opens the door, I smooth my hair and clothes, stuffing the knife in the back waist of my shorts before I push the button.

A small Polynesian looking man behind the bar is surprised to see me but he says nothing, only looking up for a second before busying himself. Saunter – hobbling over to the end of the bar with my eyes on the next car's door, he looks up with the simple look of innocence as I pull out the knife directing the point at his stomach. Eyes wide with fear, he puts his hands up and mutters something in a foreign language I don't even recognize. Quickly, with my left hand, I grab a bottle from the bar and hit him in the middle of his head. He goes out instantly.

Avoiding the broken glass on the strangely patterned floor, I drag his little body into the locker room, hoping I have not seriously hurt this man as he seems innocent to the going's on here. For all of five feet of him, he is actually pretty heavy. Thank goodness, he is small and he fits easily into a locker. This time I lock the locker with the outer latch after tying his hands and feet with socks. Looking for something to stuff his mouth with, I open the adjacent locker for arbitrary clothing. That's when I see it. *A phone!*

I have never seen a phone like this before, it's gold for starters real gold, with a patterned dark wood border along the edge. I push all of the buttons at once trying to discern the on button. Magically the screen lights up. As I push a side button on the left of the screen two small nibs pop out of the end of the phone, like boobs protruding from it. The screen is locked but luckily it has the same options I have on my phone when it's locked, photo and telephone plus one more a lightning bolt I assume means charged battery that is glowing. Quickly tapping the phone icon above the glittering touch keys, I have a line out, *but who the hell do I call? What do I tell them? I don't even know where I am!* Rubbing my face, I try to pull it together. *I'll call Grace.*

One ring, two rings, "Hello?"

"Grace! It's me, Stephanie. Listen this is going to sound crazy, I am on an island somewhere in the Pacific. H.S. has kidnapped me. I think he took Remy too. You have to call Detective Brennan for me!"

The silence on the end of the phone should have been my first sign. "Grace?"

The phone goes dead. I just stare at it blinking. *She knew! She knew this whole time!* I'm horrified. The reality of her betrayal buckles my knees. I sit on the bench. *What else has she done while I was away? The plot unfolds, that bitch took part in Remy's disappearance, she knew! What other exclusive interviews has she given? Remy knew it, he knew before he left. I guess he just wanted to be sure before he told me. How could I be so stupid? So, trusting, so eager to bring someone into our delicate world? Is there some kind of karma attached to these horrific lessons we seem to relive over and over again?*

Hands shaking in anger, I dial Laure's number, one of the only other numbers I know by heart, *I swear I will never buy another God Damn cell phone again!*

"Hello, this is Laure." Her voice is either surprised to receive a call from an unknown number or surprised she has service.

"Laure, it's me, Steph!" I spit into the phone.

"Steph! Are you ok? Where are you?"

That's more like it. "I don't know where I am. On an island. In the Pacific maybe, not really sure. H.S took me here. He's crazy!" I continue starting to lose control, "He has Remy and he's going to shoot him. There's a bunch of men they all have guns we are on a train."

"Stephanie, this is Miles. Just calm down. We are on our way, so is the FBI, we will be there within three hours, just sit tight."

Miles' voice usually such a calming factor for me, fills me with anger. **"I don't have three hours! I have to stop them now!"** I scream into the phone to a barrage of voices attempting to dissuade me, before I press end, *was that Tyler's voice? What the hell? Where haven't they infiltrated?* I can't be bothered calling back they are going to have to figure that out on their own.

Walking back into the bar car pacing I stick the phone in my back pocket out of habit and pull the little golden gun off the wall, I can see it's loaded. I have never shot a real gun, only bb guns but I 've seen enough movies to know it's not that hard. I look for a safety and click it off with my thumb then I pull down the shot gun, *if it was good enough for Teddy it's good enough for me!* I load both barrels, *nothing like a grand entrance.*

Walking through the arsenal, I spot a drawer with an explosives symbol etched in ivory. *Are they kidding me?* Stopping in front of it I grab two before running back to the locker room to nab that fancy engraved lighter. Snatching a bottle of whiskey on my way, I take a long draught out of the bottle. Holding the phone in my hand, I notice something odd about that charging icon it's pulsing, so I push it and an electric charge shoots out of the nubs at the end of the phone, like something out of Frankenstein. *This phone must be made by Tesla!*

With my head against the door, I overhear about seven voices in the next car, *if everyone is talking that's not too bad, seven against one.* Holding my head up to the cool wooden door; I see myself grappling with H.S. in the car, kicking him with my heels. I remember throwing myself off the bed in the Caymans, to find him standing there panting like a dog in heat with a look of victory on his face. *He can't have everything he wants! The world is NOT his to take!*

Moving three steps back, I jump as I hear gun fire from the next car, bracing the weighted shotgun against my shoulder, without thinking, I blast the door to bits. When the dust clears, all of the men except two have hit the deck clearing themselves from the spray of splinters and metal, one is screaming rocking back and forth on the ground, looking out the window. *I can't imagine what can be more frightening than me holding a gun!*

Recovering from the shot's kickback, dusted by the gun's outburst, I lock eyes with the two men left standing facing me, H.S. has that icky smile on his face. The man across from him, younger and dark- haired wears a look of sheer surprise.

"Get down on the ground!" I order having dropped the shot gun and now pointing the golden gun at the men. They both look at each other, I can literally see the smirk of disdain they swap, *"No reason to be afraid of a woman,"* they're obviously thinking.

"Stephanie, always the surprise. You don't actually think you can shoot all of us, do you?"

"I'd be happy just shooting one of you." Staying on the outside of the doorway in case I need cover, I smile back, "Besides, I don't have to."

Pulling one of the sticks of dynamite out of my waistband I stick it into my mouth and snap open the titanium lighter, the golden gun trained on them with my other hand. The dark- haired guy, turns toward the gun rack in the nose of the train, so I shoot him in the leg. As I raise my hand holding the lighter to my face, I feel the heat of the flame against my cheek and Boom!

70

ANGEL

The explosion is bigger than I thought! Remy thinks to himself with delight, running full bore from the first explosion at the front of the train with a goddamn coconut shell in his hand! Scaling the now incapacitated train like a monkey. "Go! Go!" he yells to the small group of freedom fighters and climbs over the nose and down the back of the train to get behind it, just as the metal monster begins to move backwards towards him. Pouring the fire onto the pile of technology, the train is now picking up speed, it's less than five feet coming straight for him, he feels the wind the train creates, there is nowhere to go but over the side, again! Without his pumpkin friend, there is no way he'll survive that a second time. "Shit!"

The majority of his group are on top of the train holding on, watching him, when the second pile explodes, not quite as loud as the first one, but the effect is right. The train stops.

Looking over the edge of the track Remy sees the words Friedland Beckett eerily spelled out in fire on the ground with Sam's lifeless body lying next to it.

It takes him three steps to get back to the top of the train, he is so pissed off, the vision of the dead woman searing his brain. The rebels go in as a wall of bodies, there aren't as many hunters as Remy thought there would be inside but it's mayhem. War cries fill the air as his group enters swinging clubs. The crunch of broken bones is unmistakable. Feeling the spray of blood across his chest without looking for it, Remy pauses as if time could stand still, the scene before him is in slow motion. Two of the hunters lay on the ground in pools of blood, while they are repeatedly bludgeoned with clubs. Two more are standing pulling desperately at guns mounted to the floor, but the guns don't turn far enough to shoot inside the train, the look of surprise is unmistakably imprinted on their faces. Veroon wildly runs up to them swinging wildly and is pushed out of the window, Remy can't even hear her scream as she falls out of the train, there is nothing he can do.

Most of the hunters are on the floor toward the left of the car, shots ring in his ears, as he watches the scared old white men crawling into the next car in an attempt to escape the onslaught.

Bare legs are on the ground twitching from behind a chair, a hunter is choking Amanda on the ground but Manning swiftly and decisively smacks the man over the head with his club, splitting the well- dressed man's skull open, his body crumples to the floor, but it's too late for Amanda.

Searching, Remy's attention falls to the face he recognizes, standing uneasily in the middle of the car with a bright golden gun gleaming in one hand and a silver one in the other. Like weapons designed for Achilles, they glow as Remy watches Bobby go down just an arms-length away from him, his eyes immovable.

Eyes lock as H.S. aims at Remy, a sick smile crossing his face. Taking his spear in his hand quickly like Tarzan aiming for his target's chest, Remy draws his arm back, but the train lurches backward and the sudden movement knocks him off balance as the gun shot fires. Falling sideways into a chair, his eyes and hands down to brace the fall, Remy sees her, eyes blinking as he drops to his knees, his heart stops. "No!" *She can't be dead!*

71

INSIDE MY MIND

The jet makes its approach for landing, Miles is repelled by the small island in the middle of the sea, like a cancer growth redirecting currents around it, heralding malignancy. The sky is blue but the air of emotions expressed in his contingency is anything but recreational. Sitting across from Laure he notes the solemn concern she silently expresses for her friends below, Tyler holding her hand for support.

Miles acknowledges the connection between the two of them. He thinks to himself that Tyler's desire to be accountable and righteous is admirable, if not timely. But questions why he himself is on board, fully aware the FBI can certainly handle all of this.

Turning to Horace next to him, caught up in the throes of storytelling like any great news reporter should be. Horace is furiously creating headlines and exposing wrong doings, a modern-day comics hero without the cape. A true steward of society. Miles admonishes himself, suddenly he feels out of place, the burden of his entitlements heavily weighing in. Can he honestly say he would never have joined a club such as this, under any circumstance? The more he thinks about it, the more he sees what bothers him, is he really so different than the men in this club? The unavoidable fact is he certainly has more in common with them, than he does the Beroes.

The difficult even questionable decisions he has made with the fates of tens of thousands of workers at his whim, come to mind. The buying and selling for profit alone, a harsh reminder he is not innocent of ignoring human interest at times. Not always having the best policy for the environment as a priority but wearing it as a badge when it is convenient, rolls back on him like a sling shot. Believing he understands his staff and employees needs and concerns when he really has no idea how they survive in a year, on less than he spends weekly. All of this adds up to one thing, he is out of touch and he doesn't like it. In fact, he doesn't like himself. With a cough, he shifts in his seat.

"What's up?" Horace asks.

"I've been thinking."

"Let me guess, feeling guilty?" The look on Horace's face is sincere and not mocking.

Miles says nothing, but the grip of his mouth tells the story to someone really looking.

"If we were going to a funeral we would be thinking about death. I believe, your taking stock in your lifestyle and business choices, old friend. It is a testament to your healthy conscious Miles, you have nothing to worry about." Horace pauses looking back to his laptop, "And if you do, now is the time to make a change."

Miles silently considers this as Laure interjects, "What are we going to do when we get there?"

"That's a good question, I am going to look around," Horace announces. "All of the souls that have been harangued there will need support, a safe harbor and perhaps medical care." Turning in his chair to push a button on the console behind him he continues, "Gentleman and Ladies please come in."

Without delay a group of half a dozen side armed soldiers enter from the rear cabin, dressed in dark green khaki from head to foot, they have a misleading casualness about them. The leader is a tall Irish looking fellow.

"I believe three of you should stay with the plane, the rest of you will join me on the ground. You have the coordinates?"

The tall blonde soldier answers, "Yes sir."

"I should have known you would be prepared Horace, you have travelled to some of the most dangerous places and incidences in the world in the last fifty years and returned unscathed," Miles comments to no one in particular, with great pride.

"I am always prepared Miles, you know that. Via satellite scanning, we have found two hot spots on the island. The first is a building not far from the landing strip, the second is in an area behind the main bay. We have set up a medical station in the rear of the plane, just in case. I suggest you stay here with Miles, Ms. Giovanni. Tyler, you are familiar with the Beroes, you should accompany me."

"Yes, of course."

Laure's concerned look is enchanting, Miles notes.

Kissing her hand Tyler reassures her, "We'll find them."

Tyler is riding a narrow line between what is right and what is crazy, Miles wonders how Tyler will be able to cope with the brutal reality they find down there. It's not every day you are privy to the fact that your Father is a sociopath but then again, maybe this isn't new news?

"Please prepare for landing in ten minutes." The pilot announces with her wonderfully French accent pleasantly distracting Miles from the gruesome situation that is before them.

Landing on the tarmac one might have expected a parade of private jets lining the runway by looking at the guest list, but there is only one.

"That's ours," Tyler confirms.

"Where is everyone else?" Horace asks out loud, scanning the area. Touching a button on his watch, "Ms. Ansange, pull up as close to the other plane as possible, block its path."

"Avec Plaisir Monsieur."

Turning back to his ground team Horace commands, "No one gets on or off that plane, understood?"

"Yes, Sir." The faces on Horace's recon team are solemn and un moveable.

Attaching a go pro to his vest and a helmet with two different kinds of cameras on the front and back, Horace laces up his boots and leaves without a word, Tyler at his side, wearing the same apparatus.

Laure looks to Miles.

"The world has become surreal, anything goes, my dear," Miles replies standing to inspect the sick bay.

72

CONCEPT TEN

The path Horace and Tyler are on is well marked, it was nice of
someone to leave all of the golf carts sitting there at the air strip.
Obviously, there was a large exodus, and from the look of the parking jobs, it
was abrupt and unorganized. Heading down the groomed small path, wondering
what they will find, Horace is hoping the fact the other planes have left is not a
sign they are too late.

"Where are we going exactly?" Tyler asks with a calm that leads Horace to
believe he is used to blindly following someone.

"The first hotspot on the satellite image is a house of some kind. Go where
the action is, I always say."

Tyler nods in agreement while Captain Sullivan drives the golf cart. There is
no line of site, only trees, vines, and underbrush, scattered with intermittent
sunlight. Crossing a small bridge, the cart path is leading up a steep mountain
side, groups of monkeys above them howl a forewarning. At several of the
crossroads there are painted signs; Beach and Club House, they stay on course.
Horace can smell the fire before he sees it. Pulling up to a large villa, they find

four unarmed men dressed in black khakis with fire extinguishers attempting to put the fire out. Caught unawares they turn around with little to no concern for Horace and his group.

"Do not engage." Horace quietly expresses to his group.

Approaching the building, a tall man in his thirties walks over to him, "We were able to contain the fire, Sir, most of the damage is in the kitchen and main living area, no one was hurt."

Horace nods, the less he says the better since the merc is assuming he belongs there. Entering the structure, it's what one would have expected. Via the large double front-doors, they head toward the area of the house that was on fire, which obviously started on the floor in the kitchen and he notes it was chemical based, looking at the scorch marks and explosion radius. From the broken plate windows Horace clearly sees a large vessel moored off shore, he looks to Tyler who observably recognizes the ship.

Sullivan brings their attention unobtrusively to the bedroom, "There are signs of a struggle." They note lamps knocked over, a painting removed from the wall, there is broken glass everywhere. The commode off the bedroom has a makeshift rope ladder that was made and used for a valiant escape. Horace smiles ruefully to Tyler.

"Sir, we have a ground team searching for people." Their new tour guide in black informs them, unintentionally aiding the enemy.

Horace and Tyler continue in silence, looking at the photographs of slaughtered big game on the walls, herds of dead animals lined up on a blood-stained savannah. Horace turns away, giving his team the sign to leave. As they breach the doorway, in a last- ditch effort of efficiency the merc adds, "We have the biped drones on standby."

Horace turns back to the man's empty face, "This is very sloppy."

"Yes Sir, sorry Sir." The merc abates.

Tyler and Horace walk back calmly to the caravan of golf carts and head to the second isolated hot spot.

"Do you know any of those men?" Horace asks Tyler without looking directly at him, understanding how precarious his situation is.

"No."

"Did you know about this place?"

"No."

It's too early to know if Tyler is telling the truth, Horace enumerates, as the GPS follows the ridiculous path signs to the clubhouse. "Are you ready for this?" He asks taking a reading from Tyler's anxious posture.

"I've been ready for this for a while," Tyler responds without moving.

"Sullivan, can we get a live feed?"

"No sir, the signal is not strong enough."

"No casualties, stun only and wound from the waist down. Do you understand? Only engage if we are attacked or if someone is at risk."

"Yes, Sir."

As Horace sits in the electric cart with its yellow and white striped canopy, driving through the pristine jungle, he could be anywhere. Without the soundtrack of war behind the visual, an unconvincing calm gnaws at him. There is always a moment when a story becomes more than text for him, it becomes human. For over fifty years, he has involved himself in the conflicts of man, the hate, and fear driven outcomes too horrible to truly convey. The irony, he considers, is that most soldiers are not pro war and most civilians are.

73

HAYLING

Dragging himself over, Remy takes her cold hand in his, feeling for a pulse, her body limp and her eyes are closed. Unsure if she is dead or alive, he holds his breath as Danielle comes up from behind him, shielding him as he moves. Manaya's small body behind the chair lies their lifeless, gently swaying with the rhythm of the train.

Looking around at the status of their mutiny, Bobby on the ground bleeding from his left shoulder, Amanda dead, Veroon gone, Galax down holding her leg, there is blood all over the floor next to the bodies of three hunters, Remy questions his motivations as the lilt of the train, deceivingly comforts him. Skylar and Manning are on either side of the door way to the next car trying to remove the guns near the windows from their mounts, as Remy attempts to piece things together. Noticing the entry to the next car, "Hang on, that's no doorway, that's a hole! When did that happen?" From his position at the nose of the train on the ground, he can see the last of the four hunters securing themselves two cars down making their retreat. But what really concerns him is the fact that the entire adjacent car is covered in gun racks! Turning from

Manaya's form Remy calls out, "Manning, you're look out."

Manning nods not taking his eyes off the now closed door of the car the hunters all hold up in.

"Everyone not wounded come to me," Remy announces surrounded by a chorus of panting in seconds. "Well, we did surprise them." Everyone sort of smirks, while catching their breath.

"I don't know where we are headed but when we stop, we have to be ready for anything."

Galax has moved close to him, her leg bleeding profusely. Grabbing a jacket that was hung over the back of a chair Remy rips it into strips of fabric with his hands before tying a tight tourniquet around it. Genevieve is doing the same for Bobby, he doesn't seem to mind, in fact, he looks like he is enjoying it. Galax then moves to Manaya, it's hard for him to take his eyes off of her, his responsibility for these people has become his main focus, and now she is dead.

"I'm going into the next car to get weapons before we get ambushed. I need someone to come with me and make it all the way down to the closed door to cover me. Once you get there you have a choice of weapons." Remy states looking at the group for volunteers.

"I'm in." Skylar accepts, his hair tussled and chest gleaming with sweat and blood, determination written all over his face.

"You know how to shoot?" Danielle asks pointedly.

"Yes, I'm a hunter, or at least I was."

"OK, Skylar stands look out, I'll push the weapons and ammo towards the hole, Manning and Danielle will load them and hand them out. I want the wounded moved to the left front of the car, out of range and someone has to guard them."

"I will guard the wounded, but what about them?" Genevieve volunteers, pointing to the three obviously dead hunters on the ground almost unrecognizable from their beating.

"Toss them out, they're dead. Alright, let's move."

Remy watches from the edge of the smattered doorway while Skylar enters the armory. Staying to the left side of the walls, he passes between overturned club chairs and plaster dusted wood paneling piled on the floor in the corner. He decides to crawl the distance next to the bench that is centered in the wood paneled car, rather than standing in the open as he makes his approach, small chandeliers glitter in defiance of the rubble on the floor from above, when suddenly the train stops.

"Fuck!" Remy reacts causing Skylar to stop in his tracks. "Keep going!" he whisper-yells, "Get cover!"

Without additional prodding, Skyler moves double time and throws himself up against the wall of the door. All of the guns within his reach are rifles, he arbitrarily picks one, opens a small drawer beneath it and loads the gun before standing sentry.

"Ok!" Skylar signals, rechecking the gun for a safety.

Remy makes his way into the car, it's filled with debris, the explosions abrupt stop must have caused the paneling to dislodge from the walls at this end, he is both drawn and repulsed by everything he sees, bits of wood and furniture are piled about, visions of the attack pressing his mind and derailing his thoughts. Hugging the left corner moving carefully from chair to chair, his eyes fight to stay focused on the door next to Skylar. Each gun is lit, individually haloed, an offering, suddenly nausea overcomes him. His head starts to spin, fever breaking through his sweat until he bends over in reluctance heaving all over the bench floor. He is purging.

Two hands wrap under his arms and pull him back into the group of the other car. Danielle leans him up against the wall, "Stay here." She says calmly, swiping the hair out of his face before she heads back into the armory car. The next thing he notices butts of guns are sliding on the floor out the door hole towards him.

Looking over to Genevieve her face foggy, Remy asks, "Is there any water?"

She hands him a gourd full of water that he pours over his head. Like a slap in the face, awakened, he rises to his feet, grabbing the butt of the gun nearest him, loading it and passing it on.

This continues until they all have two weapons each. That's when he hears it, a far- off buzzing sound like a giant mosquito, the numerous bites on his legs and arms itch on que. But the sound continues to build. *This is not a natural sound.* "It's drones! Take cover!" He yells over the whining of the motors, now hovering, just above the train. Counting six of them, their moves are jerky and awkward, the sound is menacing as their red prophetic glowing eyes come into view. They swarm over the train, only one staying within sight.

"They're flying recon, trying to see what's going on", he yells to the group as Manning pumps his shot gun and obliterates the lead drone and all the tree branches behind it.

"They're not armed!" Remy announces as the other drones fall back into a grouping out of range of the shotgun, just hovering, the sound is tremendous. Loading the rifle in his hand crawling on the floor, he perches it on top of the small pony wall. Manning throws down his shotgun and does the same, as well as Danielle, Freeman, Harli, Ora, and Arona. Haven is sitting against the door hole with Hollie from Manaya's group, holding his ears, while Skylar continues to keep watch on the next car.

Danielle, looks over to Remy, "This is new."

Remy shoots and all hell breaks loose, one drone takes off directly over the top of the train and out of range, but the rest are blown to bits. With a cry of relief, everyone is feeling pretty good. Sticking his head out the window, Remy assesses the drone above them, but there is no way he can get to it unless he climbs out the window.

"Reload we have no idea what's coming next." Taking a head count, only two of Manaya's women are left, Genevieve and Hollie. With their depleted numbers that makes thirteen but only ten can fight.

Out of the corner of his eye, Remy spots a cigar like shape. Bending over, his eyes widen as he realizes it's a stick of dynamite. Danielle moves towards it instinctually guided by his concern.

"This'll come in handy." She states placing the dynamite down the back of her skirt waist.

Remy smiles, "Of course, lighting it will be tricky. Alright, let's see where we are."

Looking out the window, to their surprise they are on the other side of the cliff face that the train usually comes out of.

"Holy Shit!" Haven exclaims facing the opposite window, Remy turns and strides the width of the car in 2 steps. The sea is in front of them through a break in the jungle canopy, it couldn't be more than 2 miles away. A moored Titan occupies the center of the small bay, *Jove's Gift*. Remy's blood boils as he paces like a caged tiger. "Son of a bitch!"

The train is still on the tracks but they are not elevated anymore, the tracks are on the ground. The jump out the window is less than 10 feet. *We need a plan,* seeing the tension and anxiety their new station has presented, freedom is a strong distraction. "Listen up, we are on the other side of this thing now," everyone turns their heads towards him, but their flight response is audible. "Something most of you thought was impossible a week ago, we have accomplished." He continues as Danielle stands closer to him in solidarity. "Unfortunately, this isn't over, they cannot afford to let us live now that we've identified them. I don't know about any of you", he adds crouching down attempting to draw the group together for one last rally, "but I recognized the son of a bitch that abducted me. I know him!" All eyes are level with him now. "Revenge must be set aside, for now, our biggest concern is getting out of here and making contact, with the outside world. If you have an idea don't let me stop you but it might be good to split up. One group finds transportation, one group finds communications, and one group stays here to protect the wounded. Who we find on the way and what you decide to do with them is up to you."

Nodding in silent unison, they start dividing into teams.

"We need one strong defender for the wounded and they need shelter. Skylar, do you hear anything on the other side of the door?"

"No, not a sound."

"Let's get that door open first, since we can't get the wounded out through the window and it's to open in this car with all these windows to protect them."

"Hmm, this might work," Danielle holds the dynamite up, "if we can light it."

"Holy crap!" Haven exclaims, "Check this out." He holds up the titanium lighter, "I found it on the floor, just sitting there."

"We must be on the right path," Genevieve confirms, her accent makes her statement more of a blessing.

"Manning, stay with Genevieve and the wounded. Move them into the next car away from the windows for protection until one of us comes back with a better idea."

"You got it. I won't run out of ammo."

Remy continues organizing, "Skylar, you take Harli, Ora, Hollie, and Arona find a computer or a phone anything that we can send a message out with and try to figure out where the hell we are!"

"We can do that."

"Danielle, Freeman, and Haven are with me. First, we find a safer place for the wounded, then we find a way out of this hell hole, we're going for the boat first."

"What boat?" Freeman asks.

Remy stands up and points, "That boat."

"That's a boat?"

"Yup and I know it's layout and all the toys on it first- hand. Skylar, you are going to want to move."

Turning to Danielle, Remy takes the dynamite and lights it with the lighter tossing it at the door at the other end of the armory car before throwing himself up against the windowless wall.

The sound is unbelievable. For a couple of seconds, no one can hear anything, ears ringing. Everyone looks dumbfounded. Pushing himself up, Remy's team rallies around him, with a glance into the next car, they can see it's empty, if not over decorated.

"Fuckin rich white guys!" Harli exclaims. "How did mankind become so fucked up?"

Manning and Genevieve grab Manaya and gently move her into the armory, layered in a cloud of dust with wood remnants and furniture bits strewn everywhere. Bobby's shoulder continues to bleed through the tourniquet, his face is becoming gaunt. Galax continues to apply pressure to Bobby's wound, with what looks like no worry for her own leg wound. The urgency of the situation is starting to make Remy anxious.

The blast has thrown debris everywhere, all of the surfaces are covered in dust and the air itself is hard to breath, there is no clear path through the car, just piles of guns and wood paneling, and furniture.

Moving quickly into the new car, there is still one door closed ahead of them. Not knowing who may be behind it Remy walks from chair to chair through the dust, Manning, and Danielle directly behind him. There are several chairs at the far end of the car unaffected by the dynamite. One half of a large bar still stands erect on the right, dismantled chandeliers hang overhead, book shelves their glass doors now shattered have exhumed pages of books on to floor.

"It's a goddamn bar!" The words escape Manning's mouth in disgust before Remy has time to register, he spoke.

"This is making revenge, seem like a whole new priority," Freeman admits with the same revulsion everyone is struggling to contain.

"Stick to the plan," Danielle states neutrally with the command of someone who has control over their emotions. Remy envies her.

Once they've made it to the end of the car, Skylar's group comes in, their faces are priceless. Remy places his ear to the next door, "I don't hear a thing on the other side. My guess is they got out. There are only five cars and we're in the fourth. "

"Now what?" Freeman requests sharply.

Taking a deep breath Remy looks around, no windows no skylights and the door is wood paneled. "Let's have a drink."

Everyone laughs. When the smiles fade, he says, "Just blast it."

Skylar steps up with a shotgun.

"Wait." Ora calls out, "What's this?" She moves up to the door and pushes a wooden button inlaid on the wooden wall panel and the door opens.

"Wow, that was complicated." Her sarcastic tone lightens the atmosphere.

The next room is obviously a changing room with lockers and benches but still very men's club. There are two doors on either side of the final exit, Danielle takes the one on the left and Remy takes the one on the right, kicking the door open with his gun pointed level.

"OH, MY GOD! Harli yells, "Is that toilet paper?"

They all crack up. The last door, also wood paneled, has the same button on the side. Looking back to his group before he pushes it Remy confers, "Are you ready?"

The door opens. There's no one there, they're inside the large plantation type building, the train's platform is a hardwood deck with a striped canopy over it. They search desperately for any signs of men; the AC is startling. There is a mechanics area for train maintenance and some photos on the wall. To the left is a double French door with curtains on the windows.

They pour out of the train, hugging the walls, listening for any sound. Nothing.

As soon as they near the wall by the doors Remy can smell food, feeling like Hansel, he pushes the door open with his foot and enters like a commando. The empty dining room is full of muzak, twirling ceiling fans, empty chairs and places set with china and linen.

"Great we've just taken a restaurant." Harli smirks.

'This is surreal, no one is here! "Remy looks back to Skylar, his team checks out the kitchen, while they look out through the windows to make sure there is no ambush waiting. Once they are sure no one is in the building or surrounding it, both groups head outside. A ceiling fan above the double doors is creaking as it sways out of alignment, offsetting the cries of birds. The warmth of the jungle air returns like an old friend. Straight ahead is a white post with three signs pointing with arrows; Beach to the left, Bridge to the right, Hospital to the right. Skylar nods to Remy and heads off to the right with his group. Remy's group turns left down a path that has been worn with small tires. They make it about a mile when he hears a familiar sound coming from above them.

"It's the drone, it's following us!" He gives the signal for Haven, Freeman and Danielle to walk just beyond the path. Although they are still a long way off from being both safe and free again, he is aware of the release and lightness in his spirit, and he senses the others feel the same way. Silently he ascertains how caging and enslaving people will drive the most sensible person to madness, and suddenly his judgment on Leeds and Packard sprouts guilt, but he has no time for remorse now.

The end of the winding pathway they are on is now only about a quarter a mile ahead, Remy notices the light is much brighter from the reflection of the sand through the arched canopy of trees framing the blue horizon line. That is when he sees shadows moving on their right, just before the path clears onto the beach. Holding his arms out abruptly, everyone stops to find cover, their concentration focused on the end of the path. Haven and Danielle at his side, he motions over to Freeman with gestures for her to scout behind them on the other side of the path that she occupies. The jungle and the drone are so goddamn loud, he can't hear a thing, so he waits.

Remy turns his head to look back towards Freeman and sees something behind her. It's frightening. A larger than man-sized, robotic droid with extended arms, rubber stoppers instead of hands, a huge box like chest that looks as if it would be top heavy, ball joint waist, and longer than average legs sticking out from Combat boots that aren't tied, the tongue of the boots flapping forward. Where it's head would be is an infra- red lens that slightly glows. Unlike the Star Wars androids, you can see through the casement into all the wiring and joints. The thing must have been dead silent to get that close to her without her knowing.

Remy grabs his rifle as the damn thing is right behind her now. Her eyes widen watching him take aim at her, in a panic she starts to move blocking his shot. The biped grabs her, turns around and takes off like a marathon runner dragging Freeman's lower half.

Before Remy has time to think, she's gone, it's gone! Everyone is silently stunned.

With a wide- eyed expression, Danielle quietly comments, "That's new."

Regrouping, Remy sticks his fist in the air with a circular motion, as everyone scouts the area, but it's too late, their path is clearly blocked by three more bipeds but these are different, they have a yellow light that flashes where their head would be. Remy impulsively starts shooting, so does everyone else. Nothing happens, the droids take the hits and just stand there. Danielle and Remy look at each other and yell, "Run!"

74

TEARDROP

My **eyes open slowly,** lungs struggling to breathe from the weight on my chest pushing me into the floor. I can only see the corner of the train car I am jammed into. *What the hell happened? I don't remember anything.* The debris covering me is mountainous and covered in fine dust. A warm sensation on my head draws my attention, my fingers confirm clearly, it's blood, and I am pretty sure it's mine. It's taking all of my energy to fight the wave of sleep that is overpowering me.

Moving backwards in time, I remember holding the dynamite and the lighter and nothing else. I feel sick and dizzy. The warm air of the jungle licking my skin is accelerating the nausea. With great effort, I manage to free my right arm that's pinned under me and begin moving debris off my chest, the fine dust in the air has coated my body and everything around me. I sit up fraught, gathering my head to my hands choking. Once I manage to catch my breath and apply enough pressure to my head to make the throbbing bearable, my vision begins to clear and the hairy legs in front of me, come into focus.

"Who the hell are you?" His deep voice bellows.

He's blonde maybe twenty- six, fair skinned, handsome, blue eyed and barely dressed. He looks haggard though, and really stressed out about, me. I don't recognize him or the two women standing next to him, I'm hoping that's a good thing. Clearing my throat, I begin hoarsely and slowly, "My name is… Stephanie." I notice the women standing behind him are dressed in tattered work clothes. The brunette hands me a gourd.

"Have some water." She says with a curious look about her.

The water feels like life itself. "What happened?" I ask," One minute I was standing here, the next I'm on the floor and you guys are here, what happened to H.S.?"

"I told you!" Hairy legs states regretfully to his obvious Scandinavian friend, turning away from me.

The woman is a stunning tall blonde, she walks over to him, and they talk, his eyes not leaving me for a second.

"Have some more water, do you mind if I look at your head? Your bleeding pretty badly." The brunette with the gourd offers.

"I am? Oh, that makes sense." *No wonder my head hurts so much.* "Please," I reply to the brunette already kneeling beside me. I am having a hard time connecting the dots, *who are these people?*

"This is going to sting a little."

I feel the cold water on my head and a sting alright.

"I just want to see where the actual cut is."

Pushing my hair around, she finally concludes, "You could use a stitch or two and you have quite a bump."

No kidding, "Who are you guys?" I ask, my voice sounding very froggy.

"If you don't mind, we'll ask the questions." He's back armed and pissed so, I acquiesce. Now I can clearly see two other people in the car next door, an injured man is leaning up against the wall across from me, he's lost a lot of blood, his face is very pale. I shake my head in disbelief because he looks just like a young Humphrey Bogart and two other women either dead or knocked out are lying on the floor next to him. The car is a mess, blood everywhere, an explosion definitely went off, but where are the hunters? Where is H.S?

Hairy legs kick me in the waist. Ok, these two, mean business. I'm not sure if they shot these people or not, but I seem to be the focus of their anger. The brunette wipes my face with her wet hand, it feels really good, a soft human touch. She has large brown eyes and a southern accent that lilts at the end of all her words, under any other circumstances she would be sweet.

"What are you somebody's girlfriend?" Both of the blondes' glare at me from above, the tone in his voice is definitely hostile.

It actually hurts to lift my head up to look at them, so I lay back down. "Actually, I'm married," I reply exasperated, the burden of my head weighing me down like an anchor at sea.

"I bet you are!" He snarls, his perfectly proportioned face in turmoil.

I turn to the nice one, as a warm stream of blood drips down past the side of my eye. Wiping it away I say to her, "I have a first aid kit in my bag in the locker room."

"Guilty as charged! What should we do with her?" Hairy legs asks the blonde smugly. She could be a supermodel, except for the grim line her lips have etched into her magnificent face.

"Guilty of what?" I reply as the nice one gets up to retrieve the first aid kit, I'm hoping. The pain from my ankle reacquainting itself. "Number nine on the right," I yell out to the ether from my back, *Wait is that my right or right of the original door I came in through? Whatever!*

"Guilty of what? Guilty of this!" He screams at me, his face contorted and turning red, arms up in the air as if I should understand what he's talking about. Like I made this mess! *Oops, maybe I did. The dynamite must have gone off, but how did I survive?* "I'm not even sure what this is," I reply looking up in earnest, pinned to the floor by some invisible force.

"Guilty by association sister, you're batting for the wrong team." The beautiful blonde woman interjects.

"What teams are there?"

"There's them and there's us, and you're not one of us." He condemns me.

The nice one returns, with my bag of tricks. She pulls out the first aid kit and starts to clean up my head as my judge and jury reconvene.

"Galax, what are you doing?" He asks with an oppressive tone to my nursemaid, "We have people in need of attention over on this side of the train, she gets what she deserves."

"What are you going to do Manning?" Galax asks, looking me dead in the eyes. She is sitting in direct view of him, blocking my body with hers.

"I'm going to tie her up in the other car and leave her here, see how she likes it." The words are ejected from his mouth in disgust.

I look back to Galax. Without moving her eyes from mine she slips the kitchen knife I absent mindedly retuned to my bag, inside my shirt just above the knot tied above my waist, before she gets up and moves over to the other side of the car.

With a jerk, I am on my feet, dizzy as charming drags me across all the debris and into the train car with the windows, throwing me into a chair covered in blood, brains rattled.

"Don't go anywhere." He calls back with a sneer.

Returning with my pillow case, he rips off two strips and drops the bag on the bloody floor next to me. Binding my hands in front of me with a short piece, he then binds my mid- section just below the knot in my shirt, *thank goodness*. Placing a gag in my mouth he ties it behind my head, and whispers in my ear, "You're getting off easy, if they weren't here, you'd be dead."

His voice is so full of hatred, I feel a teardrop fall from the corner of my eye as he walks away, and I am left with a lovely view of the jungle and my own confused thoughts.

For about thirty seconds I feel sorry for myself, then I get really pissed. I can hear them talking as they move their wounded out of the armory and into the bar car, maybe they just want to get away from me, but I take it as an opportunity. I don't know who these people are or what part they are playing in all this, but I have to get out of here. With my eyes on the door, I move my tied hands slowly to my blouse and undo the buttons one at a time with my thumbs, trying not to hold my breath. One, two, three, *I don't think I need the last button,* the oversized shirt is wide enough to allow my hands entry. In reversed heart position, *thank God for yoga*, I use the lengths of my fingers to pick up the knife blade flat between them. Navigating the shirt opening, the blade is almost out, my palms extended to the bottom of my nose when the weight of the handle drops the knife back into the shirt like a weighted dagger, piercing the skin of my chest behind the knot. Closing my eyes and wincing, I bite down on my gag, sweat stinging my eyes.

Checking first to see if anyone is coming, I try again. My chin on my chest, elbows out wide my wrists are pinched by the tie around them, if I can grab the handle with my fingers, I would be in a better position anyway. Going in again, I slide my fingertips over the blade. Stopping for a second to check the doorway before I pull it out, yanking my legs together as a safety net incase the knife falls again. I am able to wedge the blade handle in between my legs with a death grip and begin pulling my hands up and down against the blade. Sweat is pouring down my forehead now and forming a drip off the end of my nose when I become aware of a faint buzzing sound. *Is that inside my head or outside?*

Snap! My bonds are cut, I take off my gag then untie my waist, making as little noise as possible. Standing up, quietly walking over to the window, it's my only way out, unless I want to blast my way out. *That didn't work so well the first time.*

Silently, I tie the pieces of my pillow back together in a longish rope, it will give me a good five feet, cutting my drop, in half or so. After securely tying the rope on to a gun mount, I throw it out the window. Lifting my body onto the window ledge, the buzzing gets louder. Whether it's inside my head or not, it's definitely not a good thing. I hoist myself over the side hanging on with one hand and begin climbing down the side of the train. Literally, at the end of my rope, I let go.

75

RED EYE

L ong ago abandoning the claim of innocent by- stander or neutral observer, as life is too short for inaction, Horace's thoughts are a myriad of memories bumping along in the golf cart, some good, most of them incomprehensible. The dappled sunlight overhead is almost mesmerizing at twenty miles an hour. He contemplates the wealth of technology the world has adopted as the norm, seemingly overnight and that regardless of how advanced society perceives itself, or the economic status society achieves... it just never ends. Mankind is destined to forever play the tempted ingenue tasting from a tree known to be poisonous.

Reaching the site of the train clears his mind for what's ahead, the building in front of them, looks vacant. Doors wide open, the train is an impressive sight, sitting silently like the giant toy it is. The front of the bullet nose has been obviously marred by fire of some kind. The team goes in first while Tyler and Horace walk up the stairs of the porch.

Plates still on the table, music playing AC blowing. *"Where is everybody?"*

Captain Sullivan reports, "Sir, the building is clean. The train door is locked we are unsure if anyone is inside."

"Let's knock, shall we?" Horace states quietly.

Sullivan pulls a grenade off his waist and walks back into the large room off the dining room. The train is stationed at its loading dock, the rear windowless door looks marred by the same type of explosion as the front of the train, the striped canopy above, is spotless.

Taking cover, the sound of the grenade is magnified by the cavernous space that contains it. There is dead silence for a moment afterward.

"Stop, don't shoot!" A dark- haired woman standing in the new doorway of the train with the unmistakable look of terror in her eyes is waving her hands around wildly.

"All guns down!" Captain Sullivan replies to the woman, not knowing who she is.

"Yes, yes we are unarmed," Galax replies with tears, prostrated.

By the looks of her, Horace knows they have found a group of abductees. Galax leads the soldiers back into the train, with her arms up.

Several seconds later, Sullivan is on the radio to Horace, "We have six in the train, three are wounded, two dead and one is really pissed off."

"Take them all back to the plane."

"Yes, Sir. It seems one jumped out of the window before we came in."

"Shuttle the wounded first, then track the other."

"Yes, sir."

Turning to Tyler as they enter the train, Horace suggests, "Check to see if you know any of these people. It's a war zone in here, our grenade is the least of it." Horace regards the group of frightened people on the ground honestly, "We are here to help, we're friends of Stephanie Beroe's." Horace says in as calming a tone as he possesses.

Tyler shakes his head no, in response to Horace's request, he does not know anyone in the train car.

"Did you say, Stephanie Beroe?" The dark- haired Galax repeats looking guilty as hell, while she is maintaining pressure on the side of Manning's blonde head his face impaled with bits of wood and metal, he had been standing at the front of the train when the grenade hit.

"Yes, have you seen her?" Tyler responds hopefully.

"Oh, my God, we had no idea!" She responds, Manning and Genevieve look at her in confusion. Looking back to them she states, "Remy's last name is

Beroe! Stephanie must be **his** wife!"

"Shit!" Manning exclaims. "He's gonna fuckin kill me!"

Sullivan loads the bodies of Manaya and Hollie and the young Bogart, barely alive into a golf cart, as Horace asks questions.

After fifteen minutes, the recon team have all the information they need. "Let's get you all secure and see what kind of trouble we can find." Horace turns back to the door. His jaw set grimly in place.

Following, Tyler leads off, "We know where Remy is, but what about Stephanie?"

"Someone is controlling the drones, we need to find them first," Horace states matter of fact, his eyes level with Tyler's. "Cut off the head of the snake. There has to be a security office somewhere, these pompous asses didn't do all of this by themselves." Turning to Sullivan he demands, "Locate the largest energy source."

76

BASIQUE

Less than a mile from the club house, they hear the sound of an explosion, H.S. looks at Jameson, "Don't worry about that, keep the drone on the girl." he demands from the surveillance cabin, which looks exactly what you would expect a dozen men living together in the jungle to look like, junk food wrappers from food they smuggled in during their vacations and the smell of digestion mixed with permeating body odor. *Hard to believe we pay them six figures each.* Having dismissed most of the personnel before all hell broke loose. There are now only six mercs left at their disposal, he is becoming concerned. "Not ideal numbers Jameson, but there will be no escape from this island for any of the feeders. If those goddamn club deserters hadn't run for their lives off the train, we could have contained this, now the feeders are armed."

Distracted from the video monitors in front of him, his thoughts move to Stephanie, he smiles, his puffy checks creasing before he is sidetracked by whining sounds from his comrade at arms. Jameson has brutishly trained the rest of the mercenaries to command the drones with little success while complaining about his wound like a stuck pig.

"For Christ sake Jameson, the bullet is out and painkillers have been administered, what are you whining on about? Listen, we all have something to lose here if we don't play our cards right." That gets his attention.

H.S. knows Jameson has taken his own brother as his feeder. He doesn't hold it against him that he protected his billion- dollar minion by removing the only other heir, in fact, it's that type of unilateral strategy that earned him a place in the club. *But the whining has got to stop.* "Focus!" H.S. reprimands his junior club member, as Jameson snaps to without another tick.

"At least your one hundred- million- dollar price tag for the bipeds is not a complete loss," H.S. adds.

"We have captured one feeder, she's been put down. One down and a handful to go. In all actuality, the hunt has become more than we could have ever designed. Do you think Levitt and Bannock made it?" Jameson portends with more gusto, the spirit of the hunt now clearly driving his intent.

"I hope not." H.S. should be happy they are running down Beroe, who has been nothing but a soon to be removed obstacle. But what he truly desires, is for Stephanie to watch Remy die. Believing only then will she be broken. He wants to witness her resplendent face as he claims the moment, she has lost everything.

There's a loud bang at the door, "Answer it fool." H.S. dictates to the closest merc in front of him.

Standing there, panic struck is their club member, Dryson Pierce.

I thought he had left with the rest of the cowards." H.S. questions no one in particular.

"Ah, Dryson." Jameson welcomes him in, sure to make eye contact with H.S. as he turns back to the screen. "You're missing a great show."

H.S. considers Dryson, a pathetic excuse for a man. How he managed to hold two presidential cabinet offices is an attestation to purchased politics. Now in his late sixties, his paper- thin pasty skin and plugged hairline are too gruesome for public domain. Born to wealth, he never needed to do anything else, his family is famous for their extreme conservative Christian philanthropy.

Once he catches his breath, Dryson Pierce enters the surveillance room.

"You can't... kill him!" Dryson manages in between gasps of air on the verge of an attack of some kind.

"What are you talking about? You fool. Everyone goes!" H.S. replies, his tone impatient, sweat starting to bead on his forehead in the dark- temperature controlled command room.

"No, you don't understand!" Dryson blabbers, "I picked him specifically, everything is set."

"You picked him specifically?" Jameson turns to him, amused.

"Yes." Dryson now sobbing continues, "He's my donor!"

Both Jameson and H.S. are silent as they absorb this.

"Remarkable." H.S. finally responds genuinely entertained. "Honestly, I didn't think you had it in you. You abducted your organ donor?"

"The dark- haired fellow? Looks a bit like Bogart?" Jameson reasons, obviously impressed as well.

"Yes, Bobby Haskins. I have alternative storage waiting for him."

"It's not a bank account, you can't just deposit and withdraw Dryson. You know the rules."

"You would have done the same thing H.S. and you know it!" Dryson responds prostrate, the veins of his neck exposed in strain.

"I haven't seen him, he may be dead already," Jameson states perfunctorily as Dryson begins to weep uncontrollably.

"That can't be! All the tissue samples have been matched. I don't have enough time to find someone else!"

Disgusted by his display of weakness, Jameson commands the merc controlling the drone over Stephanie to go back to the train.

"What are you doing Jameson?" H.S.'s voice is even and dangerous.

"The man is weeping, either I shoot him, or take a moment to look back on the train."

Dryson looks up like a child faking a tantrum, but says nothing.

"Five minutes, you have five minutes to look for him, then we go back to the girl."

"Yes, yes I understand," Jameson answers absorbed with the controller of the drone in his hand, like a child on a play station.

No one has mentioned that one of the club rules has been broken. They all silently acknowledge the fact but it is not spoken out-loud. All three are guilty of rule breaking. The Beroe's for H.S., Dryson's donor and Jameson's brother Thaddius. Now is not the time for reprimand, it's time for action. Cool levelheaded action. Besides the only unbreakable rule is the loyalty of silence, from that, no one escapes.

The train is empty, as the drone maneuvers through the carcass of their marvelous decimated beast, there are signs of survivors among the blood-stained wreckage, but the train and facility are empty.

"He's not there Jameson, go back to the girl." H.S. dismisses Dryson's donor.

The drone instantly flies through the air on Jameson's command, returning to the coordinates Stephanie was last seen.

"Technology is so definitive." H.S. amusingly comments. "To a true sportsman, it's a double- edged sword, don't you think Jameson? Handicaps are good, but on the other hand, no one desires easy prey? She's heading to the beach. Where is everyone else? Where are the bipeds?"

Impatiently Jameson looks at H.S. from his command bar, "Relax H.S. I've got this. Your feeder is about a mile and a half off the beach path heading to the river."

"Why does he have two feeders?" Pierce Dryson whines to a deaf room. "You had a male, where did she come from, why do you get two?"

Ignoring Dryson, H.S. turns to the four mercs in the room driving the bipeds, "Gentleman, a million-dollar bonus to whomever captures this male alive." Looking, at his watch, it's twenty after four, "You have a little more than an hour before sunset."

"Yes!" The merc in front of him remarks.

Facing Dryson, H.S. replies, "She was my guest, I seemed to have misplaced her."

"I am starved H.S., let's head back to my craft. We can oversee everything from there."

Jameson started calling Jove's Gift, his craft before it was even delivered. H.S. considers, annoyed while smiling as he hears the term, ignoring the desire to wring both their necks. "Find the woman first."

"Who is she?" Jameson asks unable to recall the aged billionaire ever hosting, family or friends at the park before, at the same time Remy comes into view on the monitor in front of the Neanderthal with the joy stick.

"My new wife."

THERE THERE

Running parallel to the beach through the brush and tall grass at his top speed, the biped drone right behind him, Remy can hear it tearing branches from the trees as it barrels towards him, an abomination from another dimension. The day's light is dimming, creating shadows and hallowed places, he can't out run this thing and with the darkness of night coming he won't be able to see it either, so he stops. Turning on a dime he takes the barrel of the gun in both his hands, swinging, he does his best impersonation of Babe Ruth, knocking the monster's little flashing head off. Tiny wires sputtering as it just stands there, headless, for a moment before falling to the ground.

Could it be that easy? He asks himself, waiting a minute before running in the direction Danielle took off in, swinging the gun back over his shoulder.

Danielle made it to a river, a biped in between them. Remy looks on from the last edge of cover before a sandy bank dips down to a narrow current of murky shallow water. It's, not deep enough for cover. Danielle spots him and begins moving towards the mouth of the river to drive the things attention forward while staving it off with a large stick.

Heart racing, Remy sneaks up behind the thing and… BLAM! "Out of the park!"

Catching her breath, oblivious to his batting skills, she asks, "Where is Haven?" parental concern written all over her face.

"I don't know." Remy is wondering if he was wrong to come to her first. His instincts have completely taken over now, there may be no rational left.

Heading for the beach, Remy and Danielle are both consumed by silence. The monkeys above are completely undisturbed by their human folly until the first shot splits the air. The monkeys explode in an eruption of screams that makes discerning which direction the shot came from difficult. Freezing instantly after crouching to the ground, sweat oozing from every pore. Danielle finally points back towards the original path they were on as they both start running towards the sound. Once out from under the monkeys there's no mistaking it, Remy signals Danielle to flank off to the left as he darts off towards the right, closer to the open beach but careful to stay concealed. Finally, in front of them, is Skylar's team in tact but surrounded by four more bipeds, the sound of dogs in the distance unmistakable. Three of the bipeds have yellow heads and the fourth is the one that took Freeman.

Remy's anger turns to rage as he sees Hollie's body crumpled near a rock, he runs for the back of the closest metal creature. Just before his arms reach, it turns around and zaps him. One million volts of electricity coursing through his body, he is in a state of rigor mortis, as he watches the electric shock explode between the two small yellow darts now imbedded in his chest, lighting up the grove. Everything stops, he can only hear the electric shock that is traumatizing his nervous system, as his body is rigid with excruciating pain. Brain driven blank, all four of his limbs stiffen in convulsion, every muscle set to uncontrollable tension while his jaw clenches involuntarily. Falling on his back, he can barely see the sky above him through the leafed canopy, a monstrous green tree with long spikes on its trunk just above him. Unable to move although the shock has stopped, his body has completely shut down.

Several agonizing minutes go by, Remy's hearing finally returns, yet he is still devoid of mobility, his head can decipher the clamor of resistance around him, a low hum from the ground. Still stricken, a flash of color and blotting of the sky above him draws his attention to Ora as she flies over him in slow motion. Her blue eyes catch his just before she hits the tree behind him, impaled against the tree's armor finitely. Remy can do nothing as her golden hair dims with the fading sunlight.

Every minute, seems like an hour, unable to move anything but his eyes, when the feeling finally comes back to his arms and legs, he drags himself over to a large rock for a moment. The battle is still on, Skylar and Arona carefully keeping an arms distance from a biped, are alternately beating the body of the drone in turn with anything they can grab and throw.

Danielle is fighting two by herself. Remy stands, using his rifle as a cane, managing the two steps over to her. Taking aim, he swings at the yellow headed demon from behind with a whoosh, missing completely and almost falling down, his body weight throwing him against Ora's tree her lifeless bare feet just touching his shoulders. Pulling his eyes from her beautiful face he fixes his rifle blinking sweat, and aims at the yellow beacon as three German Shepherds jump Skylar from the brush. The drone's head is launched into the darkening brush. Turning the rifle around with three bullets he takes out the dogs, but Skylar is mangled and already bleeding out.

Screaming, Remy runs up to the machine that Arona is struggling against and knocks it's head off with the butt of his gun. Turning back to Danielle, Remy begins to move toward her as she backs up against a small rocky mound, in a flash, the last machine on the right grabs her and takes off.

"NO!" Remy screams running after her, as she is dragged through the jungle, at lightning speed. One minute it is ahead of him the next it's gone completely. Vanquished, Remy screams, silencing the jungle before reluctantly turning around and heading back to Arona. She is alone standing in the clearing with the last of the machines, as he approaches. Taking a running start with every ounce of energy he has left, Remy jumps on the back of it attempting to knock it over, sweeping Arona into the motion. As they all hit the ground, the bi-ped stops fighting. They both roll to their feet, ready, but nothing happens. Whatever they did it stopped moving.

The scene is gruesome, trampled jungle floor pooled with blood, Ora staked to a tree like an innocent victim of witchcraft. Skylar dying, his face draining quickly while he manages to look at both of them. The hard rhythm of his aspiration, the only motion his ruined body can handle. Taking three breathes to raise his eyes, Skylar smiles at both of them, while peaceful calm fights for dominance over his torn body, his shoulders descend with his last breath.

Tears run down Remy's face as he closes Skylar's eyes. Arona wraps her arms around him as they console each other. After a moment Remy grabs her shoulders, "Did you find a phone? Did you get a call out?"

"No, there was nothing there. No landline or cell phones or computers. They must have taken everything with them. Every building we found was abandoned." She pauses then asks," Where did you move the wounded?"
"I didn't." He says, dread creeping into his throat.
"They were all gone when we returned to the train," Arona replies in fear. "It looked like the door had been blown off."
Sitting back on his ass in the blood- soaked dirt, despondent, "AHHHHHH!" Remy's scream is primal. Nothing can make this right again, everyone is dead! He led these people, gave them hope that they could survive and have their lives back. He condemns himself, *Yesterday, they were all living a life, not a perfect life, but who's life is perfect? Now they are all dead, it's my fault! What have I done? "FUCK!"* His scream scatters all the birds left near the small grove, as he throws an abandoned club sideways up against a tree splintering it into wooden shards.
"Remy, what if it's just you and I." Arona whispers in between sobs, looking at him from her knees, "What's going to happen to us?" All sense of control gone, Arona melts down.
Her show of emotion, charges Remy's anger, sequestering his hopelessness, he feels it growing. "There, there. Listen, I don't care if I live or not, but **they're** not going to make it off this island alive! Hide yourself, climb up a big ass tree and just stay there, if I survive, I will find you." He says rising from his knees, his eyes hardening with anger.
"What are you going to do?"
"I'm going to end this."

78

ALL I NEED

Having left Jameson and Dryson, to return to Jove's Gift with dinner and a shower their only priorities for the night, H.S. decides to take matters into his own hands. Growing weary of both of them whining like women, one about his organ donor and the other about his wounded leg, his patience at an all- time low. Sometimes he believes, they are shooting at the wrong targets.

The multi- million- dollar bipeds of Jameson's turn out to be another cheap dollar store item for the military to buy along with countless other inferior weapons that will never work. The look on Jameson's face when he lost contact with all of them, however, was priceless. As Jameson handed him the watch controller for the visual drones, his tone was so full of defeat H.S. almost felt sorry for him, almost.

"Here, take this silly thing." H.S. recalls the defeated sound in Jameson's voice, "Just keep your hand over the screen and it will move the drone in the direction of your hand. I'm going back to my vessel to eat and regroup, they're not going anywhere." Thinking back, H.S. sniggers. Looking at the phone sized screen in front of him, following the path where Stephanie was last spotted by the drone. He is truly hunting his prize now. No more trains or mercs or military stunts; *This is how it should have always been. One on one.*

The exhilaration of the chase heightening his senses, he hears everything, feels every wisp of air and sees the evening shadows reflecting the golden hue of his favorite weapon in the last light of day. An obscured view of the events before him creates a young viral self- image, he is not just exhilarated he is aroused. It's happened before, just before pulling the trigger on a dead shot, but not like this, not like her. *Warren Bazel was right about one thing, there's nothing more dangerous than a reasoning man, or woman.*

79

RAPTURE AT SEA

W here do you think, you're going?"

His voice from behind, catches me off guard, turning around holding my breath, my hand still on the oar of the kayak I intend to commandeer, I see H.S. standing there on the beach in a jacket and tie sweating like a pig.

"Put that down like a good girl."

Facing my captor, I stand silently plotting, as he admires the day's events obviously scarred on my body.

"That was quite a little stunt you pulled on the train. You're braver than I thought."

I just stand there looking at him, my contempt obvious, as he laughs out loud, amused by it all, like this is some kind of game.

"You are quite the prize." He says moving towards me with both hands out, one with that little golden gun, the other attempting to touch me.

I am looking around for anything to change my odds.

"You realize Remy is dead."

Stopped cold, my eyes widen, while I decipher his words. Standing there frozen. *"No."* I whisper, shaking my head. *"That can't be true."*

"It's true." Moving closer, watching me respond, he adds, "He's dead. Should I show you his skin? I told you? Didn't I? I told you I would skin him alive. I have been waiting to break that spirit of yours, since the day I met you. Just like a wild horse, once you break them, they do exactly what you want, and now I have you. Two birds, one stone."

My body crumples on the edge of the kayak, limp and directionless as my mind snaps closed searching for who knows what, before spontaneously being driven by a rage that erupts from my very bone. I grab the oar and swing it around hitting him broadside across the shoulder knocking his little gun into the tide line. He's not out, but he stumbles to his right on to his knees, caught off balance. Letting my anger lead, I scramble swinging the oar back for a final blow but H.S. grabs the oar with one hand and pulls me towards him. Yanking my hair with the other hand, he pushes my face down within inches of the sand and throttles my neck, squeezing from behind. The pain is excruciating, stars swim in front of my eyes. I swing my left hand without contact while bracing my body with the other. *This can't be it! I will not let him win!* With a last effort struggling for air, I lean all of my body weight on to him, the full force of my body pushes into him for a moment before he finally yields his stance. Crying out he releases me, as we both fall back onto the wet sand. I grab his little gun glinting in the tideline and throw myself on top of him, straddling his body, barrel against his forehead.

Tears, sweat, snot and drool slipping down my sand encrusted face onto his chest. I don't care. All rationale absconded, I look into his mottled lifeless eyes, "You will never have me." My hand trembles as I grip the loaded gun resting on his forehead, but my voice is steady pushing through the pain of my hoarse throat. I cock the trigger. *I want you dead.* Wiping my face on my upper arm I focus on the barrel of the gun, it's all I can see, through absolute fury.

"You won't kill me. You have no life to return to, your company has been ruined. Your husband is dead. Your home has been defiled by your secretary, **my** employee. You have lost ever-y-thing." His words drizzling with saliva, are malicious and cruel. He is so damn sure of his intentions, but his words penetrate the depths of my soul. I am Stripped by the reality of what he is saying. *Is this just part of his sick game?* His premeditated orchestration has brought me to this place, brought Remy and I to this place. *Remy!* The rip in my heart sends a shutter, through my core and my body involuntarily ripples. Thinking his name, my mind floats away from my body for an eternal moment, I've lost the connection between visceral and physical being. I'm numb. Hovering, for what seems like hours looking up at the stars breaching the purple hue of dusk, searching for answers to all of my questions in vain. *What is the point of all of this?*

Finally, the weight of grief and despair wholly consumes me, drawing my vision down, to the pitiless smile cross his face, and in one motion my hand raises and strikes, the butt of the gun rendering him unconscious. I fall to the sand, next to the devil himself.

The sound escaping my body is foreign to me, a creature from a nether world, waves of nausea shaking my bones. *This will never end, I am swimming in an endless ocean of grief.*

Following a pervading instinct to get as far away from this monster as I can, I wipe my eyes with the back of my sandy hands, walk- crawling into the water for release and comfort. Bathing in the tears of all humanity, encouraging the mother of life to cradle what's left of me.

But there is no comfort, the outline of that cursed ship on the horizon, is a constant reminder of the anguish deliberated for us. *Remy, I can't bare this!* Swimming further out to sea, inviting the waves to crash over me, hoping at some point one of them will take my pain with its crush. There is nowhere else to go and nothing left to do. My heart is broken, I am broken, nothing and no one can fix me now.

A large gulp of sea water stingingly chokes me as I pass the breakers, burning my hoarse throat. Floating on my back, abandoned with no concern for direction or domain, empty and torn, I give myself willingly to the God of sea, as the ebb and flow flickers images of the boat coming in and out of my vision, a horrible Kharybdatic monster, the tide reluctantly pulling me towards it.

Halfway now between the shore and the ship, I can just see three people climbing on the back deck, two women and a man silhouetted against the deep red glow of the dying sun. *More gun crazed freaks.*

I watch them silently as they move out of the water and onto the platform of the boat, "Oh my God!"

Blinking my eyes, I am instantly alert. I can't see the male figure, my eyes glazed with tears, but… I know his movements… the glide of his arms… the gait of his step… the sway of his hips. Snapping like a whip, more tears covering my eyes, my heart races, and I swim for my life.

Attempting to yell, my voice forsakes me, so I keep swimming, without breathing, desperately, not allowing my eyes to stray from his form, for fear of losing him. His back is turned to me, as well as the women standing by his side, my arms burn, I have never wanted something so much in my life before. The anxiousness in my throat and chest is unbearable, *turn around! Turn around Remy!*

To my horror, they begin to walk towards the cavernous open mouth of the ship, like a black hole against the twilight. *NO! SEE ME!* I command from the depths of my soul; my voice sputtering out of breath, but he turns and looks right at me. I stop frozen by his touch. Remy leaps off the deck and into the water in one movement heading straight for me. He covers the distance between us as if being pushed by Thoosa herself. Ten feet, five feet my face breaking from my smile, suddenly covered by his mouth, his warm delicious mouth. The taste of him washing over me a thousand times more than any ocean. No words are produced by either of us, as he pulls me towards him, wrapping me in his strength and love, at long last the comfort of his body next to mine erases the world around us, we are whole again.

For several moments, we float holding one another, imprinting on each other as if for the first time. Holding my head in his gentle hands, he whispers, "You're alive." Spoken slowly as if he had feared to utter the words before now or even consider it. Tears tracking his cheeks, "Your head is bleeding, are you hurt?"

"Not anymore." I croak, looking into his penetrating eyes.

We kiss, and it's like being home. For a moment, I can almost imagine none of this has happened and we are just out for a swim when from behind him, two women swim up.

"You don't **look** like you need help, Remy." The lighter- haired gal says sarcastically while treading water behind him. A dark- haired woman who is stunning, her golden eyes piercing even in the dim light of evening, is looking to Remy for direction, when suddenly a brilliant light draws our attention from the beach, at the same time the ship fires up and starts moving away from us.

The light is born from a giant fire, a bon fire just beyond the tideline of the shore. I can see skeletons of beach chairs and palm frongs stacked within its red and yellow flame.

"Rem, I left H.S on the beach." Remy looks at me and suddenly I don't recognize him.

"Climb on." He says to me, "I'm not letting go of you, not even to swim."

I swim around to his back and lock my hands against his chest just below his arm pits, letting my legs stay free so I can kick.

"Harli, Danielle, this is my wife, Stephanie." They both nod in confusion. "We need to stay just outside the fire line, so they can't see us." He adds swimming to the right of the fire towards the beach.

Without a moon, the night sky turns black almost immediately after twilight. If it had not been for the bon fire, getting back may have been tricky, as the ink black sky blends perfectly with the land and water that's not caught in the shadows of the fire. Remy's swimming is awkward with me on his back, but it doesn't matter, I couldn't leave his side if I wanted to, my ribs are strained and my foot is useless.

As we approach the beach, I roll off Remy's back and we all crawl up the sand, staying very low. There are five men and one woman around the fire, throwing chairs and umbrellas onto the pyre like structure. Remy looks over to me, "Maybe you *should* stay here?" The other women look at each other silently.

"Not on your life, I'm not losing you again. Whatever happens, it happens to both of us."

"Yeah, well that hasn't worked out so well for everyone else." He says looking to Danielle, who looks back at me and averts her eyes.

"Look!" Harli nudges him with her shoulder. "It's Haven!"

A thin figure in barely any clothes is walking out of the tree line, one of the men in soldier khaki's, talks with the thinly framed boy for a minute before handing him something. The boy sits down close to the fire, he looks young, "Do you know him?" I ask. Everyone replies, "Yes," in unison.

He's just sitting in front of the fire eating something when two more figures walk out of the trees, both women.

"It's Galax with Arona," Danielle states biting her lip.

I recognize Galax as the woman that tended me and gave me the knife on the train. I had hoped she would be ok.

Remy takes a deep breath, "Ok, what do you think?"

"It could be a trap," Danielle responds almost immediately.

"You know all of those people?" I ask in an attempt to catch up.

"We know three of them, they guys with clothes we don't know," Harli replies patiently.

"What if someone has come to help?" I offer.

"Not possible." Danielle yields.

"No one knows we're here. We had no way to contact anyone from the outside, we couldn't find a phone or a line out." Remy adds solemnly.

"I did." I raise my eyebrows and smile as I say this, remembering the phone that had fallen out of my back pocket at some point during this maniacal experience.

"Who did you call?" Remy asks, after bestowing a kiss on my forehead.

"The only number I could remember, Laure. She was on a plane with Miles, they were on their way here. Miles said the FBI was coming too."

"Hot Damn!" Harli calls out," You did it, Remy." She says turning to him, "It wasn't pretty and we didn't all make it, but we did it. It would have never happened without you."

My husband nods his head, and a lot is left unspoken in his gesture, a lot of things I hope I would get to hear one day.

"Let's go." He says standing up, holding out a hand to lift me from the sand.

Once I am on my feet, Remy pulls me to him, and I have him in a death grip. "I love you."

"I love you too."

Heading over to the fire, wrapped in Remy, I feel the heat warming my skin as the skinny kid runs up to us, "I thought you were all dead!", he yells with relief and admiration.

Galax and Arona, join us, Remy hugs all three of them, so do Danielle and Harli.

I hug Galax, thanking her for her foresight.

"Stephanie." Galax acknowledges me.

"How do you know her?" Remy asks somewhat nervously.

"We met on the train," I add smiling, nothing can dampen my happiness, but I have definitely confused everyone.

The warm reunion feelings are overflowing just as I watch Remy's face darken. Within a second, he is bursting through the circle and on top of someone at the fires edge. The group that was just hugging is now intently surrounding his attack. Remy has a man on the ground and he is beating the shit out of him as the group watches, all of them ready to pounce, while I hobble over. As I reach the circle, an older man runs over, from the edge of the light.

"Wait! Stop! Listen please!"

He has a strange apparatus strapped around his chest and is followed by a small group of men and a woman also in khaki's, more soldiers.

Remy places one hand on the downed man's neck while he looks toward the older man, his knees pinning the man's shoulders down. Our group creates a wall between them, there is no retreat, regardless of the weapons the armed party coming towards us present. Poised for conflict, I realize the man under Remy is Tyler, "Tyler?"

"Stephanie, it's not what you think!" He squeaks out beneath my honey's choke hold.

"Please, we are here to help. I am a friend of Miles Venery; your friend Laure is here as well." The older man states evenly, as his small squad stands behind him, but makes no aggressive movement.

"It's true." Galax offers, "They came to help us. They moved everyone to their plane, your friends are on board."

"What about him?" Remy growls, nodding down to Tyler.

"He'll have to explain that to you himself. But we don't have a lot of time. We watched you from the shore and lit the fire so you could find your way back, but we have to go." The elderly man states as he offers a hand to Remy. "Horace, Horace Mendel."

"The newspaper guy?"

"Yes Mr. Beroe, it's a pleasure to meet you. Now, if you don't mind, we can fill you in on the plane."

Remy stands up brushing the sand off and returns to my side, before announcing, "There's three more out there. On the other side of the cliff."

"Actually, there were quite a few more, but we have found them all. They are all on board." Horace continues as we all walk back up near the beach path where several carts are waiting for us.

He's a giant of a man, Tyler seems inconsequential walking next to him. I question Tyler's presence here with a lot of mixed emotion, as the heat of the fire diminishes. Feeling the cool darkness of the jungle chilling my wet skin, we load up and drive away from the sea. *I've never been so happy to leave a beach in my life.*

Remy insists on driving, so I cram in between him and a soldier in the front bench seat of the golf cart. The ride through the dark canopied pathway is eerie, dim lights from the golf cart caravan catch irregular shapes of the branches that encumber the lane. Within in ten minutes, we have arrived to a lawn cleared of trees with a paved runway streaking down the middle, several blue colored lights glisten on the ground outlining the landing strip and nothing else. My hands are numb from the pressure of the men beside me, I couldn't move quickly or succinctly if a bomb went off.

BOOM!

"What the hell?"

"Everyone on the plane!" The soldiers yell at us, as if we need prompting while an actual jet is flying overhead, dropping… bombs!

Remy climbs out of the cart, scooping me up, he runs for the plane ahead of us. The soldiers create a protective walkway with their bodies, guns in the air eyes all around, while we climb the steps up to the plane.

Once we're aboard, it's like something out of a reality show, half -clad, tired, filthy, frightened men and women look up at us as we enter. All of them are strapped to a leather chair, ready to go with a look of panic in their eyes. Remy lowers me into a seat, as a very welcome face appears from the back of the plane.

"Laure!" I yell as my dearest friend runs to hug me.

"I thought you were… I'm so glad you're… I love you Sista." She finally decides on while we wrap our arms around each other, trying not to look to distressed about my appearance.

"I love you too." I manage, both of us in tears.

"Prepare for takeoff!" The female soldier with the name tag Addison alerts us over the sound system. "It may be bumpy."

The giant plane begins to taxi down the runway, while I notice Horace moving into the cock pit. We take a sharp turn and finally begin to pick up speed. Squeezing Remy's hand on the left with Laure directly across from me, I close my eyes as the g force sends my now aching head back into the plush seat. Once off the ground, I peek out the window, the land below us is melting into the oblivion of night, while two jets wipe it out of history. My mind is reeling with questions, *who called an airstrike? Why aren't they shooting at us? Where is H.S? Why is Tyler on board? Who is Horace? No wonder I have a headache.*

Tears begin to fall against my cheek again, my eyes closed, I think how lucky we are.

"Hey," Remy whispers in my ear, I feel Laure moving to another area of the plane, "Everything is ok now. We are going to be ok."

Opening my eyes to his, feeling his strong hands wrap my shoulders, I can't control my tears as we kiss softly.

Once we are at our cruising altitude, a soldier named Sullivan asks both Remy and I to check in at the infirmary in the back of the plane. While walking through the palatial private airliner, the faces of the men and women aboard tell a very serious story. Regardless of how well they may or may not have gotten along down there, they all have one thing in common, they survived and that bond is obvious. Their tattered clothes seem surreal in the executive jet.

So many people's lives have been played with. Catching the eye of all but one, a soldier in black khaki's that looks familiar, as we pass his seat, I notice terrible scrape marks on the left side of his face as he brushes his hand through his hair. I also notice a black tattoo on the back of his hand. I want to scream, *this is the guy that took you!* I turn back to Remy to explain what I know when Remy's hand on my shoulder, gives me a squeeze. *He already knows. They all do.*

One of the larger men in shorts, bare chested stands up and offers his hand to Remy, I pause for a moment to witness the exchange.

"I am so sorry." This beautiful and wounded man professes to my husband through sobs of sheer anguish.

Remy pulls the man towards him in a hug and whispers something into his ear, before patting the hulk on the back and falling back into pace with me. Two rows down, he stops to talk to the beautiful golden eyed woman, Danielle, giving her a kiss on the forehead before continuing. *Yes, we are all bonded.*

Laure is looking up at me with an expression that is difficult to decipher as we pass her club chair, next to Tyler. I cannot miss that they are holding hands. Tyler rises from his seat, stands facing us in an open area that must be used for conferencing, with several large flat screen televisions mounted on the wall and a panel of computers inlaid on wooden table tops.

"Remy, Stephanie, I know this is not the time to discuss this, but I want you to know. I had nothing to do with any of this."

I can feel Remy's restless body tensing next to me, but Tyler seems genuine in his confession.

"I had intended to tell you everything I knew, the night we met at the bar."

"But H.S. showed up and surprised you," I add, having a hard time with those initials.

"Yes, then when you went missing, I started putting bigger pieces together and with the help of Laure, we were able to fill in some gaps for Miles and Horace that led us here." Looking past me to Remy his green eyes bloodshot, Tyler adds, "I cannot apologize for my Father's actions, I can only hope you can forgive my misgivings."

Remy pauses for a moment quietly, surmising before he lifts his head as if adjusting an uncomfortable shirt collar, he replies, "Let's take this one day at a time, ok?"

"Yes, of course." Tyler bows his head and returns to his seat next to laure, who gives me a small smile.

I am confused, tired, hungry, angry and grateful all at once. I can't even hold on to this exchange, I think my brain has ceased functioning. I must be in shock, gratefully placing a barrier between the world I am viewing and the world within.

Behind the curtained area of the aircraft, there are three beds with three soldiers tending each of the wounded survivors. On the floor towards the rear are ten bodies covered with sheets, the sheets are stained with blood.

Immediately I recognize Miles, he is intently holding the hand of the man I remember on the floor of the train wounded. Miles does not seem to notice anyone else in the room, with a purse of his lips, he removes his hand and gently closes the pale young man's eyes as Galax gracefully covers his body with a sheet. Miles takes a moment to recover before walking over to me and taking my hand.

"Dear girl, I am so glad we found you."

I begin to cry. Again.

"Come sit down, let them take a look at you."

Remy and I both sit on the same bed next to one another, without relinquishing hands.

"Miles, how did you ever put all of this together?" I manage through my battered voice.

He smiles while cleaning my head with something very cold.

"It was quite a puzzle, I must say. If Horace hadn't gotten involved, I'm not sure how this would have turned out. You need a stitch or two, I am going to turn you over to Sullivan, he has the best hand at this."

Sullivan, a sweet looking young man in khakis, with sincere gray eyes moves in front of me, "Hi there, this is going to feel strange, but it won't hurt." He promises as he sprays my head with mist then starts sewing my head together. Remy is watching every move Sullivan makes. Once the thread is cut, Remy moves his hands to my throat, which is incredibly sore and from the looks of his face, bruised. "Who did this to you?" Remy asks, trying not to alarm me.

"H.S." My voice still hoarse, is not my own. Remy just nods his mouth in a firm grim line.

"Ok, I'm going to wrap up your ankle and get you set up with some ice until we can get an x-ray on that and a cat scan to be sure you don't have a concussion. The handsome soldier states before continuing, "Initially we offered sedatives to everyone, but absolutely no one has taken any pill we have offered, so I suggest a shot of whiskey, have something to eat and try to rest until we reach San Francisco."

"Sounds good." I croak, taking a crystal glass from Miles and knocking back the warm, stinging nectar.

"Your turn," I say turning to Remy, as Sullivan estimates he has a couple of cracked ribs and a large contusion on his head, but his elbows are also deeply cut, he needs stitches on both as well as his knees. I take this time to look over my husband. The cuts and bruises on his body are nothing compared to the transformation his demeanor has undergone in just a few days. His carefree wandering spirit, I had come to love is now weighted by the circumstances of greed and power. Obvious exhaustion mirrored in his now gray eyes, the slump in his shoulders will I am sure pass with time and rest, but what of his heart? Can anyone truly recover from the events he has been put through? Short of crawling into his skin and massaging his soul, I am at a loss as to how to fix him. Following my gaze, my love offers me a reassuring smile; *yes, we will start there and go slowly. It could have been a lot worse.*

"Remy, I had no idea man. Really! Please! Please don't kill me!" The injured man lying on the bed next to us yells out in fear. His head is bandaged leaving only his mouth and the left side of his face partially exposed, both of his arms are also fully bandaged. Looking closer I realize it's the guy that tied me to the chair. Galax moves towards him in both a protective and reassuring posture.

"No one is going to kill anyone." Remy asserts in a soothing voice my heart is happy to hear.

"Rest," I say to him, "everything is going to be alright."

Galax gives me a smile and sits down next to him as Remy takes two large shots of whiskey and leads me into the bathroom.

The bathroom is bigger than the bathroom we have at home, with a marble shower and all. Remy takes off his clothes, which isn't hard as he is only wearing his ripped yellow and white flower pants that are now cutoffs, and hardly yellow anymore. I do the same, looking for a place to dispose of the last material objects that remind me of *him*, as Remy starts the water in the shower. We both step in taking turns in the hot water. Attempting to rinse off the memory of our biggest fear, losing one another.

We dry each other off, not making any comments about scars or bruises, just happy we are both alive and together. *When did life get so complicated?* Before returning to our seats, we take a moment together and just hold one another privately.

Everyone gets their turn in sick bay and the bathroom, each of us wearing an array of Horace's clothing and reveling in the cleanliness of it all, as we all find our seats in the main cabin. Food is being served, and the aroma is intoxicating.

Remy has his eyes closed, I curl up next to him, until a plate of food is offered. Chicken Kiev with a Waldorf salad. There is absolute silence on the plane as everyone eats. The stewardess is dressed in a beige pant suit and she looks lovely as she removes my empty plate, all of four minutes later. Looking around me, I count the survivors including the ones in sick bay. There are twelve of them including Remy, all dressed in shredded office wear. *I wonder how many there were in the first place?*

Horace and Miles take the seats across from us, handing a laptop to Remy, something definitely on their minds. "You need to see this." Horace begins.

Remy reluctantly touches the screen. A dark image, shot from above the canopied trees is before us. If I didn't know any better, I would think it was the path to the airstrip, but it's very dark when the view opens up to the beach a bit brighter. Two people are rolling a man over onto his bloated stomach arms cuffed behind him like a criminal. My stomach lurches as I realize it's H.S. and I clutch my arm rests. One of the people is a small woman who states clearly and definitively, "FBI, you're under arrest for multiple kidnappings and murder." The sound is clear but a bit warbled. Horace interrupts, "That's Agent Navarro the other is Special Agent Spencer."

"Who are you?" H.S., who needs no introduction, demands in his pretentious monarchial voice.

"I just told you FBI." The lady agent's sassy voice denotes contempt, as H.S. strains his neck turning to look at her.

"You are making a life changing mistake," H.S. claims calmly looking around. *Probably for me.*

"I don't think so." The agent replies in what I can only discern as snarky.

Her partner walks up behind her, he is standing in the shadow of the sunset.

"This is it, this is all they could muster?" A smile spreads across H.S.'s face.

"Hold that thought, it may be the last time you smile for a long time." Navarro retorts, dragging him to his feet brutishly. Directing him back to the path, she asks her partner, "When will our back up arrive for the ship?"

"Any minute." His deep voice confirms with a firm grip on their prisoner's left arm.

"You realize, I will be free in an hour and you will be unemployed or dead."

"We've been doing a little hunting ourselves, this is some facility you've put together." Navarro clicks her tongue to the roof of her mouth in a tsk tsk tsk, while shaking her head at him like a kindergarten teacher.

"We aren't finished here." H.S. smirks.

Special Agent Spencer, pushes their prisoner forward in a bulwark motion, before jamming him into the passenger seat of a cart. Navarro drives while her partner is in the rear cargo area behind their prisoner. The cart slows to turn around the only winding curve on the path to the air strip. There is a distinctive thud as Agent Navarro's head slumps forward, her arms releasing the steering wheel as the cart slows to a stop, only the headlights now faintly illuminating the path ahead. Agent Spencer gets out unceremoniously and pulls her body over to the edge of the path with no comment, hiding her in some bushes before sitting behind the wheel.

"I'm Spencer, I'll have you out of here in no time." He states to H.S. before continuing up the path to the airstrip, after removing his cuffs.

"I can't go without the woman."

My body recoils and I can feel Miles and Horace looking at me. Remy simply places his hand over mine.

The agent stops the cart in the pitch dark of the shadowed path. "Listen to me old man, this little charade you and your cronies created has gotten way out of hand and although you have friends in high places, they are questioning why they are getting their hands so dirty for you. I am under orders that supersede your needs." The agent states with neutral calm. "I have exactly an hour to get your ass out of here."

"What happens in an hour?"

"Airstrike." The agent states as they accelerate down the path.

I am dumbstruck. Eyes blinking as Remy closes the laptop.

"My men hacked into their drone system, we took everything offline except the recon drone, it's a good thing we did, as we would have never known about the time restraint otherwise," Horace states calmly sitting back in his chair completely at home. He is unnaturally big, what seemed like extra- large seats are dwarfed by him in comparison. Miles next to him, looks small and grim.

"So that's what happened to the bipeds? Remy asks no one in particular. "Danielle has a lot to thank you for."

Horace nods.

I start rubbing my face in frustration, "What does this mean exactly. What bipeds? How is the FBI working for *them*?"

Everyone looks at me, like I'm the last one to figure it all out, which I am.

Remy turns and gently states, "It means he has immunity for his crimes. I will fill you in on the details later." Looking back to Horace, undeniably exhausted Remy continues, "Did you find anyone else on the island, that was part of the club? The members, other than the three that didn't make it on the train?"

"No, no they had obviously evacuated by the time we arrived, their ground crew left while we were mobilizing, there was only one plane on the strip when we landed, and I hardly believe they all arrived on one plane. I'm going to take statements from everyone and run a lead story, I can only list one name but I can insinuate several executives. It will run in everything I own, including overseas." This conversation is directed at Remy. "You understand, they will do the same thing."

"Yeah, I get it," Remy responds an edge in his voice, while he puts his head back.

"But we have all of these witnesses." I offer.

"So, do they, and they have a lot of clout between them. Just don't get your hopes up and watch your back." Horace gets up and returns to the cockpit.

Miles who had been silent this whole time now leans over and professes, "I am so sorry." He is obviously shaken as he places his hand on Remy's knee.

"We would all be dead, if it hadn't been for you," Remy replies, "Thank you."

Miles nods his head while getting up to return to sick bay, but turns to Remy and says," Don't be too hard on Tyler, he has proven himself a good man."

"One day at a time," Remy replies.

80

CRAZY

Packing boxes cover the floor of our office while Laure, my new assistant, and Danielle, Remy's new assistant wrap our treasures with paper and place them in the boxes. Once we came home the place just didn't work for us anymore, too many memories. Friends of ours turned us on to a small town in New Mexico outside Santa Fe, full of artists and eccentrics, maybe not enough to keep us entertained full time, but that is what our little rental in Costa Rica is for. Both of us realized if nothing else, life is short, do what makes you happy, which is being together and being creative. Danielle will come with us to N.M. and Laure will stay in CA. working remotely for us.

I will miss seeing Miles on a regular basis, his trips to the West Coast have not been complete without dinner at our home in the recent weeks. He has become a mentor for Remy and they have grown close. We decided not to take on any partners at this time, too much too soon.

New Mexico will be peaceful, a good place to heal, we found a great big old house to work on, that will hold all our crap. The views are spacious and the light is truly beautiful. When we need the water, we will head down to paradise, to a small little palapa, with running water a bathroom and an outdoor kitchen that faces the sea from atop a small hill. We spent the first couple of months there recovering after we came home, just being together. We left Mad Hatter to our ladies and really disappeared. It's going to take some time to reacquaint our new selves to each other, as both of us have changed for the better and worse. Finding a balance, we can feel good about is our new quest.

Piecing Mad Hatter back together again has not so been easy. Sure, if we could tell everyone what really happened I'm sure they wouldn't have held it against us. If I could tell them our assistant who was left in charge of their account was a paid saboteur, purposefully creating incorrect budgets and withholding tasks and information from timelines, things would be different. But that was not an option, first of all, who would believe us? No, we took the blame for others ruinous actions, started rebuilding where it made sense and narrowed our focus so we could move forward.

Our second day back a news story broke; *Several tourists on a party boat were killed after crashing onto a reef of an island off the Central American coast being used for military weapons testing.* It stated, several were killed accidently and the others were treated and returned to the U.S. with great care. Great care! I try not to get really, really, angry when I think about it. It seems the public wants to relate to stupid people doing stupid things, hence our new President.

Horace has been a true friend, the day he appeared at our door with the look of grief on his face, I knew something had gone badly wrong. On our arrival to L.A from the island, Miles and Horace took on the expense of returning everyone to their homes, once they had been treated. Horace had interviewed everyone on the plane but thought it wasn't the right time to really dig deep as the wounds were still very raw. He had planned to contact everyone at the end of the week.

Unfortunately, by the time he returned to speak with them, they had agreed to gag orders. He told us that each of the survivors except Galax, Danielle and Remy signed a ten- million-dollar gag order each. Restricting them from talking to anyone ever about the incident. At that point, we were out maneuvered. Horace had wished he had thought of it first.

The only justification we maintained, was when Horace broke his story; A luxury yacht had been found lost at sea off the coast of Mexico, the crew and passengers, top level American executives were initially charged with possession of marijuana, trafficking and under the influence of marijuana. Later they were dropped, after all of the people aboard were treated for overdose. I definitely won some points with my husband there.

Looking over to Remy, removing the Friedlander photograph and wrapping it in bubble to hand it to Danielle, I know everything will be fine. It's taken some time to get used to Danielle, she is tough, really tough, but she is quiet and fiercely protective, their relationship is special, I can honor that.

My thoughts are interrupted by the buzzing vibration of both Danielle's and Laure's phones. Remy and I are both sticking to a pledge not to reconnect directly. Their phones are literally exploding with texts.

Danielle takes a moment to sift through the information.

"It's from Burgess, your friend says he got a tip on the street from a recently fired employee from Butron, your California licensee, that they aren't going to pay the money they owe for licensing and they intend to steal your IP and replace you with their own coffee brand."

The room goes totally silent, Laure is nodding her head in agreement, she was texted the same thing. I put my pen down and look over to Remy who at the moment is staring at his desk, before he grins and announces, "Damn, it's good to be back."

Just the beginning…

About the Author

J. A. St Thomas is the co- founder of Mad Hatter Coffee & Tea Co., a cannabis infusion company. Since 2007, working in tandem with her husband they helped pioneer cannabis beverages and are presently serving over half a dozen legal states. Considered a Green Queen of cannabis, she has been profiled by The New York Times, Time Magazine and Newsweek.
A classically trained singer and co- founder of the Sire Reprise, New York City based band, The Waterlillies, she achieved international recognition with three top ten billboard hits in the U.S. in 1995. Subsequent musical projects include; Sonic Fleur, a world music trance duo and Suicide Lounge a stripped Jazz homage to obscure covers.
Presently she resides in a small magical town in New Mexico with her husband of 27 years and their daughter.

http://www.JASTThomas.com

Cat Tales Publishing

Visit our website to access a free sample of Class 7, the sequel in the Cannabis Chronicles Series by J.A. St Thomas.

http://www.CatTalesPublishing.com

Made in the USA
Middletown, DE
29 March 2019